The Black Pearl is
fascinating accounts
to emerge from the late-Victorian and Edwardian age of public morality (or, at any rate, public moralizing) and private sexual excess. The title indicates that the anonymous author was influenced by that classic journal of 19th Century erotica, *The Pearl*, and there is much of *The Pearl*'s flavour of outspoken rebellion against the official prudery of the time in these uninhibited memoirs.

But there are intriguing additional dimensions to the writings of 'Horby' (the pseudonym adopted by the author of *The Black Pearl* to disguise – very effectively so – his true identity). It is clear that the financial freedom that his independent income gave him, together with his aristocratic status, allowed him access to the inner circles of the artistic and occult worlds of his time. As a result, alternating with graphic accounts of sexual adventures are anecdotes – many of them wonderfully scurrilous – concerning some of the most famous creative talents of the age: Frank Harris, Lillie Langtry, Arthur Machen, Aleister Crowley, G. B. Shaw and H. G. Wells, to name but a few. But above all it is Horby's quest for his own sensual variety of enlightenment through the study and practice of sex-magic that provides the main theme and fascination of *The Black Pearl*, now at long last available for the first time to the wide audience it so richly deserves.

Also in paperback from New English Library

The Pearl: volume 1
The Pearl: volume 2
The Pearl: volume 3
The Pearl Omnibus
The Oyster: volume 1
The Oyster: volume 2
The Oyster: volume 3
The Oyster: volume 4
The Oyster: volume 5
The Oyster Omnibus
Rosie – Her Intimate Diaries: volume 1
Rosie – Her Intimate Diaries: volume 2
Rosie – Her Intimate Diaries: volume 3
Rosie – Her Intimate Diaries: volume 4
The Rosie Omnibus
The Black Pearl: volume 1
The Black Pearl: volume 2
The Ruby: volume 1
The Ruby: volume 2

The Black Pearl: Volume 3

The Memoirs of a Victorian Sex-Magician

Anonymous

NEW ENGLISH LIBRARY
Hodder and Stoughton

This edition first published in 1995
by Hodder and Stoughton
A division of Hodder Headline PLC

A New English Library paperback

10 9 8 7 6 5 4 3

British Library Cataloguing in Publication Data

Black Pearl: Memoirs of a Victorian Sex
Magician. – Vol. 3
823 [F]

ISBN 0-340-62570-8

Typeset by
Letterpart Limited, Reigate, Surrey

Printed and bound in Great Britain by
Cox & Wyman Ltd, Reading, Berks

Hodder and Stoughton
A division of Hodder Headline PLC
338 Euston Road
London NW1 3BH

PUBLISHER'S FOREWORD

The Black Pearl: The Memoirs of a Victorian Sex-Magician is a legendary classic of Victorian underground writing. Although the identity of the author presently remains unknown, it is clear from the text that he was a member of the aristocracy who knew all the leading figures of his age, both male and female. This eminently respectable figure obviously enjoyed the hidden and lascivious side of high life in his time: and he was also drawn to low-life. As such, we have a unique portrayal of the undertones of life in the 1890s and after.

His title obviously indicates that he was influenced by that classic journal of Victorian erotica, THE PEARL. The date of composition cannot be ascribed with exactitude though the text indicates that the author was recalling events some years after their happenstance. The edition discovered by Dr Geraldine Lamb, the editor, indicates on the publishers' notes opposite the title page that this work was privately printed in an edition of 156 copies by Van den Haagen of Amsterdam, 1925. It was set in 12pt Bembo, 1 pt leaded, printed on Japanese paper, crown quarto in size, bound in black buckram, with gold-stamped lettering which has led some bibliophiles to identify the latter work as that of Spalding & Hodge of London.

This book is of value to the sociologist, the psychologist,

the historian, those fascinated by literary anecdotes and political tales by a man who knew personally all those of whom he speaks; and above all to those who find in the study of human sexuality, a key to human nature.

EDITOR'S PREFACE TO VOLUME I

It is not often that one comes upon a classic of Victorian erotica whose very existence is a matter of speculation and rumour. Much Victorian erotica was written by debauched aristocrats in their leisure hours, then privately printed for presentation to friends. Some of these works were issued during the 1890s by the drug-addicted publisher, Leonard Smithers, who also published works of genuine literature by Oscar Wilde and works of art by Aubrey Beardsley. Others were not set, bound, printed and presented until many years later in order to protect both the name of the author and the reputations of those he mentioned.

Such is the case with *The Black Pearl: The Memoirs of a Victorian Sex-Magician*. If the publisher's notation can be trusted, it was not issued until 1925 and then only in a strictly limited edition. I came upon it in a curious way.

Following on from my B.A. at Cambridge, I went on to pursue M.A. studies at Harvard and it was there that I found myself debating issues of sexuality with distinguished men and women such as Norman Mailer and Dr Camille Paglia. Although both of them appeared to venerate the penis, they both seemed to see it as a tool of vengeance. Both, however, in their separate ways, seemed to be committed to the idea that human evolution could be advanced by sexuality. I was discerning a similar ideal in the poetry of England's Fiona Pitt-Kethley.

My essay *The Penis: Tool of Vengeance or Tool of Love? An Exploration of Socio-Phallicism* was eventually printed (1992) in *The New Rationalist*, published out of Harvard. I received a number of letters on account of it, some of them dismally predictable, but one, at least, was extraordinarily interesting. This was from an English baronet who has insisted that he remain anonymous. After a lengthy correspondence, he invited me to his castle, where he was a kind, courteous and considerate host.

It was during my stay that he showed me a copy of THE BLACK PEARL. I was absolutely astonished by this work. Most pieces of Victorian erotic writing show us simply the sleazy tenderloin of the repressed sexuality of that time. We get certain insights and there is entertaining rebellion against prevailing official mores but precious little more, even when the descriptions of the sexual encounters themselves are very well-written. Yet here was a rake who came to perceive sexuality as the holiest truth between man and woman – and as a way of advancing human consciousness.

In the text, he was at first simply a man of late middle-age recalling his youthful sexual exploits. He was reminiscing too about his encounters with celebrities such as Oscar Wilde, Lillie Langtry, Bernard Shaw, Ellen Terry, Frank Harris and Mrs Bram Stoker, among so many others. Yet he was also searching for something more and ventured into the many esoteric orders of his time such as the Hermetic Order of the Golden Dawn, the German Ordo Templi Orientis, the American Female Flagellants of New York, the Temple of the Smokers of the Sacred and numerous others. It was clear to me that in the course of his curious quest, he had become learned in many arcane techniques of expanding consciousness, which he refers to in the text as both 'Magick' and 'Mysticism'. There was much too about the use of plants and minerals to achieve a state he calls 'ecstasy'.

Who was he? My host refused to tell me, other than to state that he was the friend of a distant elderly cousin. In the text he makes it clear that he was an independently rich Viscount with access to both the rich and the poor – and the middle classes. The memories he records of his contemporaries have the ring of truth and yet it is so far impossible to identify him. My host showed me a stack of papers which had passed into the hands of the family. From these it is obvious that he chose to operate under the pseudonym of 'Horby'.

'I see that boys and "feasting with panthers" are not to your taste, Horby,' reads a scribbled card from Oscar Wilde, adding: 'but hock and seltzer should be. Do delight me at the Cadogan, 1.00, Tuesday.' The following telegram is obvious: 'LUNCHEON STOP TWO CAFE ROYAL STOP BE THERE HORBY STOP FRANK HARRIS'. Harris was then Editor of *The Saturday Review* and one of the most influential literary figures in London. Another telegram: 'SORRY CANT AND WONT STOP GBS' is obviously (and typically) from Bernard Shaw. 'Glad you appreciate poetry, Horby, but there's more to it than that,' is the inscription in the author's handwriting on Aleister Crowley's WHITE STAINS, which was privately printed (1898) and which has subsequently been criticised for its scandalous obscenity. A copy of the 1895 John Lane, The Bodley Head edition of *The Great God Pan* contains the following message by its author, Arthur Machen: 'Come to wine on Wednesday rather than to whine. And then you too, Horby, can sample the Jar of Avallaunius.' 'Absinthe any time, so get in touch, Horby, be pleased to hear from you, John Davidson,' are the drunkenly scrawled words on another bespattered postcard. 'Horby' must have stayed in touch with some of his old friends from the Nineties, for in this collection I discovered a 1921 edition, published in New York, of *Oscar Wilde: His Life and Confessions* by Frank Harris with the inscription: 'Horby, you old rogue! Don't forget your old friends! And don't you miss those glad, erect days!? – Frank Harris.'

Unfortunately for the researcher, there are no compromising documents from identifiable women. One assumes that either Horby or his family destroyed any letters of this nature. However, there are some perfectly proper signed photographs of beautiful and fully-dressed celebrities of the Nineties, such as Lillie Langtry, Ellen Terry, Florence Farr and Florence Balcombe. Lillie Langtry was, of course, the leading courtesan of her age and was for a time the mistress of the Prince of Wales. Ellen Terry was the leading actress of her era and was celebrated most in her role of Lady Macbeth. Florence Farr, a leading actress and dramatist, was also the lover of men such as Bernard Shaw, William Butler Yeats and Aleister Crowley. Oscar Wilde wanted to marry Florence Balcombe on account of her exceptional physical beauty but she spurned him in favour of Bram Stoker, author of *Dracula*. On the back of each one of these photographs, erasures have been made.

There is no doubt whatsoever in my mind that *The Black Pearl* should be published in the 1990s, giving us a quite unique insight into the 1890s. For my own part, I am still tracking down clues which will lend insight into this remarkable author. He has given us a document of great human interest which spans the academic disciplines of sociology, psychology, history, literature and sexology. It will surprise and possibly shock those who have a clichéd view of Victorian attitudes. It certainly lifts the manhole cover off a steaming underworld. The author explores every facet of his own sexuality and that of those he encounters. At times his interests are simply those of dissipation and debauchery. At other moments he relates the strange kinks of those he meets, which embroider the rich tapestry of human sexuality. For me, however, the most remarkable feature of this book is that its aristocratic Victorian author, outwardly a veritable pillar of the Establishment, comes to look upon sex as the holiest sacramental act in the known Universe.

Geraldine Lamb PhD.,
University of North Texas.

EDITOR'S PREFACE TO VOLUME II

For those who have not had the good fortune to study Volume I of *The Black Pearl*: the *Memoirs of a Victorian Sex-Magician*, a few words of explanation are assuredly in order for the approach to Volume II.

In Volume I, Horby reveals that he has inherited a Viscouncy, lands, possessions, an income from the funds of £100,000 a year 'on which a man can just about jog along these days' and letters of introduction to some of the most famous and infamous men and women of his time. He is initiated into sex by his extraordinary governess, Rosemary Radcliffe, who tutors him towards a place at Trinity College, Cambridge 1895–98. Rosemary is about ten years older and plays a prominent part in the *Memoirs*. So does the Hon. Claire Woodrough, a distant cousin he seduces when they are both in their teens and with whom he cultivates a lasting relationship. Both Rosemary and Claire, the true identity of whom diligent enquiry has hitherto failed to discover, continue to write Horby astonishingly frank letters about their manifold adventures and sexual experiences.

Horby encounters literary London, wining and dining at the Café Royale in the company of Frank Harris, Oscar Wilde, Bernard Shaw, Aubrey Beardsley, Whistler, Dégas, beautiful women and variously assorted rich drunkards. At Cambridge University he meets fellow undergraduate Aleister Crowley, poet, mountaineer and seeker after the spirit, later to be reviled in the tabloid press as 'the wickedest man in the world.' On coming down from Cambridge, he leads the life of a London man-about-town, purchasing his pornography from Leonard Smithers and discussing sex with Arthur Machen, Aleister Crowley, Ellen Terry, Mr & Mrs Bram Stoker, Bob Fitzsimmons (the Heavyweight Boxing Champion of the World), the Marquis of Queensberry, Lillie Langtry, Florence Farr and H.G. Wells, among others.

During this time, Horby proceeds to enjoy a bewildering variety of sexual experiences, both as practitioner and as voyeur. The text shows that his primary taste is for straight heterosexuality, though he clearly enjoys cunnilingus and fellatio and, on occasion, sodomy with a female and the spanking of her buttocks. On two occasions, he is bound by rapacious females wholly unexpectedly, and although the experiences excite him, he does not volunteer for them again. Indeed, when he is caned against his wish, he exacts a rapacious revenge upon the two lady perpetrators of this outrage to his manhood. Even so, he enjoys the sight of the birch being applied by women to the blushing bottoms of both males and females.

The features which distinguish this work from other pieces of Victorian erotica include an obvious love of women, however absurd some of Horby's attitudes may strike the contemporary reader as being. He loves the sight or the description of two beautiful women enraptured in the act of lesbian lust. He regards his journeys through salons, restaurants, music halls, clubs, pubs, cafés, brothels and strictly private houses as being not just a spelunking in debauchery but as a quest for the Holy Grail. He equates this Holy Grail with an ecstasy to be found within the vagina of a woman.

All the while, his perception that sex can be the holiest and most sacred ecstatic religious sacrament in the Universe is being augmented and refined by the letters he receives from Rosemary and Claire. He confesses that these do more for him than the secret magical society which he has joined, The Hermetic Order of the Golden Dawn. Rosemary, whose health appears to be erratic, enjoys erotic episodes in Brighton, Wales and Whitby, where she meets the mysterious and cadaverous 'Black Douglas', an international banker and an expert on vampirism: this intrigues Rosemary, who is a West Country hereditary witch, and she becomes his mistress. Claire, meanwhile, experiences the delights of both satanism and Rosicrucianism in Paris, then continues to Vienna for psycho-analysis with Dr Sigmund Freud and an intriguing affair with the Arch-Duke of the Austro-Hungarian Empire, Francis-Ferdinand.

Horby becomes friends with one Sir Richard Bellingham, Bart. Although to all outward appearances Bellingham is a buffoon, he has a good heart and welcomes every manner and mode of sexual and culinary experience, rejoicing in rhyme and bawdry. Horby has obviously thoroughly disguised the identity of this unashamedly scandalous gentleman since close enquiry has been unable to identify him.

After enjoying a wide variety of women, including 'the World's most beautiful woman', Lillie Langtry, mistress of the Prince of Wales – done for a bet with the aid of a phial of love potion made according to Rosemary's instructions – Horby takes the heiress and daughter of a senior clergyman, Emily Ward-Bishop, to a croquet contest with Rosemary and the enigmatic Douglas at £10,000 a side. Horby loses, Emily is spanked and stood in a corner for poor play, Rosemary relates her tale of performing fellatio upon the future King Edward VII beneath his dining table, Horby wins back his money on a bet concerning the true meaning of the word 'SNOB', sex is relished by the two couples and Douglas invites Horby and Emily to his castle near Vienna to witness a Sex Magick ritual.

Joined by Sir Richard Bellingham and a former mistress of Crowley, Horby and Emily embark on the Golden Arrow from London to Paris on a train chartered by Douglas and Rosemary. It's then Wagons-Lit carriages on a train to Vienna, chartered by Douglas, as these three couples fornicate their way across Europe. The *Memoirs* imply that this is well worth their while for they witness a solemn low mass of Sex Magick, wherein Douglas is the Priest, Rosemary the High Priestess, and Claire and Arch-Duke Francis Ferdinand are their Assistants. Horby is possessed by a trance of ecstasy but calls this 'only the end of the beginning of my sexual education.'

One can only exhort the keen student of Psychology, History, Literature and Sociology to turn to Volume I* in order fully to comprehend the sensibility with which he commences the second volume, which must surely be numbered among the most interesting documents of the period.

Geraldine Lamb PhD.,
University of California San Diego.

* Published in paperback by the New English Library.

EDITOR'S PREFACE TO VOLUME III

Some words of explanation are in order for those unfortunate enough not to have read Volumes I and II of *The Black Pearl: Memoirs of a Victorian Sex-Magician*.*

In Volume II, Horby continues to enjoy London life, seducing a suffragette he meets at a party hosted by Sydney and Beatrice Webb; attending the Rhymers' Club of Johnson, Davidson and Dowson; visiting brothels and exploring all sorts of occult societies. As a member of the Hermetic Order of the Golden Dawn, he supplies us with his own unique perspective on the quarrels between its leader, 'MacGregor' Mathers, William Butler Yeats and his curious friend, Aleister Crowley. With John Davidson, he visits the East End, smokes opium with The Smokers of the Sacred then returns to the West End to pass the evening at a strictly private club of flagellation confined to the nobility, the aristocracy, the gentry and all others who can pay its extortionate sums. He eats and drinks with Shaw, Wells, Chesterton, Belloc and Arthur Machen, recording their views on sex and society.

He visits New York twice. On the first occasion it is to witness the World Heavyweight Boxing Championship followed by a night with a secret society known as The Beautiful Female Flagellants of New York. On the

* Published in paperback by New English Library.

second, his adventures include an evening with Butch Cassidy and the Sundance Kid, along with their 'Wild Bunch.' He continues to fornicate relentlessly. On his ocean crossing, he learns much about gambling from Arnold Rothstein, future banker to the New York Underworld.

Horby enjoys a wide variety of acquaintanceship. There is Robert Ross in Paris, Frank Harris in Monaco, James McNeill Whistler in Venice; and Prime Minister Lord Salisbury with his nephew and successor, Arthur Balfour, at an English country weekend where the issues of the day are decided. He becomes involved in espionage, epitomising the English ideal of the gentleman amateur, and in Berlin encounters the intriguing international spy 'Maria', whom he will later meet in both London and Paris. He is also initiated by German sex-magicians into the Ordo Templi Orientis (OTO) which practises sex for the enhancement of consciousness though the narrator already knows this from previous experience. Back in London, he sees the humiliation of a woman by a man; then hears of the humiliation of a man by a woman. He crosses to Paris for the wedding of his old friend, Sir Richard Bellingham, and finds the links of that occasion with secret societies which enshrine the act of sex to be quite astonishing.

Bellingham plays a prominent part in these *Memoirs*, though further research has still not elicited his true identity. Nor has diligent enquiry managed to discover the name of his bride, given in the text as Mrs Davina Price-Hughes, a wealthy widow apparently worth between one and ten million pounds sterling. Nor does the text make it clear whether Bellingham is merely a fortunately-born buffoon or a holy and divine Fool in an obscure English medieval tradition, as portrayed in Tudor times by Shakespeare when writing of Falstaff.

Other prominent characters continue to elude close scrutiny of their true identities. Horby's former governess, Rosemary, High Priestess of this secret cult, continues to write him explicit letters from Istanbul, Vienna, Venice and Paris, making love with him whenever there is an opportunity to meet independently; though some of her liaisons are outrageous. The same can be said of the Hon. Claire Woodrough, another pupil of Rosemary and Horby's first young love. She journeys to New York, New Orleans and San Francisco, encountering characters as diverse as Scott Joplin, Harry Houdini, William Randolph Hearst, Ambrose Bierce and Buffalo Bill, and learns more of the mysteries of Voodoo. She is a Priestess of this secret cult and joins Rosemary and Horby in Paris for Bellingham's astounding Wedding Reception.

The names of those who appear to witness Sir Richard Bellingham's Wedding Reception in a Paris Temple have obviously been put in a code understood only by the select few to which *The Black Pearl* would be distributed privately. An especially mysterious figure is the man Horby calls 'the Black Douglas', a fabulously wealthy international banker who has Rosemary as his mistress, among many other women; who dines with the Prime Minister of England to discuss international affairs; and who is also the High Priest of the cult of enlightenment via sexuality.

There are three more men of mystery: Ram Singh, a Priest at Bellingham's wedding, has invited Claire to his ashram. 'Pierre', a very strange figure who has witnessed the lesbian activities of Rosemary and Claire, plays the peculiar role of The Monk at Bellingham's reception-come-orgy. The unpleasant Viscount Maulerby arouses a repulsion that is justified fully in the foregoing.

The intriguing Mrs Joan Smythe continues to intrude upon the narrative as the Queen of flagellation and female domination, managing a variety of sado-masochistic schemes such as The Female Flagellants of New York, The Smythe Reform Academy and the Society for the Promulgation of Petticoat Government. One Miss Emily Ward-Bishop is enthused by these pursuits; although she also relishes the pleasures of receiving chastisement from a man and to judge by the text, would like to marry Horby, a fact angrily deplored by Claire Woodrough.

'The Black Douglas' is somewhat sadistic in his treatment of women, though they do not appear to object, and, from the text, he appears to be on excellent terms with four beautiful and unusual young ladies: Lady Alison Utley and Lady Jane Fortescue, mistresses to the wealthy and powerful who enjoy their own peculiar perversities: and Lady Candida Lauderdale and Miss Amelia Edwards, an actress, friends of Bellingham's bride, the former Mrs Davina Price-Hughes, former mistresses of Aleister Crowley – in common with their friend – and both of them ensnared by a desire for the decadent.

All these questions and issues are explored honestly, behind certain necessary 'blinds,' in the third volume of the *Memoirs*, which take the reader around the world in a bizarre travelogue of sexual adventure, education and experience. In common with its predecessors, this volume is hardly 'politically correct.' The narrator was possessed of many of the prejudices of his time, although he repudiates the vice of racism including anti-semitism and continually advocates an unrestricted love of women, coming all the while closer in his obsessive quest for the Holy Grail.

Some may see merely obscenity within this document, to which one can only retort that those who dwell within a conceptual sewer tend to notice very little other than their immediate surrounds. The more educated, however, may obtain invaluable insights into the sociology, history and psychology of the period, including perceptions deriving from world-wide travel, within these pages – pages of unique literary interest.

Geraldine Lamb PhD.,
University of California at Berkeley.

AUTHOR'S INTRODUCTION TO VOLUME I

As I take up my pen to write of my life, I remain convinced that fighting and fucking are when two people come closest. You can grow close to a man either by fighting against him or by fighting with him on the same side as one slogs along through various battles. However, I am of the opinion that it is not possible to grow close to a woman unless one fucks her.

My personal view is that when fucking a woman, one should jolly well roger her brains out and give it some arse. I'm well aware that this view is thought unfashionable in our degenerate modern times. Female emancipation has indeed proceeded apace and I have never opposed it but the results have not been precisely what I wanted nor, one suspects, exactly the results desired by the fairer sex. It is indeed a delight to regard our modern young girls in their slim, short skirts but they lack the mystery and romanticism of the long, rustling white petticoats of yesteryear. These days, they all wear rosy red-leaf lip-stick and they all smoke and they pout sexily but despite all that delicious expanse of white thigh and ankle, they lack the eroticism of the women of my youth. These days one takes a girl for morning cocktails at 'The Apple Tree', goes on to luncheon at 'Pietro Le Fueno', proceeds to an afternoon session at 'Dolly's', where one's ears are deafened with jazz, takes afternoon tea at The

Connaught, goes on to cocktails at the Ritz, sees the latest play at the Theatre Royal, the Haymarket, has drinks and then dinner at The Savoy, and all the thanks you receive is 'Cheerio.'

Ah! It wasn't like that in the days of my golden, gilded youth! Women really were women in those spacious times! They certainly weren't boys with short bobs for hair, flat chests and thin skin and bone where the buttocks should have been. It is said that times have become increasingly sexually free. It is so and I welcome the development yet some inscrutable element has been lost. How is the matter best put? I am reminded of Lady Charlotte X, who always used to defend the institution of marriage on the grounds that it lent so much spice to the pleasures of adultery. Forbidden fruit does indeed taste so much sweeter. In a similar vein, one could advance the proposition that the very restrictions of my youth gave each forbidden encounter an exquisite charm that is wholly lacking in these present days that are so permissive and yet so cold.

Nevertheless, it is impossible for me to complain about a life indefatigably blessed by good fortune. I am hardly a rich man but even in these inflationary times it is just about possible to jog along on £100,000 a year. The only duties incumbent upon me are maintaining the lands, a job done most capably by the family stewards; and turning up at the House of Lords occasionally whenever there is a vital vote. My quiet position has enabled me to meet some of the most interesting men and women in the land and also to travel abroad to meet more.

Throughout my life, I have been a lover of Woman, in all her intriguing shapes and guises. Although I have enjoyed the good fortune of meeting with some of the strongest, most powerful and most intelligent men of my era, and although I have assuredly learned wisdom from their lips, I have received yet greater education from the labia of ladies. This may be thought a peculiar view but I shall demonstrate my case.

Too many men of my acquaintanceship, however illustrious, have informed me that they regard the sexual act as being merely the prodding of a stiff rod between soft thighs into a soft and welcoming female orifice. Although their joy in this glorious matter can hardly be denied and although I take a deep share in their joy, knowing of it to my own good, I nevertheless insist that there is something more to the matter.

The sexual act, properly understood, is more than merely the delights of animal gratification, splendid though these are. It is more than the doing of a deed alleged to be 'dirty' and therefore somehow sinful, in consequence of which its execution imparts a sinister thrill, an added *frisson* of forbidden pleasure. It can be the holiest, most religious act in the World when a man and a woman come together and create energy between one another as a sacrament. It can elevate one's consciousness and enable one, if one dares say so, to evolve beyond the level of the apes who originally sired us.

During my life, I have been able to acquaint myself with a number of occult groups, from some of whom I learned much and from others of whom I learned nothing at all. Most of them have taught me techniques, nevertheless, which I have found to be useful. It is my willed intention to put down here all I know before I die so that possibly some others may benefit from the recounting of my experiences.

In the beginning, I knew nothing other than my rampant rod and of its lust for a slick, juicy cunt. By the end, I had discovered the Holy Grail. I shall begin, then, amidst the mist of ignorance, continue through a hard middle and, one trusts, finish with a flourish at the end.

[illegible] I have read of them [illegible] of ladies. [illegible]

[illegible] deep sleep in [illegible] that there [illegible] to the matter.

The [illegible] properly understood [illegible] a man and a [illegible]

[illegible] I have been [illegible]

In the [illegible]

AUTHOR'S INTRODUCTION TO VOLUME II

As I commence dictation to my charming and beautiful secretary, whose name discretion forbids me to mention, and set forth the second volume of my *Memoirs*, a few more words of explanation are required if this work is not to receive more severe censure than that which it doubtless deserves.

'The proper study of mankind is Man,' wrote Alexander Pope and one trusts that his use of the generic term was inclusive of Woman. From an early age I have discerned the holy truth that the highest grace is conferred by the union of the male and the female in sexual congress. This perception was fully confirmed by my experience of a low mass at the castle of 'the Black Douglas', as I have referred to him, near Vienna. It is the purpose of this volume to explore my memory and retrieve from it the words and images of all encounters which have granted me understanding and wisdom, especially in terms of the practical application of my apperception.

O! how I sigh some mornings for those spacious days of the *fin de siècle* . . .! We were all so young then and burning with lust for the World. If that be Decadence, then I loved every moment of it! Today (1925) it strikes me that so much Romance has gone out of the World. Take the recent postcard, for example, which I received this morning from my old friend, Frank Harris.

Hope you're still keeping it up, Horby! Why not come and visit me in Nice? Know the latest rhyme about the girls today?

If the skirts get any shorter
Said the Flapper with a sob;
I'll have two more cheeks to powder
And a lot more hair to bob.

All the grimmest
Frank.

I remain fond of the former lion of literary London, though he has been savaged by critics for the first volume of his autobiography, *My Life and Loves*, which I, for one, thoroughly enjoyed, both for its literary, political and social reminiscences and for its unabashed sexual candour. One gathers that he is presently subject to a wave of puritanical persecution. His mistake, in my view, was to cast pearls before swine in this increasingly narrow, moralistic climate of opinion, where even the United States of America, once boasting itself to be the 'home of the brave and the land of the free,' has had the stupid temerity to ban the imbibing of alcoholic beverages. Ah! how I savour the memory of those spacious days of my youth! I shall describe my visits to America in the course of this volume.

The mistake of Harris was to place his private life before the profane eyes of the riff-raff and one assumes that only the pressures of financial need persuaded him to embark on so inadvisable a course of action. I shall make no such error. This work is only for the eyes of my cultivated friends.

My morning post also brought a greetings card from H.G. Wells, thanking me for the dinner I gave him the other day. Wells has of course deservedly acquired world fame – and his amorous activities continue unabated. He is too sensible, though, to soil his reputation among the respectable by publishing publicly his reminiscences of his many encounters. 'If you don't like your life, you can change it,' he always used to say and the man was certainly a living example of practising what one preaches. In my case, however, I was too fortunate to have much desire to change my life and I do not regret anything that I have done. I regret only that which I *haven't* done.

It will readily be discerned by the reader that I received much benefit from my visit to Vienna and my witnessing of a 'low mass' of Sex-Magick. Allow me, then, to essay a narrative of my further exploration in my quest for the Holy Grail.

AUTHOR'S INTRODUCTION TO VOLUME III

As I dictate these words of my Memoirs to my exquisitely efficient and charmingly pretty secretary, one cannot help remarking that some savour of the spacious days of my youth has gone out of the world. Personally, I blame the brutality of the Great War. Everything I knew seems to have become rather insane ever since the Armistice. I served my country in the Great War and I fought for freedom, justice and a better world for one and all, especially Great Britain. Where is it?

I don't enjoy seeing unemployed and disabled ex-soldiers on the streets, homeless and starving, especially since Lloyd George promised them 'homes fit for heroes.' I don't think it's right for the wages of the workers to be reduced by Government legislation. I freely admit that I am one of the lucky ones and that shrewd investments made by my assistants have made me richer now than I have ever been before. If I wanted to, even in this time of inflation, I could have a thirteen-year-old girl for the same price as in 1901: they're all out there whoring for their disabled fathers. It's just that unripe apples have never been of much sexual interest to me.

Take other aspects of modern life, for instance. Poetry? None of it rhymes or has scansion, rhythm or metre. Painting and sculpture? These 'Dada' chaps paint moustaches on a postcard of the Mona Lisa or else put their toe-nail clippings in a jam jar and have the nerve to call it Art! And some people are stupid enough to pay for it! Architecture? I see buildings being erected that look just like the Corn-Flakes packages of Dr Kellogg – and some poor people actually have to live in them. There's no grace any more and where will it all end?

Sex? These short dresses which expose lovely legs certainly arouse my carnal lusts – but why do the girls these days have to look as straight and flat in their figures as these new 'A' roads that our wretched Government is plastering everywhere across the landscape of our once beautiful countryside? The motor-car, although it has its undeniable uses, farts forth fumes that poison our lungs. They'll be abolishing the railways next! Sometimes I really do feel like those old retired Colonels who write letters to *The Morning Post* signed 'Disgusted, Tunbridge Wells', for whilst I am certainly no Socialist, I'm damned if I know which aspects of the national heritage the Conservative Party is conserving.

Ah! It was rather different in the days of my youth when it seemed as though the world was my oyster and I travelled around the globe in search of its elusive black pearl. I invite you, gentle reader – as authors used to state a century ago – to join me in my exploration of the sacred mystery of Sex.

I had thought, after the adventures I described in my second volume, that there was precious little more for me to learn. How wrong I was! And I don't mind admitting it. There was still so much for me to discover as I journeyed around the world, witnessing all manners and mores and sexual customs, in my own singular quest for the Holy Grail.

CHAPTER ONE

One thing is for certain: it was a damn good fuck that night in Paris, New Year's Day 1901. I was tumbling Emily Ward-Bishop in a four-poster bed in one of the many houses that her family owned, just off the Rue de Rivoli. Sir Richard Bellingham and his newly wed wife Davina had departed for their honeymoon and one understood that after Paris, it would proceed to Cannes and Nice, after which their voyaging would be a secret for the ensuing three months. Rosemary was with the mysterious Douglas and Claire with the mystifying Pierre. It had been a most unusual and delightful Wedding Reception and, certainly, I had no cause for complaint as Emily sucked my cock with the utmost skill and rapture.

With her mouth full of my glistening shaft, she squeezed my balls as a stream of creamy spunk hurtled out of my cock into her eager, warm, moist mouth. Gamely, she swallowed my entire gushing emission, draining my shaft of its salty flow whilst a wonderful orgasmic wave swept over me. Then she opened her lips to release my fast-deflating tadger and panted: 'Oh, your sperm has such an invigorating taste. I can hardly wait till you fuck the arse off me again, yes!'

I responded by kissing her crimson nipples as I cupped her chubby, firm buttocks in my hands, squeezing them lecherously whilst I slid all the way down until my lips were only inches away from her soft strands of pussy hair and she parted her thighs to make her moist, swollen cunny lips more accessible to me. Emily let out a delighted gasp as my tongue moved over every inch of her juicy, damp crack; and she breathed a long sigh whilst my eager tongue delved everywhere in the folds of her vagina, probing and sliding from her slit to her bum-hole, licking and lapping up the odoriferous love juices which her cunt now exuded.

I stiffened the tip of my tongue and started to lick the soft, puffed inner lips and inhaled her unique feminine aroma as she moaned again with unslaked desire. Then, suddenly, I thrust my tongue between her cunt lips, pushing within the warm, wet cunny channel. Her hips gyrated madly as I tongue-fucked this luscious girl, licking her cunt up and down and feeling her clitty grow harder each time my tongue flicked across it.

Now it was time to concentrate on this swollen bud and I nibbled at the jerking love button whilst I moved my hand upwards and slid first one and then two fingers into her wetness. Her voracious cunt was hot and tight and she bucked as I twisted my fingers inside her, arching her body with joy when I tickled her clit with the tip of my tongue.

Again and again I drove my tongue inside her, feeling her vaginal walls clutch it as my lips paid homage to her clitty, kissing and sucking the erectile flesh as Emily writhed under my erotic ministrations. The throbbing vibrations of her body excited me further and my rampant prick rubbed sinuously against her legs as my own hips worked to and fro. I continued to tongue-fuck Emily towards the ultimate peak of pleasure. She reached her climax with a throaty shriek as the orgasm burst inside her cunt in a mighty explosion and my face was flooded by a fierce, fresh outpouring of cuntal juice which I gulped down as if I were devouring oysters; while Emily now shivered all over with the force of her climactic spend.

I gave her no respite and promptly mounted her, gasping my joy aloud as my stiff, throbbing rod prodded right into her warm, juicy and welcoming cunt. My thrusts began slowly and deeply, so that the tip of my knob touched the entrance of her womb and made her quiver all over.

'Let's try a new position, Horby!' Emily gasped. 'Move in deeply – yes, that's it; now throw your left leg up over my loins, and put your right under my left leg, fork fashion . . . isn't it awfully nice? Your cock goes into the exact angle of my quim and its tip touches the very entrance to my womb! Ah! ah! Ohhh . . .! You do make me spend . . . I can't help it. Go on quicker, you darling! Ah, it drives me mad! You make me melt all over . . .'

For my own part, I was in ecstasy and my delighted prick was so sensitive to the clinging grip of her lascivious cunt that I was compelled to cry out that I could not bear it any longer as my hot spunk spurted into her quim.

Good heavens! This prim and proper – to all outward appearances – little bitch was once again quite insatiable. After a rest of only a couple of minutes or so, she once more took possession of my prick and lovingly kissed, sucked and tongued my balls, her busy fingers doing their best by teasing my increasingly impetuous shaft, causing it to re-enter her foaming vagina which was overflowing with our creamy emissions. I kept myself back before another spend and so drew out the length of that glorious fuck as she fixed her pearly white teeth in my shoulders until her lips were crimsoned by my blood. At the climax, we rolled around together in a perfect fury of amorous frenzy.

I had thought that I could do no more and so we took cognac and talked. I smoked a Turkish cigarette while she told me a joke.

'A chap went up in a balloon the other day here in Paris, didn't you know?' Emily told me. 'He went higher, it is reliably reported, than any man before him, but he came down in a shocking state. Just before he passed out and had to be rushed to hospital, he declared: "I saw God." Well,' she continued animatedly, 'the doctors and nurses saved his life, but when he recovered consciousness, his hospital bed was surrounded by journalists asking: "Did you see God?" He nodded dazedly. "And what was God like?" He refused to tell them. Finally, the room was cleared and the President of the French Republic himself came to see the gallant captain. "*Courage, mon brave!*" he exclaimed, "*mon cher monsieur*, you say that you saw God?" The captain nodded. "And," the President enquired, "what was God like?" The captain gasped a few words before slumping into a coma which would last a year, but those words were: "Yes, I saw God. And *she was black!*" '

I laughed and could not resist kissing Emily passionately, our lips glued together. My forefinger felt that her clit was trembling and tingling with reaffirmed desire. My sturdy shaft once more pressed hard against her belly as she covered my neck and shoulders with playful little love-bites. She wrapped her thighs around my hips, knowing that I was strong enough to hold her in this position, and soon enough she was once more spitted on my stiffly swollen cock. Our mouths met hungrily, again and again; then, abruptly, I bent my head down and started to suck on her titties, which so electrified her that she rocked violently from side to side, overbalanced and toppled over out of the bed.

Scrambling to our feet and shouting with laughter, we flung ourselves back upon the bed. I chose to spear her from behind with my rampant rod, easing it into her squelchy cunt: and then my belly slammed hard against her bum cheeks. I fucked her with delight as she groaned with joy.

'Oh!' she shrieked out. 'I just love it when your prick pistons in and out of my sopping cunny whilst your firm, manly hands squeeze and knead my breasts!' My tongue brushed her neck and shoulders lightly and she sighed with the pleasure of true sensuality. She pushed out her delectable bottom to meet my powerful thrusts and my balls slapped against the backs of her thighs. As I worked my thick tadger backwards and forwards, I murmured: 'Goddess! What a delicious cunt you have, Emily . . . there's no other cunny which clasps my cock so beautifully! That's it, my darling, work your arse!' My hot, wet, stiff shaft slewed to and fro, faster and faster.

'Aah . . .!' she cried out. 'Shoot your spunk, my love! Empty your balls, you gorgeous man!' And with my face buried in her neck and with my heated breath blowing upon her shoulder, I ejaculated a fountain of frothy jism inside her throbbing cunt: and her own spend arrived seconds later so that her quim was once more awash with our combined love juices. We writhed around in an undignified heap of entwined limbs as we enveloped ourselves in the delights of this simultaneous spend, and then we stretched ourselves out on the four-poster bed and enjoyed a peace which passeth all understanding.

Emily left Paris on the following morning after a delightful breakfast of exquisitely brewed dark coffee and the most crisp and buttery croissants I have ever tasted, accompanied by the conserves of the peach and the apricot. As always, she had relatives to see in England. Naturally I had hired a carriage for her transport to the Gare du Nord and she looked rather splendid as her gloved hand waved goodbye, encumbered by far too many hat-boxes and cases; the horses drew away with an appropriate jingling of bells.

I could now address my undivided attention to a further matter which had to engage my finest faculties during my visit to Paris. The reader of my second volume may recall my revelation that I have on occasion undertaken missions of espionage on behalf of the British Intelligence services. This had brought me into contact with the delectably lecherous Maria, apparently an agent for every Great Power in Europe, not to mention America. This time my mission had been given to me by both Sir Richard Bellingham and my cousin at our Berlin Embassy. It was to investigate Satanism in Paris.

It was believed in high circles, apparently, that there might be a global grouping of men and women devoted to the Devil and all the evidence pointed to Paris as being the international headquarters of this nefarious organization. Prior to my arrival, and Bellingham's wedding, I had acquired information enabling me to write and propose meetings to various personages. I had also milked Claire and Maria for further information.

'What is truth?' asked Pontius Pilate. I'm still waiting for an answer. The stories of Satanism were many and multifarious and complicated by the fact that it was difficult to tell whether one was receiving accurate information or not. For instance, it had been alleged that one Albert Pike had established Satanism in America and had sent 'the Devil's Daughter', Diana Vaughan, to strengthen its cause in Paris and in Western Europe generally. Published books had been written to this effect, especially *The Devil in the Nineteenth Century* by Dr Bataille (1892). This detailed the devil-worship of Albert Pike and his 'Palladian Order' in Charleston, South Carolina, USA, and linked it to Freemasonry in a manner expounded by Lee Taxil in *The Mysteries of Freemasonry* and *Are There Women in Freemasonry*: followed by *Confessions of an Ex-Free Thinker* by Gabrièle Jogand-Pages. *Là-Bas*, the literary novel by the celebrated author J.K. Huysmans, gave a detailed description of a Black Mass in Paris. All these works were best-sellers and set forth the notion of an international Satanic conspiracy.

At the time, this notion was plausible; and a plethora of books detailing sinister conspiracies had poured out of Paris. Now, I was hardly a stranger to secret societies, being a member, *inter alia*, of the Golden Dawn, the Order Templi Orientis, the Smokers of the Sacred, the Female Flagellants of New York (admittedly, only as an associate), various groupings of the British Intelligence services (doing my bit for Queen and Country as a gentleman amateur) and the mysterious cluster comprising Douglas, the international banker, Rosemary, Claire and other curious figures such as Pierre and Ram Singh. The difficulty lay in working out the actual significance which lay behind these sundry groupings.

Matters were not made any easier by the way in which espionage is conducted. One is given both information and disinformation and it is rather hard to tell which is which. For instance, Rosemary had written me letters from Whitby in Yorkshire concerning Douglas, only later to state that these had been fiction. Was she telling the truth or not? All I knew for certain was that she was the High Priestess of an international Order of which Douglas was the High Priest, that this Order regarded sex as being sacred, that I had witnessed its activities in a castle in

Vienna and at Bellingham's wedding at a house in Paris; and that my association with Rosemary and with this Order had brought me nothing but good. I could discern no evidence of Satanism in the rites I had witnessed; yet an atheistic bourgeois might well call these 'disgusting' and a Christian clergyman might well interpret them as being 'Satanic'.

Maria had informed me that there was 'certainly' an international Satanic conspiracy but then she might have been feeding me the disinformation she was paid to give to so many others. Claire had written me a letter from Paris in which she had given me all the lubricious details of a Satanic initiation at the hands, eager and willing, of her cousin Charlotte and her friend Jean-Charles. She had insisted upon its veracity: yet even though my loving involvement with Claire had done me so much good, and even though she had served as a Priestess at Sir Richard's extraordinary wedding, there was still the possibility that she might have been telling me an amusing piece of fiction.

At the time, I found it rather hard to make sense of it all. I was equipped with every possible advantage, having my own private agents, the full co-operation of the British Embassy in Paris and its attached intelligence services, and the names and addresses of the alleged Satanists as willingly supplied by Claire. This trail of enquiry led nowhere. Jean-Charles, who sometimes added extra confusion to the matter by calling himself Jean-Pierre, had apparently vanished off the face of the Earth, accompanied by Claire's alleged cousin Charlotte. Yes, a man and a woman answering to the descriptions Claire had given me had indeed resided at the address to which their residence was ascribed: yet their neighbours spoke of them as 'a quiet couple' who, having paid their rent, had vanished into thin air, leaving no traces behind them. I bombarded Claire with telegrams at every address at which she might be residing and of which she had informed me but received no reply.

She had left Paris, I knew, with Pierre, another mysterious one whom I desired to interview, but all endeavours to trace him were proving to be equally useless. Rosemary and Douglas, who could have helped me at that point, had vanished too. Therefore I had no alternative other than to follow the leads I possessed at that point and meet Viscount Maulerby, who did some work for the Foreign Office, and his companion, Father Armand Binoire (Society of Jesus, no less) at a café on the Rue de Rivoli over pernod.

My dislike of Lord Maulerby, with his piggy eyes and all too evident folds of bulging flesh has already been made only too clear. Father Armand Binoire was a thin, pale and skeletal individual, with hard, cold eyes and a mean, tight mouth which immediately led me to detest him even more. Maulerby was aware of the nature of my mission. I wondered how he managed to reconcile his investigation of Satanism and his acquaintanceship with a Roman Catholic priest with his lecherous behaviour at Sir Richard Bellingham's wedding.

'My advice, Horby,' Lord Maulerby pontificated, 'is that you listen to Father Binoire here. Now, he knows *the facts!*'

'What are they?' I enquired. 'I'll listen gladly.'

'Essentially,' said Father Binoire, who spoke English perfectly with only the slightest of foreign accents, 'we are speaking of a conspiracy between various groupings to destroy Christian culture and Christian civilization.'

'Down with it!' Maulerby exclaimed.

'Quite so,' I murmured.

'The threat comes,' said Father Binoire, 'from the Satanists in alliance with the Freemasons . . .'

This struck me as being absurd on one level; yet perfectly understandable on another. I happen to be a Freemason as recognized by United Grand Lodge of England, which I have found to be an innocuous, fraternal and charitable organization, enacting in ceremony various alleged 'truths' of 'The Grand Architect of the Universe.' My friend Aleister Crowley had been initiated both into this and into the Ancient And Accepted Scottish Rite and in certain conversations, conducted within the rules of all Oaths duly sworn and therefore spoken obliquely, the basic principles of Liberty, Equality and Fraternity – as enunciated in the French Revolution – appeared to be the same. A difficulty arose in discussing the French Grand Orient Lodge. English United Grand Lodge demands as a condition of initiation the acceptance of some form of God or Higher Power. French Grand Orient Lodge insists upon atheism. Ancient And Accepted Scottish Rite Freemasonry preserves 'the auld alliance' with France and admits atheists on the grounds that the human can be divine.

Moreover, many of the seniors of the Golden Dawn and the Ordo Templi Orientis were Freemasons. These Orders not only practised ceremonies but actually taught Ceremonial Magic: and what was one to make of *that*? I had discerned no Satanism at all; nor could I see how the atheists of the French Grand Orient Lodge could be Satanists either: since how the devil can you believe in the Devil if you don't believe in God?

'An alliance, Father Binoire?' I therefore queried as I sipped some more good pernod. 'An alliance with whom?'

'The Jews . . .' Father Binoire stated solemnly.

'God damn 'em!' Maulerby expostulated.

'Oh . . .?' I had always thought of the Jews as being the victims of persecution rather than the instigators of same. 'And who else?'

'The machinations of International Finance,' said Father Binoire. 'But essentially it's manipulated by the Rothschilds.' I scratched my head in puzzlement. Obviously the Jews were making money in international finance whenever and wherever they could: but so was everyone else involved. I found it rather hard to picture a group of Jews giving Satanism more than one minute of their time, still less taking part in rites of Devil Worship when they could be sitting comfortably in their offices or enjoying chicken soup with their wives at home.

The level on which I could understand the point of view of Father Binoire was simple. As far as he was concerned, *every* religion not controlled by the Roman Catholic Church had to be inspired by the work of the Devil. This was especially true of Freemasonry, which had been anathematized by the Pope well over a century ago and to which no Roman Catholic could belong. In other words, everyone who wasn't a Christian was a Satanist. This made his 'information' worthless, but I nodded patiently as he passed me a Vatican document for my attention, nodded further as he expounded his theory that the United States of America had been founded by a Satanic conspiracy of Jews, Satanists and Freemasons and nearly nodded off to sleep when he deplored women as being secondary creatures, created by the Devil in order to tempt men from the paths of righteousness.

If I were an atheist, I thought, *I'd say 'Thank God for it!'* after listening to this ridiculous fool. Even so, 'Manners Makyth Man', as they so rightly say, so I shook the hands of both my companions and departed on my way in search of sex.

I spent my evening fucking Maria. As I later learned, Maulerby spent his paying a tart to sit on his face and Father Armand Binoire S.J. enjoyed *his* whipping a thirteen-year-old choir-boy with a martinet before buggering him. I was starting to wonder just where the real Satanists were.

CHAPTER TWO

My *Memorandum 813* informs me that on the following day, I enjoyed a solitary luncheon at the Café de la Paix in the charming Opera Quarter. I have never had better *Moules Marinière*, roasted *gigot* of lamb, dripping with blood and accompanied by a portion of buttered spinach, and *tarte tatin* – all washed down by a jolly good bottle of vintage Chambertin. There is a world of difference between *eating* on one's own, whereby one suffers the pangs of loneliness, and *dining* on one's own, whereby one relishes the pleasures of solitude. One doesn't need to talk; one can simply enjoy the food and wine as one calmly surveys the world. It is said that, if you sit for long enough in the Café de la Paix, everyone you have ever known will be encountered, which makes it sound rather like the Afterlife, whether in Heaven or in Hell. Fortunately, this did not happen in the three hours I passed there, relishing my repast and the pleasures of quiet contemplation.

Lord Maulerby and Father Binoire had disturbed my mental processes with their bloody, wretched nonsense. Maria, delectable fuck though she was, had exacerbated further my perturbation of the brain by giving me more confusing information. To compound this confounded matter, there was in my pocket a letter from Claire which had been hand delivered to my hotel by private messenger service.

My darling Horby,

Surprise! Again it's me – but, as has been said before, truth is stranger than fiction.

Unfortunately, I am in a state of requiring solace since my grandmother died so unexpectedly. What a matriarch she was! It was necessary that I attend her funeral at Highgate Cemetery, the first time I have ever been an attendant at a burial. It was a solemn occasion as the grim-faced pall-bearers carried my grandmother's coffin to the grave next to that of my grandfather, who had died the year before. (I have to admit that their relationship had been volatile and sometimes even vitriolic.) It was gratifying to witness that hundreds came to pay their respects to my late grandmother, and of course we were all garbed in severe and sober black. Why do women always look so beautiful at funerals? My own hair had been styled in a petite chignon *and was graced by a black hat which sported a white ostrich plume. When the coffin of Grandmama was laid to rest, I wiped away my tears yet found it necessary that I should temporarily retire from this solemn occasion of grief.*

I meandered around the cemetery to look upon the graves of those who had died before. There was Hovis, the inventor of cheap, mass-produced brown bread. And there was Karl Marx, whom everyone within my immediate acquaintanceship appears to hate but whose books I had studied with pleasure and profit under the tutelage of Rosemary. He seemed to think that there are inevitable laws of history, that the owners of land are having power stripped from them by the owners of manufacturing industry – which may well be true – and that the industrial workers will arise, have a bloody revolution and install a dictatorship, after which the State will 'wither away', which sounds most unlikely. You know, my darling, that Politics doesn't interest me that much.

Why is it that one always feels so sentimental at funerals? And why is it also that there is usually a macabre tendency to laugh? At that moment, however, there were inexplicable palpitations within my heart. Suddenly, there was a tap upon my left shoulder. I had read and heard that this was the Sign of Death: and I dissolved into tears of grief, turning around to stare into the black eyes of Douglas, that man of mystery, secrecy and enigma.

'At last you acknowledge my presence,' he said softly.

'Douglas,' I replied, 'initially I did not see you.' I sobbed once. 'I was preoccupied with my own thoughts.'

'Let me kiss away your tears,' he replied as they dribbled gently down my cheeks.

'Did you know my grandmother?'

'Oh, very well,' he replied.

'How well?'

'You will find out soon,' was his response. We walked throughout the cemetery, arm in arm, observing the gargoyles, the angels, the seraphim and cherubim and the statues of the Spirits of the Four Elements: Michael, Gabriel, Raphael and Uriel – Air, Water, Fire and Earth.

'I am so sad that my grandmother is dead,' I said, upon reaching the garden of tranquillity and appreciating the momentary peace of our silence, where not even the doves made their presence known, staying as silent and invisible as the earthworms at their grim feasting six feet beneath us. I felt sequestered from the rest of the world. Abruptly, Douglas took me into his arms and kissed me passionately upon the lips; and I could not resist his charms. He understood the stress and tension in my life yet, beneath it all, I felt his throbbing, pulsating with a wild desire to be released.

'Madam,' he said, 'I desire desperately to fuck you.'

'Do you think that this is the most appropriate time?' I responded, adding a sarcastic, 'Sir . . .?'

'I assure you that it is.'

'But there might be an intruder!'

'Only mine,' he replied.

I lifted up my skirt hem, rolled down my silken stockings and removed my suspenders. Off came my thigh garter, too; this was of scarlet with engraved gilt buckles and frills of taffeta.

I am so ashamed to say that we fucked upon a tombstone. How he did prod his rod into me and how stiff it was! Yes! A mighty ram-rod with the power of a steam-engine piston, pumping and pumping as my thighs trembled. How my clit twitched! And how my toes did tingle as my breasts heaved beneath my tight corset and my nipples stood erect like two little guardsmen.

To my stunned stupefaction, he produced a wicked, gleaming knife from his trouser pocket and proceeded to slit my corset in two down its middle! Then he took my left teat into his mouth and proceeded to suck upon it.

'This is rather like the Matterhorn,' he murmured.

'But now you must enjoy the pleasure of my other mammary,' I sighed, 'for you might find it to be like Mont Blanc.' He nuzzled his head between my breasts before ascending the next mountain. I delighted in his kisses as he gently bit upon my right bosom, finally to reach my right areola.

'Mont Blanc . . .?' he growled. 'This, my dear, is what I would call Mount Everest!' His voice became gentler. 'How many men have conquered this mountain before?' Too many, *I thought. 'What a sublime elevation!' I felt the same way as his mighty member thrust within my cunt to shake me with its rhythm, prior to its*

spurting of his love juices into me – but abruptly we were rudely interrupted in our final copulation. How could anybody behave so discourteously at my grandmother's funeral?

Whack! whack! whack! *That was the sound of a parasol beaten upon the naked and twitching slim buttocks of Douglas.* Whack! whack! whack! *again – and how his prick and his sperm did penetrate me! It was as if the barriers of a dam had been burst wide open and his secretion of juices entered my vagina as if I were the sole recipient of the indundation of some fearsome deluge. How he did emit his sperm from here to eternity! He shot his juices inside me as if he were a mighty fountain – or perhaps a volcano such as Mount Etna might be a more accurate analogy.*

At that moment, I looked into the eyes of my former tutor, Rosemary. They were sparkling blue, bright and alive as she thrashed Douglas upon his bare bottom as he recovered swiftly to fuck me once more in the quiet of the garden of remembrance, city of the dead and valley of dry bones.

'Rosemary!' I exclaimed, in between gasps of pleasure, 'what is the connection between you and my grandmother?'

'I have known that great matriarch for many a year,' she replied coolly, then carried on calmly whipping Douglas's bottom with her unfurled parasol. 'In my youth, I attended her finishing school in Switzerland and was one of her star pupils. I learned . . .' whack! *'. . . ah, so very much from her, including . . .'* whack! *'. . .the finest disciplines in life.'* Whack! whack! whack! *she went; and Douglas groaned and gasped in a curious admixture of agony and ecstasy as my cunt unambiguously enjoyed the jerking thrustings of his*

prick. 'Also matters such as riding a horse, cooking a dinner fit for a gourmet, figure skating, needlepoint and making a bed with proper hospital corners.' Whack! *'Oh, and she also taught me the craft of embroidery.' She lifted up her black skirt of satin to reveal the finest pair of white silk knickers that I have ever seen. They came down to the backs of her knees and were adorned with frills of lace.*

Douglas turned his head and was visibly amazed by her finery, her fal-de-lal, her frills and furbelows, her crimson suspender belt and her black, silken stockings. The tight lacing of her corset made her breasts thrust forward as if they desired to be eaten and her bottom thrust backwards as though it desired to be kissed. Suddenly I realized the nature of the situation between them. It was so obvious that they now wanted to be together that I gracefully retired from my recumbent posture atop the tombstone, taking up a new position behind an old yew tree with red berries in full bloom. It was a joy to be a voyeur as they made an exhibition of their mutual ribaldry, hedonism and debauchery. Douglas licked her cunt, sodomised her bottom and rejoiced as Rosemary sucked his prick before he thrust within her and they both screamed out their shared joy as they came together.

Afterwards, Douglas lit a Turkish cigarette and produced a silver flask of brandy and we sat merrily upon the tombstone, reminiscing about the life of my grandmother, Dorothea. They spoke of her acquaintanceship with that great American poet, Walt Whitman, for she had enjoyed her travels throughout the world. She had been a good friend of Pierre and Marie Curie, only now receiving their just share of recognition after years of neglect. Amidst tales of adventures among the Russian aristocracy, I was not expecting Rosemary to lift up her frock.

'Would you not say . . .' she murmured languorously, 'that my cunny is not unlike the shape of a Russian samovar? Douglas, would you not like to drink of my hot tea?' His head darted forth eagerly to suck greedily upon her quim.

I realized that I should leave them to their own devices and so wandered on to the wake in Hampstead, the cries of lascivious lovers ringing in my ears. What strange obsequies! I departed to the house of a relative, there to utter my condolences before those festivities which customarily follow a funeral.

I believe that my grandmother has left me certain properties in her will, one of them being in Rajasthan, India, the city of the Holy Men, where I believe that the intriguing Dr Ram Singh has his ashram. *One gathers that the most sacred of Temples are there.*

My darling, I must conclude this letter now. The past few days have just been so exhausting for me. But one cannot complain too much about necessary matters of grave concern. I miss you.

All my love,
Claire

My whirling mind was put into further fevers of perturbation that evening when I saw Maria.

'That Douglas,' she said, 'do you know who he really is?'

'Who is anyone *really?*' I enquired as I poured cognac for both of us in my hotel suite.

'He is the Count of Saint Germain!' Maria exclaimed fiercely. 'Do you not know of him?'

'Of course I do,' I replied. 'He was a mysterious

eighteenth century gentleman heavily involved in the esoteric arts and in international espionage, working both for Louis XV of France and Frederick the Great of Prussia. He claimed to have discovered the Elixir of Life via his practice of Alchemy, stating seriously that in common with his pupil, Cagliostro, he had walked and talked with Nefertiti and Cleopatra in the days of Ancient Egypt. A fascinating man, indeed, Maria, with a charming gift of implausible phrase, but I cannot see how or why you identify him with Douglas, since Saint Germain is dead and buried.'

'No, he isn't,' she answered. 'After his death I am reliably informed that he was seen twice in India by travellers from both France and England. Moreover, your Lord Edward Bulwer-Lytton, that politician, novelist and magician, friend of your Dickens and Disraeli, met him in London and made him the inspirer of that most notable novella: *The Haunted and the Haunters: or The House and the Brain*.'

'That's a wonderful story,' I said, 'but surely you are joking?'

'No,' she returned coolly, 'I am not. Nobody ever really knew how the Count of Saint Germain managed to appear so carelessly wealthy. The same is true of Douglas.'

'Maria,' I responded, 'I find it easy enough to believe that mysterious people make much money in mysterious ways and become involved in secret societies. What I don't believe is that the Count of Saint Germain as an old man faked his own death and burial and then returned rejuvenated in our time as Douglas.'

'Then all the more fool you,' Maria retorted with a classically Parisian shrug of her nubile shoulders. By this time, I had had enough of trying to make sense of all these matters and so seized her unresisting hand and, fired by the stare of her deep, dark eyes, I placed it upon my trousered prick and was at once rewarded by the gentle pressure of her slender fingers, which assured me that she quite understood my need for delicate attention. Adroitly unfastening my buttons, she grasped the stiff and naked truth, which twitched under her delicious fingering in such a way that a very few motions of her delicate hand brought on a throbbing state of bliss.

Instinctively our lips met in a long, impassioned kiss. Tongue to tongue, we revelled in a gorgeous osculation. It was ecstatic having this lascivious girl close by my side, with my right arm around her waist, whilst my left hand found no resistance in its voyage of discovery underneath her petticoats. What mossy treasures my fingers searched out! Whilst for her part, one arm was draped around my neck and the warming touches of her right hand amply repaid my investigations into her regions of passion. My fiery kisses roved from her lips all over her face and neck, until I took possession of the heaving globes of her bosom. How she shuddered with ecstasy as my lips drew in one of her nipples and gently sucked the delicious morsel. A very few moments of this exciting dalliance was too much for her. She sank back on the bed.

Then followed delicious kissings and toyings; no part of Maria's person was neglected, and when, as a finale, she surrendered the moist dewy lips of the grotto of love itself to my warm tonguings, the excess of voluptuous emotion so overcame her that she screamed out her delight, when the crisis came again and again in rapid succession.

I still didn't know much about Satanism, or the similarities between the Count of Saint Germain and Douglas; but I cried out my joy in orgasm when I prodded my rod deep inside this perplexing bitch and this latest act of love became an accomplished fact.

CHAPTER THREE

It was on the ensuing afternoon that, as previously arranged, I met Joris-Karl Huysmans at a *Salon de Thé* on the Rue de Rivoli. Any Englishman who protests that one cannot enjoy a good pot of tea in France has obviously not been there. My own preference that day was for Darjeeling with milk and sugar; Huysmans took Lapsang Souchong without any accoutrements though we both agreed that that delicate little piece of *patisserie*, the *japainais*, would be a suitable accompaniment.

Huysmans was a tall, lean man with a gaunt face and haunted dark eyes, dressed in sober, clerical black. There was an element of the cadaverous about him. If anyone had overheard the first half hour of our conversation, it would have been assumed that Huysmans was a civil servant relaxing after a relatively easy day at the Ministry, a man who led a life both conventional and conservative. This was perfectly true: yet his imagination had caused him to create two of the most remarkable novels that I have ever read.

A Rebours or *Against Nature* had caused a sensation on its publication over ten years before and had inspired both the Aesthetic and the Decadent Movements: it was the 'book that corrupted Dorian Gray' in Oscar Wilde's memorable novel. Its hero, Des Esseintes, is a decadent aristocrat of independent means who chooses to live largely within his own imagination, influenced in his life-style and interior decoration by Edgar Allan Poe's *The Fall of the House of Usher*: and also by the bejewelled paintings of Gustav Moreau, most notably *Salomé*. In one chapter, he orders his servants to pack his bags for a trip to London, where he has never before been. Then he sits and imagines what London might be like, using the words of Dickens to paint a mental picture of beefsteak and oyster pie enjoyed in a roistering tavern as a thick yellow fog swirls about the window panes. Having explored this vision fully, as if in trance, he tells his servants to unpack his bags, for there is no longer any point in going to London.

His later novel, *Là-Bas* or *Down There* had also caused a sensation, especially upsetting all those who knew of it only by evil repute. Here, a rather cold writer called Durtal researches the life of the alleged Satanist, pervert and child-murderer Gilles de Rais, also a brave warrior, a friend of Joan of Arc and Marshal of France, who was eventually burned at the stake. In the course of Durtal's research, he discovers that Satanism is alive and well in the Paris of his time: and the closing chapter consists of a detailed description of our hero witnessing the Black Mass.

This was why I was keen to see Huysmans, quite aside from my genuine admiration for his writings. I asked him to what extent there might be Black Magic and Satanism in Paris and whether he had actually witnessed the matter which he described so well in his fiction.

'Lord Horby,' he said, 'I can only tell you of my own experience.' He sipped his tea thoughtfully. 'Have you heard of a half-mad prophet called Vintras?' I shook my head. 'He claimed to have been visited by the Archangel Michael who apparently informed him that his task was to inaugurate the coming "Age of the Holy Ghost". He travelled around the country, preaching his doctrines of redemption, declaring that even Satan would be ultimately redeemed, and soon built up a considerable following. He was a powerful preacher – he could never remember afterwards what he had said so one presumes that he spoke while in a state of trance – and his disciples included not only unlettered men such as himself but priests and aristocrats. He founded the Church of Carmel and, clad in vestments decorated with an inverted cross, proclaimed that "the reign of the suffering Christ is over and the reign of the Holy Ghost has begun."

'This Vintras has had quite an influence,' Huysmans continued coolly. 'He used to celebrate *The Provictimal Sacrifice of Mary*, a mass of his own devising, and during these masses his followers became totally hysterical. They declared that they saw empty chalices suddenly brim over with blood, smelled wondrous perfumes, beheld the consecrated host bleeding and even witnessed the Holy Ghost, in the form of a dove, perching on Vintras's shoulder. It was hardly surprising,' Huysmans smiled wryly, 'that the Roman Catholic Church quickly condemned Vintras for heresy or that, in 1842, after an unfair trial, he was sentenced to seven years of imprisonment on a charge of fraud. On his release in 1848, he passed some time in London then returned to his native land of France to die in 1875. You may be wondering about the relevance of this matter, *mon cher monsieur*, but allow me to explain.

'Vintras had influence upon Eliphas Lévi, author of *The Ritual and Dogma of Transcendental Magic* and *The Key of the Mysteries*.' I nodded. I had read both books and had been rather impressed by Lévi's insistence that the mysterious pack of cards called the Tarot is a pictorial exposition of the data contained in the Jewish Qabalah. The

Hermetic Order of the Golden Dawn had always praised Lévi as a master of esoteric wisdom; and so had Aleister Crowley, who would later translate Lévi's *The Key of the Mysteries* for Rider Books, adding his own sardonic footnotes. Moreover, I knew that Lévi had visited Lord Edward Bulwer-Lytton in England, which latter was stunned by the former's knowledge of esoterica. I shook my head bemusedly, for Maria had mentioned Bulwer-Lytton in connection with the Count of Saint Germain on the previous night. 'Vintras,' Huysmans continued, 'also attracted sexual deviants into his sect, for unorthodox mysticism frequently goes hand-in-hand with unorthodox sex. One ex-disciple, a priest named Gozzoli, accused Vintras of being homosexual, conducting secret masses at which both priests and people were naked, indulging in group sexual activities and masturbating at the foot of the altar. *Moi?*' Huysmans shrugged. 'Gozzoli was a most unpleasant character who was inclined to charge other people with vices to which he himself was inclined. Yet Vintras did exert an influence upon that most peculiar character, the Abbé Boullan, who had been unfrocked and who had previously been imprisoned in France for fraud and in Rome for heresy. In 1859, he had founded The Society for the Reparation of Souls whereby he cured and exorcised demon-possessed nuns by feeding them a mixture of consecrated communion wafers and human excrement.' Huysmans's thin voice dripped with acid sarcasm. 'I have evidence that on 8th January 1860, Boullan conducted a Black Mass at which he ritually sacrificed his own bastard child born to one Adèle Chevalier. After meeting Vintras, he declared himself a convert to the teachings of the Church of Carmel and after Vintras's death, he proclaimed himself to be a reincarnation of John the Baptist and the new Supreme Pontiff.

'His doctrines were curious,' said Huysmans, 'teaching as they did a form of sexual magic. He held that the Fall of Man had been caused by an act of love on the part of Adam and Eve and that, as he said to me "it is through acts of love accomplished in a religious spirit that the Redemption of Humanity can be achieved." He claimed that the evolutionary ladder could be climbed more speedily by humanity if we partook of sexual intercourse with celestial beings. One might think, Lord Horby, "Yes, and lead me to them" but he held also that mankind could accelerate the evolution of brute creation by copulating with animals. He moreover urged his disciples to enjoy sexual relations with incubi and succubi, the male and female spirits one arouses in the act of onanism. Some of his disciples thought that they were enjoying lascivious relations with archangels, angels and the spirits of Alexander the Great and Cleopatra. He also taught his female disciples a method of having sex with his astral body.'

'He sounds rather intriguing,' I remarked. 'Can you introduce me to him?'

'*Non*,' said Huysmans, 'for he is dead. It was as a result of a magical duel, part of which I witnessed. In the course of my own research into Satanism, I came across Boullan and his reputation. It was when I was breaking away from the influence of Emile Zola. Are you familiar with his work?'

'Yes,' I replied, 'and I agree with Oscar Wilde. He finds life crude and leaves it raw.'

'*Eh bien*,' Huysmans finished his tea and looked unconcerned, 'I wrote to Boullan, thinking it likely that he was either a Satanist or else could put me in touch with them, asking for reliable information on the subject of devil-worship and offering to depict him in my forthcoming novel as "the Superman, the Satanist, the only one in existence, far removed from the spiritism of the occultists." Boullan replied in a friendly fashion, assuring me that he was "an Adept who has declared war on all demoniacal cults." He also offered to loan me documents "which will enable you to prove that Satanism is active in our time and in what form and in what circumstances." Subsequently I received a great mass of material from Boullan's home in Lyons, a hot-bed of Freemasonry which has enjoyed a reputation for unorthodoxy ever since the Middle Ages. It all gave me a somewhat favourable impression of Boullan and inspired me to portray him as the saintly Dr Johannes, enemy of all Satanism and respected theologian in my novel *Là-Bas*. Unfortunately, I was reckoning without the influence of his enemies, the *Kabbalistic Order of the Rose-Croix* of Stanislas de Guiata, Sâr Peládan and their associates. I became involved in a magical war . . .' he arose. '*Excusez-moi, monsieur, je vais au pissoir*,' he remarked with eloquent French simplicity.

I remained to ponder both his words and the extraordinary scene in which I had eagerly participated on the preceding night.

After our fuck, Maria had informed me that, unless I objected, a friend of hers called Dominique would be arriving shortly. This was a proposition to which I had assented gladly and the eventual appearance of Dominique fully justified my anticipation. Dominique was possessed of a beautiful pale face surmounted by rich dark brown hair. Her delectable figure had been accentuated in the fashionable 'S' curse in a manner which would have been preposterous, were it not so erotic. After a good round of stiff brandies, Maria lost no time in stripping Dominique of her evening dress and unlacing her tight basque, enabling her to breathe freely once more. My penis was still flaccid but Maria's response was to pluck a pink India-rubber dildo from her bag and she giggled wickedly as she addressed the other ravishing young girl.

'They call this The Ladies' Comforter,' she informed Dominique. 'And I'm truly looking forward to fucking you with it.'

'It's very lifelike, isn't it?' Dominique giggled as she made herself comfortable on the bed next to me, lying back with her soft thighs spread open, her long, lissom legs stretched out and her exquisitely well-manicured finger-nails diddling her pussy.

'Yes, this is one of the best-made dildoes I have ever seen,' Maria remarked as she smoothed the imitation rubber cock over Dominique's hardening nipples. Dominique and I laughed lightly as Maria took a firm grasp upon the superbly fashioned instrument and pressed its bulbous knob between the pouting cunny lips of Dominique. It slipped in easily and I found it quite thrilling to see Maria's busy fingers nipping and pinching Dominique's finely developed clitty, which stood out so proudly as Maria manipulated the dildo with a truly feminine subtlety.

Dominique started to moan, twisting and turning as Maria plunged the dildo in and out of her gaping honeypot; and then they changed positions, with the young girl now brandishing the rubber prick. This new tableau made even my sated shaft twitch and, slowly but surely, it began to swell up. Dominique noticed this happy state of affairs and, with a little cry of joy, she swooped her head down to my cock and started to suck noisily on my knob until my tool was standing up hard and stiff as she swirled her wet tongue around my uncapped helmet.

Maria was now writhing from side to side with a blissful smile of satisfaction on her face as Dominique continued to wield the dildo in and out of her tingling passion-pit; and both girls were frigging their own cunnies as I hauled myself up and positioned myself behind Dominique. I parted her legs: I could see the love juice dripping down her inner thighs from her quim, and I licked my lips as I regarded that rosebud of an arse-hole which winked at me from within her cheeky bum-globes. It was in my mind to bugger this delectable young girl and so I eased my rampant shaft towards her tiny, puckered rosette.

'No! Ah, *non!*' Dominique cried out as she felt the tip of my prick nudging her sweet sphincter. Yet she did not miss a beat of her rhythmic dildo-fucking of Maria's cunny. 'I would far rather you fucked my dear little cunt instead.'

'By all means,' I whispered as Maria rubbed my cock until it was at its fullest length. Then I made Dominique bend forward and stick her deliciously rounded backside high into the air. 'But I really must insist first on paying your delightful *derrière* the merest token of a compliment.' So saying, I grasped her hips firmly and returned my rock-hard knob-end to her shy nether entrance. She must have realized by now that further protest was useless for, apart from an involuntary gasp of shock, Dominique made no further sound as I gently but firmly eased the head of my rigid cock through the wonderfully tight flesh-ring of her secret hole before sinking its whole stiff length on into the warm depths beyond. Having, I felt, made my point about who was in charge here, I then allowed chivalrous impulse to overrule carnal instinct and decided to withdraw – albeit with some reluctance – after this one marvellous deep stroke.

I slid my engorged shaft out of Dominique's arse and

without further ado plunged it below the voluptuous curve of her soft white bum cheeks. We both purred with pleasure as I at last embedded my throbbing rod inside her clinging cunt.

'Go on, you two!' Maria gasped, fully discerning the nature of what was transpiring as she wrested the dildo from Dominique's hand. 'Have a wonderful fuck! And do not worry, Dominique, my sweetheart, I can easily bring myself off.'

Thanks to this generous gesture, Dominique was able to concentrate fully on enjoying the delicious sensations of my cock see-sawing a squelchy passage into her welcoming quim and of my balls bouncing against her pubic fleece. She jerked her hips forwards and backwards in time with my pistoning strokes in and out of her juicy love-sheath and she gasped: 'Aaah! Aargh! How scrumptious! Push your prick in harder, Horby, further in, that is the way!' Her rounded backside responded to every shove as I drove home, excited to fresh, raging peaks of pleasure; and I almost fainted away as the sweet friction of her cunny lips against my stiff shaft made every nerve tingle with that exquisite, unique, amatory delight until the thrusts from my lusty prick coupled with the electric contractions of her cunt finally sucked out a frothy emission of spermy jism from my cock.

At this point, I wanted to relax but these young ladies appeared to be quite insatiable. Maria stretched Dominique across her knees, stroking her bare buttocks as I lay upon the bed and gazed at them with gradually renewed erotic interest. I could hardly refrain from gloating over the tight little bum cheeks which were so rudely exposed to my lascivious gaze.

'Go on, my love,' Dominique said to Maria as the latter stroked her bare white buttocks and she grinned cheekily.

'Give me a nice little spanking – not too hard, though.' Maria was not unwilling to oblige her and commenced gently to smack Dominique's firm flesh until a pink blush showed on her superbly rounded bum cheeks. Maria paused and Dominique murmured: 'Go on, my mistress, give me a neat spanking for my naughtiness.' Maria began to spank her hard, transforming the pink blush to one of crimson. 'Oooh! Oh la la!' the girl squealed. 'My arse is really tingling.'

Maria responded by slapping Dominique's beautiful bottom more lightly yet with increasing rapidity until her jiggling bum cheeks changed colour from crimson to burning scarlet: and my cock was once more rock-hard as the victim winced and wiggled under the spanking.

'Ouch! Ouch! That's enough, quite enough . . .!' Dominique gasped and Maria relented as the girl turned her head to me. I seized her within my arms and as I took one of her protruding nipples within my mouth, her slender fingers caressed the other one whilst my hold upon her clitoris aroused her amorous flame in all its intensity. My lips imprinted hot kisses upon her face, the cheeks of which were burning with a fire as strong as that which warmed her bottom.

Higher and higher crept my insinuating hand, till I had got fair possession of her chink, all moistened as it was with warm, creamy emission. Dominique sobbed slightly on my shoulder, owing to the spanking, as her legs parted slightly and a perceptible shudder of suppressed emotion informed me surely enough that my success would soon be complete. As I withdrew my hand from that burning spot, she lifted her naked foot so that it rested upon my rampant tool, stiff and hard as iron; and my prick throbbed beneath the heel of that caressing foot as it gently frigged me.

From her face, my lips found their way to Dominique's bosom once more and her sighs too plainly uttered her feelings. My tremendous truncheon was stiff against her belly. Now Maria placed her cool hand upon it and directed it into Dominique's cunt. We commenced a delightful side-fuck, our lips again glued together, 'tip-ping' one another with the ends of our tongues. I kept up the strokes until she spent in an agony of delight. Resting for a few moments, I went on again, with her legs entwined over my waist as she heaved and writhed in all the voluptuous ecstasy of her lecherous nature, to the intense delight of my prick, which revelled in the joyful moisture, becoming firmer and more excited moment by moment.

'Ah!' Dominique shrieked, barely able to catch her breath. My bounding strokes were making the bed creak as Maria laughed with a deep, throaty chuckle. 'Drive on, push it in, balls and all – oh – fuck me, fuck me! Oh! I'm coming again! . . . so do you . . . what a spend yours is! . . . how to you shoot it into me, you grand fellow! . . .'

I was aroused from my reverie by the return to the Salon de Thé of Monsieur J.K. Huysmans, my estimable companion.

'*Eh bien, monsieur*,' he remarked with severely clerical sobriety. 'Now, where was I?' I dragged my mind back from my memory of a memorable encounter with the daughter of one of the most influential men in France. What had *he* thought about in the *pissoir?*

'I was wondering . . .' I said.

CHAPTER FOUR

'Let us refresh ourselves with Chinese Green Gunpowder Tea,' J.K. Huysmans suggested courteously, 'as I proceed to tell you my tale of Black Magic. Ten years before, I might have offered you absinthe, but as I have seen, it is the drink which drives men mad.' I stared at the two looking-glasses, full-length mirrors between which our table was positioned and which reflected our images forever unto Infinity, and was glad that we were not having absinthe. 'Green is a curious colour,' he continued meditatively. 'Why, green tea can make a man mad. You are assuredly acquainted with the story of that name by that exquisite Irish writer, Sheridan Le Fanu?'

I nodded an uneasy assent. In this tale, a devout clergyman drinks copious quantities of green tea which leads to his being haunted by a monkey-like figure whom no one else can perceive and which destroys his sanity.

'My mood is a little green today,' Huysmans announced, coolly regarding the small emerald embedded in a gold ring which adorned the little finger of his left hand. 'So let us enjoy pernod, the legal equivalent of absinthe. It is green: and to accompany this, let us enjoy a portion of green plums, which you in England call greengages. However, *mon cher monsieur*, let us restrain ourselves from the debauchery of green *sauce menthe* with which your countrymen choose to ruin roasted lamb; *je n'aime pas ça*. It reminds me that green is also the colour of slime. A man must be sparing in his choice of green.' The refreshments he ordered came swiftly and proved to be delicious as this intriguing man continued with his tale.

'Have you heard,' he asked me, 'of Stanislas de Guaita, Gerard Encausse and – or – Sâr Peládan?'

'Yes,' I responded as I stiffened involuntarily, for I recalled Claire's epistolary description of her initiation into an allegedly Rosicrucian Order in Paris, done in terms of Sex Magick.

'Permit me to explain,' said Huysmans. 'Stanislas de Guaita was a Marquis and a poet of great promise with a wide literary acquaintanceship. Around 1884, he became friendly with another poet, editor and novelist, Catulle Mendés, son-in-law of the immortal Théophile Gautier, whose novels were brilliant, most notably *Mademoiselle de Maupin*. The novels of Mendés were less distinguished, using the themes of incest and other sexual peculiarities, but this man urged de Guaita to read the works of the great French magus, Eliphas Lévi. The Marquis did so and was immediately subjected to what he himself termed the *coup de foudre occulte* – the "occult thunderstroke".

'As a result, he changed his way of life completely,' Huysmans continued calmly. 'He read magical and alchemical works rather than poetry, attempted to contact the spirits by Magic in his scarlet-draped study converted into a magical Temple and took hashish and cocaine to assist his communion with deities and demons. In 1885, on making the acquaintanceship of Encausse and Peládan, he founded the Kabalistic Order of the Rose-Croix with the objectives of studying and practising magic, spreading a knowledge of occult principles among the French public and revivifying the artistic life of Western Europe. Leading members included that extraordinary composer and

'An interesting question.' Huysmans gave me a dry smile. 'According to Boullan, spells and curses were exchanged between Lyons and Paris with great spiritual struggles taking place on "the astral plane": yet de Guiata and Wirth claimed that these "astral" struggles existed only in Boullan's imagination. However, Boullan died three years after I met him. Partly I blame myself.'

'How so?' I really did need my green pernod, never mind my green tea.

'Boullan believed our friendship had drawn me into his struggles,' Huysmans answered. 'He was anxious to protect me, and twice in the summer of 1890 he performed magical operations designed to protect us from our enemies. They proved insufficient.' The man spoke as if he were describing a visit to the dentist. 'I suffered from bouts of fluidic fisticuffs.'

'Sorry . . .?'

'My cat and I were struck blows by an invisible antagonist.' He finished his tea in one gulp. 'I took Boullan's instructions, isolated myself and burned a pastille of Boullan's Paste of Exorcism, a mixture of camphor, cloves, frankincense and myrrh, and then, brandishing a miraculous host of the Prophet Vintras within my right hand, I clasped the blessed scapular of Carmel close to my body and recited conjurations which dissolved the astral fluids and paralysed the power of the sorcerers.'

'I see,' I said. I didn't see at all.

'During the summer of 1891,' Huysmans continued, 'I spent several weeks in Lyons where more elaborate ceremonies were performed for our protection. The battles of Black and White Magic had begun again. Boullan was jumping about like a tiger whenever he held one of his hosts. He invoked the aid of St Michael and the eternal justiciaries and standing before the altar, he cried out:

"Strike down Peládan! Strike down Peládan!" Unfortunately, the powers of Satan prevailed and it was Boullan who was struck down. The day before he was due to go to Paris to lecture of Mysticism, he collapsed and died suddenly, on 3rd January 1893, the victim of Satanism and black magic!'

'Was he previously in good health?' I enquired.

'Ah, Lord Horby, I see that you don't believe me.' Huysmans looked mildly disappointed. 'Yes, there was the matter of heart trouble and a problem with his liver . . . but I assure you that it was Black Magic of the deepest dye. Why, my learned acquaintance Jules Bois, a journalist and former member of the Church of Carmel of Vintras and Boullan, why, he shares my opinion. In an article published in *Gil-Blas*, Jules Bois, a severely rational man, accused de Guiata and Peládan of astral murder. It is indisputable that de Guiata and Peládan practised Black Magic every day. Poor Boullan was perpetually in conflict with the evil spirits they sent him from Paris. My poor friend Boullan succumbed to a supremely powerful spell: and on the evening that he died, my cat and I were subjected to a particularly severe infliction of what the Americans would term "fluidic fisticuffs".'

'But you're still alive,' I said.

'For reasons I shall explain,' Huysmans replied. He glanced briefly at our empty glasses. 'Let us take green Chartreuse now.' I agreed. 'De Guiata was still determined to kill me. He publicly denied that he was a diabolist and murderer and challenged both Jules Bois and myself to a duel. I will not fight a man who has black magic in his gunpowder and so thought it prudent to apologize via my seconds, stating that I was not responsible for the statements of Jules Bois. But Jules Bois has always been a stubborn one and he publicly repeated his allegations, this time also implicating Dr Gerard Encausse in his accusation of astral homicide. Two duels took place. You look sceptical, Lord Horby, but allow me to tell you the truth.' I sipped my chartreuse and nodded.

'When Bois left his home for the duel with de Guiata,' Huysmans informed me, 'some very singular things occurred on both sides. On both sides our allies were praying for us and practising conjurations. And on the road to Versailles, for I heard this from Bois's second, Paul Foucher, one of the horses pulling Bois's carriage stopped suddenly and began to tremble, then it staggered, *as though it had seen the Devil in person*. It was impossible to proceed. The trembling lasted for twenty minutes. The duel took place eventually and two bullets were exchanged without result.'

'Honour was satisfied . . .' I murmured.

'But there is a curious fact or two.' Huysmans smiled wryly. 'My words can be verified by Paul Foucher, Bois's second, and by Gastine-Renette, the leading gunsmith of Paris, to whom the pistols were taken for examination later in the day. "What happened?" the famous gunsmith demanded. "The bullet of one of the duellists didn't leave the barrel." Paul Foucher said: "I was sure that the pistol of Jules Bois had not missed fire. As for the pistol used by the Marquis De Guiata, it is quite unbelievable that neither he nor his seconds, one of whom was an officer and the other Laurent Tailhade, should not have noticed that the pistol did not fire." The occultists could therefore pride themselves on having terrified the horse of one of the opponents and having prevented the bullet from leaving the pistol of Monsieur de Guaita.'

'There was a second duel,' Huysmans informed my

bemused ears in between sips of his green chartreuse, 'between Jules Bois and Dr Gerard Encausse, this time to be fought with rapiers, and it took place three days later. *Encore*, horses were involved. The horse drawing the carriage of Bois to the duelling field collapsed. Bois engaged a second carriage but *encore*, the horse collapsed, this time throwing Bois violently to the ground. Even so, a bruised, cut and bleeding Bois insisted upon keeping his appointment with a formidable antagonist. "I remember Papus taking off his coat," Bois told me, "I remember the words, the gypsy eye of my adversary, the impatient wrinkle in his forehead, his beard and jovial lips, his heavy build. He was a bull among these improvised evangelists." '

'What happened?' I asked, not being a bad swordsman myself.

'Both antagonists were wounded in the encounter but neither seriously,' Huysmans replied. 'As Paul Foucher told me, although the swords were magical, the wounds they inflicted were slight and have long since healed. Shortly afterwards, they were reconciled as friends . . . but Stanislas de Guiata died in 1897 from an overdose of drugs.'

'And you . . .?' I queried.

'Some time ago, a very learned Jesuit priest told me that at some moment in my life, I would have to choose between the point of a pistol or the foot of the Cross. I have chosen the foot of the Cross.' I could now understand why that although I had relished *A Rebours* and *Là-Bas*, I had found his *En Route* to be a monumentally tedious account of the follies of the Christian Mysticism he had misguidedly chosen to embrace. 'Have you had the good fortune to meet Father Binoire S.J.?'

'I have encountered him, yes,' I replied, 'but you

obviously know him rather better than I do. And since it is a green evening, allow me to confess that I feel quite green with envy.'

'Lord Horby, do I detect a slight trace of sarcasm in your attitude? It is the lowest form of wit.' He sipped the last of his green chartreuse and shrugged his shoulders dismissively. 'Satanism or Catholicism, that is the only choice for those of mystical persuasion.'

'Is it?' I queried innocently. (Today, in 1925, I recall Aleister Crowley's saying: "J.-K. Huysmans tried to betray the Secrets to the Roman Catholic Church and died of cancer of the tongue", which he did a few years after our meeting.)

'It is,' Huysmans retorted with dogmatic defiance. 'Now drink up your green chartreuse, *mon cher monsieur*, and if it be your wish, kindly accompany me to a sanctuary of The Church, therein to witness the punishment of a female penitent convicted of the crime of Witchcraft.'

CHAPTER FIVE

J.K. Huysmans swore me to secrecy concerning the precise location of what we proceeded to witness, though I am permitted to say that the event to be described took place in the Jardin des Plantes Quartier at a Convent School for young ladies. We journeyed there by cabriolet and he led me into a grim and forbidding building just as the moon was rising. A nun admitted us through a bare hall into a luxuriously furnished anteroom. I wondered if I were at last to witness Satanism but instead saw Lord Maulerby and Father Binoire sipping *fino* sherry. We greeted one another and they were obviously well acquainted with Huysmans. The nun filled and replenished our glasses as we conversed inconsequentially about nothing in particular. Eventually, the Mother Superior was ushered in by two more nuns and we greeted her.

It was difficult to discern her figure beneath her habit though she possessed a plump and pretty face, marred only by the tightness of her mouth and the hardness of her eyes. I was introduced to her as an English *milord* who was contemplating the taking of Instruction in the Roman Catholic faith and saw no cause, at that instant, to disillusion her, so intrigued was I by the proceedings. She had the nuns usher us into another antechamber, where she left us. I followed the example of my companions in taking a white, hooded robe as indicated by the nuns, who promptly departed. All four of us changed our clothes and we looked as if we were inspectors from the Spanish Inquisition when Father Binoire knocked once upon the door. A nun re-entered to admit us into a central hall.

The air was thick with the smoke of frankincense and myrrh. A hidden organist was playing some of Bach's more gloomy compositions. We were given sofas at the back of the hall, upon a raised platform, which gave us a perfect view. Before us, there were rows of empty chairs and, beyond them, a stage. The hall was illuminated throughout by tall white candles. At the back of the stage, nailed up high on the oak-panelled wall, was a statue of Jesus Christ upon the Cross and, directly below that, a white marble statue of the Virgin Mary. There were two cages on either side of this statue and each one contained a young girl, certainly no younger than eighteen and no older than twenty. One girl was slim and blonde, the other one was pleasantly plump and brunette and the hair of both had obviously been elegantly styled for this auspicious occasion. Both wore yellow ribbons in their hair and their heads had been crowned with the white dunces' caps; they had also the adornment of white frilly blouses; knee-length skirts, pleated and in grey; white socks which reached to just below the knee; and shiny black shoes with silver buckles. The cages were labelled: CATHERINE for the blonde and JEANNE for the brunette.

Both girls stood with their heads bowed and their hands tied behind their backs. Each girl had had a placard hung around her neck and the slogan, immaculately lettered, on each was: I AM A WITCH. I AM A WHORE. I AM TO BE BIRCHED. I AM GRATEFUL FOR MY JUST PUNISHMENT. As the organ music continued to play, around fifty girls dressed in white blouses and long black skirts entered backstage, filed past the penitents, then stepped down the stage steps to take their seats, though not before taunting the girls in their cages. I heard comments such as: 'You thought you were so important, didn't you?', 'You've always been such a snooty bitch', 'Look at you now' and 'That'll teach you to be cheeky.'

The nuns filed in silently and took their seats in the front row. I could hear much rustling of petticoats among the seated convent schoolgirls. The Mother Superior mounted the stage and led us in a hymn to the Mercy of Christ. After that, we knelt and prayed for the souls of the sinners. On arising, I saw an eager, flushed anticipation upon the cheeks of the schoolgirls. The Mother Superior proceeded to make a speech. She informed one and all of the crimes with which Catherine and Jeanne had been charged and found guilty. The principal crime was Witchcraft but it was compounded by sexual immorality: Catherine and Jeanne had been found in bed together. There was a slight gasp from the girls, instantly suppressed as the nuns turned their heads. Their private belongings had been searched in consequence and two nuns now entered upon the stage, bearing the grisly exhibits.

The evidence, in terms of the Convent, seemed to be incontrovertible. Both had hidden photographs of a Parisian music hall star called Le Pétomaine, whose speciality consisted of farting musical tunes out of his arse. Both had scrawled obscene words in their Bibles: Catherine had scrawled FUCK THIS over the passage in which Jesus Christ declares: 'I am the Way, the Truth and the Life.' Jeanne had written BUGGER THIS over the verse: 'Suffer little children to come unto me.' They had not denied that these words had been lettered in their handwriting. Moreover, in addition to holding up the disfigured pages of the Bible for our inspection the Mother Superior asked if anyone would deny that the scripts had indeed issued forth from the pens of the culprits: no one did. Finally, she held up a wax figurine of a woman with obscenely gross breasts and buttocks, bearing an observable resemblance of the Mother Superior. The word BITCH had been painted in what could have been blood across the thighs and belly of this figurine and two pins had been inserted into the vagina.

'What is your verdict, my children?' the Mother Superior asked earnestly.

'Birch them,' the girls chanted in unison. 'Birch them! *Birch* them! BIRCH THEM!!!' The girls writhed in semi-hysteria.

'Thank you, my children, but we must consider the case for the defence. After all, the good God is merciful and just.'

'NO!!!' the girls screamed.

'I insist upon hearing the case for the defence,' the Mother Superior insisted calmly. 'Sister Agnes,' she turned to the nun upon her right, 'kindly conduct it.'

' "Father forgive them for they know not what they do," ' the slim Sister Agnes quoted from the Bible as she raised her eyes to heaven. 'Looking at their confessions made to you and me, Mother Superior,' she consulted a sheaf of papers, 'Catherine and Jeanne claim that they were the innocent victims of demonic possession. This must be true, for only the demonically possessed could possibly be guilty of such disgraceful acts of blasphemy. I therefore beseech you, on their behalf, to show them the greatest possible mercy by increasing the strokes from the customary six to a round dozen in order to ensure a gracious exorcism of these penitents.'

'Nobly spoken, Sister,' the Mother Superior declared, 'and your plea for mercy is granted.' The whole school cheered at the justice of the decision. 'Sister Elizabeth, kindly bring me the penitent Catherine.' Sister Elizabeth gladly obliged, unlocking the cage and bringing the girl to the front of the stage. Sister Agnes pushed an altar on wheels to the centre of it, then lovingly covered it with a white linen cloth, on the front of which was emblazoned a red cross. 'Catherine!' the Mother Superior commanded sharply, causing the girl's bottom to quiver visibly within her pleated skirt, 'you have heard the verdict of the School. Fetch the rod, which you have spent the morning making.' The trembling girl briefly left the stage to return with a pliant birch, neatly trimmed and adorned by a yellow ribbon. She then knelt at the feet of the Mother Superior, offered the rod for approval and begged softly and tearfully for a good whipping.

The Mother Superior graciously granted her request and Catherine was led to the altar by the two Sisters, Agnes and Elizabeth, who bent her over and secured all her four limbs with leather straps. Her skirt and petticoat were lifted and her drawers pulled down to her well-turned ankles, revealing one of the loveliest curvaceous pouting rears that I have ever seen. Her bare flesh was displayed to the entire girls' school and the masked male 'inquisitors' in what must surely have been a supreme humiliation. Her bottom appeared to be blushing with shame before the birch even reached it.

The Mother Superior tapped the birch across the buttocks of Catherine. Instantly they tensed and clenched.

'Present your bottom properly for punishment, Catherine,' her mentor commanded sharply. The girl raised her trembling fesses into the air. After an almost audible silence, the Mother Superior swished the birch down hard and smartly across the centre of her victim's bottom. It made a soft, smacking sound but it left no mark, although

Catherine sucked in her breath and nervously jerked, perhaps more from the torturing suspense than from the first stroke itself. I feasted my vision to the utmost, for it was extraordinarily, mouth-wateringly tasty, this sight of a young girl's twitching, punished buttocks.

The second stroke descended with a hiss, landing just below the centre but well above the slender thighs and I enjoyed the sight of the birch thwacking across those tender hemispheres. Catherine gasped a little more loudly this time, nervously tried to shift from foot to foot and visibly dragged on her bound wrists. From the way her sides were trembling – and I could see the lovely ribcage plainly outlined against her taut white skin – I knew that she was lamenting the long duration of her atonement. The third lash whistled through the air to land about an inch below the place which the second had punished.

Catherine's hips gave an involuntary swerve to the side and her head tilted back a little as she sighed softly. At this moment when the makings of stripes and weals could be discerned, the Mother Superior commanded Sisters Agnes and Elizabeth to wheel a large looking-glass upon the stage and to place in it before the penitent as a gasp of pleasure from the girls in the audience ascended up to heaven, no doubt.

'You see, my darling child, Catherine, what the practices of witchcraft and immorality have brought you to?' the Mother Superior demanded. I could see that Catherine's eyes were full of tears and her nostrils were beginning to dilate rather rapidly. She was not kept waiting for the fourth swish which was applied almost instantly thereafter, yet exactly over the last place attacked. A reiterative stroke on bare flesh which has already been sensitised produces much more than a double effect of irksome heat, which radiates throughout the entire feminine nervous system and thus aggrandises the punishment and, also, the voluptuous titillations which a whipping always produces in a female in any sensitivity whatsoever, as any connoisseur of flagellation can tell you from experience.

The fifth swish took a little longer and Catherine nervously glanced back for a second, then again bowed her head and stiffened herself. It cut directly across the plumpest curves of both her naked arse-globes, producing a faint sob and a convulsive squirming which I found maddeningly stimulating to my roused and savagely excited cock. The Mother Superior made her wait almost a minute for the sixth lash, which wrapped the pliant birch around the base of that wonderfully contoured backside of the girl, and a twig may possibly have darted in toward her furry gap, for she lunged to the left, sticking her bottom out in straining fashion with a plaintive groan of entreaty.

The Mother Superior paid no attention to the penitent's sighs and cries. She promptly applied several more strokes, placing them straight across the jounciest region of the summits of Catherine's naked, striped behind. I was enraptured by my contemplation of this spectacle. For all I knew, Catherine might be a most delightful and charming girl, albeit a naughty one; but I could feel no pity. I was fascinated by the sight of her scarlet glowing bottom as it twisted and turned.

As the final stroke was applied, tears poured out of her eyes. She groaned and sobbed, writhed and jerked, but in the main I had to admit that she had borne her dozen strokes with relatively good grace, far better than many an English girl would have done if bent over a desk to receive chastisement for poor lessons or inattentiveness or rudeness to a schoolmistress.

The punishment completed, the girl who had been so well whipped was released from her bondage and the

Sisters restored the state of her drawers and brushed down her petticoat and skirt. She then had to kneel once more, kiss the rod – by now bearing all the markings of its contact with her tender flesh – thank the Mother Superior for her just chastisement and implore forgiveness and permission to retire.

'You are forgiven, my child,' the Mother Superior replied gently. The whole school applauded in a frenzy of excitement. 'Arise.' Catherine obeyed. 'Curtsey.' She did so graciously as she sobbed. 'You will now go and stand in the corner for an hour and quietly contemplate both your sins and your way of being forgiven.'

Catherine was led to the back of the hall by Sisters Agnes and Elizabeth, who placed her in a bleak white corner, face to the wall, with her hands behind her back. Sister Agnes drew her white, lacy drawers down to her ankles and Sister Elizabeth pinned up her skirt and petticoat once more to reveal her scarlet, punished buttocks. It struck me that one could spent a delightful hour watching her bottom change colour as it trembled and shivered, and the other schoolgirls seemed to be of the same opinion; but after a few minutes, the drawers were raised and the skirt and petticoat lowered. A card was hung upon her back declaring: I HAVE BEEN RIGHTLY BIRCHED FOR MY INSOLENCE. Her bottom continued to twitch, causing the pleats of her skirt to quiver quite enticingly.

Jeanne was then released from her cage and a similar performance ensued. There was one noticeable difference, though: her buttocks were much more round and plump and took longer to redden. When that happened, however, and it would have been at about the sixth stroke that they blazed with a fiery glow, one was amazed both by the thrusting and writhing of her hips and sighs and gasps of her fellow schoolgirls. I noted also that the facial cheeks of the Mother Superior and her fellow Sisters were almost as red as the bum cheeks of their penitents. Nor could one avoid noticing that the schoolgirls who had not surreptitiously placed their hands actually within their skirts were rubbing their palms hard against their covered pubic mounds or else were squeezing their thighs so tightly together that I feared they might shriek out as loud as Jeanne at the end of her birching.

I shan't forget my disrobing in the antechamber with the men, once Jeanne had been placed in her corner to be teased with Catherine by the schoolgirls after a hymn and final prayers, when I couldn't help spotting that the white underpants of Lord Maulerby, J.-K. Huysmans and Father Binoire S.J. were soaked in semen.

'I trust,' said Huysmans, as Maulerby and Binoire gazed approvingly at a rampaging erection which I could not hide, 'that you are beginning to discern the joys of penitence and Christianity.'

'Oh, indeed,' I replied. 'But I'm bloody well damned if I know the differences between a brothel, Satanism and this.'

CHAPTER SIX

The following morning brought a letter from Claire, postmarked southwest London. Why the hell hadn't the bitch answered my telegrams? I needed to communicate with her now more than ever and so I ripped the envelope open with some irritation.

My darling,

I have met an interesting elderly gentleman recently and, according to my estimation, he is of the same age as my father. I do not think that I have ever suffered from an Electra 'complex' as Dr Freud would have it, that feeling of sexual attraction to the father with hostility towards the mother, yet this gentleman had great magnetism; and my father is renowned for his own charm.

Upon this auspicious occasion, I was attending a dinner party at the home of a friend. A total of ten guests had assembled in Knightsbridge to enjoy the banquet thoughtfully prepared for us. Six of the guests were married couples and sometimes I wonder if I will ever marry. Most of my friends have accepted a proposal, have been led to the altar as lambs to the slaughter and have become living embodiments of the old proverb: 'Marry in haste, repent at leisure.'

I hope that wedlock will never be forced upon me but

such was the case with the hostess, Maud, a dear friend from my schooldays, who had stood at the altar when eight months pregnant to join her life to that of a gross but wealthy country squire, Sir Toby Downshire. On their honeymoon in Ireland, she gave birth to twins and a cousin who was present swore that she saw the leprechauns present in the room, the little people, those mischievous spirits. The twins were both born with cauls upon their heads, which is a good omen as they will develop the inner sight and powers of perception.

My dinner companion to my right was Pyotr Alexeyvich Kropotkin, known in London Society as Prince Peter Kropotkin. I could not take my eyes away from him. He spoke with such a strong Russian accent, even though it emerged that he had lived in England as a political exile since 1886. He talked in a fascinating fashion about his life and about his passion for Geography and Geology, in which he had achieved a respected reputation, though he did not at that point mention that he was also a notorious anarchist. I had fondly imagined that all anarchists wore black, broad-brimmed hats with black cloaks and carried incendiary devices bearing the label BOMB.

I had never met a Geologist before, let alone an anarchist, yet I knew that they have a desire to penetrate the crust of the Earth, to prod into the layers of granite and basalt and ultimately to penetrate our planet's burning core. He spoke of his travels in the Siberian tundra and of the savage cold of the winter weather.

'I wish I had been there to keep you warm,' I remarked over the sixth course (of beef and Burgundy) as I allowed my hand to rest upon his knee. 'It must have been terrible for you. Did you suffer from frostbite at all?'

'My toes turned blue.' He looked into my eyes and his

piercing gaze burned me within. My hand crept up his thigh.

'How miserable it must have been,' I responded sympathetically.

'Yes, my dear, it was, but if I had had the pleasure of the company of a beautiful and intelligent woman such as yourself, it would have been much more tolerable . . .' My hand reached his scrotum, appreciating the feel of his bulging testicles through the cloth of his trousers. My thumb stroked his pulsating ram-rod and I knew then just how much his throbbing member wanted to penetrate my pussy. 'We must fornicate!' *he roared in the voice of a mad Russian.*

There were shock and amazement upon the faces of one couple at the dinner-table and I'm afraid that I forget their names. Poor dears, they were so dismally middle-class and simply didn't know how to behave. They stared aghast at our hostess who knows my nature intimately well and who carried on eating as if nothing untoward had occurred. The hideous nature of their social faux pas *slowly dawned upon them as they turned their heads to stare at Squire Toby, who was tucking away wine, as usual.*

'Bloody good idea!' he bellowed in a voice like *thunder. 'The trouble with this country is that there's not enough fucking!'*

'Quite agree,' his wife returned icily. I looked coy.

'Let us drink some more!' Prince Kropotkin declared, accepting another glass of La Tache. 'And then a good rogering, as they say in England. A splendid expression!' He glared at the middle-class couple who were shrinking into their seats. Pulling a revolver from his pocket, he glanced for permission at our hostess, who nodded once. The hapless couple dived beneath the table as Prince

Kropotkin promptly shot a crystal off the overhanging chandelier.

'Damn good shot, sir!' Squire Toby exclaimed approvingly. 'Never seen it hit so accurately yet. Damnit, sir, you and me must go tiger hunting some time.'

As the bourgeois couple crawled miserably back into their seats, perpetually to be a laughing-stock in London Society, Prince Kropotkin replaced his smoking gun, the other guests carried on chatting about the theatre and the servants continued to pour more wine as if this sort of thing happened every evening. What insolence, arrogance, haughtiness, cockiness, brashness, bumptiousness he had, and with such a flagrantly self-assured manner!

The atmosphere relaxed over treacle pudding with whipped cream, followed by a compote *that seemed to consist mainly of cherries. I am sure that some specks of dried* cantharides, *popularly known as Spanish Fly, had been sprinkled over the top, and there was the royal jelly of the bees and flowers. This sweet, viscous, yellow fluid had been applied liberally to soak into the mellow fruit. As the ladies left the table to withdraw for coffee and liqueurs, leaving the men to their port and nuts, I heard Squire Toby say:*

'Think you're a damn fine fellow, Kropotkin, damn fine fellow. But I don't hold with any of this anarchist nonsense of yours. Isn't it all about a bloody revolution or some such rubbish like that?'

'A revolution, certainly, Sir Toby,' Kropotkin replied, 'but it need not be a bloody one provided that we all see sense in terms of the next step of Mankind in terms of evolution.'

'Humph!' Squire Toby snorted. 'Intellectual balderdash. Still, you shoot straight, I'll give you that. But look

here, Prince, don't take it too far. Why, you'll be wanting to abolish the House of Lords next . . .'

The ladies left the gentlemen to sort out the world, which on the whole they do very badly, and concentrated instead in our conversation on local, practical matters, which on the whole we do very well. I enjoyed my mocha *coffee topped by dollops of Guernsey cream sprinkled with flakes of chocolate and a pinch of cinnamon, and the glass of Drambuie was a welcome addition. It was a joy to sit around the roaring open fire of wood and the men appeared genial when they joined us. Squire Toby kept seizing the poker and prodding it into the coals beneath the wood to encourage the flames further, just as my father was wont to do. For a nightcap, we were served brandy, kindled by a flame of lambent blue. Some guests left, including* 'les nouveaux riches' *who were now* 'les misérables.' *Others had been invited to stay the night and I was ushered to my chamber, whereupon I discarded my clothing, attired myself in my silken night-gown and covered myself with the eiderdown.*

I lit the oil lantern beside my bed, enjoying the strange optical illusions it created upon the ceiling and on the walls. Suddenly there was a knock upon my door as I was settling down to read some short stories by Arthur Machen.

'Who is it?' I queried gently.

'It is I, the Prince Peter Kropotkin and I have been requested to deliver you a deoch an doris, *a stirrup cup,' his strong Russian voice boomed, 'so that you might have a peaceful sleep tonight.' I removed my nightcap and quickly combed my hair, then opened the door.*

'Do come in.' Within seconds he had seized me in his arms.

'You do not know how long I have been waiting for this moment!' he sang out passionately and, he held me close and tightly to him, my belly was pressed against his rigid member. His shoe shot back to slam the door shut. 'You have nothing to fear, my dear,' he sighed within my ear. 'In Russia, we men love to treat a lady well.' Thereupon, he lifted me up and tossed me onto the bed. I bounced upon the springs as he quickly removed his clothing and then he tore off my silken nightie with one mighty rip! *He sprang to suck my bosoms eagerly then took his tongue down to my quivering thighs. Gooseflesh trembled up and down my legs in a deliciously tickling sensation.*

Suddenly he entered me. As he penetrated further into the deep heart within my labia, I entered into a world of fantasy, ecstasy and wondrous imagination as his empowering hands closed tightly upon my wrists to hold them down, spread upon the bed.

'Give it the rhythm, bitch,' he growled, 'yes, definitely give it the rhythm . . .' I did so and he swived me as I have rarely been swived before. His rhythm was that of a piston and the shot of his juices, that of a pistol. Afterwards he gratified my tender sensibilities in that my essences had trickled down my thighs and he slurped noisily upon my fine nectar as if he were a bear devouring the wild honey of Siberian bees.

Afterwards he offered me an Imperial Russian cigarette, a long, thin object, half of which consists of the filter; and then he produced a flask of polished silver.

'This is what we like to drink in Russia after our sacred act of love,' he rumbled. It was as if mingled fire and water were passing down my throat and yet I recognised the aphrodisiacal qualities immediately. We sat upon the bed and discussed sundry matters. He told me that he

had joined the Russian Anarchist Movement during the 1870s.

'Doesn't that imply a radical evolution?' I enquired.

'Yes,' he responded simply. 'You cannot believe the oppression that I suffered in consequence of advocating the proposition that Man is essentially good and that governments are instruments of repression, not evolution and hence I advocate revolution. *My autobiography will be entitled* Memoirs of a Revolutionist.*'*

'Perhaps one day I shall write my *autobiography,' I answered. 'Possibly I shall call it* Memoirs of an Aristocratic Whore.*' He gave me a wicked grin and a deeply rich chuckle. 'May I include you?'*

'If you so desire.'

'I desire you,' I replied. He graciously accepted my invitation and this time we made love with laughter and tomfoolery. Afterwards he produced a balalaika from a deep inside pocket of his evening tail-coat and sang me Russian songs. I asked him to translate them and they all seemed to be about sex and violence. As the early morning sun arose, we fell asleep in one another's arms and I awoke in the afternoon to find that my anarchist, geological, geographical and royal lover had silently left: leaving his balalaika behind.

All my love,
Claire

This was all very well: but why the devil wasn't she assisting me in my search for the truth about Satanism? I was glad when Maria visited early that evening.

'Still engaged in the pursuit of Satanism, Horby?' She shrugged her shoulders and laughed mockingly over our *bocks*. 'Well, I have ensured that Gabriele Jogand will indeed be present at Le Chat Blanc in Montmartre tomorrow at luncheon to inform you of the unvarnished truth. Meanwhile we have more pressing matters at hand. Do you have your pistol?'

'I always do,' I replied.

That said, I sprang upon her, pushing her down upon the bed and kissing the inviting globes of her firm breasts with their pert, upstanding nipples, having roughly pulled her low-cut blouse down to her slender waist. Maria responded by moaning sweet endearing words, as if she was being caressed by one for whom she genuinely cared! My right hand pushed her coyly protective arm aside and took possession of her tender muff-cleft, squeezing it through the thin material of her skirt. Then I gently placed one leg over hers, pressing my rigid penis – by now almost tearing its own way out of the constraining trousers that held it back from its goal of Maria's tantalizing cunt – close to her delectable and voluptuous body. We looked into one another's eyes, nodded and proceeded instantly to divest ourselves of our outer clothes.

I noticed at once that Maria wore a red silk basque that she could untie from the front and very brief white lace panties that hugged her cunt so tightly that her pouting vaginal lips and dark-haired pubic mound were clearly outlined. Sheer black silk stockings, held up by a red-and-black lace suspender belt, sheathed her long, shapely legs high up her smooth thighs, leaving a breathtakingly enticing span of naked flesh between stocking-top and pantie-edge. The whole ensemble was clearly designed to focus the male gaze with burning intensity on the magic triangle of Maria's wondrous quim.

What thrills of delightful expectation shot through my whole frame! With my rod stiffly erect, I quivered from head to foot, for this luscious temptation and the intensity of lustful feeling it inspired produced an urge to ravish that would stand no further delay. So I glued my lips to Maria's in a long, lecherous kiss, holding the whole length of her marvellous lithe body tightly against mine. I ran my hands down her back, over her slender waist and on down to cup the firm flesh-globes of her superbly shapely buttocks. I squeezed them hard through the lace of her panties, pressing Maria's barely-covered cuntal mound roughly against my own bulging crotch at the same time as I rasped the hairs of my chest across her stiffening nipples. Breaking off our kiss, she arched her head back and moaned softly. I continued to squeeze her delectable arse hard, and forced both hands beneath the tight lower edge of the panties until I had two handfuls of smooth, warm, naked bumflesh in my grasp. Kneading them savagely, I insinuated the middle finger of my right hand into the fleshy groove between them until it reached the puckered portal of Maria's anus. After a preliminary circular stroking that caused her to shiver all over, I stuck the qucsting digit up to the second joint into her arse, relishing the sensation of the tight grip of her sphincter. 'Horby, you devil,' Maria breathed as I withdrew my finger from her bumhole, 'whatever next?'

My answer was not verbal but was certainly direct. Gripping Maria's tight, brief panties in both hands – one hand holding the flimsy item by its front, the other grasping it at the rear – I wrenched hard and ripped them off her in one quick movement, flinging the torn white lace aside. Maria shrieked in outraged surprise and instinctively tried to cover her suddenly revealed dark-haired muff with her hands. Gently but firmly, I forced her hands away from her pubic mound and held both of them easily behind her back in one of mine, using the other to fondle her now defenceless quim, preparing the way for my raging cock's assault upon her honeypot.

Maria gasped, struggling and trying to twitch her cunt, by now well lubricated, away from my clutching hand. I recognized the signs: Maria liked, on occasion, to pretend that she was a reluctant victim of her male partner's lustful desires. She gained extra excitement from the fantasy that she was helpless and at the mercy of a heartless rapist. I was more than happy to play along with her in this charade of the flesh.

I pulled Maria close against me and leant forward to speak softly in her ear. 'Maria,' I murmured, 'you beautiful, cockteasing bitch. It's me, Horby. You should know that you can't lead me on like you have been and expect to get away with just a friendly hug. And you *certainly* can't flaunt your wonderful body in that provocative underwear in front of me – or any man worthy of the name – without getting what you're asking for and getting it hot and hard. Just *looking* at your cunt lips bulging through those tight panties (before I ripped them off you), framed by your smooth thighs in those stockings and suspenders, nearly made me come on the spot. Which would have been a real waste of the flood of spunk I'm going to drench the depths of your jellybox with in a few minutes' time. My pork sword is going to teach your teasing twat a lesson it won't forget in a hurry. Whether you want me to or not, I'm going to fuck you senseless right now.'

Maria breathed in deeply and opened her mouth wide. I thought she was going to scream in mock terror so I sealed her lips with another soul-sucking kiss which seemed fairly to shut her up. When our lips disengaged, she muttered tearfully. 'The fancy underwear isn't for *your* benefit, please believe me. I only wear it for my *real* lover. You were never supposed to see me in it: I never intended to excite you or any other man apart from him. How can I help it if you assault me, undress me forcibly and like what you find so much that you want to rape me? Oh, show some pity and let me go, please. Oh, *please*.'

Maria was certainly getting into the spirit of the charade and no mistake. Her *ad lib* (or was it?) dialogue was a nice twist to the proceedings. But if I was going to be as good as my word about fucking her senseless, it was now time for action rather than dialogue. Otherwise there was likely to be an embarrassing case of premature ejaculation on stage, so to speak.

'Too late for pity, I'm afraid, Maria,' I said. 'If I don't get up you in the next five minutes, my balls will explode. I don't imagine that's the kind of interior decoration you want for this place, eh?' I pushed Maria back down onto the bed and knelt over her, my massively engorged member swinging stiffly from side to side above her breasts, before lowering myself onto her quivering form. She did not speak this time but appeared awfully discomposed nonetheless: long drawn-out sighs came from deep within her bosom as her breasts trembled (actually with excitement) and her hands feebly and increasingly unconvincingly tried to push away my intrusive fingers as they tweaked her nipples and pubic bush, kneaded her bum cheeks and thrust urgently between her cunt lips and into the depths of her quim. Desire eventually overcame her entirely false modesty; her return of my passionate kisses became more ardent and her straining, wonderfully firm and smooth thighs gradually gave in to my efforts to penetrate between them and parted with only a token reluctance. Instead of playing at repulsing my advances, her arms were now entwined around my body.

But, once again, Maria recollected the fantasy of rape in which she was engaged. She suddenly abandoned her embracing of me, beating at my chest – albeit weakly – with clenched fists and clamping her slender legs so tightly together that her cunt lips were hidden from view and only her dark pubic bush could be seen, framed enticingly by her trembling suspendered and stockinged thighs.

Obviously the citadel of Maria's pretended chastity had been stormed successfully many a time before yet she certainly acted as though it hadn't. Reaching the limits of my own self-control, I thrust my hands between her thighs and forced her legs apart, pushing them up and back, brutally exposing her quim to the battering ram of my lust – which still had to be vigorously applied to supposedly reluctant pussy-portals before a breach was made sufficient to effect a deep lodgement. Although Maria's cunt lips were actually sopping with love-juice, her amazingly developed vaginal muscles were able to keep the entrance to her joxy clenched tight. Not that she had the ghost of a chance by now of keeping me out. The sight of her plump pink honeypot lips and damply glistening pubic hair laid defenceless at last between her splayed, shapely thighs, and this whole fantastic target area so arousingly framed by suspender belt and stocking-tops, raised my surging desire to boiling point.

I grasped Maria's firm, beautifully rounded buttocks with both hands in a kneading grasp of iron, slipping a middle finger deep into the rosebud of her arse. Next, I leant the weight of my upper torso on the backs of her raised, frantically thrashing thighs, stilling them and forcing them yet further apart and back, so that her silk-sheathed knees now almost pressed against her shoulders. I manoeuvred my groin into position and placed the swollen tip of my poker-hard prick against the outer lips of Maria's damp cooze, relishing briefly the delightful sensation of the grip of the flesh-ring of her cuntal entrance around my bulging glans. Then, unable to delay a second longer, I savagely thrust the whole length of my rigid, engorged cock into the inner reaches of her warm, moist quim. I shouted in triumph – and Maria screamed a horrified 'No!'

So now, what anguished pleas for mercy and sighs of submissive despair!' What involuntary murmurs of real erotic joy, mingled with moans of pretended protest! As for me, I kept a tight hold of Maria's wonderful arse-globes, pulling her crotch tightly against my thrusting rod-root as my hips proceeded to move with a driving, pounding rhythm of their own, plunging my stiff dick to its hilt into Maria's vanquished, stockings-and-suspenders-adorned cunt time and time again. Soon enough I felt the familiar welcome rush of tingling, electric sensation from the depths of my balls through my pistoning shaft and out through the tip of my prick as I came explosively in a spurting tidal wave of jism, pulse after pulse after pulse. As my tadger shot its liquid load, Maria tossed her head from side to side and gasped an incoherent mix of grateful endearments alternating with tearful cries of outrage at the successful climax of my 'violation' of her innermost fleshy depths.

'That was *most* enjoyable, my darling Horby,' Maria said over the customary cognac which we both liked to take after a fuck, 'but it was not *quite* what I meant when I referred to your pistol, you hateful rapist, you.'

'Oh, if you mean something with which one shoots men rather than women, yes, I think I have a useful revolver somewhere,' I responded.

'You will need it,' Maria returned, 'for I have information that may shock you. You are, I believe, acquainted with a Viscount Maulerby, yes?'

'I have that particular misfortune,' I sighed.

'Are you aware,' she enquired, arching a thinly-pencilled eyebrow, 'that he is a double-agent, working in the interests of the German Empire?'

'Surely not! I mean, I know the man's a complete shit,' I expostulated, 'but a traitor . . . impossible!'

'Then look at this.' She extracted a sheaf of documents from her bag and passed them to me. I leafed through them with growing amazement though, thanks to my cousin at the Embassy in Berlin, I was not entirely unfamiliar with their contents. Here were detailed plans in the event of war with France, which had nearly come about due to the Fashoda clash in Africa 1898.

'How did you obtain them?' I queried.

'Simple.' Maria shrugged. 'I slept with Maulerby and took them from the ridiculous fool as he slumbered. And here is a letter to him,' she passed it over to me, 'from the deputy chief of the Prussian Secret Service congratulating Maulerby on subverting British interests in German East Africa.' I looked and there was no denying this most disturbing matter. 'I am endeavouring,' Maria said, 'to bring about peace through a maintenance of the balance of power on the Continent of Europe. This can best be done via closer relations between the British and the French. To this end I have been sleeping with two leading British Generals: John French and Douglas Haig. Both of them are obstinate, unimaginative fools. French thinks that any war in Europe can be won by a cavalry charge by the British dressed in red coats; Haig thinks that repeated assaults by massed infantry can do the trick. Neither of them appear to have heard of railway trains, minefields, barbed wire, poison gas or machine guns, such as I have heard about from my German lovers. Also they are both useless in bed. Even so, if the English idiots speak with the French idiots, then perhaps there can be an *Entente Cordiale* to block German Imperial expansionist ambitions peaceably.'

'This makes sense, Maria,' I said. (By God, it did! With the hindsight of 1925. There *were* 'informal military discussions' between the General Staffs of England and France; there *was* the *Entente Cordiale* of 1902; and when the Great War unfortunately came, Sir John French and Douglas Haig proved themselves to be even more useless than Maria had declared them to be.) 'But what are you proposing with regard to Maulerby?'

'Expose him as the traitor that he is,' Maria replied, 'one who is trying to spoil plans for peace between Great Britain and France by working for Germany and who is harming British Empire interests in Africa. Now, he thinks tonight that I will be walking into his trap; but given your co-operation, he will be walking into mine . . .' I listened to her proposal and smiled, fondly fingering my Harris tweed jacket.

'Let's go,' I said, smiling sadistically.

CHAPTER SEVEN

The British Secret Service can be damned good in action: it's its intelligence gathering that's the problem. I don't suppose that the relevant chap at its French HQ, obviously in the British Embassy in Paris, would have given me the time of day had it not been for my various social connections. The instant that some possibility of action was discerned, however, there was a definite stirring and plans were made.

Later in the evening, Maria entered the apartment block where Maulerby had rented a flat in Montparnasse. As she informed me later, he ushered her through the hallway and into the drawing-room where he produced a revolver, fondly imagining that as a British agent he was in one of our many 'safe houses'. Five minutes later, I came through the door with the key I had been given in my left hand and a revolver in my right to find Maria bound over a block, stripped naked, and Maulerby grinning gleefully as he poised and switched a martinet in his hand.

'The game's up, Maulerby,' I said. 'You and Maria will be changing places. Drop the martinet and untie the lady.'

'Stay out of this, Horby,' he snarled back. 'This woman is a spy and I'm working for British Intelligence. Just don't get involved in matters which don't concern you.'

'Oh, a spy, eh? Just as you are?' I responded. 'British Intelligence services will be here soon enough: how do you think that I have the key?' I waved it in the light of the oil-lamps. 'Unfasten the lady or I shall shoot you in the balls, with my gun going off by unfortunate accident.' Maulerby dropped the martinet and untied Maria, whose bottom was still a lustrous pearly white, owing to my arrival in the nick of time. 'Over to you, Maria,' I said as I picked up Maulerby's martinet and revolver, handing them to Maria as I kept him covered.

'You'll be hearing from High Command!' he spluttered. 'I warn you!'

'Dear me,' I retorted, 'and poor you.' My left hand slipped the keys into my jacket pocket then pulled out a Cuban panatella. I lit the cigar from an oil lamp as I continued to keep Maulerby covered with my pistol. 'Over to you, Maria.'

Maulerby stood there and looked foolish as Maria put her clothes back on. Eventually she rustled her skirts angrily and in return he quivered more than her petticoats.

'Take down your trousers, you traitor!' she snapped, her eyes ablaze. Lord Maulerby looked so foolish as his trousers tumbled to his ankles. 'Now pull down your drawers. Bend over that block where you intended to flog me. O! you were so sneeringly sadistic, weren't you? Now it is my turn.' She smiled gleefully as she clicked the handlocks and footlocks upon his wrists and feet, leaving his white behind perfectly positioned for punishment. She twirled the martinet in the air.

'This is an implement of French design,' she declared, 'invented by the French Major Martinet for use on the bare bottoms of negligent officer cadets at St Cyr. It closely resembles a cat o' nine tails, does it not?' She flicked it against his buttocks and he shuddered, his small, piggy eyes bulging at the unexpected and alarming reversal of roles. I took a glass of the champagne he had intended to sip as he flogged Maria and offered one to her, which she graciously accepted. 'It is a curious implement,' Maria continued as she suddenly lashed his bottom. The six thongs went *tsuck!* and Maulerby squealed. 'I suppose that the French simply have to be different,' she observed airily as she flicked him again and his hips twitched in response. 'You chose the martinet to punish me, you foolish boy, and now *I* shall use it to punish *you*.' She brought it down with a solid *thwack* in a stroke reminiscent of those ladies who have recently chosen to play tennis, raising two blue welts upon Maulerby's bottom and extracting a squawk that came from the depths of his throat. 'Painful, is it?' she laughed.

'Now look here . . .' Maulerby gasped. 'Don't. The consequences will be dreadful. I am highly connected, I warn you . . .' Maria responded with a further fierce lash and I watched with detached interest as the six thongs of the martinet raised marks all over his twitching buttocks. He shrieked and writhed as Maria giggled and I puffed upon my cigar. 'Highly connected, indeed,' Maria observed.

'And you had no compunction about doing this to me, did you, Lord Maulerby?' She whipped him again and he shouted out his pain as his florid face turned puce. 'On the whole,' Maria remarked casually, 'I find the martinet to be less useful than the birch, and considerably more inaccurate. In common with all whips, even the properly tapered varieties, it has an unfortunate lashing effect . . .'

'Ow!' Maulerby shrieked as the thongs lashed him.

'I find,' said Maria, 'that the tips of the thongs curl around the far flank and inflict the greatest punishment, not on the bottom, but in the region of the hip.' A further stroke which indeed landed on the side of Maulerby's hip made the man squirm. 'The answer,' Maria continued evenly, 'is to stand a little. Further. Back.' That enunciated, she extracted a phial of lipstick from her bag and wrote in scarlet upon his buttocks: 'I AM A TRAITOR TO GREAT BRITAIN. PLEASE WHIP ME.' There was a mirror in front of the flogging block in which Maulerby was confronted by his wretched and perspiring face. Maria now took a hand mirror from the bathroom and held it up so that the traitor could see her words scrawled in scarlet upon his whaled, twitching bottom. The next stroke landed on his upper thighs and he shrieked. 'It is a different instrument to control,' said Maria, thoughtfully surveying the damage, 'but the night is yet young.'

These deliberations were interrupted by an expected knock upon the door of the apartment and I admitted our operatives. The British Secret Service was among the first to employ female agents and Agnes, Maud and Beatrice, who entered, certainly did credit to the process of selection. Agnes bore a camera, Maud had the tripod and Beatrice carried the photographic plates. Maulerby writhed in pain and shame as the infernal device was swiftly set up in order to portray his disgrace.

'I believe, Lord Maulerby,' Maria sneered, 'that you are financially embarrassed and are proposing to solve this particular difficulty by being a traitor to Great Britain; and also via your engagement to Lady Sarah Hogg. Lady Sarah,' she commented acidly, 'who is an heiress, might change her mind were she to see the ensuing photography.' That said, she draped a pair of her own drawers around his sweating neck. 'It suits you, this dog collar!' she laughed merrily. Agnes, Maud and Beatrice took a dozen photographs of Maulerby in his somewhat undignified condition. 'If ever you betray British interests again,

Lady Sarah Hogg will be seeing these photographs, so you had better be a good boy and behave yourself, hadn't you? *Hadn't* you??' She whipped him again with her martinet; he gasped and squirmed as the girls giggled then proposed to depart as swiftly as they had arrived, declining my proffered refreshments on the grounds that they were on duty.

'Oh, my dear girls, do stay for the *finale*,' Maria insisted. They looked at each other and smiled briefly as Maria released Maulerby from the flogging-block, though she kept his wrists handcuffed. 'Now dance before us.'

The girls hooted with laughter as Maulerby proceeded to dance with all the grace of a clumsy bear. Every time he made a false step, which was uncomfortably often, Maria lashed him on his legs, thighs, arms or bottom, causing him to shriek volubly as the ladies chuckled appreciatively. 'By using my whip on limbs that go astray,' Maria observed, 'I ensure that not too many mistakes are made.' Maulerby danced obediently, ladies' knickers around his neck and flinching from the flick of Maria's martinet as further photographs were taken. Then he had to lie down upon his back and, in turn, each woman lowered her drawers and proceeded to sit upon his face for five minutes; and he had to lick each separate arse-hole and kiss their bottom-cheeks. Now it was the women's turn to writhe and squirm, but with pleasure rather than pain.

When every woman had come upon his florid face, Maulerby was led back to the flogging block he had intended for Maria and chained down there once more. A dog-bowl, lipsticked with the words 'FIDO', was put in front of him and Maria proceeded to pee in it. 'You might be needing some water,' she remarked. Taking a feather from her hat, she proceeded to tickle his prick until he screamed with a curious mixture of agony and ecstasy. As his rod spurted forth, his face plunged involuntarily into the dog-bowl of women's piss and another memorable photograph was taken. 'Wouldn't your family just like to see this?' Maria taunted him as the magnesium-powder lights flashed. 'It could persuade your father to change his will. So just be an obedient one in future.'

We then departed, leaving him bound and helpless, to be rescued, no doubt, from this awkwardly humiliating position by the maid of the apartment block on the following morning.

Maria had once again kept her word in arranging my luncheon on the following day with Gabriele Jogand at Le Chat Blanc in Montmartre. This was a café for artists and, to employ a slang expression that has recently come into vogue, 'piss-artists'. Monsieur Jogand turned out to be a man with a charming manner, dressed in immaculate clerical black though sporting a floppy bow tie in mauve and yellow. His figure was short and tubby and he radiated pleasantness until one looked into his very hard blue eyes, which nevertheless twinkled as though the irises were gemstones. A thin, waxed moustache adorned his smiling mouth with its full lips. We agreed to drink St Emilion, accompanied by a variety of nuts.

I was interested in Jogand because he had for a time been hailed as Europe's leading master Satanist who had repented and turned to Roman Catholicism, exposing in his many best-selling books the evils of Satanism and its twin, Freemasonry. His views had furthermore received confirmation from the authors Leo Taxil and Dr Bataille.

After our elementary pleasantaries, I broached the matter and I have rarely heard a man laugh so hard, wiping tears away from his eyes in between in copious quaffing of wine.

'*Mon cher monsieur* . . .' he grinned broadly as he dried his eyes with a napkin, 'do not please say that a man of your intelligence has also been fooled by my ridiculous tricks?' He chuckled and lit a slim panatella, which he proceeded to smoke with evident enjoyment. 'My books are a complete fraud,' he said. 'Leo Taxil is simply a pseudonym I use and Dr Bataille is an old friend of mine, a former ship's surgeon whose name is Charles Hacks and to whom I offered the opportunity of making money on my idea. Why, do you not know the full story?' I shook my head. 'I can tell you the truth,' he chortled, 'now that it is over.'

'I wish someone would,' I responded.

'*Eh bien*,' Jogand puffed out a perfect smoke-ring, 'I was educated in the Roman Catholic faith and I grew to hate it beyond belief. When I saw the attacks of the Church upon Freemasonry and its scattering of the accusation of Satanism too freely and loosely upon all who dissented, I saw my opportunity both to make money and to exact revenge. After a course of reading, I invented an international, world-wide conspiracy of Freemasons and Satanists.'

'Why not bring the Jews in too?' I asked.

'I may need them in a future volume,' he replied. 'In any event, I then confessed my sins to the Church and they welcomed back their prodigal son, especially since I was giving them what they thought to be 'top secret' information about Satanism and Freemasonry. How I do pity poor Albert Pike of New Orleans! By every account, he is a quiet and pleasant scholar, sincerely dedicated to the ideals and ceremonies of Freemasonry. I accused this innocent fellow of being the International Head of the global Satanic conspiracy.'

'Bit dirty, isn't it?' I murmured, 'to accuse an innocent man?'

'Not at all,' Jogand retorted. 'He had about three members in his grouping before I accused him in my books. Now he receives hundreds of applications to join his allegedly notorious society and, in consequence, thousands of dollars. So he is happy. I made a small fortune through the books of mine which accused him: so *I* am happy and my publishers are happy. My readers are happy for they bought my second volume. And the Church is happy because at last it has discerned the man who is the Devil's representative on Earth. Of course, in order to complete the happiness of the Church, I had to produce the Devil's female representative, the Whore Babylon from *The Book of Revelations*; so I invented Diana Vaughan, who was in fact my charming and delightful secretary.

'I gave this beautiful, rampaging and rampant bitch a post as High Priestess and 'Daughter of the Devil' at Albert Pike's allegedly infamous Lodge, which idea excited many. Then I announced that she was repenting and was desirous of joining the Roman Catholic Church, therein to pour out all the secrets of her sins, her fornication and her iniquity. The Church became itself quite frantic with lascivious desire for me to produce Diana Vaughan. They ached for my confirmation of their false beliefs and I wanted their money: so it was so far an eminently satisfactory transaction.

'Did you not read about it in the papers? Dear me, the Church must have exercised all its influence to suppress the story. *Non*, on April 19th, 1897, at the lecture hall of the Paris Geographical Society on the

Boulevard Saint-Germain, it was announced that Diana Vaughan would be present in person. The matter had been primed well by the *Memoirs* of Diana, published the previous February. The hall was packed; there was not even standing-room at the back. It made me smile to see that the audience was evenly divided between the Catholic and Masonic camps, with Bishops sitting in uncomfortable social promiscuity with Masonic Grand Masters – there was also, unsurprisingly, a large journalistic contingent present.'

'What happened?' I asked.

'Why, I told them the truth, of course!' Jogand roared with laughter. 'I blew the entire *gaffe*. I explained to the Church precisely how I had managed to take their money and fool them for twelve years and to the Masons precisely why I had done so.

'Then I removed my gold pince-nez, bowed politely to the astounded gathering and walked away from the platform. I left the building by a side-door, walked across the Boulevard Saint-Germain to a café opposite, ordered a cup of coffee and a glass of cognac; and awaited developments.

'The instant that I left the hall, pandemonium broke out, the booing and whistling of the embarrassed Catholic party mixing with the jubilant jeers and catcalls of the Masonic supporters. Shame soon turned to fury and blows were traded. Cleric and Grand Master brawled with total loss of dignity and only my prompt summoning of the police prevented a full-scale riot. In consequence, it is nowadays impossible for anybody in France to take Satanism seriously as a threat. For let it be stated definitely,' Jogand smiled wryly, '*Satanism as an organized conspiracy has never, and does not now, exist.* Those who claim to have attended Black Masses are either deluded, liars or the victims of fraud.'

'What about white Masses?' I enquired, 'which celebrate the sex act as holy and which some say are celebrated by international orders such as the Rosicrucians?'

'*Mon dieu . . .*' he groaned wearily, 'you have obviously been mixing with the occultists of Paris. I know them well, Lord Horby, and to which one do you refer? The late Stanislas de Guiata? Why, he was simply a drug addict making endeavours to realize his fantasies, the same as that crazy Jesuit priest, Father Binoire. Huysmans is these days a Catholic penitent looking for an evil enabling him to expiate his guilt. Pelādan is mad and Encausse is boring, even more so whenever he writes under the name of "Papus". Believe me, sir, these occultists are fools. I know. I've made my money out of them so this atheist says thank God for their folly! And you English are no better. Have you heard of a Doctor W. Wynn Westcott?' I nodded in acknowledgement of his mention of a senior Founder Member of the Golden Dawn.

'Nice but naive.' Jogand leered at me. 'I persuaded him to give me a specimen of his signature for "spiritual" purposes. I then forged it on a Charter for an Order which I sold to a gullible American for thousands of dollars. Ha! ha! no fool like an occult fool!'

'So you don't think that anyone can harm anyone else by Black Magic?'

'Ha! ha! ha!' His ample sides heaved with mirth and merriment. 'I have received so many curses in my life that I could paper my walls with them: that is all they are fit for. Please, some common sense, monsieur. You *can't* be magically attacked unless you *want* to be magically attacked, and then it is your own mind that does the tricks.'

Jogand was a charming companion over luncheon though I never saw him afterwards. One gathers that he retired to a life of comparative luxury in Provence and died there in 1907. I shan't forget his words of departure:

'Forget Sin and Satanism, Lord Horby. Life is merely made up of fleeting moments of joyous sex and raucous laughter.'

CHAPTER EIGHT

'And this is the thing, to run away from a lady?!' the Countess of Salzburg exclaimed. 'I shall now take great liberties with you, young sir.' Helena proceeded to take possession of my manly jewel as it now sprang forth in all its grandeur when she opened the front of my dressing-gown. I had tired of Satanism and Paris and, needing a change, had taken the night express to Munich. In the dining-car I had discerned a delightfully voluptuous brunette, styled at the height of fashion, and evidently her motives for travel had not been entirely dissimilar to mine.

'The love!' she shrieked out and a button burst upon her blouse. 'Now it's mine! What a beauty!' The Countess Helena leaned over me and implanted hot, wanton kisses on the head of the rampant prisoner within her kid-gloved fingers. I fairly sighed and heaved with excitement under such skilful osculation. I had rarely felt such an ecstatic thrill before it was altogether a new sensation. The tonguing and pressures of her sucking lips and the tickling tips of the gloved hands of this wanton woman opened up such a new source of delight that I almost fainted under her caresses. She did not even blush as she withdrew her scarlet lips from my glistening knob, drew me to the side of the bed and, as the Wagons-Lit carriage clattered on into the European night, raised her skirt-hem and petticoats to expose her lovely cleft to my amorous gaze.

'My fanny always expects a little kiss first,' she whispered to me as at last her face flushed slightly, which added considerably to her beauty. I was kneeling in a moment, paying my devotions to that divinely delicate-looking pink slit. She turned her body and I adored her vagina, shaded by golden hair, as soft as the finest silk. My tongue divided its juicy lips, searching out her pretty clitoris, which at once stiffened under my lascivious probing. My tongue-tip flicked across its rosy head as I gently licked it, sucking at the same time. A perfect shudder of emotion thrilled throughout her body.

'Oh! *oh!!* Fuck me quick! Your kisses have set me on fire!' Suiting the action to the words, she threw herself backwards across the bed and I rose to the charge in a moment, hurling myself over her, gluing my lips to hers as my stiff sex-weapon forced its way between the moist but yielding lips of her tight little quim.

A quiver of delight enlivened her face as I gained complete insertion. Her lovely legs, encased in drawn-down, delicate, white and silken knickerbocker drawers, fringed with lace, and sheathed to her firm thighs in rose-coloured silk stockings, spread wide and she cried out as she threw her high-heeled Parisian boots amorously around my waist.

'O, your fine, manly buttocks!' she shouted. My own hands were clasped around her lovely rump as it rose in agitated heaves in response to my vigorous thrusts.

It was a wonderful night of sex and I had no occasion to escort the lady into her own bedchamber. Early on, she swooned with joy: my own hands beneath her bottom were bathed by her copious flow of love-juices. Ah! how we profited by our intercourse! I went on my knees between her legs and made her stretch her white satin thighs wide apart. Just before I entered, she took my vigorous fleshy firebrand within a hand still kid-gloved in fawn. The flicks of her fingers made it harder than ever. She squeezed and stroked it for some seconds, then pushed it gradually into herself while I savoured slowly the delightful pleasure. When the arrow had completely disappeared within its quiver, I leant over her and, lifting her two legs over my arms, forced the Countess backwards, upturning her arse, and thence went to work so lustily that soon a second ejaculation became added to the first.

I do not intend to retrace moment by moment all our delicious passages. I will limit myself to a description of the most striking facts of this adorable *liaison* which I wished could last all eternity. My lover knew how to vary our pleasures without ever reaching satiety, she felt a singular pleasure in the arts of enjoyment and emission and she found in me a keen and eager student. Sometimes a woman in her mid-forties can be the ripest fruit of all.

The Countess taught me all the obscene European names for genitalia, sometimes making me say them, but only in the whirl of passion. She used them herself in supreme moments of bliss, pretending, and rightly, too, that such a high spice should never be too much hackneyed, else 'twould lose its flavour. As I write on, I forget myself in these sweet recollections . . .

What cunning caresses! What lecherous postures did she not teach me! What innocent play and prolonging of pleasure on both sides! And what *refinements* of pleasure did we not realize as soon as thought of! I made such progress under such a good mistress that at moments I surpassed her.

We kept changing the way of doing it. For instance,

when she was plugged from behind, one of my favourite positions, she would mischievously unhorse her cavalier, turn around quickly, give a kiss to her rosy conqueror, wet with her spendings, and escape to the other end of the railway chamber, lit only by a dim blue light. She would place herself upon the *cabinet* which concealed the wash-basin, her legs upraised and her pussy quite open, giving it provocative, twitching movements. I was hardly in her again when by a fresh whim, she would draw my prong out, turn her bottom upon me and then, seizing my courser, lead it to plunge within her body up to the very hilt until my burning jet completed that part of our sweet operation.

During that unique night, as the train rattled onwards, her cunt, this splendid vessel of my joy, became my abiding passion, the object of true worship. Helena responded by admiring and delighting at the thickness of my rod, its strength and its length. '*Formidable . . .*' she sighed dreamily as she handled it, dandled it, sucked it, licked it as if it were a sugared lollipop, caressed it in a thousand different ways, rubbed it between her titties, holding it there between them by pressing hard with her gloved hands. When my prick was held captive within this voluptuous cleft, it threw forth all its dew.

My lover returned all my caresses and with added interest. Her pussy became my goddess and idol; I assured her that no woman had ever possessed a more perfect one. I loved to open it, like the petals of a flower, and frig her clitty and fuck her cunt in every conceivable way. As my prick finally began to weary of the sport, it was nevertheless still a supreme delight to apply my lips to her quim and extract, so to speak, the quintessence of voluptuousness by titillations of the tongue which led her to exclaim: '*Moi! Je suis fou!*'

Was she mad? I have only a dim and hazy memory of the last hour before which the train steamed into the Bahnhofstrasse station at Munich; and that is unfortunate in view of the ensuing consequences. I have led, on the whole, a quiet and retiring life, remote from the fields of front-line adventure, and remain unused to the unusual. I have to tell now of one of the strangest things that has ever happened to me.

I suppose that in my usual fashion, I would have escorted Helena, Countess of Salzburg, to her compartment, enabling her to prepare herself for our arrival. After all, we had been drinking vintage champagne and the finest cognac all night. Naturally I would have ordered porters for the lady's luggage at the station but I have no memory of the fact, if fact it be. All I know for certain is that I have a visiting card before me, here, now, as I write, with a Hapsburg crest announcing the Countess Helena of Salzburg at some castle near Munich: the lengthy German name of this castle is beyond the wit of any sane Englishman to pronounce soberly. On the back of this visiting card, a spidery feminine hand was written in hard but delicate pencil an invitation to dinner at an address overleaf for the night following my arrival in Munich.

I imagine that I escorted my fair lady to a carriage and bade her a sweet *au revoir* until the evening. Certainly I went directly to a good hotel opposite Munich's grotesquely baroque yet massively impressive Palace of Justice. Once settled, I was determined not to be late for this enchanting lady and so resolved to ascertain the swiftest method of transportation to her for the magical moment when dusk would fall, for I had been invited to arrive at 8:00 pm. Unfortunately, absolutely nobody in Munich had ever heard either of the castle in question or of Helena, Countess of Salzburg. Finally I tried the

British Consulate, the staff of which proved to be courteous and efficient. According to my description and their information, I had been mildly duped by an international confidence trickster known to the police as Helena Zuttendorf.

The expressions of the helpful consular officials became progressively more fixed as they studied some newspapers. Eventually I was ushered into the presence of the Consul, a Major Bull, officer and gentleman of the old school, who gave me a stiff whisky.

'Do you realise, Lord Horby, that the corpse of Helena Zuttendorf, alias the Countess of Strasbourg – who is not called Helena, incidentally – was found by the railway line at the precise spot reached by the Paris-Munich night express one hour before it gets into Munich?'

I could not quite believe that I was hearing this.

'I have it here.' Major Bull tapped the newspaper before him with a questioning index finger. 'The lady you intended to see tonight at a non-existent castle . . . this confidence trickster and lady impostor died at 7:00 a.m.'

'Oh . . .' I turned pale.

'So far,' Major Bull said it calmly, 'it appears that her death was a suicide. All the evidence points to her flinging herself from the door of the moving train. Probably couldn't take her life of crime and espionage any more, poor girl.' I froze with horror, to furiously deny within myself the possibility that I might have had anything to do with the death of this wondrously enchanting woman. 'But don't worry about it, old chap, you did the right thing and nobody will ever be able to pin this one on you,' Major Bull continued blithely. 'You're in the clear. Every document, including relevant newspapers, concurs with the fact that Helena Zuttendorf died at 7:00 *two days* ago. So the woman you were with was probably pretending to be

Helena Zuttendorf, who was herself pretending to be Helena, Countess of Salzburg.' His fingers flicked to a photograph upon his desk and he held it up before me. 'Recognize her?'

'Yes,' I said. 'That was the woman I was with last night and this morning on the Paris-Munich express.' I dug my railway ticket out of my pocket for impartial verification.

'Can't be, old boy,' the Major responded. 'As I've told you, she died two days ago.'

'And you're asking me to believe that I slept with the impersonator of an impostor?'

'Possibly . . .' Bull murmured thoughtfully. 'Although we old Munich hands do have a curious legend among us. It's that there's a ghostly lover on the Paris-Munich night express, that she gives a man a quite incredible fuck and that she is compounded of all the ghosts of adventurous women, disillusioned and despoiled in love, who have committed suicide on that particular journey.' He coughed. 'More whisky?'

'A ghost could not give me a visiting card.'

'It was a false one, though, wasn't it?' Major Bull said.

As Christopher Marlowe has it:

Thou hast committed
Fornication: but that was in another country
And besides, the wench is dead.

CHAPTER NINE

I had a further motive in going to Munich in early 1901 as my *Memorandum 993* informs me. My cousin in Berlin wanted me to meet and report on two gentlemen going by the names of Guido von List and Lanz von Liebenfels, based in Vienna, and my membership of the OTO of Karl Kellner and Theodor Reuss, as described in the second volume of *The Black Pearl*, made the matter readily easy to secure in terms of channels of communication. There was some sort of international convention of European occultists taking place in Munich, enabling me to encounter the gentlemen in question.

I had arranged to meet them for 'a light supper' at the *Höfbrähaus*, a celebrated beer hall which can seat between two and three thousand people. The atmosphere was jovial as lusty Bavarian wenches smilingly served steins of excellent beer, though I confess that I had my doubts about my companions. This was not on account of the fact that the 'light supper' they had proposed consisted of mountains of sauerkraut topped by bockwurst, bierwurst, bratwurst, weisswurst, knockwurst and frankfurters, which were delicious. I was perplexed both by their demeanour and by their attitudes.

List looked like a grey-bearded magus in his flowing black robes. In 1875, he informed me, he had celebrated the Summer Solstice by burying a number of empty wine bottles on the summit of a hill overlooking Vienna. These wine bottles had been placed in the form of a sign which had not been seen in the land before: it was Tibetan in origin; it was a symbol exclusive to the Aryan peoples; I had learned of it in the Golden Dawn as The Hermetic Cross and the Hammer of Thor; and it was the Swastika.

Liebenfels looked like an elementary schoolteacher in his ill-fitting light grey suit of cheap cloth, the crumpled jacket of which came half-way up his arse, yet he concurred fully with List in venerating the sign of the Swastika. This, they agreed, stood for Light, as I had learned in the Golden Dawn, and also, they argued, for abandoning Christianity, an embracing of neo-paganism, an affirmation of Aryan racial superiority; and a desire to become or create something called 'the Superman.' Both deplored Satanism as 'a childish excrescence' and affirmed that they were 'fighting for the Light, the future and *der fuehrer*, a leader for whom they were waiting – rather like the Orthodox Jews who wait for their Messiah. Obviously the *von* was false: they weren't Barons *von* anywhere, merely lower-middle-class autodidacts fond of high-sounding titles. Still, the beer provoked them into talking.

'I renounced the Catholic faith at the age of fourteen in 1862, and vowed to build a Temple to Wotan,' List told me. 'And I have done so. Furthermore, there is now a flourishing Guido von List Society. Lord Horby, you may be interested, with your credentials and connections, in joining the Inner Order of Armanen Initiates.' I looked enquiring and earnest. 'I have been clairvoyantly inspired,' List declared proudly. 'I have been given true visions of the ancient race of German Supermen called the Armanen and I am the last surviving member.'

'Kindly excuse my ignorance,' I queried innocently, 'but how can this be so when by your own account, you were born in 1848 . . .' and added, 'if you would be so kind as to answer me, Baron von List.' At the mention of this title, List shuffled his robes and preened himself.

'That was in a previous incarnation,' he replied, 'but now I have returned to fulfil the mission I swore to Wotan. WOTAN!' he shouted. 'We must study the runes and you know what the runes tell us?' I shook my head. 'They tell us that the Jews are the sworn enemy of the Aryan race and that this scum can only be extirpated from the face of the Earth when the German Empire includes also Austria. We must study, to this end, the sagas of the Teutonic tribes and the occult folklore of our people.

'I am presently working,' List continued relentlessly, 'upon my masterpiece, *Laws of the Aryan Germans*. (*Editor's Note: This was finally published in Vienna in 1908, the year Adolf Hitler took up residence in that city*.) If the German people are to be saved from their enemy, the hydra-headed international Jewish conspiracy, which enslaves them with capitalism on the one hand and communism on the other, then we must construct a racial state in which inferior peoples become the slaves of the Aryans. This new *Reich* must be divided into units called *Gaue*, each one with its *Gauleiter*.' He drank deeply of his beer as his eyes blazed with fanaticism. 'The Leader will be a self-chosen *Fuehrer* to whom each German willingly submits but bound to his followers by a sacred oath. Their will be special, racial laws exalting the Aryans and degrading their inferiors, including stringent marriage laws to prevent mongrelization. The symbols of the new Reich will be the Swastika: and also the double '*Sig*' rune to be adopted by its warrior élite, whom I would like to see called: *The SS*. WOTAN!

'The Reich,' List declared feverishly, 'will then be ready to annihilate the enemy . . . all military preparations must be made in the most complete detail in order to fight this inevitable war to build a Greater Germany, which will come because it *must* come. Then there will be established a racially pure community that will destroy both Democracy and Jewry. *Mit Armanengruss und Heil!*' he screamed, raising his right arm in a rigid salute.

(*Editor's Note: The U.S. Library of Congress contains a book taken from Adolf Hitler's private library, the flyleaf of which is signed by List: 'To Adolf Hitler, my dear brother in Armanen.'*)

'Very interesting,' I said. An Englishman, after all, always says that he is interested whenever he is bored. 'And do you agree, Baron Lanz von Liebenfels?' I asked the little fellow in the crumpled suit.

'*Jawohl*,' he replied firmly. 'I have the utmost respect for my brother and colleague.' List looked pleased as Liebenfels ordered more beer. 'I am a proud member of his Armanen Order and I hope that he is proud to be a member of my Order of New Templars.' List inclined his head. 'The Aryans are responsible for all creativity in history. This is what makes racial purity a necessity.' He spoke in harsh, cold, clipped tones. 'I advocate forced labour and a starvation diet for any and all who indulge in inter-racial sexual relationships. In addition, citizenship should be denied to non-Aryans for we are opposed in all we do by the Dark Forces of Jews, Slavs and Negroes. The best remedy against race pollution is the castration of male offenders: and give the females a clitorectomy.' He drank more beer, ate another sausage, rubbed his hands with joy and appeared to relish the prospect.

'Why this obsessive need for racial purity?' I queried.

'Because the coming race of Supermen can be *bred*,'

Liebenfels replied firmly as List nodded agreement, 'and bred only from pure Aryan stock. Why, I openly propose the establishment of special breeding colonies.' (*Editor's Note: The Book of German Psalms: the Prayerbook of Arios Racial Mystics and Anti-Semites by Adolf Lanz as 'Lanz von Liebenfels' became part of Hitler's private collection, preserved in the U.S. Library of Congress*). 'You are English, Lord Horby. Ponder upon the significance of future Anglo-Saxon racial supremacy. *Natürlich*, the British Empire and the German Empire can rule the world together.'

'And you have rites, ceremonies and rituals of Magick to attain this goal?' I enquired.

'JA!' they both affirmed. 'Come and join us in the present for our creation of the past and our celebration of the future.'

'Plenty of good-looking German girls, I hope?' I responded cheerfully with a wicked grin, for actually I felt that I could do with a fuck. They glanced uneasily at one another.

'Lord Horby,' List explained patiently, 'we do not admit women to our sacred rites and ceremonies. A woman should be a tender, cuddly thing, soft, sweet and stupid. We call it KKK: *Kinder, Kirche, Küche*: the children, the church and the kitchen – that is where women belong.' The pair of them looked as though they hadn't enjoyed a good swiving in ten years and I had had enough of their bloody nonsense. It was expounded recently, of course, by one Corporal Adolf Hitler who recently endeavoured to take over Bavaria by occupying one Munich beer hall but this ridiculous idiot is now in prison after which he will vanish into a richly deserved obscurity.

'Gentlemen,' I said as I drained my mug and arose,

'thank you. I shall ever afterwards think of you as Biffo and Boffo.' They both looked exceptionally puzzled.

'*Vas ist das?*' List asked.

'It's an Old English saying,' I replied.

'And what does it mean?' Liebenfels queried.

'It might be unkind to tell you.' I smiled. 'Have a good time, as the Jews would say; and *Auf Wiedersehen.*' I walked out into a refreshing blast of cold, crisp air.

I took a carriage to the Schwabing, an area of the city peopled mainly by artists and poets and students and general riff-raff. I had been told that by walking through its twisted cobbled streets, I could enjoy a much more interesting encounter than if I went to a respectable brothel. This turned out to be the case, for in a bar I encountered two delightful girls, Astrid and Heidi, who were more than happy to be bought drinks and dinner and to listen to my proposals.

'Are your intentions honourable?' Astrid asked over her mountain of sausages and sauerkraut, which is all they ever seem to eat in these places, not that it tastes badly. She was an artist's model who aspired to be an artist and who, having run away from her no doubt stiflingly petit-bourgeois home in Hanover, was also waiting at tables and tending bars with her friend Heidi, an angular brunette from Hamburg.

'Extremely *dis*honourable,' I said genially and ordered the best wine which the house had to offer. How I enjoy a really good hock! The upshot of the matter is that the three of us returned to my hotel. These charming German girls needed precious little encouragement, I can tell you! In no time at all, Heidi was sitting naked on the sofa, sipping fiery German brandy as she watched me tumble Astrid.

I threw my arms about this strapping wench and,

drawing her to me, pressed her to my heart, our lips joined so that there was a long and audible kiss.

'My delightful, darling Astrid!' I exclaimed. 'Allow me to embrace you again . . . Give me your beautiful eyes, your lovely teeth, your divine white neck! O! how I could eat them!' Astrid gave herself up to me, returning kiss for kiss and caress for caress as her colour heightened and her eyes sparkled.

'I am all yours . . .' she sighed gently. One may judge the effect that such gentle verbal and physical caresses had upon me. My temperament ignited as if struck by an electric spark, for I could sense the nature of the joys to come. What charms I had exposed! Under Astrid's fine cambric chemise were legs worthy of Venus, encased in the silk stockings I had now removed, secured above the knee by garters of the colour of fire; then two adorable thighs, white, round and firm, surmounted by a fleece of black and lustrous curls.

'How I love it!' I declared. 'How young, beautiful and fresh it is! Open yourself a little, my angel, that I may kiss those adorable lips!' Astrid did as I demanded. Her thighs opened to display her rosy slit to its fullest advantage. I glued my lips upon it and Astrid writhed in ecstasy, shutting her eyes and speaking broken words, then thrusting up her hips in response to my kissing and licking which had transported her so.

'*Auf!*' she shrieked. '*Wieder!!!* . . . *ich schön* . . .' she gasped. 'Go on! . . . *er macht* . . . It's coming! . . . *Ai!* . . . I . . . *ich* . . . *I'm coming!* . . . *ICH KOMMT!!!* . . . Aargh!!' Good God! How she writhed and rocked and rolled upon the bed!

Now Astrid turned over and proudly presented two voluptuous globes of dazzling white for my delectation. By now, my instrument was enormous and I had no hesitation in my introduction of its tip between the two crimson lips my eyes had already perceived. Astrid did not flinch and opened as much as possible the part which she presented, which seemed without the aid of her willing hands to open itself and at length absorb my long and mean machine tool, which penetrated so well that it disappeared entirely.

'Ah!' Astrid shrieked as my happy belly became glued to her luscious bottom. There was then a conjunction of combined movements followed by broken words. 'I feel you . . . push it all well into me . . . softly . . . let me come first AH! . . . I feel it . . . I'm coming! . . . Quicker! I come . . . stop . . . there you are! I die . . . I . . . I . . . Ahhhh!' With my eyes half-closed and my hands holding her hips, I felt inexpressibly happy.

'Hold . . .' I sighed. 'My angel, my all, ah! How fine it is! Push well! Do come again . . . there; it's coming, is it not!? Go on . . . I feel you're coming . . . push well, my darling!' We both stopped for a moment. Astrid appeared momentarily exhausted but she did not change her position, lightly turning her head at length to give me a lover's kiss.

'Now both together!' she shouted out, adding: 'You let me know when you are ready.' Thence she thrust upwards quite wickedly.

'AH! . . .' I cried out in return. 'I feel it coming . . . you are ready, my love? Yes . . . yes . . . there I am . . . push, again . . . go on . . . I spend . . . I am yours. I . . . I . . . Ah! What a pleasure . . . I . . . sp- . . . *spend!*'

A long silence followed. Eventually I recovered my senses to find myself lying upon the ample bosom of Astrid. Turning my head, I saw that Heidi had just come over the slim forefinger she had employed to pleasure her cunt.

Now Heidi joined me upon the bed as Astrid took her seat and helped herself to copious quantities of brandy.

As Astrid sipped, there was Heidi naked before my delighted eyes. No one could dream of a finer sight! Her nipples, firm and high, stuck out boldly in bright rose-pink; the line of her back and her backside were both admirable. At the base of her white and polished belly, her luxuriant dark fleece could be plainly seen. Suddenly she knelt before me and almost reverently imprinted two or three ardent kisses on the object of her desires. My hands parted her willing thighs, yielding another delicious view of her dark, bushy mount, with just a discernible vermilion slit beneath the slim belly.

My ramrod, refreshingly renewed, was thrusting between those slender thighs quicker than it takes to say so and, throwing my body over hers, I proceeded to kiss her face and neck in the most impassioned manner, being too well within her body to lick her heaving bosom, though I caressed and moulded her right breast with my left hand. The girl seemed instinctively to open her thighs wider. She gasped as I withdrew abruptly, then sighed as I put forth the swelling head of my tremendous cock, opening her quim lips until the throbbing head had re-entered about an inch.

Her hands pressed my buttocks downwards – and both of us quivered with joy and spent at this moment. We lay motionless for a few moments as Astrid stroked herself noisily; but there was to be no peace for the wicked.

'Horby! Milord!' Heidi gave my bottom two slaps with her hand. 'Again, my love . . .' she whispered. 'You did make me feel nice as you spurted into me just then. I shan't be so tight now. Go on – go on – oh!' My abruptly renewed ramrod plunged within her cunny to its full depth. She shrieked out her joy as if in agony and I withdrew to give it another hard push, and thrust again and again, clasping her fainting body as she uttered a piercing scream and lost consciousness.

This sound and the sight of my still throbbing instrument aroused Astrid to action for, in response, she heaved up her rump and writhed in a perfect state of erotic frenzy, inviting me to fuck her on the sofa, to fuck her well, to shove it all – balls and all – into her cunt as she used every international bawdy expression of which she was plentifully capable. She was a demon at the game now and to judge by her languid sighs and alternating screams of rapacious delight at my thrusting, she was coming continuously.

She appeared to gain in strength as I weakened. Without warning, her flanks thrust me away, then she rushed me to the bed, pinned me on my back and in rampant triumph and beside her lascivious girl-friend, straddled and bestrode my still stiff penis. I roared like a lion as I came.

Ah, yes! They can keep the men of Munich! I'll fuck their women any day!

CHAPTER TEN

It was a very good idea of mine to answer the sudden telegram received from Douglas in Cairo and to join him on a river cruise along the Nile. Sometimes a man really does need to get away from it all: This was the case with both of us, and it was a pleasure to enjoy his company on a river yacht he had chartered. He had also hired two beautiful whores, Nina of England and Leila of Turkey, for our pleasure. Abdul, the Turkish chef, proved to be excellent, fulfilling his proud boast that the cuisine of his country is equal to that of the French and has influenced the cooking of the entire Eastern Mediterranean.

'*Réculez pour mieux sauter*, my dear fellow,' Douglas said on our first evening aboard. 'Really, the French have it right: step back so as to jump forward better.'

'Quite agree,' I murmured as I watched the silvery crescent moon and its exquisite reflection upon the waters. 'I'm finding it rather hard,' I continued, puffing on an excellent Hoyo de Monterey cigar, 'to make sense of Satanism.'

'That's because there is no sense there, only non-sense,' Douglas replied. We drank our Armagnac thoughtfully. 'If there *is* any Satanism out there, it's done either by perverted Christians or else by some bunch of wealthy perverts who delight in ritual and want salt with their sex and pepper with their perversions.

The genuine Rosicrucians know that sex is the holiest act in the Universe if done with love under will but we have no time at all for occult fools. Look!' he suddenly exclaimed. 'Crocodiles.'

I looked to see that these reptiles infested this particular section of the river.

'The Ancient Egyptians venerated this prehistoric creature,' Douglas continued. 'They seemed to realize that the crocodile had been around during the age of the dinosaurs and so personified its spirit as Sebek, crocodile God and God of Time.' Douglas gazed fondly upon these creatures, some of which lay like rocks in the waters of the Nile, looking as though they had lain still for one hundred million years and were ready to do so for a further aeon of time. Others lazed upon the river bank, their jaws open as little birds popped inside to peck at their teeth and eat all insects and decay within their gaping cruel mouths.

'When they wish to move, they can be so swift,' Douglas resumed his discourse and grinned at me wickedly. 'But soon enough now, we'll be coming into hippo country. These mammals hate the crocs and that's why they divide the river between them and the reptiles. A hippo has little to fear from a crocodile, whose teeth will make little impact on a hippo's thick skin. As for the deadly whack of a crocodile's tail, this will make little impact upon a mammal that weighs well over two tons. The crocodile cannot harm a full-grown hippo in the water and once on land the hippo simply stomps the croc to death with its hooves. However, the crocodiles do occasionally try and poach a baby hippo and that is why the hippos hate them. There's not a croc that won't turn tail when faced with an angry adult hippo.

'I'd love to be a hippo,' Douglas sighed wearily, but added: 'Sometimes. Just think on it, Horby, for if you were a hippo, you wouldn't need to think at all. What creature attacks a hippo? Hippos can sprint at up to thirty miles per hour and they can bite a man in half – and a crocodile too, for that matter. Even men leave 'em alone. Hippo meat is totally disgusting to eat. And would you want to give your mistress a purse or bag made of hippo skin? They're quite useless for the purposes of humanity. All they do is laze around in muddy water. They eat vegetables and weeds and occasionally surface to capsize a boat unintentionally. What a life!' The boat cruised past a mother hippo coming to the surface with a smiling baby hippo upon her back.

'Nature . . .!' Douglas breathed enthusiastically; and I must record that I am appreciative of the matters he showed me during our cruise. I saw a deer come to drink by the river. Instantly, what looked like a rock moved with the speed of a crocodile and sank its teeth into the deer's belly. A hippo that had been drinking some hundred yards away instantly charged in a gesture of mammalian solidarity and stomped upon the crocodile, driving away one sorely battered reptile. The deer sagged to the ground, bleeding badly from its belly. The hippo tried to cure the wound with huge, sympathetic licks but the damage was done and the deer died. As the sun set, I saw a dead deer and by it, a hippo hanging its head in mourning and grief.

'The rhino is a much maligned creature,' Douglas said to me on another occasion in the course of our cruise. 'It simply eats vegetation and, apart from man and wild dogs, no other creature dares to trespass on its territory. They can be very bad-tempered beasts and I certainly wouldn't want a two-ton rhino coming at me at twenty miles an hour. But they're extremely stupid and forgetful. Sometimes they charge in a rage, then they stop that charge and trot away because they can't remember what it was that they were becoming so angry about. Sounds rather like some human beings, doesn't it?'

'Wild dogs?' I queried.

'Oh, yes,' said Douglas, giving orders for the boat to anchor. 'Look at that.' I looked and saw a female rhino protecting her baby from the attack of ten wild dogs. 'Dogs are so nice and cuddly when domesticated,' said Douglas, 'but in the wild, they're truly vicious.' I saw them jumping nimbly between the slashing horn and pounding hooves of the mother rhino as they chewed bits out of the baby. Mother rhino managed to spear one dog with her horn and to scrunch two more with her hooves but meanwhile her baby bled to death from the wounds inflicted. The mother appeared to go mad and charged at the dogs, who used their superior agility to avoid her clumsy lunges. She settled down to watch over the corpse of her child and the dogs settled down around fifty yards away, knowing that she could not transport it. Behind them, a pack of hyenas had gathered, one could discern a few jackals and since it was merely a matter of time before the meal, vultures already wheeled in the sky.

'As Oscar Wilde said,' Douglas remarked, 'the only tyranny that ever lasts is that of the weak over the strong.' On a succeeding evening, we cruised into lion country. 'Extraordinary, isn't it?' my host commented, 'if you're a lion, all you have to do is marry for an easy life. A lion usually has three lionesses in his pride. They go out and do the hunting whilst he lazes about all day and, I suppose, cuffs the cubs occasionally. His wives drag the kill back to his kingdom and the lion gets the first bite of the best. What a lazy brute the lion is! He normally sleeps for eighteen hours a day. That's probably why lions don't mind life in a circus: they perform and they get fed and after that they can go back to sleep. Have you ever heard of a lioness tamer?' I shook my head because the idea was too ridiculous. 'So how come the lionesses put up with this?' Douglas demanded. 'Simple. In the mating season, the lion can do it twenty-six times in twenty-four hours. There's a moral in there somewhere, Horby, wouldn't you say?'

I agreed with him and still do; and I cannot forget the sight of a lion and a lioness crossing a shallow stream together. Suddenly the lioness looked at the lion and with one swish of her massive paw, sprayed him with water. He looked at her as if to say: 'You lovely, silly bitch,' and they walked on contentedly together. I am sure that the higher mammals have a sense of humour.

When I wasn't chatting to Douglas or fucking Leila or Nina, or eating and drinking, I sat on deck with a drink, a pipe of hashish and a good book. 'A good book is the precious life-blood of a master spirit,' said Lord Macauley. They can be even better than friends: you can put them down when you are bored and they will not take offence. I also perused my correspondence and arched an eyebrow as I read the following letter from Emily, presently in Tunbridge Wells. After opening with greetings and expressed affection, it read:

The last time that we met, my darling, I seem to recall that you enquired after the progress of the Society for the Promulgation of Petticoat Government. Allow me to assure you, my dear boy, that it is flourishing.

Do you recall my tale of young Jeremy, scion of one of the noblest families in the land, who was petticoated in a fashionable ladies' department store in Bournemouth on account of his sexual misbehaviour? Young Lady Charlotte had complained of his unwelcome importunings, impolite behaviour and lustful glances: and they were both pupils at Mrs Joan Smythe's Academy. Well, after this purchase of his female attire, Jeremy was put back into a red tartan kilt, with silken knickers and a petticoat beneath and, carrying the shopping bags, had to follow Joan Smythe and I along the sea-front. She had strictly instructed him to walk ten paces behind us with his head submissively lowered and his eyes gazing in homage upon our hips. Both Joan and I found it to be such a spiteful joy to tease him by switching our bottoms in ladylike triumph. Jeremy blushed positively crimson as he endeavoured to conceal his erection and also his shamefully petticoated condition from the ladies who passed by. The wind blowing off the sea made his kilt flutter prettily, causing him to catch its hem continuously, though at one moment it blew upwards and his frilly white petticoat was exposed to the enquiring eyes of two dear old friends of ours whom you know, Lady Alison Utterley and Lady Jane Fortescue. Joan and I made Jeremy curtsey to them on the sea-front as the waves splashed in.

Jane and Alison, with whom I believe you are intimately acquainted, are of course notable ex-pupils of Mrs Smythe's Academy in Tunbridge Wells and I gladly accepted the invitation to visit that institution. This took place a few days later. It's about five miles from the town itself and set in rolling meadows flanked by thick woods. It is inaccessible unless one has a horse and carriage. To all outward appearances, it is a rather grim neo-Gothic building, surmounted by mysterious domes and turrets. One also notices beautiful flower-gardens, an immaculate croquet lawn, a fine court for lawn tennis and the cheerful faces of most of the pupils in their smart navy blue uniforms.

I was greeted at the front door by Jeremy and instantly

noticed the contrast in his uniform. The boys wear white shirts with ties, knee-length navy blue shorts, white socks to just below the knee and shiny black shoes with silver buckles. The girls wear the same, except that the heels of their shoes are elevated by an inch and, in place of trousers, they wear knee-length, knife-pleated skirts beneath which the lace of a white petticoat was peeping. Jeremy was wearing the girls' uniform.

He curtsied to me most politely, then obeyed my request to conduct me to the Headmistress. Joan Smythe was enjoying dry sherry with Alison and Jane, all of whom welcomed me as if I were one of their own, which I suppose I am. After some more sherry, I was taken on a tour of the school, founded, I was informed, 'to cure the recalcitrant habits of incorrigible boys and girls.' The conditions of the pupils were certainly comfortable and I sampled their luncheon and found it delicious; moreover, what I saw of the teaching was thorough, caring and altogether excellent, done well by smartly-dressed, well-educated women. However, discipline was very strict.

Any girl who misbehaved would be stood in the corner or spanked privately, strapped in front of the class or birched in front of the whole school. Boys received the cane instead of the strap; and for them there was a worse punishment. If there was any insult to a girl, the boy would be deprived of his trousers, put into girls' uniform and assigned to fag for the Girls' Prefects Common Room, which was given permission to spank him should he prove to be sullen or unwilling at his servile duties.

'Jeremy, of course,' Mrs Smythe beamed smugly, 'is rather a special case. He is being punished for his unwelcome sexual advances to Charlotte, our Head Prefect, and so is under petticoat discipline and must fag for her, gratifying her loftiest whim in the minutest

particular. This will fit him for marriage, which tonight he will be proposing to her before our senior gels and,' she smiled graciously, 'our most distinguished graduates and visitors to the Academy.'

After devouring an exquisitely tender goose with bottles of vintage claret, we filed in with our liqueurs – yellow chartreuse, as I recall – to a hall with a platform and a grand piano. This piano stood to the right and in the centre there was a throne with two grand oaken chairs at either side of it. The walls had been painted in shocking pink: so now *I know what goes on in these peculiar turrets!*

Jeremy, still dressed as a schoolgirl, was standing obediently in the corner, face to the wall, his hands holding up his skirt and petticoat to reveal a crimson bottom that glowed from a previous spanking; girls' frilly bloomers encumbered his ankles.

Now Mrs Joan Smythe took her throne at the centre of the stage, placing her voluptuous rear upon the cushion as though it were the face of a grateful male lover. She was followed by the Junoesque Jane and the willowy Alison: together they plucked a golden crown out of a potted thicket of thorns and placed behind the throne. Alison laid the pot of thorns at the feet of Joan as Jane placed the crown of gold upon her head. The Headmistress responded by plucking two silver coronets from beneath the purple velvet drapes which adorned the sides of her throne. Each lady knelt before her and was graced by a coronet.

The ladies took their seats. A clock chimed 8:00. Eight schoolmistresses entered. They all wore tight, white, fussy blouses and severe black, ankle-length skirts, the cloth of which appeared to have fallen in love with their hips. A gong resounded. Eight young female Prefects entered, immaculately dressed in school uniform. They were bare-headed whereas the schoolmistresses were wearing elegant straw boaters adorned with flowers. Your friend Sir Richard once said to me: 'Any man who likes women's hats is either a fashion designer or a pervert. Hats are things women wear to impress other women.' Possibly so; but being a woman, I love the sight of other women's hats.

We all stood as Jane and Alison rang bells and Joan stepped forward to speak to us. As always, her voice was high, clear and hard, with every vowel and consonant strictly enunciated.

'A very happy event has transpired,' she declared. 'There was a time when this boy here,' she gestured at the penitent in the corner, 'was ever so badly behaved. Now that he has been brought under petticoat rule,' she preened herself proudly, 'he will never misbehave himself again. For the yoke of marriage is about to be put upon him and after that,' she laughed lightly, 'he will always be governed by his wife's petticoat.'

A gong was struck by someone unseen. A beautiful young lady entered to mount the platform, whom I correctly surmised to be Lady Charlotte. She wore a vivid dress of shining black silk which accentuated her perfectly proportioned figure. Upon her feet were high-heeled, laced boots of shining leather. Her face was quaint, piquant and sexy rather than conventionally beautiful but one could not help noticing her shining hazel eyes and her slightly spiteful mouth, nor the taunting way in which she switched her taut bottom.

Oh! what a darling Jeremy was! He had to hoist his knickers at Charlotte's command, approach her and curtsey as Joan Smythe sat down at the grand piano and began to play airs and graces from the Piano Concerto

No. 2 in G Minor *by Saint-Saens. Then he had to kneel on the floor before Charlotte, kiss her shining black leather boots, lick them and promise evermore to be faithful and obedient to her if only she would condescend to marry him.*

Charlotte responded by flicking out her fan as he lay at her feet and Alison and Jane swept forward to bring her red and white petticoats. Charlotte commanded Jeremy to arise and step into them, which he did. Charlotte smoothed his skirt down and kissed him upon the lips. Joan Smythe ceased her skilful playing of the piano.

'Jeremy's going to be such *a good boy now that he's marrying and put into skirts.' She chuckled throatily. 'Aren't you, Jeremy?'*

'Yes, Madam.' He curtsied to her.

'Oh, what *a pretty curtsey, Jeremy!' Joan Smythe exclaimed. 'Your affianced will be* so *pleased with you.'*

'Curtsey,' Charlotte commanded and as he obeyed, his prick fairly threatening to tear through the ladies' attire that so delicately imprisoned it, she clapped her hands for joy in witnessing his subjugation. 'Now remember, my husband-to-be, you will always walk respectfully behind me.' With that, Charlotte swished and swisked her skirts, turned upon her heel and left the stage arrogantly, with Jeremy following humbly behind her.

'Oh! *What a beautiful petticoating!' Jane exclaimed.*

'Quite exquisite,' said Alison; and the delicate hands of all schoolmistresses, schoolgirls and visitors present came together in applause. What a hoot! Must dash. More next time. Loads of love,

Emily.

After reading Emily's letter, I really needed a stroll on deck and as our boat glided past the river banks and my ears were enlivened by the night-time sounds of the jungle all around us, I was pleased to see the silhouette of Douglas, smoking a Burmese cheroot.

'Oh, glad to see you, Horby,' he said. 'Sometimes a man can do with a spot of good company. Just been thinking about women.'

'So have I,' I said.

'Know old puce-faced Belloc?' Douglas queried sharply and I nodded acknowledgement. 'Women are like hippos in one way and in one way only.' He threw back his brandy in one gulp. 'Allow me to alter one word of Belloc, my dear fellow, and this verse of his will reveal the secret of my success with women:

I shoot the hippopotamus
With bullets made of platinum,
'Cos if I use leaden ones
Her hide is sure to flatten 'em.

'Ha! ha!' he laughed cruelly and raucously. 'Now let's go and have another brandy below decks. The old serpent of the Nile can be quite chilly at night.'

CHAPTER ELEVEN

On the first night that I entered Leila's cabin as we cruised along the Nile, I was delighted by the sight that greeted my eyes. She stood there, the olive skin of her beautiful thighs set off to perfection by the black silk stockings high along them, with flouncy rosette garters holding them up on her lovely long legs. Otherwise, she was magnificently naked; and the sheen of her bare flesh, the deep chiseled hollow of her supple back seemed all the more alluring and libidinously enticing against the contrast with her nudity which those silken stockings made.

And now that she was naked, I could feast my eyes unimpeded upon her charms and compare her with Nina, my second choice, who had been preferred by Douglas, though we had both fucked the pair of them. Nina's legs were a trifle too short for her but this very defect added to the fascination of her figure. Her plump and rounded thighs tapered to the neatest of calves and ankles and tiny patrician feet. Her waist was dainty but not too small and she had fine rounded arms with small well-shaped hands. Nina's magnificent curves of hips and haunches, the graciously swelling belly with its deep navel and the full, fat, fleshy and prominent mound of love together with her rather full, firm and outstanding breasts had made her wholly mouthwatering.

Yet Leila was visibly more mature and slightly taller,

which added further to her seductiveness. She turned around to display the jouncy, full ovals of her naked bottom which fairly invited pinches and slaps; and the beautifully pronounced curve of her back and the dimple at her chinkbone which marked that beginning of the sinuous shadowy groove separating her superb buttocks set my cock to aching all over again. I seized her, tumbled her upon the bed and fucked her swiftly.

I wanted the second fuck to be done in a more leisurely and thorough way. When a man initially takes a beautiful and spirited girl, the excitement of the procedure very often defeats him and he cannot withhold himself to make the conquest as complete as he would like. This had been the case with me, for the ecstatic feeling of my rigid prick inside Leila's choice warm cunt had overcome even my own excellent staying powers, and I had spurted a veritable come-flood into the juicy flesh-depths of this gorgeous, exotic young female. But now that the first furious libation to Venus had been poured out, I knew that I would be able easily to prolong my pleasure with this brown-haired beauty.

Leila's coiffure added an ambiguity: along the top of her high forehead was a little fringe of frilly curls which suggested a saucy, rather coy girlishness, an almost juvenile ingenuousness. Yet at the back of her stately head, the mass of her glossy brown hair was fixed into an exaggeratedly large oval-shaped bun, which resembled a kind of crown. That portion of her coiffure indicated her innate and insolent wish to dominate and to 'lord it over' even her betters. And that was why I reached up with both hands and began to unknot that arrogant crown.

Once again I had hit home directly. Leila started and uttered a husky sobbing after perceiving my action in the mirror before her, then tried to turn her head. I gave her hair a little yank.

'Hold still unless you want to feel pain,' I commanded. This momentarily quelled her and when she saw me loosen her hair and rumple it out with my fingers until it fell in a rich dark cascade to her shoulderblades, she caught her breath again and closed her eyes and bowed her head in resignation. Decidedly I had attacked her vulnerability. Now there was a wonderful femininity and grace to her which she had not had before. Now she was much more softly alluring.

I lay there for a long moment behind her with my cock in full erection as if pondering her fate. Actually, I had long since decided on it but this pause was purposely chosen to tantalize her, to heighten her suspense, to weaken her nervous whore's resistance to the point where she would be frantically willing to grant me what I yearned for from her lusciously olive-tinted, vibrant flesh.

I now passed my hands round and in front of her, grasping her beautiful bubbies and squeezing them lingeringly as I moved up close behind her so that the tip of my aching cock just brushed the base of her behind and suggestively prodded the warm, slightly humid furrow that divided that magnificent posterior. Once again, Leila caught her breath and stiffened, uttering a long, heartrending sigh. She also closed her eyes so that she would not have to be shamed by watching my sinewy strong fingers close like tentacles over her swelling, glorious breasts. Whores have their pride.

'Are you feeling a little more humble now, my dear?' I demanded sarcastically. I felt her bottom twitch and contract against my gently, slyly prodding cocktip and I stared over her right shoulder to follow her reactions in the huge mirror placed before her. A wave of scarlet suffused her lovely, haughty face and her chin was trembling as she bit her own full lips, unable to answer. Her breasts rose and fell with violent turbulence now. She drew a long, shuddering breath, lifted her head and bowed it and then, while my cockhead lightly nuzzled at the shadowy groove between her luscious bare bottom cheeks, falteringly responded with a sigh.

Turning Leila around, I gripped the backs of her stockinged thighs and, lowering my head, put my tongue to the warm twitching and palpitating olive skin of her left thigh, just above the rosette garter. How warm and tasty it was to savour! Not only was there the subtle perfume of musk with which she had evidently sprayed herself; there was also the stronger and more exciting compound of perspiration and the tang of her feminine scent from her delicious Venus-vent.

In an involuntary reflex, Leila dashed her bottom backwards. But my fingers rose up to grip the base of those olive-sheened nether ovals and I forced her back to me as my tongue rasped upwards again until it attained the sensitive, soft twitching flesh of the groin as I made my way towards the sweet fig of her voluptuous cunt.

My instrument stood up proudly for the fray, rearing its haughty head and boasting of its uncommon length and thickness; Leila's thighs opened wider. She slid her head down slightly, hiding her face on my shoulder and gave herself up to me, fully offering herself to me.

'I desire . . .' she moaned, 'and yet I fear the entrance of such a handsome guest.' She soon enough felt the head of my penis between the lips of her grotto; and then I thrust inwards, and deeply. My lips pressed softly against hers as my prick pressed to her very vitals. 'I am beside myself . . .' Leila sighed. 'I feel that I am going mad.' The supreme moment arrived for both of us and she writhed about, uttering inarticulate sounds.

I withdrew my prick from Leila's quim with a feeling of quiet satisfaction – yet also with an awareness that I had unfinished business with her that required attention sooner rather than later. She had rolled over onto her stomach as soon as I had pulled out and the sight of her delightfully rounded buttocks above her stockinged thighs caused a fresh surge of lust to course through my groin. My cock began to swell once more. But after two climaxes in swift succession, I knew that this time its staying power would be equal to the task that lay before it.

I reached out and stroked Leila's back from the nape of her neck to her wonderful arse, where I allowed my hand to linger, cupping and squeezing the lower curve of one delectable flesh-globe. At the same time, I insinuated a finger into her cunt – she moaned softly – and gathered a quantity of love-juice from Leila's well-rogered joxy-depths onto the digit concerned. Taking it out, I transferred my ministrations to her bumhole, thrusting my slippery finger past the tight flesh-ring of its entrance and on into its secret regions.

'Ah! No!' Leila gasped, seeking to clench her buttocks tight against this unexpected intruder. 'What are you doing?' She tried to turn onto her side to escape my grasp. I restrained her with my other hand, pinning her fast to the bed.

'I am endeavouring, madam, to show some small measure of gentlemanly courtesy and consideration by lubricating your back passage with a *soupçon* of spend from your placket before paying your delightful backside the compliment of a visit from Lord John Thomas,' I replied.

At this, Leila renewed her struggles, twisting desperately to free herself from my grip. But to no avail; if anything, her movements – the jiggling of her firm breasts, the frantic motions of her stockinged thighs – heightened my state of arousal. And they definitely made my determination to penetrate her bumhole all the stronger.

'Lord Horby, please desist, oh, please, I beg of you!' Leila pleaded as I raised myself to straddle her lithe form. I grasped both her wrists in one of my hands and held them firmly. Sitting back on my heels, I surveyed the wondrous prospect before me: Leila's beautiful if apprehensive face in profile against the pillow, her tousled, lustrous hair, the smooth olive skin of her back and buttocks and her thighs (squeezed so tightly together now in futile resistance to the coming assault) emerging from the enticing sheer black silk of her stockings. Desisting was the last thing I intended.

'I don't imagine for one moment that Douglas intended any restriction or limitation to be put upon the use of your and Nina's sundry orifices when he signed you up for this cruise,' I said. 'That being so – and, of course, your arse being of such overwhelming attractiveness – I fully intend to ensure that he gets his money's worth. By proxy, as it were. And, by the by, a word to the wise and all that, I wouldn't advise any unseemly screams of protest from here on in, so to speak. Douglas won't appreciate having his own session with Nina interrupted. And – who knows? if he *was* to look in on us he might decide to avail himself of your bottom-hole facility too. Then you'd be getting two for the price of one. Not quite the kind of bargain you might have in mind, eh?'

Leila strained against my grip on her wrists. 'Oh, no, no, *no*. I can't . . . You mustn't . . .'

'Oh, mustn't I? I shouldn't have to remind you who's in charge here but it seems as though there's a lesson *you* must learn, my girl,' I responded. With my free hand, I picked up the silken cord of Leila's negligée from the coverlet and briefly released her wrists before seizing them again and binding them together – securely but not tightly enough to cause discomfort or to restrict the flow of blood – behind her back. 'Now, you might as well attempt to put into practice the old adage about relaxing and enjoying it because nothing you can do or say will dissuade me from my course.'

That said, I proceeded to run my hands down Leila's smooth sides, sliding them around and under to knead her breasts and tweak her nipples before moving them down to her thighs, relishing the sensuous feel of the contrast between silken stocking-top and warm thigh-flesh. I thrust one hand between her thighs, forcing them apart and pressing my palm against her moist cunt-lips before moving it to her bumhole with its fresh load of lubricant. Then I took an arse-cheek in each hand and gently but firmly prised them apart sufficiently to expose Leila's shy sphincter to my gaze – and to the narrow eye of my bulging purple cockhead, surmounting by now a rigid, thick length of beef bayonet that was raring, – nay, raging – to go.

Leila still sought to escape the by now inescapable by pressing her pelvis hard down into the coverlet in a futile attempt to put as much distance as possible between her bumhole and my rampant cock. Briefly releasing her luscious bottom-globes, I reached behind me and grabbed a small cushion of Turkish (how appropriate!) design, one of several scattered about upon the bedspread. Raising Leila's hips quickly by pressing strongly upward against he cuntal mound with one hand, I stuffed the cushion between the bed and her pubic region so that, even when I had released my hold upon her Venus mount, her derrière remained raised slightly – but sufficiently – from the bed's surface.

Leila made one last desperate effort to plead with me. 'Lord Horby, oh milord, I beg you to ravish my cunt or my mouth instead of my bumhole. Your weapon is so monstrously huge that . . . aaaaaah, oh yes, yes . . .'

Seized by a sudden urge to mischief, I had indeed at this point gone along with Leila's suggestion of an alternative approach to the extent of swiftly plunging my engorged flesh-shaft to its hilt between her slick pussy lips. She sighed with relief – until she felt me withdraw completely from her cunt after the one stroke and once more grasp a bum-cheek in each hand. As I manoeuvred my hips to guide my swollen glistening pricktip into position against her private entrance, she whispered in final submission, 'Oh, cruel, cruel . . .'

'Sorry for the momentary false sense of security there. Couldn't resist the opportunity for a bit of trickery-pokery, what? Anyway, joke over, back to business. Here comes Old One-Eye!' So saying, I urged the taut glans of my ramrod into the snug entrance to Leila's sweet bottom-hole, resting it there a moment to relish the supreme sensation of its tight grip. Leila gasped and groaned but made no further movement of attempted avoidance. I pressed on in, savouring to the full the delicious constrictive feeling as the whole length of my prick became engulfed in the secret reaches of this beautiful, exotic whore's arse.

I am sure that if I had not already experienced two orgasms within the past hour I would have spent within seconds of penetrating Leila's bum, such was its grip. As it was, though, the stamina bestowed by those earlier climaxes enabled me to thrust on and on into her wonderful arse, increasing the force of my plunges steadily as I sensed her relaxing when the sensation of the fleshy intruder up her jacksie grew less unfamiliar. Keeping a strong hold on one firm, rounded arse-globe, I slipped my other hand around to Leila's cuntal mound, running my fingers through her silky pubic hair and locating the bud of her clitoris which I proceeded to frig gently as I continued thrusting into her bum-depths. This combination of sensations caused her to buck and shudder in an ecstasy of sensual delight – and to my own great satisfaction it also induced spasms in the flesh-ring of her anus which squeezed and clenched around my cock in exquisite fashion. As a result I soon felt the spunky floodtide gathering in my balls, building its pressure up to the point where no further holding back was possible. I surged down the length of my pounding prick to explode in a volcanic release of pulsating sensation in Leila's innermost secret flesh-depths – just at the moment that she herself cried out in the unmistakable tones of female orgasm.

'So, you see,' I said as Leila's no longer so shy sphincter relinquished its grip on my finally shrinking member, 'this butt-fucking business isn't necessarily such a pain in the arse. I hope you won't give the next punter who fancies a bit of your bum such a tough time. Well, I'm for a celebratory snifter – care to join me? Bottoms up!'

After a drink and some kisses and caresses, I went up on deck and gazed at the Nile for a while, graced as it was by a crescent moon. After a time, my reverie was interrupted by the clack of balls and, turning around, I discerned that Douglas was playing this new-fangled game of snooker on a billiard table which he had had the forethought to install.

'Care for a game?' he asked. I nodded and entered the cabin. 'Had a good fuck?' he enquired. We looked one another in the eyes and smiled, then Douglas potted some coloured ball. 'Glass of port?' He indicated a decanter of old tawny on a sideboard and I took my fill from one of the crystal glasses. 'Can't travel anywhere without port,' Douglas murmured as he potted another ball. 'Obvious, isn't it, why England has Portugal as its oldest ally. Ready to play?'

'Let's just talk for a while,' I said.

'All right.' He placed his cue on the rack and took another glass of port. 'Enjoying the cruise?'

'Immensely, thank you. Rather reminded me of one of my heroes, Sir Richard Burton. Didn't he discover the source of the Nile with Speke?'

'Yes,' Douglas replied, 'and he discovered many other things in addition, most notably in matters of literature.'

'Of course,' I concurred, 'there's his wonderful translation of *The Arabian Nights*, also known as *The One Thousand Nights and a Night of Sheherezade*. I tell you, I could curse that wretched widow of his for burning his private papers. What a forlorn, Presbyterian prude! Why the fuck did he marry her?'

'Fortunately she didn't burn all his works,' Douglas responded. 'There's still *The Perfumed Garden*, translated from the Arabic; and *The Kama Sutra*, which he translated from the Sanskrit. Got 'em, Horby?'

'Of course,' I replied truthfully.

'Read 'em?'

'I've glanced through them,' I answered, 'and discerned no matter worthy of close study. *The Perfumed Garden* seemed to tell me that I should eat bread and raw eggs to keep my erection thick, long and strong, also that I should try not to come too quickly; the latter I did know before. *The Kama Sutra* appeared to give me unenjoyable and anatomically uncomfortable sexual positions.'

'Then you have missed the truth and the beauty.'

'Evidently,' I said. 'Kindly explain it to me.'

'*The Perfumed Garden*,' he replied, 'refers to the vagina

and its varying emissions during a 28-day cycle of the moon. It is a manual of instruction concerning how to pleasure it, arguing also that in this way, you will increase your own pleasure. *The Kama Sutra* declares roughly the same proposition but proposes the use of advanced yoga postures so as to increase sensory enjoyment. There is a cultural difference insofar as the author of *The Perfumed Garden* discerned women as being lazy but greedy to be pleasured, the author of the Hindu *Kama Sutra* saw women as being only too willing and eager to join in. Such is the sexual difference between the male Muslim and Hindu minds, my dear sir.'

'And the Rosicrucians?' I queried. 'Where do they fit in here?'

'Depends to which Rosicrucians you refer,' he replied coolly. 'The English Masonic Societas Rosicruciana is honest and harmless and makes no false pretences. If its members happen as a rule to be pompous busy-bodies, enlarging the borders of their phylacteries and scrupulous about cleansing the outside of the cup and the platter, that is their affair. But those orders run by persons *claiming* to represent the True Ancient Fraternity are common swindles. The claims of "Papus" (Dr Encausse), Stanislas de Guaita, the late, and Sâr Pelâdan merit respect as serious, but lack full knowledge and authority. I have respect too for Mathers but it remains to be seen where it will all lead and the same is true of Crowley. The "Ordo Rosae Crucis", presently chartering Temples in America, is a mass of ignorance and falsehood, though this may be a deliberate device for masking itself. I can't say that we're worried, Horby. Fancy a game of billiards?'

I joined him in the billiard room and over our games, he informed me that Rosemary had gone to visit a relative in Montreal but would be writing to the pair of us and she hoped that her letters would arrive at the British Consulate on our return to Cairo. Douglas was a good player but I'm quite skilful with a cue and we were three games all when we agreed to break for more port.

'You know,' he said as he poured more velvety port for both of us, 'I'd like to tell you a story with a moral about a billiard table and a man.' I nodded acquiescence. 'This man, an acquaintance of mine, went to London's leading department store to purchase a billiard table. He was an explorer and he asked them to have it ready for him by the time he came back from the Himalayas. They did. "Your billiard table, sir."

' "What's this?" he protested. "A billiard table with six legs? Everyone knows that a billiard table has *seven* legs. Never known such tomfoolery. I'm off to the Andes. Have it ready for me next time I come back."

' "Your billiard table, sir," they said on his return. "*What?*" The Duke was outraged. "Never known such nonsense!" he expostulated: 'You have given me an oblong table and everyone knows that a billiard table is round. I'm off to the Arctic. Be sure to have it ready for me next time I come back."

' "Your billiard table, sir," they said on his next return. "*Ri-diculous!*" the Duke shouted. "You have given me round balls when all the world knows that in billiards, the balls, so-called, are square. And what're these funny long wooden things? Cues, eh? Oh, for heaven's sake, one plays billiards with proper bone clubs. And do get rid of that useless blue chalk; can't see the slightest use for it. Hah! Billiards? And I thought that this establishment knew its business. Well, I'm off to explore the outback of Australia. Have it ready for me next time I come back."

'Unfortunately,' Douglas continued evenly, 'the dear Duke was eaten alive in the Australian outback by a pack of wild dogs. So do you know anyone who wants to buy a round billiard table with seven legs, clubs of bone and square "balls" . . .?'

'No,' I said, 'but what's the moral?'

'Never deal with lunatics,' said Douglas. 'Fancy another game of billiards?' On this particular game, which we both agreed would decide the 3-3 issue, he proceeded to outplay me with greater skill. He was ahead and about to pot a perfect shot when the boat lurched and caused him to muff it completely, putting me back in the game with a winning chance. According to the crew, it was a hippo that was responsible but the accident rather upset his concentrated play and I managed to take the win and the thousand pounds that we had bet.

'Tales of the unexpected,' Douglas said as he paid the bet and poured more port for us. 'Always like that, isn't it? However well you may plan anything, there is always that random factor, infinite and unknown . . . how d'you fancy swopping girls for tonight?'

'Fine,' I answered.

CHAPTER TWELVE

After an exceedingly enjoyable cruise, Douglas and I were both pleased to receive letters from Rosemary in Montreal. Mine read:

Mon cherie, mon petit choux,

Comment allez-vous? Très bien? *Please excuse my terrible French for I am now in the most delightful city of Montreal. I gather meanwhile that you have been cruising along the Nile with Douglas and one trusts that you enjoyed the experience.*

When my godmother invited me to her mansion in Westmount, I could hardly refuse it. Her house overlooks the western slope of Mount Royal, often referred to as le petit montagne. *I believe that it was volcanic at one time. It rather reminds me of my godmother. She is getting on in age and often in the afternoon likes to have 'forty winks', or as she often says as she retires for her* siesta *'to lie in the arms of Morpheus.' Then she declares: 'Jacques, would you please bring me* le thé avec l'orange pressée? Je suis très fatiguée. *Rosemary, excuse me, my darling, I must retire for a while.'*

I am certain that the strong, handsome young Jacques is a housecarl but he does treat her well. On my first afternoon, I sat and contemplated the view before me. In 1842, Charles Dickens had visited the place with his wife and had written well of the city. Montreal is pleasantly situated on the margin of the St Lawrence and is backed by bold heights around which there are charming drives and rides. The streets are generally narrow and irregular. Yet as I sat in quiet contemplation, I was amazed by the sounds of the activities which were taking place overhead. I had always thought that sounds did not carry within a colonial building of this nature but evidently this one was an exception.

'Fuck me! Fuck me!' my prim and proper godmother was screaming at Jacques, 'but first of all, let me suck your cock.' I could not help but eavesdrop whilst the floor vibrated overhead.

'My love! My beautiful coquette!' Jacques roared. 'Let me lick upon your quim, upon your beautiful cunty, upon the lips of your marvellous labia!' Then the doorbell rang at the instant that my godmother was yelling words of orgasmic relief. I knew that guests were vaguely expected and also, obviously, that Jacques was presently in no condition to admit them; therefore I opened the door to reveal a young gentleman who was in possession of the slightest trace of a moustache and with his hair shiningly pomaded and parted down the middle. Bidding him welcome, I led him into the main drawing-room and helped him to a glass of wine, thereupon introducing myself.

'Rosemary, Rosemary . . .' he enthused, 'that evergreen, fragrant shrub, Rosemary taken as an emblem of remembrance,' and he softly blew me a kiss. How formal he was! And how he did blush!

'My name is Smith, yet you, Ma'am, can call me by my first name, which is Robert.'

'Robert, it is so apparent that you are an educated man.'

'At the present time, Ma'am,' he flushed furiously, 'I am pursuing my studies at McGill University. My desire is to achieve a degree in Philosophy; yet my greatest wish is to excel at hockey.'

'A hockey *player . . .?'*

'Indeed, Ma'am. I have invented the puck *by cutting off the sides of an Indian Rubber Ball!' he announced proudly.*

'How fascinating . . .' I murmured as Catherine, my godmother, swanned into the room, followed by Jacques.

'Mr Smith . . . .!' she greeted him. 'What a pleasure it is to see you again!' She smiled at him graciously. 'You simply must introduce my god-daughter Rosemary to the delights of skating! It is,' she remarked as Jacques served her with wine, 'such a joy to see how much you already appear to be enjoying one another's company.'

'Madame Vigère,' Robert Smith replied, 'it is such a pleasure to enjoy your hospitality once again. And I am greatly looking forward to the arrival of the other guests.'

'Ah, yes,' she responded, 'I am sure you will find them all as interesting as you find yourself.' She smiled bitchily as he blushed. 'Age before beauty, I always say,' giving him another smile to show that the shot had been executed without malice. 'Although I am a devotee of beauty.' She glanced at Jacques, who was busy uncorking more wine. 'One fellow you must meet desires to build the most beautiful hotel in Montreal, combining the glamour of the Ritz in Paris with the splendour of the Carlton in London . . .' her flow was interrupted since the guests suddenly arrived all at once as they are wont to do.

Eventually, eight of us were finally seated around the dining table to relish the cuisine of Jacques. His potage de pois, tortières, *molluscs simmered in cream and calvados,* le biftek *and an unusual accompaniment of* fruits de mer *were among outstanding highlights. I was reminded of an old French Canadian folk song:*

There are some who love good food
Beans with pork and also green peas;
And plenty of pork also with beans.
There are some who eat; others who don't.
The spoiled gherkins in the salad . . .
There are some who eat them and make themselves sick!
But to eat pea soup?
The Canadians are always ready!
Ah! Ah! The Canadians are always ready!

This somewhat banal nationalist anthem did not augur well for the future of Canada as a Great Power; but it certainly did not interfere with my enjoyment of Jacques's excellent pea soup; and it was a delight to sit opposite Robert. I could not take my eyes away from his. He had a double set of eyelashes which I have never seen before on a man; I think it is the sign of the second sight. Occasionally, he winked at me, an indication, one hoped, of something further to come.

After the occasion ended, I retired to my room, one that is always set aside for me, and put on my nightgown, sipping my hot chocolate and gazing into the glowing coal fireplace, both services which had been rendered by the attentive Jacques. The snow fell that evening, crystals dancing upon the ground as the moon glittered upon each ballerina falling from the sky. There was then a tap upon my door – a tale of the expected.

'Who is there?' I enquired in a voice of 'sauve qui peut'.

Of course, it was Robert and I was delighted to welcome him and to give us both a glass of apple brandy which Jacques had thoughtfully placed upon the bedside table. We talked pleasantly until he said:

'Rosemary, have you ever played the game of Smacking Bottoms?'

'I thought that only happened in Public Schools in Great Britain.'

'Possibly so,' he smiled, 'though there are their imitators throughout the Empire. Would you care to participate?'

'Yes?'

'This is a game of strength and skill . . .' We both removed our attire and squatted on the bed with our legs intertwined, each one of us holding a towel in the air. Abruptly, I shoved and twisted Robert over onto his abdomen and I slapped him viciously upon the buttocks. How they did redden and quiver! I knew that I was setting fire to his loins. Upon this cold winter's night, it was assuredly essential to raise the temperature. Droplets of steam appeared upon the window as, outside, the white flakes from heaven fell ever quicker and quicker.

As the coals glowed, we made love again, again and again. It was such a blazing inferno, this incandescence of heat between our loins. In the course of our outbursts of passion, we were both in a fever of pyrexia. My darling, I was suffering from violent ebullitions. Towards the early hours of the morning, he announced his intention of temporarily retiring from this bliss to his room.

'Mon chérie,' *he said, 'I would love to teach you the art of skating when we can have the whole rink to ourselves but first of all, I must exercise in my sport.' I agreed to watch him practise his 'hockey' on the following afternoon at McGill and then fell asleep. Around midday, there was a gentle knock upon my door. I called out my assent to entrance and was greeted by Jacques, who was bearing a tray.*

'Bonjour, Madame,' *he smiled, revealing wickedly white teeth. 'I come to bring you* le petit déjeuner.'

'What have you brought me exactly?'

'Le café avec les crullers.'

'Come in, then' I replied, suddenly feeling so abashed to realize that my left breast was exposed. Before I knew it, Jacques and I were frollicking upon the bed together. How he did tickle my cunny! What a young stud he was! Any farmer would hire him to breed!

Horby, you do not know how exhausting some activities in life can be. As you know, I am a very orgasmic woman. The French can be such paramours . . . and Jacques is a golden example. However, I had made an arrangement to be with Robert later that day yet I did not want to appear too distinguée.

I went to Eaton's to purchase a skirt of vermilion, the frills of which were trimmed with ermine, that fur which changes colour throughout the year – occasionally marked with black spots. My outfit included a warm vermilion pullover of wool, a little red hat, a furry brown muff to keep my hands warm and a pair of thick, red stockings of wool in addition to a pair of figure skates.

On my arrival, and on greeting Robert Smith, it was a pleasure to see that we had the whole rink to ourselves. I had learned figure skating at St Moritz during my teenage years and so it was a joy to glide upon the ice once again. It was an even greater pleasure to be served hot mulled wine which he had made. We toasted one another's health.

'I hope that you become the greatest hockey player that

Canada has ever known,' I said. (Editor's Note: Robert Smith is regarded as the Founder of Canadian Ice Hockey.)

'So do I,' he replied, 'but now I must change into my costume. 'Unfortunately, it is necessary that I change in front of you.' I wondered just why it might be necessary since there was a clear sign stating CHANGING ROOMS on the EXIT door. Yet I could not help but look as Robert removed his clothing, down to his combinations. They were bright red with a flap for his bottom.

The combination of the ice upon the surface of the rink, the warmth within the room and the mulled wine put me in such a jovial mood. How we did frolic! We even sang a few chansons de geste. *As we danced upon the ice together, I began to feel the throbbing between his thighs, yes, I could feel a major protrusion under his cardinal red undergarment.*

'Turn around,' I said teasingly as we slid along the ice, 'and then bend over.' He complied and I released the flap to see his firm young buttocks, which initially I nibbled gently with playful bites. I can never have too much of a mouthful of ham, especially that of a fine, young gentleman. I did gently rim him, at the same time flicking my fingers upon his posterior, the haunches, hunkies, hindquarters of a fine young stud. I have never seen such a fine pair of hunkers in all my life, apart from yours, my darling.

Outside it was so cold in terms of temperature as Montreal froze under the intense brunal *of Winter.*

'How much longer do I have to wait before we can once more glide upon the ice together?' I asked.

'If you are going to be so attractive and alluring, it could be forever. Allow me to serve you another negus,*'*

he added as he sped away to refresh our glasses. What spices he had put into this concoction!

We then fell into one another's arms, with sparks flying and the room numinous with light. He was scintillating as he caught me on the ice, then slowly unlaced my boots and gradually removed all my attire and there and then did penetrate me with his marvellous art. What a slow fluidity there was between the two of us! He rammed it in sufficiently hard for me to forget temporarily the pleasures of skating. I was so looking forward to gliding upon the ice with an exquisite ease and yet, in another sense, this was taking place here and now as his prick throbbed within my cunt.

Douglas tells me that you have gone on a Nile cruise with him. I hope that the pair of you are misbehaving yourselves. I've made my own arrangements to meet Douglas; my advice to you, Horby, is: 'Go East, young man,' and don't be like my grandmother who always used to say: 'I don't want to try it because I might like it.'

All my love,

Rosemary.

Douglas and I finished reading our separate letters from Rosemary simultaneously. The British Consulate in Cairo provided an excellent smoking-room in those days.

'Remarkable woman, isn't she?' I said.

'Oh, indeed,' he answered firmly. 'So now let's do what she'd want us to do and pick up some good girls and fuck their brains out.'

CHAPTER THIRTEEN

It proved to be relatively easy to attain our desired objective. We were staying at a certain hotel in Cairo, the name of which, even now, discretion forbids me to mention. for it is still in being. If I mention the small golden pyramid within a glass case housed just to the left of Reception, then some of my readers may know of it. Essentially, it was – and, I believe, still is – an excellent rendezvous for wealthy and respectable gentlemen and ladies.

As was customary with him, Douglas had spared no expense for his every whim to be gratified. We had adjoining suites with a connecting door and even Tutenkhamen or Queen Nefertiti would have been gratified by the gaudy splendour. It was in Douglas's drawing-room that I smoked the *hubble-bubble* of hashish with him and also took copious quantities of gin-and-tonic. This is not, in fact, my favourite drink but the quinine in the tonic is a most advisable protection against the dangers of malaria.

When we wandered somewhat airily downstairs and into the dining-room, I had become so used to his eccentricities that I was not at all surprised by his choice of menu.

'All influenced by North Africa, Horby,' he murmured; and the fact is that in Cairo's finest establishments, they will bring you whatever you want as long as you can pay for it. We therefore took a glass or two of *arak*, a hot, white, burning spirit and commenced with a Tunisian speciality, *brikl*, thin pastry folded over a filling of vegetables and raw egg, deep-fried and served with a side salad, and observing the custom of the country, we ate it with our right hands. 'Watch that you don't end up with egg on your face,' said Douglas. I did not; though I was watching two extraordinarily attractive young women who were dining at a table across the room from ours. Douglas noticed my appreciative glances.

'Ah, that's Juanita and Alicia,' he murmured over our *chorba*, a spicy soup with lemon. 'All is easy as ABC here, as you may have discerned from the menu I have chosen, for our next course will consist of *dolmades*. We've having an alphabet dinner. Just enjoy it, old chap, this'll keep your pecker up.' I nodded my appreciation of the spiced minced meat and rice wrapped in vine leaves. With it we were drinking a young Turkish white wine which truly did taste of the grape. 'Anyway, Juanita, the *Marquesa*, and *Doña* Alicia are long-standing friends of mine from Spain and they'll be only too delighted to join with us for a good fuck later.' My sense of appetite was rising, since both ladies were exquisitely dressed in silk, Juanita in black and Alicia in white. 'And so that's my letter 'e': *e*ager.' He chuckled wickedly. 'Takes a whole alphabet of ingredients to make a good dinner and a good occasion, wouldn't you say so, Horby?'

I nodded assent since my prick was rising at the sight of these two exquisite women who were speaking together quietly yet eating voraciously. Juanita, the *Marquesa*, had long, wavy dark hair and high cheek-bones which set off to perfection her flashing eyes. Lady Alicia had masses of flaming red curls and her expression was somewhat haughty and disdainful. Juanita was beautifully buxom whilst Alicia was delectably slender. I wanted to fuck the pair of them there and then but turned back to my gaunt, cadaverous and curious host.

'*E* is also for eggs,' he smiled as a small plate of one of my favourite delicacies, plovers' eggs, appeared upon our table. This dinner was certainly memorable. For *f* there was a delicious fish stew to accompany our *g* for grain, a North African speciality called *couscous* and this was excellent. 'You may well be asking what I'll be doing for *h*, *i* and *j*. Why, *h* is for that delicious dish of mashed chick peas that is coming, called *hummus*, *i* is for *I* since *I* am the host and you still find me *i*nscrutable,' (which was true), and *j* is the *jambon*, for we will be enjoying a few slices of exquisite smoked ham from France. *L*,' he continued, 'is for the *l*adies present, for we'll be wanting a good fuck after dinner and meanwhile we admire the view; *m* is for meat, since we shall, one trusts, enjoy a dish of exquisite, thinly sliced raw fillet of beef in the Lebanese fashion; and chopped cashew *nuts*, as in *n* are a fitting accompaniment. After that, we shall require an *o* for orange, sliced into four quarters, to refresh ourselves for the next dish.

'This will commence,' Douglas informed me, 'with *p* for peppers spiced and roasted to accompany our *q* for quails roasted within the same dish and accompanied by a small portion of *r* for rice, plentifully flavoured with the world's rarest spice, which is *s* for saffron. There is of course a *t* for twist in this tale of our dinner *together, for it is a t*ale of the unexpec*t*ed, a *u* for the indispensable *u*tensils we employ to eat it, a *v* for our victuals generally – and let's not forget our e*v*entual *v*ictory over those *v*oluptuous women – a *w* for our wine; and I've ordered plenty of robust Moroccan red to go with it.' He drew a deep breath then smiled benevolently. '*X* is simply the factor infinite and unknown which informs every encounter, *y* is for the yogurt appropriate to so many of these dishes, and as for *z*, that's when we invite the ladies to our table to join us in partaking of that magical Italian dessert, *zabaglione*.'

'Sounds splendid, Douglas,' I returned with genuine enthusiasm. 'But as we proceed to enjoy this feast, can I ask you a couple of questions which continue to puzzle me?'

'Be my guest.'

'Is Emily Ward-Bishop really your niece?'

'If she says so, then she is,' Douglas returned with a wry, dry smile. 'I wouldn't doubt her word and heaven knows, if you were to research the matter, you might well find that we are related by marriage between a wide variety of relatives. Next question.'

'About a year ago, the Hon Claire Woodrough wrote me a letter from Paris in which she described Satanism as practised by her cousin Charlotte with her paramour Jean-Pierre. This mysterious and intriguing couple have left Paris without a trace. What is your opinion?'

'My opinion,' Douglas replied, 'is either that Claire was having you on to excite your libidinous fantasies; or else that it was not a Mass but a mess. There sometimes are these pieces of theatre staged in Paris to sort out the wheat from the chaff; and Claire is definitely among the wheat.'

'Any idea where she might be now?' I stared into his eyes, which were like cold gun-muzzles.

'Out in India with Ram Singh, I imagine,' he answered casually. 'And that's where you ought to be, as I keep telling you, my dear fellow. You keep on looking for Truth, don't you?' He laughed harshly. ' "What is truth?" asked Pontius Pilate; and you're still waiting for an answer. Why, Hasan Al Sabah, leader of the Sect of

Assassins, also called "The Hashishin", declared: "Nothing is true; everything is permitted." And I say to you now: "Truth is what you believe." Incidentally, don't believe *me*. You never know, I might be lying. Make up your own mind, Horby, and come with me tomorrow to the King's Chamber of the Great Pyramid. Meanwhile, enough of this intellectual nonsense. Let us invite Juanita and Alicia to our tables – incidentally it's rumoured that they made their fortunes by marrying and killing aged, wealthy, titled men – let's enjoy *zabaglione* and let's fuck!'

Fifteen minutes later I had no cause for complaint as I fucked the voluptuous Juanita. Her every cry was in tune with mine. Next door, I knew, Douglas was fucking Alicia. I was enjoying a very good fuck indeed. My right hand assaulted her delectable bubbies as my left advanced towards her navel, flicking all around into that delightful nook, and then with the same hand, I swept a peacock plume at the socket of her sweet and quivering left hip, tickling the shivering skin with a lingering peroration. She gasped and wriggled, bit her lips and then closed her eyes, delighting in her submission. My fingers glided down her stockinged thighs and stroked the fine black silk sheath about the knee and then on up to where that lovely column joined her hip, thence to brush against her lower abdomen where the curls of her pubis flourished. As I lowered the tip of my finger toward the top of her cunt, Juanita uttered a low sobbing groan.

Upper class ladies are so easy to seduce, provided that one has the right surroundings. As for one's behaviour, I concur with Beau Brumell: 'I treat all the chambermaids like duchesses and all the duchesses like chambermaids.' That is why I suddenly slapped her face, a quick flick to the right cheek. Her eyes blazed with anger.

'Why did you do that?' she demanded furiously.

'Because you're such an insolent, snooty bitch, aren't you?' I replied. And with this, I lowered my right hand down toward the very tip of her cunt and began to tickle her.

The bourgeoisie fail utterly to realize that the aristocracy and gentry behave like farmyard animals, which is why we usually get on so well with the working classes. If ever royalty pretends to ape middle-class behaviour, that will be the eventual doom of it. In any event, Juanita's eyes widened as she stared down at herself and all of a sudden, a fiery blush suffused her contorted, flushed cheeks. Then she gnawed her lower lip and stiffened herself but she could not help a sporadic trembling which shook her body from head to foot.

I stared greedily at the thick verdure of her crisp silky growth which so luxuriantly and protectively fleeced her slit. And I prodded my finger until its tip touched through the curls to open her outer labia, then began very slowly but deftly to rasp it up and down the lip nearest to me, so as to sensitize it. Meanwhile my left hand continued with its gliding touches all along her trembling thigh, abruptly visiting her leg with long and deliberate caresses. A tiny whimpering gasp escaped from my naked victim and lover.

Now the fingers of my right hand moved over to the top of the other fleshy outer lip which helped to form that lovely fig, that sweet miniature conch-shell which was her voluptuous vagina and I proceeded to tickle it in the same way. But now I glided the feather that I had picked up again down to the very base of her slit and then back up again along that crinkly, fleshy pink lovelet, while my left now moved to the inside of her right thigh, very near to that furry grape which I was so intent upon peeling.

'Ohh . . . oh! what are you doing, oh my Lord for I thought you were an English Gentleman. I'm only a helpless woman . . . ahhh!!! – oooh! – oh! no more, no more, in the name of mercy!'

"Between a woman's yes and a woman's no, I would not care to put the point of a pin," wrote Cervantes in *Don Quixote*: and who am I to disagree? Naturally I deplore rape: but the point of the pin is when you put your finger into a woman's cunt. If it is wet, that means an affirmative. If it is dry, that means a retreat in good order with chivalry. And let us not forget that if there is sufficient chivalry, she may yet change her mind. After all, that is assuredly a woman's prerogative.

As it happened, I continued to tickle this delectable, small, wet cunt and Juanita began to jerk and twist, swaying her hips from side to side in a coy endeavour to disengage my hands from their stealthy and relentless attack.

Now, and slyly, I moved my left hand over to her cunt and in a trice had the soft downy lips moving up and down, caressing these fleshly portals which concealed the road to paradise. Juanita uttered a shriek as I touched an acutely sensitive spot and lunged her bottom backwards to escape my dual siege of her most sensitive and sacrosanct regions. She really did excite me with her convulsive gyrations and her buckings and lungings which made her thighs and bubbies jounce and jiggle and express the luscious resilience of her naked flesh. The fingers of both my hands directed their diabolically persuasive caresses up and down the outer labia of my lady's twitching quim.

'Ah! – oh! – God in heaven – oh! – you'll drive me crazy – oh, please, sir . . . – oh! in the name of heavenly mercy . . . I beseech you . . . DON'T! . . . oh, DO . . . stop! eeeowow! – oh! Lord, oh! . . . it's too much! I can't bear it any longer!' she gasped. 'Oh! Sir, do have mercy upon a poor helpless woman and spare me, milord!' Her soft vibrant voice was choked with sobs and gasps and groans as she twisted and arched and wriggled back and forth, her eyes now fixedly staring down at the prick aimed at her crotch, that very prick which now proceeded with its swollen head to tickle the quivering coral petals of her love-slit.

I drew my prick away so that I could have a look at the threshold of my coming attunement. Yes, the curly thicket of Juanita's pussy-hair was ruffled and here and there I could perceive the exquisite crinkly surfaces of that voluptuous membrane which was her temple of Venus, her nymph's grotto of satyr's delight. And then, with a cool little smile as I stared down at her, I thrust my cock deep into her cunt and worked it back and forth.

The effect was magical! Juanita emitted a wild, piercing shout of '*Aaaah! Ohh! nooo-o-o-o-o!!!*' as she madly jerked her glorious bottom backwards.

This was a perfect cue for me to push my mid-finger up her arse and she writhed with the pleasure of it. I cupped her glorious bottom within my palms and relished the sensation of her soft, young and tender flesh. Initially, I moved my stiff prick slowly in order to make a gentlemanly acquaintanceship with her ladylike cunt. Once gracious admission to her more inward recesses had been granted, I began to step up the pace and the rhythm.

First, I gave it to her in the long way, which is to draw your cock in and out at its full length, and on the odd inward thrust, follow the advice of *The Perfumed Garden* and try to make the tip of your cock touch the outer lips of her womb. Once she has sighed her signal to sexual surrender, slam in hard. I suddenly moved very fast, whipping my prick in and out and surprising her with my speed. Then it's *slam*. That is a sequence to the sexual dance which I find increasingly hard to repeat as I age – though it is still possible on occasion – and it consists of grinding one's rod-root against her pubic bone. One wants her to be walking around with the feel of your cock up her cunt for at least a week even though you're miles away; and certainly, that way, the lady will not forget you.

Slam can be so exciting to both man and woman that the man might well come but it is best not to do so. I returned to long, loving strokes within her warm wet cunt as Juanita writhed and twisted her swan-like neck with the pleasure of it. There was a moment when she realized that I was about to come and she made it glorious by gripping her creamy thighs around me. When I shot my load of spunkshot into her, my hips went into a spasm, my spine tingled from brain to balls and in my mind, the glory of my seed spurted forth unto the stars within her.

CHAPTER FOURTEEN

There is no doubting that the sexual act is the holiest act in the Universe. The male conjoins with the female in ecstasy, celebrating all creation. One should therefore despise anyone who opposes this noble movement of Nature as a fool, charlatan and bearer of foul mental diseases.

I am hardly an expert in scientific matters but it seems to me as though the research and discoveries of our present scientists confirm the statements of Ancient and Renaissance philosophers who declared that everything is relative, depending upon the point of view of the observer; and that everything in the Universe is somehow connected with everything else.

Philosophy, however, was not in the forefront of my mind on the following morning. After good, strong coffee with Juanita, we joined Douglas and Alicia for a light breakfast of more coffee and bread and eggs. Both of them looked as though they had enjoyed a marvellous time, which caused me to wonder increasingly about Douglas. Although I had spent weeks in his good company and he had been and was being an excellent host, I still did not know very much about him and he had pointedly declined to answer all my questions of a personal nature. Nevertheless, I acceded to his proposition for the day, which was to take camels to the Great Pyramid.

It was a curious procession. Douglas was surrounded by fierce tribesmen, all of whom seemed to be devoted to his welfare. They were the sort of chaps who might slit your throat for one bad word and think nothing of it: and if you were to touch their sisters in a disrespectful manner, they would chop your balls off and stick them in your mouth. Aside from this, they were dignified men of the utmost courtesy.

I was also baffled by the fact that they had brought two sorts of camels: the Dromedary with one hump; and the Bactrian with two. They gave the one-humped Dromedaries to Juanita and Alicia, assuring them that they would be more comfortable that way; the men rode the two-humped Bactrians. Camels really are extraordinary desert creatures. They store their food in their humps and their water in their bellies and they can go for weeks or even months without either as they plod along at a slow and steady pace. Juanita and Alicia initially found it difficult to master the knack, as I did, but since we were accustomed to horses, the matter only required a period of adjustment and the Bedouin friends of Douglas rendered us every possible assistance in the course of our learning process. After a couple of hours, I was sitting well in my saddle and so was everyone else.

'Extraordinary, isn't it, Horby,' said Douglas, 'that Mohammad was for a time an illiterate camel driver. Nothing more. Then, by his own account, while he was quietly meditating in a cave, endeavouring to seek the Truth of God, the Angel Gabriel came to him and dictated *The Qu'ran*. This Book made of him the Prophet of Islam and he restored Civilization to the West, then suffering the Dark Ages of totalitarian Christianity. Mohammad restored Art, Science and the rights of Woman.'

'Quite agree,' I replied, for I had read a translation of *The Qu'ran*. 'Isn't it a pity, though, that this holy scripture can be misinterpreted as a tool of foul oppression?'

'True,' Douglas sighed heavily. 'As Schiller has it: "With stupidity, the Gods Themselves argue in vain." '

We trekked on our way towards the Pyramids. There was nothing to see except sand. Does anything ever happen among those burning dunes or does it remain as uneventful as a cricket match upon an English village green?

Will Eternity be like this? I wondered as we continued with our bumpy ride across the endless dunes of sand. It's been said that cricket is the closest knowledge that any Englishman will ever have of Eternity. Even cricket is more interesting than this endless vision of sand. It was a joy when some pyramids came into view. There was also the Sphinx and I thought of Her Riddle of Man. The sun really does addle one's brain sometimes; and so did the conversation of Douglas.

'Have you ever considered, Horby,' he asked me, 'the fact that there might be alien creatures among us?'

'Is that a fact?' I replied. 'It sounds like something from the scientific romances of H.G. Wells.'

'I didn't say it was a *fact*. I said that it *might*, be a possibility. After all, there are billions of stars within our own galaxy, some of which may support planetary systems. For all we know, there are billions of galaxies. Some form of intelligent life might have sent alien beings to this planet in order to accelerate human evolution.' I nodded my assent to this possibility. It was conceivable that it might explain the behaviour of Douglas, not to mention Rosemary and Claire. 'Now look at the Great Pyramid coming up ahead of us.' I looked with astonished admiration at this magnificent sight. 'Did you know that if you multiply its height by a million, you get the distance from the Earth to the Moon accurately to two decimal places?' I didn't. 'The pyramid also exemplifies *pi* in its structure,' Douglas continued remorselessly. 'The fact is, my dear fellow, that it would be virtually impossible even for us, with our modern technology, to construct a building possessing such minute mathematical exactitude in the plain truths about the physical Universe of which it plainly informs us. It is not impossible that alien intelligences may have informed a primitive but hard-working people of knowledge well beyond their ken.'

'Not impossible . . .' I muttered as this magnificent structure came into full view.

What followed was one of the most extraordinary experiences of my life. The four of us spent a night in the King's Chamber of the Great Pyramid after dismissing the servants at the foot of the Great Gallery.

By the light of a single candle placed on the edge of the coffer, Douglas began to read: 'The Preliminary Invocation' of *The Goetia*. This was a fragment of a Graeco-Egyptian papyrus, discovered in the British Museum and edited for The Cambridge Antiquarian Society, with a translation, by one Charles Wycliffe Goodwin (1852), as Douglas informed me, and it was given to the Adepts of the Golden Dawn once they had entered into the Inner Order of the Rosy Cross. The original, which he kindly gave me, follows:

> An address to the god drawn upon the letter.
>
> I call thee, the headless one, that didst create earth and heaven, that didst create night and day, thee the creator of light and darkness. Thou art, Osoronnophris, whom no man hath seen at any time: thou art Iabas, thou art Iapōs, thou hast distinguished the just and the unjust, thou didst make female and male, thou didst produce seeds and fruits, thou didst make men to love one another and to hate one

another. I am Moses thy prophet, to whom thou didst commit thy mysteries, the ceremonies of Israel; thou didst produce the moist and the dry and all manner of food. Listen to me: I am an angel of Phapro Osoronnophris; this is thy true name, handed down to the prophets of Israel. Listen to me . . . .
. . . . hear me and drive away this spirit.

I call thee the terrible and invisible god residing in the empty wind, ...
thou headless one, deliver such an one from the spirit that possesses him. . . . .
. . . . strong one, headless one, deliver such an one from the spirit that possesses him . . . . .
. . . .
deliver such an one . . . .
This is the lord of the gods, this is the lord of the world, this is he whom the winds fear, this is he who made voice by his commandment, lord of all things, king, ruler, helper, save this soul . . . .
. . . . angel of God . . . . .
. . . . I am the headless spirit, having sight in my feet, strong, the immortal fire; I am the truth; I am he that hateth that ill-deeds should be done in the world; I am he that lighteneth and thundereth; I am he whose sweat is the shower that falleth upon the earth that it may teem; I am he whose mouth ever burneth; I am the begetter and the bringer forth; I am the Grace of the World; my name is the heart girt with a serpent. Come forth and follow – The celebration of the preceding ceremony – Write the names upon a piece of new paper, and having extended it over your forehead from one temple to the other, address yourself turning towards the north to the six names, saying: Make all the spirits subject to me, so that every spirit of heaven and of the air, upon the earth and under the earth, on dry land and in the water, and every spell and scourge of God, may be obedient to me – And all the spirits shall be obedient to you . . .

As he went on, I noticed that he was no longer stooping to hold the page near the light. He was standing erect, yet the manuscript from which he read was not less but more legible. Looking about me, I saw that the Kings Chamber was glowing with a soft light which I discerned as being at the violet edge of the spectrum. If I had to affix a conventional label, I should probably call it pale lilac, though the quality of the light was much more striking than that colour. Here the word 'phosphorescence' occurs to the mind. It is one of the mysteries of physics that the total light of the sky is very much greater than can be accounted for by the luminous bodies in the heavens. There are various theories, but I personally believe that the force presently called radio-activity, which we know to be possessed in some degree by every particle of matter, is responsible. Our eyes are affected with the impression of light by forces which are not in themselves recognized as luminous.

However, back to facts. The King's Chamber was aglow as if with the brightest tropical moonlight. The pitiful dirty yellow flame of the candle was like a blasphemy and Douglas rightly put it out. The light remained during the entire session of all that ensued.

Douglas had obviously ordered his servants to place couches in the chamber prior to our arrival. These were carved, ornamented and fashioned with every extreme of oriental luxuriance. I gazed at Alicia, with whom I had not yet made love. She was as beautiful as an earthly Venus, with eyes that were large, dark and dreamily voluptuous, in whose depths true love had evidently found no place. She was clothed in some sort of light, flimsy garment, showing the charming slender curves and displaying the mobile undulations of her lovely form. At my beckoning, she placed herself beside me as Douglas fixed his own attentions upon Juanita.

Ye Gods of Ancient Egypt! What a maddening sight

now met my enamoured eyes as they feasted with insatiable delight upon the supreme beauty thus given to my view. Her rounded, softly moulded chin merging into the white column of her neck, this gradually widening until it indicated two round, swelling breasts, crowned each with a delicious pink bud, and their very colour, which was a dusky brown . . . all of this added to my delight. What tides of ecstasy thrilled through my maddened spirit as my hands wandered unrestrained over the soft expanse of her breasts as they swelled to meet my gentle, kneading pressure.

The light was leaving me in a delirium, though I knew that through some mysterious power, Alicia would fully respond to my endeavours as I fastened upon her lovely mouth and sucked in her fragrant breath. As if in answer to my prayers, her face suddenly flushed and her breasts began to heave with innocent bliss. With what joy I saw her body tremble in ecstasy! Her efforts to respond to my fond pressures had somewhat disordered her dress and I now perceived that it had fallen entirely from her limbs.

If I had been excited before, this was increased threefold when I moved back to the other end of the couch and saw her most secret beauties revealed in all their maddening luxuriance: her legs had opened wide and as I gazed my eyes dwelt on each softly rounded limb, from tapered ankle to glowing thigh. Her hand, meantime, prompted perhaps by the light aroused within the Pyramid, wandered down until it rested between her quivering thighs, and almost unconsciously, played with the short, silky, curling hair that covered this delectable slot.

Excited and aroused by this unusual occupation, a pair of scarlet, pouting lips opened, whilst the soft mound above thrilled and throbbed as if longing for some unknown pleasure. I watched fascinated as she brought herself to some kind of dreamy climax. Her whole body heaved upwards as if to meet some responding pressure, whilst her breasts rose high and her nipples visibly engorged with the exquisite ecstasy of love's enjoyment. At last, unable to bear this unusual pleasure, she lay back, her cheeks flushing and her eyes half-closed in delicious languor, still disorientated by the effect of her orgasm.

Maddened by the sight in the violet light, I embraced Alicia with frantic eagerness and kissed her breasts again and again until, prompted by my unruly desires, my hand suddenly plunged through her panting mounds of pleasure and took possession. All this rendered her nearly helpless in my arms. Both her arms were now joined around my neck and she was lost in the mazes of her warm imagination. She now encouraged my hands to rove unrestrained all over her lovely neck and breasts, now and then wandering to her slender waist and softly rounded belly. Her mouth was half open like a ripe pomegranate, returning my burning kisses whilst her tongue darted between my lips.

'This is like nothing earthly!' she gasped. My desires had now reached a height entirely beyond my control; and indeed, she seemed to be in almost a like condition. We lay stretched face to face now, our bodies pressed together in frantic embraces and our limbs disordered. I threw myself upon her and clasped my arms around her waist whilst hers embraced my neck. Alicia pressed closer and closer amidst humid kisses and soft murmuring, as if she wished to incorporate our bodies into one.

Whether by accident or by remembering the movements of her own masturbation, Alicia's limbs by degrees opened to admit my pulsating prick, her legs twining convulsively about my loins. Nearly fainting with the unaccustomed ecstasy of our still raging and as yet unappeased desires, we heaved and pressed frantically against one another. She resisted so as to prolong the delicious torment but could feel my member pressing against that lovely spot between her thighs, determined to force its imperious way despite all impediments; and with longing, her cunt pouted wider at each instance of assault, longing despite itself to admit the dear invader.

All thoughts of modesty or maiden diffidence within the King's Chamber of the Great Pyramid was now completely overwhelmed and forgotten amidst the rampaging impulses of her unappeased desires. She sank down before me, her eyes half closed with love, her breasts thrusting high, as if willing to be pressed, her legs thrown apart, impatient to clasp my body. I prepared to consummate our mutual bliss. With trembling eagerness, she aided and abetted my every endeavour.

My invading weapon now entered the open gates of my longing partner and pressed onward. Her breasts heaved upwards against my chest, as each eager thrust sent a thrill of heavenly delight through her frame. Her thighs quivered and clasped around me while she seemed to dissolve in an agony of enjoyment.

Now wriggling with her hands clasped around my loins, all at once we suddenly struggled more fiercely, clasped tighter and tighter, till with one hot kiss, we came together and sank fainting into one another's arms.

When I recovered consciousness, my prick was still in the cunt of the slumbering Alicia. I looked around to see that this was the case also with the seemingly somnolent Douglas as he lay aboard the tender Juanita. The curious light, which had no natural, physical explanation and which I have since heard called 'astral light', remained; though it lessened in intensity as we composed ourselves to sleep.

In the morning, it had completely dissipated and the only sound was the flitting of bats.

CHAPTER FIFTEEN

There was a parting of the ways in Cairo after this extraordinary event. Douglas had urgent matters of business in Europe which called for his urgent attention; Juanita and Alicia had to return to Spain to administer their estates; and I had decided to take the advice of Douglas and go East. As I bade farewell to this excruciatingly enigmatic man, whom perhaps one day I would understand, I thanked him for his lavish and astonishing hospitality.

'I hope you've received a good letter from Rosemary,' were his last, jovial words to me before I boarded a French steamer, S.S. *Dupleix*, for a passage to India.

The voyage was actually atrocious; the ship stank of oil, partly from the engines, partly from the cooking and partly from the crew. But the consolation, there was indeed a letter from Rosemary:

My darling

How I miss you so much! I have never known such a long, arduous, onerous, toilsome train journey as that across Canada. I am so glad that I had brought some interesting literature with me; for instance The Ballad of Reading Goal *by the late Oscar Wilde; and other words of litterae, humaniores, a veritable chrestomathy; and* belles lettres.

I felt it so necessary that I bring my needlework with me also in order to wile away the hours. I am working upon a rich arras as a gift for you upon my return. How I do like to be so meticulous, attentive and accurate with my stitching! I so much loathed doing samplers when I was at school, especially when I did accidentally pierce my finger with my sewing needle and the blood would slowly ooze out upon my fine white linen.

The weather is so cold and the daylight hours so short . . . I thought that my railway journey across the Prairies would never end. However, I must tell you, my darling, of how spectacular the sunsets were, the most lavish and amazing display of lights in the sky that I have ever seen: hues of reds and orange, crimson, carnation, pink, even a touch of imperial purple with the transparency of garnet.

It is believed by some that the period of sunset, shading into twilight and dusk, is the declining period of life: yet I know it is not so, as the great Sun God Mithras gradually falls down unto the Earth to meet the arising Goddess of the Moon, known under a variety of names such as Luna, Phoebe and Selene; and they kiss and touch with reverence before they part until their next meeting on the following evening.

When the world stands still, the Blind Man's Holiday is the instant of the day just before the lamps are lit.

What was even more brilliant and histrionic was the sight of the Aurora Borealis, streamers of light radiating from the northern sky. Am I wrong in stating that the Aurora was named after the Roman Goddess of Dawn?

Upon my first evening within this train, I wanted to delight in the beauty of the night sky, enjoying a brandy in the observation car prior to retiring to my Pullman compartment. Admittedly, I was desirous of company, especially that of a gentleman and stag, such as you are. Midnight approached. I felt so reluctant to depart, even though I was the last customer. Suddenly, a man entered and approached me, swaggering with bravado and with the odour of whiskey upon his breath. However, the sight was a delight. His hair was long, jet black and long, and it was shining; and he wore an outfit similar to that I have seen in picture books: that of the Native American Indian.

We spoke; and he told me that he was the son of a chief of the Blackfoot tribe in my destination, the Province of Alberta. He expressed surprise when he learned where I was going.

'I'm going to see a Great Aunt of mine,' I explained. 'Recently there has been a discovery of oil upon her land.'

'Do you not think that there is more to life than mere financial gain?' he queried.

'Would you please explain?'

'Yes. You people are expropriating our *land and putting* us *on reservations.' I could see that I was talking to a very angry young man and I started to feel somewhat intimidated by his audacious and impudent manner.*

'I must go now,' I said.

'Sit!' he demanded peremptorily whilst producing a proffered flask of whiskey. As we sat and drank, I could not look away from his eyes that affected me so hypnotically.

'Really . . .' I smiled. 'Now I must retire.'

'And so you may,' he smiled back with gracious condescension.

I made sure that the door to my compartment was safely locked. The clickety-click *of the railway wheels had a somnolent effect upon my body. Yet within my compartment, there was a greater resonation, such as that of tom-toms, hand-beaten drums. To my stupefaction, I came out of my sleepiness to see a young, naked man with feathers in his hair with an eagle poised atop his head.*

'Do you not remember me?' he asked. Abruptly I recalled a certain Initiation.

'How could I forget you, ATOTARHO?' I replied. I stared upon his naked, bronzed, muscular, almost hairless body, possessed of a throbbing, very erect penis, which I immediately took into my mouth, sucking upon the knob before I allowed his complete member to plunge down my throat. His juices were as tasty as those of pemmican, a dried and powdered meat that is flavoured with currants.

'Now stand up,' he demanded. 'I will do you no harm; as I am the Great Shaman.' He fondled upon each breast and took each nipple gently into his mouth. Then he started to kiss me with a wild rapture that made me feel so excitable. I winced and flinched as his tongue gradually approached my cunt. When his tongue finally did enter me, it was like that of a fire-breathing dragon. How my knees did tremble as he rampantly drank my juices and I felt ablaze within! 'Your cunt is hotter than a prairie fire,' he said. 'You even arouse more heat than the dog days, the heliacal rising of Sirius, the Dog Star!' Then he added very gently: 'Please do lie down since I would really like to make love to you.'

I could not resist. I was aware of the bald eagle flapping its wings overhead with the sound of drums beating as ATOTARHO again penetrated my cunny, but this time with his penis. I could not believe the smoothness of his skin against mine as he pumped into me. His orgasm almost left me exhausted. However, he produced a piece of tobacca *that was inserted into a pipe and once smoked, this had the effect of a renewing aphrodisiac.*

As the sun rose, we again made love with a greater intensity that was even more fulfilling in its alacrity. I clung on to his muscular biceps and to all the other contractile fibrous bands of nerves in his body; and kissed those of his inner thighs and calves and his firm young buttocks which gently quivered like some well-set raspberry jelly; and maybe there was a spot of whipped cream and a maraschino cherry on top, just demanding to be eaten!

You cannot imagine how much I delighted in the morning light which daybreak brought! Then, after I came, weariness swept over me and he could see it in my eyes as he gently laid me down upon my bed and kissed me tenderly upon each eyelid. His powers appeared to be greater than those of the Sandman as I sank into a deep slumber. I recall dreamily his final words: 'We will meet again soon.'

I wonder if we ever will. He has left the train. Anyway, in a day's time, all being well, I shall have reached my destination and will correspond with you again as I do miss you so much.

All my love,
Rosemary.

After reading this intriguing letter, I went up on deck and gazed at the sea for a time, then retired to the bar in search of good company, though the hope seemed somewhat forlorn. To use the words of Samuel Taylor Coleridge in his *The Rime of the Ancient Mariner*: 'We were a dismal crew.' Yet to my delight there suddenly entered a chap whom I'd met in London and with whom I was vaguely acquainted, the psychologist Dr Harry

Maudesley. He seemed to be as despairing of good company as I was so we readily agreed to dine together.

Dinner was as awful as everything else on the voyage. Anyone who thinks that the French regularly eat well has not endured the misfortune of travelling to the East upon the *Dupleix*. There was a bowl of hot water with swimming vegetables, a limp and tasteless fish in powdered cheese sauce, a pork chop upon which one could break one's teeth accompanied by overcooked cabbage and 'sauce piquante' – mustard seeds with water – then Bombe Surprise – an ice-cream with chocolate made so badly that no sane man could eat it; hard cheese followed that, even though it was supposed to be camembert. The wine tasted as though it were sweat scraped away from the feet of the peasants who had pressed it.

'What are we doing here . . .?' I sighed.

'Studying humanity, I suppose,' Dr Maudesley sighed back in return. He was a tall gaunt man with hollow cheeks and a morose expression. He became slightly more cheerful when the brandy was brought, although this turned out to be only barely acceptable. I tried to cheer things up by quoting my acquaintance, Chesterton.

'If a thing is worth doing,' I said, 'then it is worth doing badly.'

'Such is the course of evolution,' he replied. I thoroughly enjoyed the conversation of this fascinating man who went on to found one of London's most celebrated psychiatric hospitals. Maudesley thought that every psychological matter could be reduced to problems of Cerebral Neurology.

'What about altered states in consciousness?' I queried.

'You remind me of a curious chap called Crowley,' he answered. 'Once went on a sea voyage and he was one of the passengers. Come across him at all?' I signified my assent, mentioning that we'd been at Cambridge together. 'Crowley thought that these altered states you mention could be a cue to propel the billiard balls of human evolution.'

'And what did you think?'

'Well,' said Maudesley, calling pointedly for more brandy and relighting his pipe, 'it was hard for a man of science such as myself to ascertain the precise nature of his terminology. How on earth does one equate the propositions of Science with those he termed "Magick"? The methods he described to me obviously stimulate the brain and therefore results in consciousness alteration are more than likely to follow. How is one to explain this curious phenomenon? I put it to him that the "demons" and "spirits" he "evoked" by his peculiar methods were merely cells of his own brain, stimulated sufficiently so as to cause him to enjoy particular hallucinations. I must admit, however,' Maudesley continued, 'that his techniques could be valuable in our understanding of the brain's functioning and he did not disagree with me.'

'What about sex, though?'

'Sorry . . .?'

'Sex in terms of furthering human evolution,' I said. 'Sex with intention. Let's face it, Dr Maudesley, no biologist knows why something which squanders energy as much as sex was ever necessary for the purposes of breeding. (Nobody still does, 1925). (*Nobody still does, 1995: Editor's Note*). 'Yet,' I continued remorselessly, 'the union of the human male and the human female, when done with appropriate ritual, seems to bring about altered states of consciousness. How do you explain that?'

'I will give you in reply the three most honest words in the English language,' said Dr Maudesley. 'These are: *I DON'T KNOW*. We have insufficient data. But believe me, sir, it is a question upon which the scientists will be working. You strike me as being quite an artistic sort of chap, Lord Horby. The trouble with Art, it strikes me, is: how do you measure it, save by like and dislike? And that's entirely subjective. Science, however, tests everything by experiment. That's how we advance.'

'So then, let us make an experiment,' I replied. 'See those two bitches there?' He looked and saw an English mother and daughter suffering a bad dinner at a table a few feet away from us. They were wearing somewhat tawdry finery and were obviously lower-middle-class 'ladies' going out to India to join some wretched subaltern. They both had dyed blonde hair and hard but sexy faces. 'Let's go for some Cerebral Neurology,' I said.

It was so easy to enter into their company. All I needed to do was send a magnum of the ship's bad champagne to their table, accompanied by my card. It's rare to see mouths gape so wide and one could sense their itching cunts as Maudesley and I crossed the room in response to their eager invitation, written on a card which declared The Larches and was somewhere in Middlesborough. Yes, Gladys Tracey (Mrs) was indeed going to India in order to join her husband Wally in Calcutta and meanwhile hoped to sell off her daughter, Victoria, to the highest bidder, in that cattle market known as marriage.

Anyone who chooses to undertake a sea voyage on the *Dupleix* is either as careless and crazy as I am; a keen student of human nature such as Harry Maudesley; or very short of money. Clichés are tiresome but true: to charm Mrs Gladys Tracey of Middlesborough was but the work of a trice. She was enchanted to be in the company of a Lord and a Doctor, and I feared that Harry Maudesley might be wearied shitless by her account of her ailments and her pleadings for his prescriptions. However, one cannot deny those sexual attractions to which we are all susceptible.

I enquired as to whether young Miss Victoria Tracey ever behaved badly and was informed by her mother, with a fluttering of eye-lashes, that to her regret, this *was* sometimes the case. I ventured my opinion that naughty girls should be punished and chastised by their mothers, doing so while young Miss Victoria was visiting the Ladies. At the same time, I made sure to slip an envelope of banknotes into the bag of Mrs Tracey. Victoria returned to be informed that her bad behaviour on the cruise was so insupportable that she would receive a sound spanking in their cabin in front of two stern gentlemen.

Victoria saw the look in her mother's eyes, pouted charmingly, wiped away a tear from her eye and obviously decided that the exposure of her buttocks for punishment before two well-established men could either make a match of the matter or else lead to suitable connections. Blushing deeply and charmingly, she curtsied graciously to us, all aflutter in a sea of skirt and petticoats, and walked away with a sexual rustle.

It really is quite amazing how so many mothers are willing to prostitute their daughters but I don't care as long as I receive sexual pleasure. Maudesley and I walked into the second class cabin to see Mrs Gladys Tracey preening herself as Miss Victoria Tracey stood obediently in a corner with her hands above her head. We took our seats and our brandy. At a stern command from her mother, Victoria turned, curtsied to us once more and confessed to the crimes of insolence, impertinence and impudence.

'And insubordination?!' Mrs Tracey snapped. Victoria confessed obediently and submitted to her chastisement. Her mother arranged her black skirt and then the daughter lay over her lap to receive maternal punishment. Mrs

Tracey crossed her thigh over her daughter's and, looking cross, whipped up the skirts and petticoats of Victoria to expose knee-length, lace-trimmed white knickers which had obviously been purchased at the best department store in Middlesborough. I overheard Dr Maudesley sigh quietly as Gladys pulled down the satin knickers to reveal a pearly white bottom of surpassing excellence.

'Now, my girl!' the mother commanded sternly. 'You will present your bottom for appropriate punishment.' Victoria edged her bottom a few inches higher, almost as if she was aching to be fucked, which, I reflected, she probably was. Mrs Tracey proceeded to don leather gloves of elbow length. 'You will receive a dozen strokes,' she said fiercely.

Maudesley and I smoked our cigars and watched the discipline of the Midlands with considered fascination. The girl writhed and jerked upon the older woman's thighs as the sound slaps came down with a heavy *smack!*

'Victoria is a high-spirited girl,' said Mrs Tracey as her leather-gloved hand came down hard to impart a faint pink hue to her daughter's white and trembling buttocks. 'On occasion, therefore, maternal chastisement is required.' *Smack! smack! SMACK!* Victoria writhed as her beautiful bottom changed its shade to a bright crimson. I heard a groan of ecstasy from Maudesley and assumed that he had creamed. Victoria started to jerk her bottom around in a wild and crazy spasm as it came to glow in bright scarlet.

I really cannot imagine a better advertisement for the marital prospects of a young and beautiful girl. When he arose from her mother's lap and executed a gracious curtsey for her deserved chastisement, her bottom glowing red beneath the frills of her white, pleated skirt, I really wanted to fuck her so badly. Her mother's forbidding look made it obvious that her daughter was a virgin on the market and as such could not be shop-soiled until the night of her marriage, probably to a subaltern as boring as her mother's Wally.

I was hardly prepared to make that particular marital commitment and therefore suggested that Victoria should be sent to bed in order to recover from her public spanking. Dr Maudesley looked in need of bed on his own. I suggested to Gladys that she might care to enjoy a coffee and a brandy in my cabin and she looked only too eager to accept my invitation. After bidding goodnight to Dr Maudesley and to the soundly spanked young teenage girl who, in truth, looked chastised indeed but only too willingly, ready and eager to masturbate, I took the mother to my cabin.

It hardly took me a moment to tip her over my knee, whip up her skirt and petticoats and pull down her drawers in order to redden her bottom as scarlet as she had made her daughter's. My hand came down time and time again upon her plump, womanly bottom, deriving a malicious pleasure from its smacking contact with her glowing flesh, a glow which contrasted so pleasantly with the creamy whiteness of her thighs. As she wriggled and writhed, I took a sadistic pleasure in smacking her harder, turning the colour of her behind from scarlet to puce. She cried out for me to stop but I would not, gaining much pleasure from the sight of that firmly rounded bum jerking around in squirming pain.

She had a good thin slit of a cunt, covered with a fair and luxuriant brush and so it was a pleasure to turn her over and ram my rod within her. This prim, prissy and pretentious bitch sighed, shouted and shrieked obscenities as I pronged her. Her cunt, which smelled delicious, oozed all the oils of womanhood. My prick rammed in up to the very hilt and she sighed and cried amidst the throes of her orgasm.

'You bossy little tart,' I growled as I shot my load deep into her. She responded by scraping my back with her long, red, manicured finger-nails.

As I held her in my arms, 'to sleep, perchance to dream,' I could not help reflecting upon the curious bond which obtains between mothers and daughters.

CHAPTER SIXTEEN

'So how d'you feel about the death of Queen Victoria, Horby?' Aleister Crowley asked me. We were drinking tea inside a bungalow at Kandy, Ceylon, and outside it was pouring with torrential rain.

'What am I supposed to feel?' I asked. I had left the ship at Colombo since I couldn't stand it any longer, much as I had enjoyed my conversations with Maudesley and my erotic experiences with Gladys and Victoria. 'I don't feel anything at all. Nothing whatsoever. How about you?' It had been a relatively easy matter to locate Crowley. Enquiries at the British Consulate had directed me to Sri Parananda, accomplished yogi and Solicitor-General of Ceylon. This gracious and kindly man confirmed that he had hosted both Crowley and Allan Bennett, giving instruction in Yoga to 'two of the most astonishing students of Yoga that I have ever encountered.'

'*I* felt joy,' said Crowley. 'And I have never forgotten the occasion.' He sipped tea calmly. 'I went mountaineering in Mexico with Oscar Eckenstein, inventor of the crampon, or climbing iron, and unquestionably the greatest rock climber and mountaineer in the world. The pair of us now hold every mountaineering record, especially those for pace uphill at high altitudes. We proved that to a sceptical journalist on Popacatapetl, lugging up this lazy bastard like the dead weight he was; but he should have seen us race up Ixtaccihuatl, which is the Aztec word for "sleeping woman". Eckenstein, provided he could get three fingers on something that could be described by a man far advanced in hashish as a ledge, would be smoking his pipe on that very ledge a few seconds later and one could not tell how he had done it. Whereas I, totally incapable of the mildest gymnastic feats, was able to get up to all sorts of places that Eckenstein could not attempt. On Ixtaccihuatl, we established a camp at 14,000 feet and remained there for three weeks, climbing this beautiful mountain from all sides and living off canned food and champagne. You don't believe me? No one does.'

'More tea?' Crowley offered and I accepted. The rain poured down outside. 'Now, when we returned to Amecameca to celebrate our triumphs, we were greeted by our charming host with a long face. He broke the sad news as gently as he could; Queen Victoria was dead. To his stupefaction, he saw us fling our hats into the air and dance for joy. Let's face it, Horby, to all artists and thinkers, Queen Victoria was sheer suffocation, a vast thick fog which has enveloped us so that we were unable either to see or to breathe. The spirit of her age had killed everything we cared for. Smug, sleek, superficial, servile, snobbish, sentimental shopkeeping has spread everywhere.'

'Quite agree,' I replied. 'So have you come out here for more mountaineering in the Himalayas?'

'Of course,' he answered. 'In due course, Eckenstein and I shall lead an expedition to climb the second highest mountain in the world: K2. The only reason that we're not attempting Everest is that access to it is presently denied by the King of Nepal. Meanwhile, as Eckenstein organises the expedition and chooses the team, I am studying Oriental Philosophy and practising Yoga.'

'Kindly explain.'

'The main idea,' he replied, 'is that the Infinite – God, the Oversoul, or whatever you may prefer to call it – is always present; but veiled or masked by the thoughts of the mind, just as one cannot hear as individual heart-beat in a noisy city . . . then to obtain knowledge of That, it is only necessary to still all thoughts.'

'That's easy enough,' I said. 'Just go to sleep.'

'True, perhaps, roughly speaking,' he answered, 'but the perceiving function is stilled also.'

'Then you wish to obtain a perfect vigilance and attention of the mind, uninterrupted by the rise of thoughts?'

'Absolutely, my dear Horby.'

'And how do you proceed?'

'Firstly, we still the body by the practice called Asana and secure its ease and the regularity of its functions by Pranayama, a process of breathing. Thus no messages from the body will disturb the mind. Secondly, by Yama and Niyama, we still the emotions and passions, and thus prevent them arising to disturb the mind. Thirdly, by Pratyahara we analyse the mind yet more deeply and begin to control and suppress thought in general of whatever nature. Fourthly, we suppress all other thoughts by a direct concentration upon a single thought. This process, which leads to the highest results, Dharana, Dhyana and Samadhi, grouped under the single term, Samyana.'

'I'm sorry,' I said, 'these technical terms baffle me and I haven't the faintest idea of what on earth you are talking about.'

'My apologies also,' Crowley responded. 'Yama means DO and Niyama means DON'T. It's a simple code of behaviour which leads to self-respect and calms the mind, emotions and passions. Dharana is concentration, utterly one-pointed and single-minded; Dhyana is the trance of stillness in contemplation; Samadhi is when you unite totally with the object of your contemplation. Samyana is the knack of putting all these three things together at once.'

'How's your progress?' I asked casually, almost as if he were practising P.T.

'Not too bad,' he replied; and promptly proceeded to sit on his hard, straight-backed chair for two hours without moving a muscle, his spine erect, his knees together and his hands laid upon them, rather like those statues of Egyptian gods that one sees in the British Museum. All endeavours to distract him, including speech, jokes and the public school trick of flicking paper pellets from an elastic band, proved to be futile. He was as immobile as a lump of finely-chiselled stone.

'That Maudesley fellow you mentioned is a fine chap,' he said after a while. 'He thinks that all problems of expanding consciousness and human evolution can be reduced to propositions of Cerebral Neurology, and he may well have something there. After all, what is Pranayama other than control by breath over the central nervous system?'

Crowley proceeded to demonstrate his point by breathing in and out via alternate nostrils and holding his breath on the climax of inhalations and exhalations, timing it all at fifteen seconds each by his stop-watch. I drank tea and watched his activities with no little fascination. I saw firstly, a peculiar kind of perspiration, that smelled very sweet. After an hour of this exercise, I discerned that his body had attained a notable rigidity of the muscles. There then occurred a most curious phenomenon. His body, whilst still absolutely rigid, was taking little hops in various directions without the slightest sign of perceptible conscious effort. It seemed as if he were somehow raised, possibly an inch from the ground, and deposited very gently a short distance away. Yet he did not seem to be at all conscious of the fact.

'Just jumping about like a frog, Horby,' he told me when he came out of his trance. 'That's what the yogis call it. Oh!' he exclaimed as he relaxed, sighed and lit his curved, briar pipe. 'Yoga, properly understood, is a simple psychological method of attaining a definite psychological state.'

'So is sex,' I replied.

'Possibly so but I wouldn't know,' he responded, 'since I haven't had any sex in three months. Never thought I'd be celibate but there we are. Had any good fucking, Horby?'

'Yes,' I responded. 'Gladys and Victoria.' I explained to Crowley how I had witnessed an exquisite spanking and enjoyed a good seduction of the mother. 'My money and position persuaded them to get off that dreadful boat and join me for a weekend in Colombo, and I paid for the next stage of their journey. Ah! how rich, how soft, how peaceful is Colombo, "the place where four winds meet," the crossroads of the civilized world. The palms, the flowers, the swooning song of the surf, the dim and delicate atmosphere heavy with sensuous scents, the idle, irresponsible people purring with placid pleasures . . .' Crowley nodded his benign agreement. 'Anyway, in the best suite of the best hotel, Mrs Gladys and Miss Victoria were true to their appointment. Mrs Tracey had decided, after all, to accept my handsome but discreet offer for her daughter's virgin cunt even though no marital commitment accompanied the purse of sovereigns that changed hands. (How could it?) As Gladys drank some good Bollinger, Victoria and I sat down on a quiet seat for a few moments and enjoyed some kissing and groping. The bed was prepared.

'I found the amorous Victoria so difficult to enter on account of the narrowness of her passage,' I continued, 'that she had to bite her lips in suppressed agony from the pain of my attempt. But courage effects everything and she was so determined to be rammed at last that I found myself most deliciously fixed in the tightest quim I had ever entered. It was simply most voluptuous and the pressures of this girl's sheath upon my delighted instrument made me come in a moment or two. Then, the lubricant applied, things went easier; and a most luscious combat ensued.

'Victoria was perfectly beside herself with erotic passion whilst her mother Gladys, instead of standing on guard, lasciviously handled my shaft and appendages in her soft hand, until the excitement was more than I could bear, making me actually shout with pleasure at the moment of orgasm. Mother and daughter repeated the game without interruption and Victoria had me place the head of John Thomas just between the lips of her pussy.

'After spending an hour or so upon this slow and delectable amusement, we all agreed to dress and visit the City Park.

'Say what you like about the British Raj – and who doesn't eh, Crowley? But from what I witnessed, it's hardly sexually repressive. There were so many unblushing games going on. Our soldiers were rogering young girls, old fellows were fumbling servant girls and there was no end of the most unblushing indecency on every side. Why, it could have been the Green Park in London! Remember that? If couples could only get into the Green Park before the gates closed at ten p.m., they might stop there all night, or could at any time go out by the turnstile at the end of Constitution Hill into Grosvenor Place.' We smiled fondly at the memory. 'The one or two bobbies who patrolled the park seemed to take no notice, or were easily squared by the girls who used the place for business.

'This stout old British tradition is maintained, I'm glad to say, in Colombo. In fact, I saw one stalwart officer of the peace doing a glorious grind on the grass until a Guardsman came up and, slapping his naked rump as hard as he could, told him jovially to set a better example, which caused great fun to several who were looking on, especially when the soldier challenged the policeman for half-a-crown to exhibit his civilian prick against his military one for the amount he had paid, the girl to be the judge. The policeman evidently decided that discretion was the better part of valour.

'These sights produced an extraordinary effect upon young Miss Victoria Tracey, y'know, Crowley. On our return to my hotel, we all separated temporarily for our ablutions, but I know what she told me subsequently. "The hand of my mother refreshed with care all the parts which had been so well worked earlier by you, Horby. All at once I saw her stop still, then a finger fixed upon a little eminence which showed itself prominently; this finger rubbed lightly at first, then with a kind of fury. At length she gave the same symptoms of pleasure which I had so often seen before. I understood it all now! My head was on fire, my bosom palpitated, and my steps tottered, but I was determined at once to play by myself the last act I had seen and which required no partner." '

'You have,' Crowley commented, 'a remarkable memory for a young lady's words.'

'Certainly,' I returned. 'They are so remarkable that they are etched upon my mind. (1925: Unforgettably so; Victoria bore me an illegitimate child in consequence of which she has enjoyed rich pickings from me ever since, precisely as her mother Gladys had accurately forecast and for which the scheming bitch had plotted.) But to continue with her words: "I arrived in my room in a state of madness, threw my hat on the floor, shut and double-locked the door to my hotel bedroom and collapsed upon the bed. I turned up my clothes to the end, recollecting in the minutest details what Gladys – my mother, my self – had done, and as she had done with her hand, so I placed mine between my legs. Some essays were at first fruitless but I found at length the point for which I searched. The rest was easy: a delicious sensation seized me. I continued with fury and soon fell into such an ecstasy that I lost consciousness. When I came to myself, I was in the same position, my hand all moistened by an unknown dew." '

'And . . .?' Crowley queried, adding: 'That's rather sweet.'

'Well, when Victoria and Gladys re-entered my chamber, I lost no time in kissing that young girl's two pure globes as she reclined backwards, shuddering beneath the caresses that seemingly caused her to shiver in every vein. Profiting from this movement, I toyed for a moment with her lovely, silky pubic hairs. Then, slightly opening the nook they were hiding, I let my finger slip upwards a little to renew the playful friction which had caused us such enjoyment. I also displayed my splendid member and neither mother nor daughter could take their eager eyes away from this sight. Victoria opened her thighs once more and therefore stretched her slit, which did not appear longer than my little finger. *How is it possible?* I asked myself, that an instrument of my size can penetrate entirely into such a little place? Yet she received this great machine with gladness and for a while we continued with a silent and joyous clicketing.

' "Ah!" she shrieked suddenly. "My darling! . . . go on . . . Ah! I am so happy! . . . How lovely you are, Horby . . . Oh! how I shall spend! . . . It's coming now! . . . Do it a little longer! . . . Ah! I die . . ." There was a long and silent pause while Victoria seemed to be quite overcome; her beautiful form thrown back, her head hidden upon my shoulder, her glorious thighs still wide apart. I gazed at her intently, ravished at the sight.'

'Great stuff!' Crowley exclaimed with a chuckle. 'And did you fuck the mother once again for good measure?'

'Yes, she was a good fuck and I'm just coming to that.'

'In a moment,' my host returned. 'As you know, I'm sharing this bungalow with Allan Bennett who is presently my guru in Yoga. Presently, he's meditating, as usual, and it's my duty to bring him his food. Incidentally, it is very rare to encounter Europeans who can sit in the attitude called Padmasana, which is that usually seen in seated images of the Buddha. Yet Allan can do it. He can knot his legs so well that, putting his hands on the ground, he can swing his body to and fro in the air between them. Anyway, enough of that; I've made him a good salad of okra. Let's go and see how he is.'

I can only record what I saw. Earlier, I had seen Crowley 'jumping about like a frog', contrary to all known Laws of Physics. When we looked into Allan Bennett's room, we found him, not seated on his meditation mat, which was in the centre of the room at the end farthest from the window, but in a distant corner ten or twelve feet off, still in his knotted position, resting on his head and right shoulder, exactly like an image overturned. Crowley set him right way up and he came out of his trance. He was quite unconscious of the fact that anything unusual might have happened. But he had evidently been thrown there by the mysterious forces generated by Pranayama.

The rain poured down outside.

CHAPTER SEVENTEEN

There was a young man who said: "God
Must find it exceedingly odd,
If he finds that this tree
Continues to be
When there's no one around in the Quad."

'Heigh ho!' said Crowley. 'And here we have the Hindus saying exactly the same thing as Bishop Berkeley in Western Philosophy, which is that something can exist only if someone perceives it.' He smiled genially over his tea and tobacco at an impassive Allan Bennett and myself. 'But of course, gentlemen, there is an answer:

"Dear Sir: your argument's odd.
I am always about in the Quad.
And that's why this tree
Will continue to be,
Since observed by Yours truly, GOD."

'What if there is no *I* and no GOD?' Allan Bennett enquired. Allan looked so much healthier since when I had last seen his asthma-attacked and drug-ravaged body in London. I supposed that he owed his continuing life either to Crowley's Ceremonial Magic or else to the money freely given by a Crowley mistress, arguably

Davina Price-Hughes, now Davina Bellingham. Crowley responded with:

Let me die in a ditch
Damnably drunk
Or lipping a punk
Or in bed with a bitch.
I was ever a whore.
Dung? I am one with it.
Let me die in a ditch . . .
Die and be done with it!

'Well, that's no good, is it?' said Allan Bennett. 'You'll only come back to reincarnate on the Wheel of Suffering and Illusion. Fancy a walk in the jungle?' His lean body hauled itself to its feet as we nodded assent, arose and followed his sandaled feet, their bareness oblivious to the thorns that tore at his bare flesh. I had no idea at the time that this was the man who, as Bikku Ananda Metteya, would bring Buddhism in its purest Theravada/Hinayana form to Great Britain. However, I shall never forget the moment that I saw a krait in the grass.

This snake was lying just beside the sandy road. I had been warned by Douglas about the krait. It is, in terms of poison, the deadliest snake in the world. It is not a case of once bitten, twice shy; no, you can die in agony within an hour. Crowley spotted that snake too and promptly drew his Webley revolver, only to have his arm stayed by Bennett.

'No, Brother,' he said. 'I know that you are skilful enough to shoot the snake's head away, even at this distance, but kindly allow me to deal with this matter in my own way.' With that said, this intriguing man walked up to the krait, stared it in the eyes and said: 'Little krait, it is not good to bite the innocent and kill them. But let me tell you all about Buddhism and of how we can all evolve and improve . . .' The serpent, so deadly, turned tail and slithered away.

As we entered the jungle, Allan Bennett motioned Crowley to put aside the machete he had drawn for the appropriate purpose of chopping a passable walkway through the dense and lush vegetation. Allan Bennett led the way through a writhing and weaving of his lean, lithe body, declining to harm even so much as a stick of forest life. Three times Crowley drew his revolver and on each occasion, he was right, for even my inexperienced eyes discerned dangerous animals: a tiger, a panther and a buffalo. Each time Bennett brushed away his gun, then snaked forward through the undergrowth to face the deadly danger. He was so far ahead of us at times that I cannot swear to what I saw, so swift were his movements; and in subsequent conversation, neither of us felt that we could swear to the matter either: but both of us *thought* we saw, through the curious quarter-light of the jungle, Allan Bennett joyfully hugging a tiger. It was only a glimpse and then the image was gone.

'Can you believe,' Crowley asked me on our ten-mile march from the jungle along the dirt track which led to his bungalow, 'that this man,' he indicated Bennett who was this time walking peaceably behind us, '*terrified* all occult circles in London with his blasting rod?' Was Bennett laughing behind me? 'Yes, Allan used to carry a *lustre* – a long glass prism with a long neck and a pointed knob such as adorns old-fashioned chandeliers. He used this as a wand. One day, a party of theosophists – you know, the sort of wets who think there's some sort of "new age" coming, but even if there is, they simply cannot face its implications – anyway, they were chatting sceptically about the power of the "blasting rod". Allan promptly produced his and blasted one of them. It took fourteen hours to restore the incredulous individual to the use of his muscles.'

'He seems to have mellowed,' I commented to Crowley.

'Yes and no,' Crowley replied. 'Remember the Golden Dawn?' I nodded. 'Personally, I find it very easy to adapt to Hinduism, since their deities equate with the Egyptian ones we worshipped in the Golden Dawn. Yet there is one thing I find to be very odd about Mathers. I had honestly thought that whatever his faults might be, he was Head of the Rosicrucians and my principal link with the Gods. Then I heard a disturbing story and Allan has confirmed its truth.'

'Oh . . .?' I murmured.

'Yes, indeed, "O!" If I may resume my tale?' Crowley returned. 'One trusts that you are familiar with the Gods who are the prime manifestation of the Infinite Brahman, which in itself is All and Nothing: Brahma the Creator; Vishnu the Preserver; Shiva the Destroyer. Now, back in the London days, Allan became a particular devotee of Shiva. Bennett said to Mathers of Shiva: "If one repeats His name often enough, He will open His eye and destroy the Universe." Mathers disagreed. The thought that his life should depend on Shiva keeping his Third Eye shut was too much for him. Allan retorted by assuming his Padmasana yoga posture and repeating the mantra: *Shiva*, *Shiva*, *Shiva*, *Shiva*, *Shiva*, *Shiva*, *Shiva*, *Shiva* . . . "Will you stop blaspheming?!" roared Mathers, worked into a rage by this quiet man sitting there and chanting: *Shiva*, *Shiva*, *Shiva*, *Shiva*, *Shiva*, *Shiva*, *Shiva*, *Shiva* . . . and let's face it, Horby, Shiva is the Great God of the Mysteries of Sex and Death.

'Well, Horby, Mathers produced a revolver and yelled:

"If you don't stop, I'll shoot you!" But Allan, totally concentrated, took no notice and merely carried on chanting: *Shiva*. Wonderful, isn't it? The man who claims to be our link with the Secret Chiefs is terrified and infuriated simultaneously by the chanting of the name of a Great God. He *wanted* to pull the trigger on Allan: what a disappointment and disgrace! Fortunately, before Mathers could cock back the hammer, Moina Mathers entered the room and may possibly have saved Allan's life . . . not that he cares.'

On our arrival back at the bungalow, we found a rain-soaked messenger with a letter for me; for I had used telegrams and my paid staff to facilitate communications wherever I ventured upon the globe.

'So what's this, then, Horby?' Bennett chuckled pleasantly. I chuckled back and proceeded to read out Rosemary's letter, written in Alberta, Canada:

'My darling,

'Finally I have arrived in Calgary. It is so cold. The weather is so fierce, brumal and hiemal. A continuous wind blows across the prairies and I am now suffering from chilblains. How my hands and feet do itch!

'Yesterday there was a chinook, *which is a warm, dry wind that blows east of the Rocky Mountains, raising the temperature suddenly as much as 50 degrees Fahrenheit within a couple of hours and it can evaporate a snowfall of several feet within a day. This can make the most sane person suffer from* non compos mentis, *quite deprived of one's wits; and can lead even to hysterical and psychotic behaviour.*

'This town is so strange and is completely different from the East Coast of Canada. It is so good to see my Great Aunt Catherine again, however eccentric she might

be. Her father was one of the early Scottish settlers out here and when he died, he left his property to her: the old homestead; a large cattle ranch not too far from Calgary. The reason that he chose to settle here is that it had the attraction, allurement and (to him) charm of the moors and lowlands of Scotland.

'Upon her arrival, Great Aunt had found the life harsh and she had felt lonely and isolated. A number of beaux had courted her in London but only my Great Uncle had attracted her. A new life in the New World, after the death of her first husband, had appealed to her. Initially, she had gone with a gold prospector, who promised her life-long riches. This nuptial bond did not last long and before the promised gold came, he was killed in a gunfight. She married again: Tom is my step-Great Uncle.

'It appeared to me that her life was a series of ingerminate occurrences in continuously repeated sequence. However, I hope that this will not happen to me. She told me of how difficult life was, especially for the early homesteaders. They had to plant crops and she told me of the blazing sun and the devastating grass fires and of how the land had to be cleared, restored and ploughed using horses and oxen. Mind you, as she told me when the Donkhobors settled here, they hitched women to their ploughs in order to till the land.

'It appears that Great Aunt does love her third husband, Tom, the cattle baron, though they have to spend much of the year apart from one another. Tom does amuse me. When I arrived, he tipped his hat, bowed slightly and clicked his heels.

' "Good afternoon, Ma'am," he said with the greatest politeness when he met me at the railway station. He has such bandy legs! He also has a six-gun in his holster and

I imagine that he is fully capable of using it well. And even though he doesn't have to do it these days, he seems to enjoy spending many hours of the day in the saddle.

'Great Aunt Catherine has married well. I was amused to see her applying wax to his moustache. I enjoyed our first evening together, for the meal included venison and marinated and tenderised buffalo meat. Around the dinner table, with the log fire blazing upon the hearth, I was told wild and wonderful stories about Tom's son John.

' "He sounds rather fascinating," I remarked. "I hope that I may experience the joy of his company at some future occasion."

' "Unfortunately," Tom replied, "he's kind of a – uh – kind of what an educated lady like you would call – uh – yeah – a 'dilettante'; and I figure that he does not take life too seriously."

"Where is he?" I asked.

' "In some bar," Tom sighed, "probably brawling or else trying to engage the attentions of some beautiful young woman, even if she has committed herself to another. He likes to flirt, bill and coo; even poodlefake."

'Suddenly the door burst open and in entered one of the most attractive men that I have ever seen. He just stormed *in.*

' "Do not call me licentious!" he yelled. "Anybody round here been calling me licentious?" At that moment, Great Aunt and her husband decided to retire to their bedroom. "Glad they've retired for the evening," he said as he pulled out a cigar. "What does this remind you of?"

' "A cigar," I replied.

' "Yes, my dear," he returned, 'it is indeed a cylindrical object with a pointed end and yet let me tell you,

before the evening is over, you will see and experience an even larger cylindrical object." He gazed momentarily and reflectively at the six-gun in his holster. "I have a trunk, bole, column . . . that has satisfied too many women." What insolence! *I thought. "Do you know what a Calgary Red Eye is?" he demanded.*

' "No, not really."

' "Then let me make you one." He proceeded to mix a concoction of beer and tomato juice, a drink that I have never experienced before. What a brew! and it's such an erotic stimulant! The juices were soon stirring within my cunt and I could feel that my silken knickers were wet. He was a man of bravado, boldness, and bellicosity, a braggart and a swaggart. "I am a warrior and I can tame anything and anyone, including you," he boasted. It appeared to me that this was an angry young man with a giant ego and an even larger erection. It was so obvious that between the two of us, the lust of carnal knowledge had been aroused.

'Instinctively, we both decided to remove our clothes together in front of the fireplace, that burning inglenook. Then he stood before me wearing bright red combinations; my cowboy, cowpuncher, bronco-buster and gaucho! I opened the buttons and took his firm rod into my mouth. He penetrated so deeply within my throat that my murmurs went from: "Oh, that's lovely," to "Ohugghhrrr!" Then he shot his juices in: and how saline they were! Brackish and salsuginous.

'Then, gazing upon my exposed breasts, he kissed my nipples lovingly and there was such a throbbing within my inner thighs. My vagina was aching for a penetration. He kissed each nipple so gently; and then suddenly he stopped.

' "Please carry on," I requested.

' "You have a third nipple here." He pointed out my extra mamilla. As you know, Horby, it looks like a rather enlarged freckle.

' "Yes . . ." I sighed, "I am well aware of this."

' "You are a witch . . . an enchantress . . ." he gasped as I took his throbbing penis into my cool and delicate hands.

' "Occasionally, I have some powers of perception," I murmured; and then he was upon me in a riotous act of coitus, copulation and capitulation. The resulting heat of our fuck, yes, the tornado we engendered, was greater even than that of the chinook.

'I must close now, my darling. I miss and love you so much.

Rosemary.'

Bennett was silent and smiling.

'Introduce me,' said Crowley.

'Slam! Bam! Thank you, Ma'am!' I said. 'That's Canada.'

CHAPTER EIGHTEEN

'Ah! The Romance of Lust!' Crowley declared heartily. 'And I haven't enjoyed it in what seems like ages.' He sipped more tea. 'Did you find Colombo to be as good for that as I did, Horby?'

'Yes, I did,' I replied, 'for in one brothel I saw something most erotic.' Crowley sat up attentively and Bennett looked quietly indifferent. 'I saw two slim young women, Pabloo and Naznin, lying upon a bed together. "I must have it all!" Pabloo cried out as she writhed naked upon the bed, twitching her slender buttocks this way and that. "I want it all!" she shrieked. "Come, I am on fire. I burn, Naznin, so quick, you must flood me with your bounteous liquor."

'Naznin threw off her dressing-gown,' I continued, 'and stretched herself beside Pabloo upon the bed. How beautiful she was, built like a slender Athena to her partner's Aphrodite: or perhaps I should speak of Shiva's consort, Parvati and of Lakshmi, the consort of Vishnu. Anyway, don't you find that one of the greatest mysteries of Womanhood is the clitoris? I could see that proud instrument of Naznin stiffly growing out of a wide slit and thick bush that showed it off splendidly.

'Pabloo was lying on her back, her legs parted and lifted a little. Naznin got on her knees between her thighs, and their naked forms were exposed to my gaze. For an instant, Pabloo turned her backside to her lover in a flirtatious gesture, then Naznin turned her back over and stretched herself upon her. Pabloo lifted her legs and crossed them upon Naznin's back, in such a manner that no detail escaped my vision. I could distinctly see Naznin's fingers capture Pabloo's clitoris, directing a forefinger to the centre of the little slit that opened to receive it. Naznin gave her partner a vigorous rubbing of her pudenda and Pabloo sighed lazily, jerking her hips upwards with an energetic stroke of the loins. Naznin answered her by the insertion of her forefinger into the little hole, which dilated and began to engulf it. A few more movements completed the insertion, and I saw their two growths of pubic hair mingled together. Now there was nothing but movements, sighs, inarticulate words and maddening shivers.

' "Let me have it all . . . Pabloo sighed: "Ah! How fine your clitty is . . . Go gently . . . let us spend slowly . . . hold me tight!"

' "My sweet darling," Naznin sighed back, "Lift up your thighs, so that we can be right in . . . There! Do you feel it? Ah! how delightful!"

' "I die . . .!" Pabloo squealed. "Are you ready? . . . My Naznin! I'm going to spend . . . I . . . I . . . make haste!"

' "I'm ready . . . It's coming . . . There it comes.. spend now . . ." Naznin murmured: ' "I'm spending . . . Ah! . . . I've come! Oh . . ."

'Both remained quiet for a moment. Pabloo remained longer without giving signs of life but she got up at last and after smothering Naznin with kisses, went for an instant to the lavatory. I thought that it was all over and began to arrange my retreat, but a secret presentiment made me stop. Pabloo re-entered, went to the bed again, embraced her lover in her arms and then they engaged in sweet conversation.

' "I have been so happy, dear!" Pabloo exclaimed. "It is so much better when we are at our ease and you do it so well."

' "My darling," Naznin responded, "there is not a more perfect woman than you in the whole world . . . and I want to eat you up bodily!"

And once more, tickling the breasts of Pabloo, Naznin covered with kisses the whole of her beautiful body that trembled beneath her caresses; and when she arrived at the centre of bliss, she opened it, bit it gently and kissed it passionately.

' "Stop, dear!' Pabloo cried out. "Stop! You will fatigue yourself. Rest, rest!"

' "No, darling, look!" Naznin waggled her pretty pink tongue at Pabloo. "See, she once more asks permission to go into her little companion. You won't refuse her?"

' "Let me see, my dear. So your tongue continues in its exquisite state, Naznin? Well, well, I'll let you put it in the prison of my cunt once more in good time. There, place yourself like that and don't move!"

' "What you are going to do?" Naznin demanded.

' "You know, dear, how I like a change." Pabloo picked up a thick, white dildo from beneath the mattress and brandished this erect phallus in the air. She promptly proceeded to plunge it into Naznin, up to the hilt, then she moved it gently in and out. Naznin was fairly spitted by this enormous spindle. Pabloo teased her, blew her kisses and showed Naznin her adorable titties, smiling and pouting at her all the time. ' "'Tis *I* who have *you* now," she said, "You are my little wife. See how well I do it!"

'After a few instants of this dalliance, it was easy to see that the supreme moment was being reached. Pabloo fell upon Naznin, who received her in her arms and pressed her lover's flesh to her own, as Pabloo took hold of the olive cheeks of Naznin's shapely bottom. Pleasure mounted to an ecstasy which seized them together: then Naznin left Pabloo's embrace and lazily stretched herself out at her lover's side. This was not enough for Pabloo.

' "My bosom is panting!" she cried out. "An active fire is coursing through my veins." She alternately touched each of Naznin's breasts; and the nipples swelled up. Feeling her partner's body, Pabloo reached her exquisitely delicate spot and rummaged there with great curiosity. It seemed to me as an observer that a slight change had taken place. The lips of the little nook were plumper; and Pabloo was singing. "I seek the place that is greedily swallowing this monstrous dildo!" she cried out as Naznin gasped with pleasure. "There is a little spot here which this tool cannot touch without admixture of pleasure and pain," she cooed, pushing up the dildo a little and then rubbing it in.

' "Ah!" Naznin ejaculated. "An indescribable sensation invades my entire being." Pabloo used the dildo to rub softly first, then quicker, afterwards slower, then again with more vigour as Naznin shrieked: 'I spend! . . . Ah! I come . . . I come . . . Ah!"

'At length, a nervous spasm overtook her. I felt transported with an immense pleasure which I only fully appreciate now. I wasn't expecting Pabloo to place a big cushion in front of the wardrobe and to kneel upon it, her head and arms much lower than her ravishing buttocks, which, thrown out and developed by this magnificent position, presented the path of pleasure well in view and largely open.

'Naznin placed herself behind her, commencing to stroke Pabloo with her slender fingers.

‘ “Oh, you can see too much of me!” said Pabloo.

‘ “How can I see too much of such beauty? Look in the glass!”

‘ “Oh, no; it’s too bad! . . . Ah!” Pabloo gasped as she stared into the mirror before them. “You’ve taken my bloody dildo, you bitch! . . . It’s going into me! Stop a little . . . Ah! What a fine girl you are!”

‘ “My adored one, how lovely you are!” Naznin retorted as she toyed with the dildo and her lover writhed. “What admirable hips! What an adorable – ARSE!”

‘ “Oh, Naznin!” Pabloo sighed. “What is that naughty word?”

‘ “Don’t be frightened, darling,” Naznin cooed back. “Lovers can say anything. These words, out of place in colder moments, add fresh relish to the sweet mystery of love. You will soon say them too and understand their charm.” Whilst she spoke, she continued with her delicate movements. Pabloo, in silent enjoyment, said naught, but devoured with eager eyes the lustful endeavours of Naznin. I was somewhat stupefied to hear her say a minute later:

‘ “Do you love it so very much?”

‘ “What!” Naznin exclaimed.

‘ “Why . . . my.”

‘ “You *what*?”

‘ “Well . . . my . . . arse!”

‘ “Ah, Pabloo, how sweet you are to me. Oh, yes; I love it. Your beautiful arse. I adore it!”

‘ “Feel it, then. It’s yours – yours alone” Pabloo cried out. ‘My arse . . . arse!! . . . arse!!!” ’ As she concluded her broken utterances, she let herself go until she reached the rapture of complete enjoyment. Naznin, who was herself rapidly arriving at the height of sovereign pleasure, reached the desired goal with her and fell upon her completely overcome.'

'A good time,' Bennett muttered.

'Allan,' I said, 'do I detect a slight trace of sarcasm in your attitude?'

'Yes,' he answered. 'Where does all this sex get us? It just further snares us in illusion.'

'Typical!' Crowley laughed.

'*Everything* is an illusion,' Bennett responded impassively. 'And it's no use committing suicide for you'll simply come back to face the same problems in your next incarnation. The Gods and Goddesses of Hinduism and the Golden Dawn, and their attractively erotic interaction, are an illusion too. Mathers is simply dancing well amidst these veils of illusion. And so are we unless we improve ourselves.' He smiled slightly. 'And the way to do that is Yoga. Hinduism is false in stating that there is a central "I" or *atman* which is the essence of *Brahman*, or God or the Supreme. Buddhists are right in declaring that there is no Self, that there is no God and that there is no "I". Is there the same water in the repeated waves which roll in upon a sea-shore? No. No. There is only the wheel of Existence, which is Suffering or Samsara: and there is Deliverance from Suffering, which is Nirvana.'

'And what is Nirvana?' I asked.

'Ultimate cessation of Existence,' Bennett answered.

'Wishing you a speedy termination of Existence, Horby,' Crowley chuckled. 'And it'll take you quite a while.'

'Thank you very much,' I replied. 'Your kind remarks are truly appreciated,' I added sarcastically, 'but I'm quite happy here and now, thanks again.' I accepted Crowley's offer of more tea. 'Though I'm most impressed by your astonishing feat of apparent levitation, Allan.'

'Another illusion,' he murmured dismissively.

'Yet there is no doubt whatsoever about this phenomenon,' said Crowley. 'It is quite common. But the yogis claim that the lateral motion is due to lack of balance and that if one were in perfect equilibrium, one would rise directly in the air. I have never seen any case of levitation and hesitate to say that it has happened to me, though I have actually been seen by others on several occasions apparently poised in the air. Unfortunately, I can form no theory as to how the practice of Pranayama could counteract the force of gravitation, which makes of one a sceptic. Yet, after all, the stars are suspended in space. There is no *a priori* reason why the forces which prevent them rushing together should not come into operation in respect of the earth and the body.' He lit his curved meerschaum pipe and I promptly detected the aroma of latakia and perique. 'You see, I had an extraordinary experience only the other day. I was practising Dharana and concentrating on the tip of my nose.

'Well,' Crowley continued animatedly, 'I obtained a clear understanding of the unreality of that nose. This persists. An hour later whilst breathing on my arm as I was asleep, I said to myself, "What is this hot breath from?" I was forced to *think* before I could answer "my nose". Then I pinched myself and remembered at once; but again breathing, the same thing happened again. Therefore the "Dharanization" of my nose dividualizes me and my nose, affects my nose, abolishes, annihilates and expunges my nose. What do you think, Horby?'

'I think you're talking incomprehensible shit,' I said. Crowley and Bennett burst out laughing.

'Probably,' Crowley retorted. 'I often do. It's impossible to put into words that which lies beyond them. If you don't believe me, suck it and see.'

'Still on for stricter measures?' Bennett asked Crowley, adding, 'despite the sceptical remarks of our friend here?'

'Definitely,' Crowley answered.

'Good,' said Allan Bennett. 'Oh, and by the way, I've brought you this as a present.' Whipping up his robe, he smilingly produced a dead five foot cobra. 'You trod right on its neck with your heel on your midnight stroll last night and never noticed it. You should be more careful in future. But never mind. Tomorrow, let's go for *it*. That means no more tea and no more tobacco.'

'You're stopping my baccy and my tea?!' Crowley cried out in mock-horror. 'No, no, not that! Anything but that!' Bennett just smiled and nodded.

'Anyway, if you gentlemen would kindly excuse me,' he said, 'I am off to bed.'

'With him that means two further hours of strict meditation,' Crowley commented.

'Ouch!' I suddenly shrieked. This was because some mosquitoes had battened onto my bare arms and were biting.

'Oh, those . . .' Bennett sighed wearily. 'You can prevent the things from biting you by certain breathing exercises. Hold the breath in such a way that the body becomes spasmodically rigid and insects cannot pierce the skin. Here, allow me to assist.' To my absolute stupefaction, Allan offered the veins on his wrists and the mosquitoes flitted from my arms to his. As he breathed, his body became rigid. My vision blurred momentarily but when I looked again, the dratted insects were gone.

'It's one of his favourite party tricks,' Crowley observed. 'There's a pool near here and we often put our hands together into the water. His always comes out free and mine has a dozen leeches on it. Well, Allan, a coyote will not eat a dead Mexican.' Bennett remained impassive. 'You see?' Crowley demanded. 'Even I can't annoy him.' His discourse was interrupted by the whining of new mosquitoes in the room.

'I wouldn't worry about them too much, Horby,' Bennett said. 'Simply love them and invite them to make a feast out of your body and blood, wishing them well all the while. The first night is hell, I assure you; but after that, they leave you alone.'

'I can vouch for that.' Crowley concurred. So can I: after one night of absolute hell. Yet mosquitoes have left me alone ever since that ghastly night of absolute torture.

'So it's no sex for you, eh, Crowley?' I jested after Allan Bennett had gone to bed. 'Most unusual.'

'That's Yoga,' he replied. 'I'm racing for results like an athlete and I don't want any impedimentia. Let's just say that I'm Off Games for the time being. Sure you don't want to join me in this honourable quest for superconsciousness?'

'Thanks but no thanks,' I responded. 'I think I prefer sex.'

CHAPTER NINETEEN

For about a month, I wallowed in the flesh-pots of Colombo, Ceylon, finding life to be lazy and pleasant, with many sensual diversions. I felt like one of Tennyson's '*The Lotus Eaters*'. In common with the people of his poem, I could not summon up the energy to tear myself away and press on with my design to visit India.

Now, I have often found that in life, it is always a case of 'either too much or too little'. There was a place of refreshment I used to attend regularly called simply Parvati, the name of the consort of Shiva. Here they served excellent cocktails in the bar, superlative curries in the restaurant, opium of the finest quality upstairs and, on the top floor, there were some of the island's most exquisite whores. I walked in one mid-day, expecting it to be just the same as every other day only to find an horribly familiar figure declaiming his verses to a group of polite but puzzled Indians. Yes: it was that deplorable poet, Wilfred Sedgewick.

Each perfectly see it is so
And yet the fool to logic go.
He only taking in as sent
Away will reason increment.
Not faith but knowledge would lead man
Did he himself but see as can.

'There's the true gold!' roared a familiar voice. 'Until the very last word you think it's going to mean something; and then – smash!'

'Bellingham!' I bellowed. 'What the devil are you doing here, old chap?!'

'Suffering same as the natives, Horby,' he replied, and we greeted one another warmly. I also greeted Sedgewick, for after all and no matter what our quarrels, Englishmen abroad must jolly well stick together. I was genuinely pleased to encounter Sir Richard.

'But what are you really doing here, Bellingham? I thought you were on honeymoon.'

'I *am* on honeymoon,' he returned indignantly. 'It's just that Davina takes all day to decide which outfit to wear for the evening and a man needs a drink and some company.'

'And how about you, Sedgewick?'

'I,' he responded primly, 'have a position here with the Colonial Service,' after which he preened his waxed, handlebar moustache.

'Oh,' said Bellingham, 'so *that's* why the natives listen to you.'

'Bellingham,' said Sedgewick, 'you have no ear for poetry.' He proceeded to order three absolutely delicious drinks, served in halves of scooped-out pineapple and consisting mainly of strong spirits and coconut milk: rather more pleasing than his verses. 'And anyway, you've only just arrived here and so you don't know the ropes. They respect my poetry here. Why, only the other day, I wanted the best table and at first the Head Waiter was most disobliging, but when I told him who I *was*, then naturally, I had a table at once.'

'And who *were* you?' Bellingham yawned.

'What do you know about life out here?' Sedgewick

sneered. 'Javed!' he shouted at the slim, dark barman. 'Do you know who I am?'

'No, sir,' came the reply, 'but I can find out for you.'

'Oh, just give us a bloody table, Mr Javed,' said Sir Richard; and we were promptly escorted politely to the best that the restaurant had to offer. The resulting meal was excellent and confirmed my view that Indian cuisine can be superb. There was a mixed grill of chicken, lamb chops and sausage in the North Indian *tandoori* style; then a prawn *biryani* in the South Indian style, accompanied by a delicious porridge of lentils with garlic which they call *tarka dhall*; there was a delectable dish of lambs' brains so hot that it made Sedgewick choke, so that he had to be brought the cooling fruit of the mango; nor shall I forget the exquisite lamb with spinach, which I believe they call *Sag gosht*. We drank plenty of good, strong beer with it too.

'Nothing like this sort of stuff,' Bellingham chortled as he spooned copious quantities of mango chutney and *raita*, yoghourt with onion and cucumber, onto the brains of the lamb. 'Oh, and Mr Javed, could I have some more of those little green chillies, please?' Mr Javed gaped at him with open-mouthed astonishment and turned so pale, I swear, that in that instant, he could have passed muster as an Englishman.

'You want, sir . . .' he faltered, '*more* green chillies . . .?'

'Well, obviously,' Bellingham returned briskly, 'since I've eaten them all. Why else should I be wanting 'em, for heaven's sake?' He quaffed more beer. 'Some people just don't see the obvious. Ah! Jolly good!' he exclaimed when the plate of chillies arrived and he proceeded to offer them around the table. Sedgewick coughed and declined; I took two which burned my mouth and throat but which otherwise caused a pleasurable sensation; and in his typical fashion, Bellingham greedily scoffed the rest and called loudly for more beer, then wiped away copious quantities of curry sweat from his brow. 'Good place, Colombo. Delicious food. Mind you, it's full of perverts. Why, there's one part of this town that's just packed jam-full of men in womens' clothing and blatant homosexualists. I mean, if you drop a rupee, you have to kick it for ten streets before you bend down to pick it up. Mind you, that doesn't worry me, chaps. I always wear a pair of stout English trousers!'

'Can we get away from these sordid matters and return to the sublime?' Sedgewick demanded.

'Oh, very well, if we must,' returned Bellingham. 'Yet more poetry, is there? I shall eat and suffer in silence.'

Sedgewick proceeded to declaim:

Ere was condition manifest,
The unconditioned was at rest.

'Yes, certainly,' I concurred. 'That I did know before.'

Relations of rest with unrest
Hence did conditions manifest.

'Um. Seems to skate over the difficulty a little,' said Bellingham. 'But go on.'

To such relation specify
We use the word velocity.

'Do we?' I queried.

Velocity sole history
Of uncondition's mystery.

'But this is only the Introduction,' said Bellingham. 'This is all mere mashie chips on the green. Let's see what he can do with a wooden club, this plus-four Wilfred Sedgewick.'

While man trains up the child in way men go,
It goes without saying that man's way
In life convention only will display.
As each one by himself can surely know;
Hence may these notes that light of rush-light throw
Where glares so-called, civilization's day.
Without night's darkness chasing once away,
Perchance as simple truth for some one glow.

'Yes . . .' Bellingham nodded cautiously. 'I think I would almost swear what these lines mean to my knowledge. Education leads to conventionality, lines 1-4, therefore these notes may glow as simple truth for some one. I'm afraid that:

Each perfectly see it is so
And yet the fool to logic go

is one on me. But all speculations are futile. Carry on, Sedgewick.'

If seen the curse, if be a curse, on man
Is taxing self to understand, amid
Environment that ever keeps its place,
What shape may take his life, if any can,
That haunting foolishness not bid
Him to endure, with pain, but for disgrace.

'Where's your subject now?' I burst out indignantly. 'Where's your principal sentence? Where's any vestige of connection with anything? I cannot imagine in my wildest moments any nexus with the last three lines of the sestet. I cannot see the merest germ of an apodosis for that majestic protasis.'

'Horby, you're just an ignorant, aristocratic, philistine,' Sedgewick retorted acidly.

'I personally find more poetry in the letter I recently received from young Miss Emily Ward-Bishop,' said Sir Richard, handing an envelope over to me. 'She asked me to pass on this enclosure whenever we met. I was happy with my letter. Go on, Horby, why don't you read yours out to us?'

'Very well.' I ripped open the envelope, read through the contents quickly and proceeded to read them aloud.

'My darling Horby,

'One trusts that you are well but what with all this gallivanting all over the globe that you're currently doing, I thought it best to entrust my missive to Bellingham. Many thanks for your telegrams: but do *let me know where your next port of call will be, otherwise I shall be sorely tempted on your return to these shores to take you by the ear to the Reform Academy of Mrs Joan Smythe, thence to be subjugated to Petticoat Government.*

'The place is so popular at the present time. Mothers of the country's most distinguished families are eager to enrol their sons and daughters; and I have recently taken employment there as a teacher of French and an Assistant Housemistress. As part of my apprenticeship, Joan Smythe invited me to witness her lesson in Biology.

'I entered the classroom to see ten girls sitting up attentively and expectantly: one could breathe in the

heady perfume of wet knickers and female excitement. Lady Jane and Lady Alison, who are Governesses of the School and Official Visitors, had taken up their places in armchairs to the left and the right of the blackboard. A bell rang: and the Headmistress entered, wheeling a push-chair. There was a young man manacled to this push-chair whose name was Clarence and I must say that I was pleased to see him chained as he was since he had behaved rather badly during my French classes and I had duly complained to the Headmistress.

'I also sensed that Clarence had behaved badly to the girls, to judge by their behaviour. They arose promptly and obediently upon the entrance of Mrs Smythe, curtsied submissively, then, on received permission, sat down with a fluttering of skirts and a rustling of petticoats as they smiled wickedly at young Clarence and then exchanged glances of glee. Clarence had been forced to wear a frilly white blouse with a pink bow tie, a pink, knee-length pleated skirt with flouncy white petticoats, white silken stockings and shiny, black, high-heeled court shoes. His face was blushing a perfect crimson with the shame of his public humiliation. Alison and Jane took the push-chair from Joan and wheeled it into a corner, so that he faced the wall during the first part of the Biology lecture and a yellow dunce's cap was placed upon his head by Alison in order to emphasise his disgrace.

'Mrs Smythe then gave the girls a straightforward account of human reproduction with diagrams, explaining precisely what occurs in the process of generation between the male and the female. She gave wise advice on matters of contraception before proceeding to sketch expertly an immaculate diagram of the vagina, etched lovingly in glistening wax crayons. She pointed out the

clitoris and stressed its importance when it came to female pleasure.

' "There is also another spot within you which can lead to ecstasy, gels," she continued evenly, "but this can only be found by yourselves through trial and error, which is why I warmly recommend the practice of masturbation. As you should know by now, practice makes perfect. Once you have located it, you must train the male you capture to titillate it at all times." Skirts swished and petticoats crackled with excited approval among her audience. "However," she continued, "there is no denial of the fact that a stiff, thick, hot male penis within the vagina gives the greatest of pleasure to ladies."

'At this point, she nodded to Jane and Alison, who promptly wheeled the scarlet-faced Clarence to the front of the class, whipped up his skirt and petticoats and pulled down his silken, white, knee-length knickers to expose a full-blooded and pulsating erection.

' "Now regard Clarence's tool closely," the Headmistress urged the girls, who were only too willing to obey her instructions. There were audible gasps at the size of this thick, monstrous dick and I noticed that a number of pupils had slipped their fingers up their skirts and were listening to the lesson in a dreamy and, alas, rather clearly dissolute sort of way. "Unfortunately, most males are brutes," Joan Smythe continued, "and their sole desire is to prod their rod into any female they can find. The secret that I am about to teach you is that you should never be frightened of the masculine sex organ. Rather, you should learn how to manipulate *it." At this instant, she touched the tip of Clarence's penis with her black, leather-clad, elbow-length-gloved hand and he sighed and shuddered.*

' "Now!" Mrs Smythe snapped, dipping her hand into

a black leather bag to emerge with thirteen exquisite peacock feathers. "I want you gels to see just how easy it can be to control the penis of the male; there really is no need to be frightened. Take a feather from this desk and proceed to stroke it. As you know, Clarence has been petticoated for sexual misbehaviour and disrespect to girlhood and womanhood. It is now your turn to have power over him."

'One by one, Anita, Cynthia, Diana, Elaine, Georgina, Harriet, Lola, Nina, Suzanna and Teresa took a peacock feather from the desk and proceeded to stroke the rampaging penis of the chained and bound young man, who shuddered and writhed in the grip of his torment of agony and ecstasy. His chair shot forwards, backwards and sideways as Joan laughed spitefully. When Alison, Jane and I tickled his organ simultaneously, he emitted a hoarse cry as his rod shot a jet of ripe spunk straight into the lap of my new, navy-blue, pleated, bell-shaped skirt – aimed perfectly at my cunt! Can you not imagine *my vociferous outrage?*

' "My apologies for the bad behaviour of Clarence," Mrs Smythe hastened to reassure me. "I'm afraid that he is wholly lacking in sexual manners. He thoroughly deserves a sound caning from you for this singular atrocity. And he shall endure your punishment tomorrow." The schoolgirls rubbed their thighs together with gladness and glee. "Clarence may be jolly good at rugger but he still does not have the faintest idea about how to conduct himself in the presence of young ladies."

'This might well have been the case for, to my astonishment, John Thomas began to rise again, throbbing in all his glistening and pristine glory. The young ladies were thrilled by this intriguing sight and so was I.

'Mrs Joan Smythe responded to it by producing a yellow ribbon about three yards long from her shining black-leather handbag; and she proceeded to knot it in a bow around the rampant prick of Clarence. The ends of the ribbon she thence fixed to her own slender wrist. It took just one jerk and two twirls amidst the silk before the young man shot his seed again, this time straight into the pleated skirt of Anita.

' "Anita," said Joan. "Do you take this male to be your lawful, wedded husband?"

' "I do, Madam," she replied as Clarence sighed and sagged within the chains of his bondage.

' "So be it," the Headmistress declared, "and never forget the importance and effect of petticoat power." With that, she snapped her fingers, Alison and Jane wheeled Clarence away to bed, thence to contemplate my caning of his bottom on the morrow; and Anita, a hale and hearty lady who shone on the hockey pitch, though hardly in the classroom, caressed her own buxom body and positively glowed with pleasure at the thought of marrying and governing one of the wealthiest landowners in England.

'I shall tell you more of all these doings in a subsequent letter. Meanwhile, Goddess bless; and if you can't be good, be careful.

'All my love,
Emily.'

'Poetry indeed,' I murmured.

'No!' shouted Sedgewick. 'That's not poetry at all. To quote my own noble verse:

All other were mere vanity
Save, sadly, 'tis profanity.

'Thank you,' I said. 'Most grateful for your illumination.'

'Glad you see it, Horby,' Sedgewick went on remorselessly. 'For:

For other than what is may not say 'tis
But to impose on blind a fool's design
As thorns about the brow of Christ define
Not him, but those who mock, with emphasis:
Less puncto see and pundit silent pass
Mankind from truth will ever wander on.

'And so on, almost intelligibly,' came another familiar voice. I looked up to see Aleister Crowley descending the staircase with his arm around an exquisite whore within whose slender limbs I myself had derived great profit and enjoyment. 'With a single word, our dear Wilfred Sedgewick knocks down our castle of cards. Who or what is "puncto"?'

'Crowley! You old bastard!' Bellingham roared. 'What the fuck are you doing here?'

'I couldn't stand celibacy any longer,' said Crowley.

CHAPTER TWENTY

Naturally we invited Crowley to join our table and he told us all about his Yoga practices with Bennett, informing us that these had occupied sixteen hours each day, every day, without tobacco, alcohol, sex or even tea.

'I was very alarmed one day,' he told us, 'to find that I had completely lost the object of concentration. I could not think what I wished to find or where to find it. I naturally thought something was very wrong. Here was an occasion where Allan's experience proved invaluable. Without it, I might have been frightened into giving up the practice. But he told me the result was good, showing that I was approaching the state of what is called "neighbourhood concentration".

'Another experience,' Crowley continued excitedly, 'was this: I found myself at one and the same moment conscious of external things in the background after the object of my concentration had vanished, and also conscious that I was *not* conscious of these things. To the normal mind this is of course sheer contradiction, but Buddhist psychology mentions this peculiar state. The higher faculties of the intelligence are not subject to the same laws as the lower.' He attacked the dish of lamb brains quite greedily, as though he had not eaten meat for a month. 'I continually increased the number of hours which I devoted to my work.'

'Jolly interesting,' said Bellingham, 'but what on earth are you doing here, then?'

'Oh . . .' Crowley sighed and gulped some strong beer, 'I just need to go "on the bust", so to speak, prior to returning to this rigorous austerity.'

'Well, *I*'ve never been one for rigorous austerity,' Bellingham declared. 'Good luck, old chap. Anyway, Horby, I've not only brought you a letter from Emily; here's one from Claire, presently in Rajasthan. Why don't you read it out to us?' I proceeded to comply with his request:

'My darling,

'I do apologize for the utter negligence on my behalf in replying to your missives. Sometimes one can be rather remiss and thoughtless, even insouciant in one's duties. Please do accept my tergiversation.

'I am now in Jaipur yet took a detour upon the way to Agra in order to visit the Taj Mahal, the globe's greatest monument to love. How beautiful it is! When Shah Jahan's beloved Mumtaz Mahal died in 1631, his grief and despair were beyond belief and he wanted to create a mausoleum for her. He hired 20,000 labourers and craftsmen and it took 21 years to build. When I saw this sight, it took my breath away, what with the four rising minarets. The dome is so magnificent. That unjustly neglected painter, William Hodges, wrote in 1876 that it was "like a most perfect pearl on an azure ground."

'Ram Singh is such a delightful host; however, I am rather baffled by such strange coincidences in Life. As you may recall, we first met by chance in a Parisian café. It was such a strange coincidence that subsequently he was a Priest at Sir Richard Bellingham's excellent wedding; and then he invited me to his ashram. *An invitation*

of such distinction was hardly one that I could refuse.

'He recognised that I was a trifle fatigued after my railway journey but this did not impede the excellence of his hospitality. For the evening meal I was served Khargosh Mokal, *shredded hare sautéed with chillies, cumin and cardamon; followed by Venison in the* Nizami *style, the flesh of the deer having been marinated in papaya and then simmered in a curry. I must admit that* Gosht Achari *was my favourite dish – lamb cooked with lemon juice, curd, mustard seed, chillies and tamarind, which latter is a spice used often in medicinal beverages. I was also appreciative of the spinach and the bread, this air-light* Methi Puri, *enhanced with fenugreek.*

'It is necessary that one should use the right hand to eat, never the left – which is customarily used to wipe one's bottom – mixing mouthfuls of rice with meat and vegetables. I am reminded of the old Indian proverb: "Eating with a knife and fork is like making love through an interpreter."

'Upon the ensuing day, Ram Singh insisted upon a day of fasting in order to celebrate the Festival of Shivarath, a day dedicated to Shiva, the male principle, who represents bliss yet who is sometimes portrayed as the Destroyer, and his female counterpart, Shakti, the mother of the Universe.

' "Let me take you to my Temple," Ram Singh demanded of me. I could not resist his offer. Once therein, he requested: "Anoint my lingam."

' "I will, on one condition," I replied. "That you arouse, energize, stimulate and quicken the pulse within my yoni."

' "The world is bound by lust and it is only this animal desire, sexual indulgence, lasciviousness and passion that

can release us from our trappings . . ." And so he took me into his arms and slowly removed my attire, an outfit which, he remarked, binds us too much to the material world. He then applied oil to my forehead, breasts, knees and feet, finally anointing my finely trimmed pubic hair with an unguent. A garland of jasmine encircled my neck; yes, it was the flower of the moonshine, small white flowers that are so pungently fragrant at night.

'After that, he produced a hookah, an elaborate hubble-bubble pipe, and he filled the bowl with bhang.

'What a gradual build up it was to making love! It was a leisurely progression in andante *timing, leading up to a* crescendo. *I have never felt such soft lips upon mine; and simultaneously, he was stroking my young breasts and I could feel my nipples being aroused and becoming erect under his beautifully manicured fingertips. When he began to kiss each breast, I could feel an arousal within my loins. How I did want his male projectile to penetrate my hinterland! What a delight it was when he began to lick upon my quim!*

' "Your cunt," he sighed, "is like the flower of bougainvillea with a cerise blossom within." His tongue shot in and out; and then his palpus savoured and relished my flavoured juices, as they poured within his mouth and slid down his oesophagus. "This is better than lassi," he sighed. "There is both salt and sweetness, the true essence of your body."

'At that moment, I could sense the nature of his throbbing penis. I do not appreciate conjectures; however, I feel that this was not one. There would be a conjunction, an ultimate collision, the violent encounter of two moving bodies, male and female. The heat between the two of us was intense, zealous, torrid – and then he plunged his penis into me. Within seconds I had

my first orgasm: such a tarantism, a dancing mania.

'He kept on penetrating deeper and deeper in order to reach the quintessence, which as you know is the purest and most perfect form and force whenever heavenly bodies meet with no perversions. Until the early hours of the morning, we made love. We embraced and cherished one another, taking pleasure in each others' bodies. Oh! What a flame of passion and bedazzlement! Mr Ram Singh had the power to ingratiate himself with the treasure he possessed.

'Finally he said to me: "We must go to sleep as it is necessary that we prepare for the Feast of Kali, which will begin within the next twenty-four hours." I awoke in the early afternoon to the sounds of ululation; the high-pitched screeching, piercing notes of the peacocks in the garden. The male bird has always been somewhat more extravagant than the female. He has such a brilliant plumage of lapis lazuli, sapphire and emerald whilst the female wears mere tawny brown, reminding me of my aunt, the dowager duchess. As the male courted the female, fanning his feathers, there was a knock upon the door.

' "It's Josephine," said Ram Singh. "Please do enter." A slim and attractive girl obeyed his wish.

' "Mr Singh," she said, "I have brought tea for you and your guest." Not only was there a salver with a silver pot of Indian tea but also there was an epergne. What a delightful ornamentation! There was a vase containing rose flowers, jasmine, yellow champa and laburnum; and a bowl of fresh fruit with limes, guavas, chickoos, kinos and petias *– a large pumpkin whose flesh is cut up, pricked and cooked in syrup until it becomes white and then transparent.*

' "We must celebrate the Festival of Holi together,"

Ram Singh declared, leaving me a little puzzled, since I had thought he had been referring to Kali. "But until noon tomorrow, all customary social conventions are in abrogation, completely suspended."

' "Tell me more," I requested.

' "It is the rebirth of Spring," he said. "We will have a bonfire tonight to celebrate the destruction of the demon Holika by the infant Krishna."

' "Then," I queried, "will there be rockets? O! those lovely projectiles in cylindrical casings that are fired to ignite the night sky!"

' "You are right," he muttered, once Josephine had left the room, "but I would like once again to penetrate you."

' "Let me be your fizgig," I said.

' "You are much more than that," he replied swiftly. His thick, erect penis once again entered me and moved slowly and strongly in and out. Our orgasms were completely uncontrollable as our bodies tremored and twitched. We then showered each other with pink powder and water, which produced a pleasing, cleansing fizzing upon our light and dark skins. How we did dance and flirt and sing!

'He invited me to join the festivities within the ashram and upon the street and, my darling, it was so beautiful to experience the chanting and the beat of the big chang *drum.*

'I hope that all goes well with you and that you will respond to me soon enough.

'All my love,

Claire.'

'Ah, yes, a splendid gel,' Bellingham muttered as he tucked into more curry. 'Mind you, I've always been rather fond of Ram Singh.' He drank more beer. 'Splendid fellow!'

'I am not impressed,' Sedgewick replied stiffly. 'And I have summarized the matter in my poetry. My *Sonnetical Notes on Philosophy* under my pseudonym of Wm Howell Williams has now been published. And I summarize the matter well:

Through aggregation form, as semblance place,
Where mere sensation will substantial find
Unseen relation force conditioned mind
Form aggregation ever set to face
Perception shall be as fixed for the case.
Example: Huxley nihil bonum screen;
How . . .

'Parse *screen*!' Bellingham demanded.

'And what can it mean, this Fragment of Ozymandias?' Crowley queried. 'It stands there, absolutely isolated from any reference to Huxley; as an "example", but of what, who can say? On all sides, boundless and bare, the lone and level sonnets stretch far away.'

'Did Huxley put a screen on the market called the *nihil bonum*?' I asked.

'Did he give shelter to "nothing good"?' Crowley demanded.

'Or did "nothing good" save him from exposure?' Bellingham suggested.

'Or was Huxley's screen no good?' asked Crowley.

'Or is it no good to screen Huxley?' I wondered aloud.

'You are all idiots, gentlemen,' Sedgewick retorted. 'And I leave you to your idiocy. Myself, I am going upstairs to make love with Naznin and Pabloo.'

'Well, at least you'll be doing something useful in your

life,' said Bellingham. 'Really!' he exclaimed as Sedgewick went upon his intended mission, 'that fellow is such a bore. Anyway, chaps, I've been travelling around the world with my dear lady wife, Davina. Allow me to order another round of these excellent drinks and then I'll tell you all about an extraordinary piece of flagellation, a woman's most delectable bottom being flogged from the colour of black to lobster red, yes, on a sugar cane plantation in Jamaica.' We settled back in expectation to hear his tale but we were abruptly interrupted by the sound of gunfire. We sprang to our feet and sprinted up the stairs to find Pabloo nodding us towards a bedroom. The three of us burst within to find Wilfred Sedgewick face down upon the floor – and Naznin with a smoking gun in her hand.

'Who shot this man?!' Bellingham roared.

'I did,' Naznin answered.

'Congratulations,' said Bellingham.

CHAPTER TWENTY-ONE

'Why did you do that, Naznin?' I asked.

'It was his poetry,' she replied solemnly. 'Anything he did to me I could take; but not his terrible poetry. This is too much for a young girl to endure.'

'Quite agree,' Crowley murmured in a rather bored tone of voice. 'It's just a question of what we do with all the mess and of how we'll handle the various authorities.'

'Simple,' I said; for I had discerned the true nature of the matter. 'This is just one of Bellingham's jokes. If you look at Naznin's gun, I think you'll find that it actually contains blanks and poor old Sedgewick has fallen down in a dead faint. Look! He's stirring into life again!' This was undeniable as Sedgewick hauled himself to his feet and we all started to laugh.

'Sedgewick,' said Bellingham, 'I've just heard news from the Colonial Office that you're due for a transfer, *old chap*. So why don't you just piss orf out of here . . . Jolly good!' Sir Richard bellowed as Sedgewick slunk away. 'Must say that Naznin and Pabloo did their jobs well. Utterly unsuitable for Ceylon, that man!' he snorted disgustedly. 'Best place for him is probably teaching English to Arab boys in Aden; and from what I hear of Aden, the punishment fits the crime. But allow me to continue with my tale which my own practical joke so rudely interrupted. Now look here, Horby, and you too,

Crowley . . .' He called for brandy, 'I was about to tell you of my time in Jamaica. There's a friend of mine called Geoffrey who runs a sugar plantation. Now he's not nearly as bad as his grandfather, who was an extremely cruel man. Why, when one nigger was so hungry that he nibbled at a piece of sugar cane and – poor bugger – got caught, Geoff's grandfather flogged the fellow to within an inch of his life and then forced another nigger slave at the point of a whip to drop a huge cockroach in his mouth. Disgusting! And I don't hold with it. Yet I have some sympathy with the treatment Geoffrey meted out to a black woman working in the sugar fields upon his plantation. He had made her a manager of molasses processing, the condition being that she didn't fuck with anyone apart from him. What did she go and do but – no, not give it to some raw black stud, no, far worse: she started to give away his trade secrets of molasses, treacle, golden syrup, sugar and rum in its forms of white, dark and golden to his nearest white business rival for money. Well, he felt that he had been betrayed. Now let me tell you about his revenge:

'Davina and I entered the main part of a tiled barn which stank of horses' shit and where a padded leather bench stood at the centre of the floor. Joanna, an exquisitely voluptuous female, had been stripped, made to kneel at one end of the bench and lie forward along it. Her knickers had been pulled down around her ankles. Geoffrey's servants had tied her glossy dark hair into a short pony-tail.

'Joanna's arms were strapped to the far end of the bench, her waist was buckled down and her legs were belted tightly together just above her knees.

'All this will sound so severe to you, gentlemen, that you will scarcely credit how much pleasure there might be for Joanna in her punishment. Yet some women have the sense to realize that they have done wrong, surely? And then they ought to accept the punitive measures they receive.

'Myself, I squatted down behind her and studied the area which offered itself as a target to Geoffrey. Joanna's buttocks, firmly and fully presented by her posture, were stretched hard apart. Both the rear pout of her vaginal purse and her anal cleft were in full view.

' "You've been making love, haven't you, Joanna?" Davina teased the punished girl since she was a second cousin of Geoffrey. He, meanwhile, stroked her down the length of her cleavage, between the dark-skinned sturdiness of her buttocks, tickling the rear of her vaginal pouch and finding it visibly moist. She was far away in mind by now, her eyes glazed, her mouth open a little, and her imprisoned bosom heaved.

'Now, Davina is a lover of that delight known to us as "Birching in the Boudoir". Every caning is an occasion for her pleasure. It is true, is it not, that certain girls have found a succinct pleasure under the rod? And is it not so that certain women find an exquisite pleasure in the fact of it? I could discern that Joanna's black, firm thighs, in all their stocky power, were squeezing rhythmically together. It was impossible to prevent it, except perhaps by ordering her thighs to be strapped apart. To tell you the truth, my curiosity was so great that I could not bear to request it.

' "No wonder you've been watched as you were set out on a harness display," said Geoffrey to Joanna. "You have been misbehaving most dreadfully."

Joanna, it seemed, had no shame, She continued with her thigh-squeezing and buttock-clenching as though she could not have stopped for dear life. Geoffrey promptly cut the air with a trial swish of his bamboo cane; our young black masturbatrix stopped, frozen in a moment which mingled apprehension with self-love.

'A dozen strokes across your bare bottom, Joanna,' Geoffrey growled as he began the punishment with a long and supple cane of bamboo. How the first stroke of his cane rang out across the firm, dark cheeks of Joanna's bottom! She gasped, cried out; but never ceased to squeeze her love-lips hard between her thighs. Again the cane lashed across her seat, and again. She uttered a soft cry but it was hard to say whether pain or pleasure drew it from her. Geoffrey was quite pitiless with her. Believe me, chaps, any true disciplinarian who might have watched Joanna displaying her bottom would have approved of that.

'Six times the cane raised a weal across the cheeks of Joanna's buttocks – with a gratuitous lash across the backs of her thighs. She cried out with the hurt – and with the curious pleasure of her own thigh-squeezing at the same time. The vicious bamboo was a smarting agony across the bare cheeks of her backside yet the swelling balloon of pleasure within her own loins enabled her to take it with commendable insouciance. This irritated Geoffrey.

' "Almost at the summit of your climb, Joanna?" he sneered. He waited until her thighs seemed to beat quickly together in their squeezing, like soft, black wings. Then he caned this impudent woman without compunction. I was conscious that Davina was watching with a hot flush upon her cheeks and with her eyes focused upon every nook and writhing cranny. Joanna screamed out and her dark, soulful eyes brimmed over with tears. The anger of Geoffrey brought thin ruby trickles from the renewed weals across her bottom cheeks.

'At last Joanna lay limp and gasping, her black behind

now glowing as red as that of a hot, cooked lobster and marked by swollen stripes.

' "What do we do with this punished bitch?" Geoffrey demanded as Joanna sobbed and her beautiful bottom twitched and writhed in a series of spasms.

' "Quite simple," said Davina. "D'you have any oils?"

'It turned out that he had some oils of benzoin and patchouli. Davina proceeded to amaze the pair of us as she soothed Joanna's twitching bottom with soft strokes; then, by inserting her deft fingers into the young lady's cunt, my wife brought her to orgasm. Joanna's head twitched and turned as much as her bottom.

' "She needs gentle discipline for her wrongdoing," Davina said as Joanna waved her bottom in the air and appeared to implore it. Now, I might well argue with my wife on major things but it's a foolish chap who argues with his wife on minor ones. When, therefore, Davina demanded the finest of soft, silken underwear and clothing for Joanna, I nodded to Geoffrey that I was in absolute agreement.

'The punished girl was released from the block at Davina's request and made to stand in the corner with her face pressed against the wall while we discussed her fate. She had to hold her dress and petticoats above her waist: and it was indeed a positive pleasure to sip our drinks and watch the state of her wealed and whaled bottom as the stripes slowly changed colour. Eventually, Davina put her into the softest of clothing, she had to curtsey to us and thank us for her justly deserved punishment; and then Davina put her to bed. I don't know precisely what happened at that moment but Davina was away for quite a while and I can guess.

'Anyway, gentlemen!' Bellingham threw the contents of his glass down his throat, 'that's my story. Anyone got a better one to tell?'

CHAPTER TWENTY-TWO

I caught a rather ordinary steamboat to Madras a couple of days later, though at least the cabin was moderately comfortable and the food was adequate. It was a pleasure to stroll upon deck and gaze at the Indian Ocean, all the while reflecting upon my experiences. Crowley had returned to Kandy, there to practise more Yoga under the capable tuition of Bennett.

'The trouble with you, Crowley,' Bellingham had said, 'is that presently you're too bloody austere. All this asceticism of yours does no good, you know.'

'That,' Crowley had replied, 'remains to be seen.'

'Oh, well, please yourself,' Bellingham retorted. 'Don't know if you'll be pleasing anybody else.' He had then continued on his way with Davina, sailing to Bombay.

'You seem to be enjoying the sight of the ocean,' said an unfamiliar voice. I turned to see a tall dark man with a thick moustache, who introduced himself as Amin Shah, from Persia. One always needs an interesting man to talk to on a sea voyage, I find, and I had no cause for complaint. He informed me that he was a Sufi going to visit a friend who was a Yogi.

'What exactly *is* a Sufi?' I queried. 'One's informed that the Sufis – and the word means "weavers" – are part of Islam as some sort of mystical sect.'

'Sufis adapt themselves to times and changes,' he

replied. 'Every description of our activities is at least a century out of date. Essentially, we are about learning how to learn so as to advance human evolution.'

'Most laudable. But can you give me an example?'

'Yes,' said the Sufi. 'Sir, I would like to put the light on for you. Please do not be like one of the many fish who swam to a reputedly wise old fish and said: "What's this *water* that we've heard so much about lately?" Allow me to illustrate my point regarding learning how to learn by telling you a joke. Actually, it is two jokes, and I have yet to meet a Westerner who finds the first joke to be funny. However, the condition of the telling is that however much you may deplore the first joke, you must agree to listen to the second.'

'Agreed.' At that moment, there was fuck-all else to do.

'There is a shepherd,' Amin Shah commenced, 'and among his flock, he has a sheep called Lucy, of whom he is particularly fond. Now one day he wakes up, goes to the meadow and Lucy the sheep is missing. So he goes into the village and tries the tavern. "Any of you seen Lucy the sheep?" he asks. No, nobody has. He tries the grocer. "Have you seen Lucy the sheep?" No. The confectioner. "Have you seen Lucy the sheep?" No. He tries the baker, the greengrocer and the cobbler, all the while asking: "Have you seen Lucy the sheep?" and all the while getting the same answer – No. Now, he has tried every shop in the town and nobody has seen Lucy the sheep – except the very last shop, which is the butcher's.'

'I think I know what's coming,' I murmured.

'So he goes in there,' Mr Shah continued, 'and says: "Mr Butcher, have *you* seen Lucy the sheep?" And the butcher says . . . "No".'

There was a pause.

'Please go on,' I requested, adding: 'I'm terribly interested.'

'That's the joke,' he responded. 'I didn't think that you would find it to be humorous.'

'It's not funny at all,' I said indignantly. 'In fact, I think it's the worst joke that I have ever heard.'

'No, I suppose it is not terribly good,' he smiled regretfully, 'but I assure you that the second one, to which you promised to listen, is much better. There are two men in the compartment of a railway train. One of them has a pet monkey sitting next to him. He also has a box of cigars and is greatly looking forward to smoking them. Well, he lights a good cigar but the other man says: "Excuse me, my dear sir, I suffer from bronchitis and asthma and although you are permitted by law to smoke in this compartment, I wonder if here and now you would be kind enough to refrain." Now, the first man is a little irritated but he is a gentleman and so he stubs out his cigar. Then he thinks that there is precious little to do except go to sleep. He does: and so does the other man. And while they are both asleep, the monkey takes the box of cigars and disappears. After a while, the first man wakes up to see that his monkey has vanished. That perturbs him – and his cigars have vanished, too. He wakes up the second man who declares that he was asleep throughout these events and knows nothing. The second man goes back to sleep as the first explores the train, entering every corridor and enquiring within each compartment, looking for his monkey and his box of cigars. "Have you seen my monkey and my box of cigars?" is his question to everyone he encounters but all the time he receives the same answer – No. Now, sir, the very last carriage of this train is where they have the buffet and the bar. He enters that compartment – and there, sitting at the bar, wearing his glasses, reading a newspaper, drinking beer and smoking his cigars . . . whom do you think he sees?'

'The monkey,' I answered smartly.

'No,' said the Sufi, 'Lucy the sheep.'

After that, of course I bought the fellow a brandy and invited him to dine with me, mentioning only that it could not be tonight since I was previously engaged at the Captain's table.

'So am I,' he replied, 'so we shall be dining together after all.'

I started to wonder just what sort of boat I was on that night when I sat down to dine at the Captain's table. Captain Jack Rivers was a genial, fat, florid-faced buccaneer who had been sailing the South Seas for many a year and who was also surprisingly well-read. Although there were some attractive women on the voyage, only Amin Shah and I sat with Rivers. 'I don't often get the chance to have a good men's evening of congenial and intelligent conversation,' the Captain explained.

'I'm quite interested in Sufism,' Captain Jack Rivers declared, 'having listened to Amin here on a number of previous voyages.' It was the end of a good and satisfying meal based largely around hot lamb curry, and he poured generous quantities of brandy for both of us. 'I love listening to people who talk sense or make me laugh. Why, on my last voyage, I was listening to a Chinese Zen Master. "What is Zen?" I asked him. He told me the following story: "One day Chan Tzu-lin was walking in the sunshine and was greeted warmly by Wu Pei-fu. 'Hot weather,' said the Master. 'A good day for work.' Thence Wu Pei-fu was enlightened." '

'Yes . . .' I muttered. 'Go on.'

'That's it,' said the Captain. 'That is Zen. At least,

that's what he told me. Frankly, gentlemen, I can't make the slightest sense out of it. Can you?'

'No,' I said.

'I can put the same truth to you in another way,' Amin Shah interposed gently. 'Chan Tzu-lin one day took Wu Pei-fu to a meadow in order to show him Enlightenment. This was in the form of a cow grazing. The Master pointed and the disciple looked and the sacred cow went: "MU". And thereupon absolutely nobody was enlightened. Would you like to know why?'

'Yes,' I said.

'Nobody could speak Chinese,' he retorted.

'I think I'm beginning to comprehend,' I said smilingly as the Captain roared with laughter and poured more cognac for all of us. 'Both Zen and Sufism are about different ways of perceiving the obvious.'

'Why do you think I sail the seas, sir?' Captain Jack Rivers demanded. 'I listen to all my more interesting passengers, gaze at the ocean waves and am thrilled each day at perceiving the obvious all the time. There're so many who just can't.' He lit a huge *Corona de Corona*, offering us his box of Cuban cigars, then glanced pointedly at one of three young ladies dining together. She appeared to be thrilled by his sharp glance. 'A very good night to you, gentlemen. Personally, I *love* the obvious!'

I retired to my cabin and re-read the most recent letter I had received from Claire, finding it to be as paradoxical as everything else I had heard this evening.

My darling,

I miss you so much and hope that you received my last letter. Upon the Festival of Holi, Josephine, a 'younger sister' of Ram Singh, insisted that I be properly decorated and applied henna *upon my hands in a lattice pattern, with lines, dots and triangles forming diamond figures like those of heraldry. She applied this concoction of nut gallis, ashes, spices, all heated by fire at the point of a* calema, *a piece of sharpened wood. Throughout the ritual of ornamentation of my body, she chanted with such a goddess-like, transcendent voice.*

'You will be the most beautiful at the Festival,' she sang softly, 'for your skin is so pale. The darkness of the henna *contrasts so delicately with the pallor of your skin.'*

She then produced a sari for me to wear, woven of the finest gossamer red silk and exquisitely embroidered; such fine ornamentation in gold thread, a filament so delicately fashioned . . . I had never worn a sari before with so many folds of fabric held together in such a simple and sensible style of elegant dress. Upon my forehead, Josephine applied tikka, *a spot of red appropriate to a Brahmin priestess; and she dotted my chin with a* siyala, *a lucky charm; and finally there was a circle drawn upon the end of my nose to ward off the evil eye.*

'Do you not know . . .?' Josephine asked me, 'that the Singh family have been the rulers of Jaipur since the late 16th century and that includes the father of Ram Singh. The family is highly distinguished.'

'He never told me of the history of his family,' I replied with astonishment, recalling my initial encounter in a Parisian café and our subsequent roles as Priest and Priestess at the wedding of Sir Richard to Davina in Paris.

'Mr Singh is a very modest man,' Josephine observed. 'His family is putting great pressure on him to marry diplomatically so that he can produce many fine sons. Let us not forget that his great-grandfather had 300 wives

and a harem of 5,000 concubines, occupying two-thirds of the palace.'

'Josephine, how did he manage to satisfy them all?' I asked with bewilderment. Suddenly the door flew open and in strode a man dressed in the most magnificent oriental finery. Josephine silently left the room.

'Later on, Memsahib!' he cried out proudly, 'I shall show you how he managed to satisfy, please and content them all.'

'Please show me now,' I requested, recognizing Ram Singh.

'First of all you must catch me!' he roared.

'Oh, do stop teasing me . . .' Suddenly, and to my complete stupefaction, he proceeded to perform a series of somersaults and handstands.

'If you want me, then you must chase me,' he teased as he tempted newly excited and aroused desires of the flesh within me. 'If you can ambush and trap me, then I will be compliant, devoted and submissive to your demands: heh! heh!' Then, without warning, he dashed down the stairs and into the street. I pursued him. It was annoying, upon my entry into the street, to see so many people in festive attire blocking the way. Cows were ornamentally decorated and I had to push and thread my way through the throng. The chanting resonated throughout the air as the women hunted and stalked their men.

I was the quester, seeker and searcher after Ram Singh. I prowled and pursued his every pervading scent that permeated and saturated the air. Yet it was virtually impossible to push my way through the multitudes assembled.

Unexpectedly, there was a kiss upon my lips: it was curious; it was not rough; but it lacked the tenderness of Ram Singh.

I stared into the eyes of Douglas.

'What are you *doing here?' I asked.*

'Everyone has to be somewhere,' he replied lightly, 'and I would like to ask the same of you.' Again he kissed me resplendently upon the lips and vanished as swiftly as he had arrived. I turned around to face Ram Singh.

'At last I have found you!' he exclaimed warmly. 'It is the end of the chase. The hunter is the hunted and the biter bit.' Amidst the dancing and the chanting, we kissed so passionately. 'I only desire to give you even greater pleasures this evening,' he informed me. 'Let us rid ourselves of this maddening crowd.' I gladly agreed as we strolled leisurely through the winding side-streets, enjoying the various festivities. There was an intensity in our walking and a greater magnetic field that would bring us even closer together. Finally we arrived back at his ashram, *and when the doors closed behind us, he took me into his arms. 'What magic power do you possess that you should find me so quickly?' he asked.*

'You found me,' was my response. 'It is the Goddess within me.'

'Let us now make love,' he said, 'and we must retire to my sanctuary, the inmost recess, the shrine to penetralia.'

Within the confines of this sanctum, he embraced me again.

'You have never looked more beautiful,' he remarked, 'so now I shall show you how a man can satisfy over 5,000 women.' He lifted my sari and within seconds his penis had entered my moist cunny in a gradual, leisurely and meticulous build-up to a forthcoming climax; yet much faster than the pace of a piaffer, even developing his rhythm up to that of a canter and thence to the gallop of a stallion. How his ramrod did shoot into me! And

when his orgasm did occur, it was a total immersion, an inundation of his manly fluids, a saturation of my vulva. I have never known such a plenteous and precious spurting of semen!

These festivals appear to carry on for days – or "Daze", it might be said – for there is continuous dancing and chanting, with the accompaniment of gaily caparisoned elephants and camels; yet it was our choice to remain within our doors and to watch from the balcony and the windows. I think I began to generate more power within his phallus, a veneration such as that between Shiva and Shakti or between Vishnu and Lakshmi. Throughout the night, we made love, yet I think I want more than what he has offered to me, including a proposal of marriage.

I cannot deny that there is a powerful passion within his loins. He can make love so many times a night but I think he also wants to scatter his seed around a harem.

There is a wishing-pond in the garden. It contains so many beautiful fish. I threw my robe into the pool to watch it gradually ripple and to hope that my deepest desire comes through.

All my love,
Claire.'

After reading that, I went up on deck and was glad not to hear any further words of insight. Instead, I picked up a stupid but beautiful French tart called Jacqueline, who had gorgeous, glossy, black wavy hair; upstanding tits; a voluptuous, rounded, firm bottom; and, yes, I thrust my stiff rod within her, and as she writhed and moaned just before she came, I fucked her brains out.

CHAPTER TWENTY-THREE

I found Madras to be sleepy, sticky and provincial; yet there were compensations. I continued to dine with the intriguing Amin Shah and it had been warmly recommended to me that I visit Lady Joanna Featherstonehaugh – pronounced 'Fanshaw' for some indiscernible reason – who received me warmly and turned out to be everything that Bellingham had described: a beautiful and stylishly-dressed voluptuous redhead. Within thirty minutes of my arrival, she asked me if I liked riding, and when I assented she exclaimed: 'Then I'll ride upon you.'

Only a fool would refuse so gracious an offer from so lovely a lady: and so I undid my trousers and sat upon a chair. Joanna pulled up all her petticoats and proceeded to set herself in the saddle. She then seized my vigorous implement and commenced the physical introduction by pushing down her bottom as it slowly entered. I was so placed that I could enjoy the sight from behind and consequently could not miss the slightest detail. My enormous tool soon disappeared completely. Joanna lifted up her legs, placed her high heels on the bars of the chair and began to rise and fall with frequent gasping.

The accustomed sighs and words rose to her lips as our souls melted together in mutual enjoyment.

'Ah! how finely you do it!' said she. 'Gently, my angel . . . Uncover him well . . . Now quicker. Stop! Go on again! Ah! I feel it coming! Quicker! . . . I . . . I spend . . . I come!'

She could not help opening up her thighs wider and elevating her petticoats in a sheer transport of delight. Her hands gripped my thighs fast in her embrace, impatiently desiring the supreme moment. The lips of her womb soon enough felt the tip of the head of my instrument. I shoved it in as far as was possible and she uttered a raucous cry: 'I am spending!' So violent were her convulsions that I almost lost my senses. I stopped for a second or two, astonished at her transports, then returned to the performance of my sweet duty. What a remarkable woman! She poured out her delicious dew upon my penis at least four times! All the while she was pushing out her bottom as if she were riding a stallion. As, in a sense, she was. At last I shuddered and sighed and a fiery, flaming jet of jism inundated her flesh-depths.

After a period of silent embracing, she arose, rang a bell and summoned a slender maid called Laura, all the while smoothing her skirt.

'Laura, you've been a very naughty girl,' Joanna informed her with a severe crackling of her petticoats. 'Now be a good girl and go and fetch my birch.' She chuckled wickedly. 'You need another erection, Horby, and the tender rump of Laura will give you much satisfaction. She's such a coward and the first cut will make her wince yet we all know how nice and delightful the finish is. This will excite your cock to another great fuck.'

A timorous Laura returned, holding the birch requested by Lady Joanna.

'Would you kindly be the horse, Horby?' she asked me; and I acceded to her demand, which entailed bending over as the fanciable Laura was placed upon me with her wrists bound to mine by thongs of brown leather. There were four mirrors upon each wall of the chamber of milady, enabling me to watch the progress of the punishment from a variety of perspectives.

'I am very much obliged to you for your kindness,' Lady Joanna addressed me, 'but Laura's bottom will soon be *aglow* for your delectation once I begin to apply some of Mrs Martinet's scientific touches to it. Laura is a bonded maidservant and so she shall remain. This is a serious business,' she declared, swishing both her skirts and the birch within her hand. 'Thin ticklers are only useful just to touch up a man in the act of fucking. Laura's whipping must be *much* more severe in order to stimulate your presently languid tool and rouse it again to a state of lustful fury by the exhibition of the reddened flesh, weals, and dripping drops of the ruby, as it is distilled from the abraded skin.'

'Oh, pray don't be as bad as that, Milady,' Laura pleaded apprehensively.

'No, Miss Pert, no nonsense, no drawing back, or I really *will* make it worse for your wicked bum!' exclaimed Lady Joanna, standing up straight and looking fiercely at her helpless victim, firmly fastened over my manly back. The birching commenced: and my cock was in a state of glorious stiffness.

'Oh, it stings so!' Laura gasped. 'Ah, not so hard, Joanna, darling,' Laura sighed as the first two or three swishes made her buttocks tingle under the smart.

'Is that better, you rude girl?' Joanna retorted. 'Didn't I catch you frigging yourself in bed this morning?' she demanded with a spiteful smile upon her face.

'Ah, ah, oh, no! My God, how you cut me! I shall die of it. I never frigged myself. I should be ashamed to do such a thing,' she sobbed, the tears trickling down cheeks that were blushing more scarlet than the twitching bottom I could see in the looking-glasses. Her exposed bottom was being fairly reddened beneath the smarting cuts and this love-canter quickened into an impetuous gallop so that, when the emitting crisis came, the three of us fairly howled and shouted with excess of delighted emotion, while Laura went into a fit of hysteria, laughed, cried and stiffened herself over me, almost throwing me out of position as her teeth closed convulsively upon the flesh of my neck.

'Just listen to this hard bitch!' cried Lady Joanna. 'It's as bad as saying I'm a liar.' She let fly with two vicious cuts that made Laura squirm in agony and drew the blood up under the skin of her rump. 'Ah, you bad girl, I'll whip the frigging fancy out of you. Wouldn't it be nice to be frigged just now with your cunt rubbing against Horby's back?'

'Oh! Oh!! Oh!!! I didn't!' Laura screamed back as she squirmed. The cuts fell in rapid succession on her devoted bum, which now began to exhibit weals upon the broken skin. The victim still writhed and struggled upon my back and under Joanna's scathing cuts yet her head fell forward upon my shoulder, her face suffused with crimson flushes, and her eyes closed in a voluptuous langor.

I had decided to act on the frigging accusation and by the light pressures of my lower back on her excited clitoris, had made her close to fainting under the combination of excitements, as she spent so profusely that her thick, creamy emission trickled down my back.

'Lay her down upon the bed and let's have her later!' Lady Joanna commanded imperiously, flinging down the rod which was considerably worn by its work. 'Who'll have *me* on the horse-hair sofa? Will you, Horby?'

'I'm randy enough for anything, my love,' I exclaimed as the bonds were untied by her and a sobbing Laura was tucked into bed. 'Ah! Horse-hair throw-rug, eh? It's just how Adam and Eve must have shagged on the grass in Eden.'

'Oh, it does prick the flesh so,' Joanna exclaimed as she plumped her bottom on the horse-hair. 'But it's the finest thing to stimulate a woman that you can think of: the little prickly ends of the stiff hair are like pins and make your arse bound under every single stroke. It's simply delicious. No one but those who try it can appreciate the delights of a horse-hair sofa-fuck.'

How she bounded and writhed as I fairly and furiously pounded my prick into her swimming cunt, which seemed to be perfectly appositioned and quite insatiable. She was spending again and again, every two or three minutes, until at last, with a perfect howl of delight, she drew upon my pent-up emission, which shot up into her vitals like a stream of liquid fire.

Kissing and billing, we lay entranced within each other's arms until the soundly birched Laura remarked that it would soon be time for breakfast.

Dinner was my main concern when I met Amin Shah, who invited me to sample delicious Southern Indian vegetarian cuisine, eaten with the right hand off a huge banana leaf. The *dosa*, something made of wheat and rice which was betwixt and between a piece of crisp bread and a pancake proved to be particularly notable. The *thali*, a selection of dishes in each of which a blend of spices has made the crisp vegetables deliciously picquant, added to the memory of this meal. With it we drank something called *lassi* or *lhasi* – who knows and who cares about the minute exactitude of its spelling and translation? Anyway, it's a jolly good beverage made out of yoghurt. Amin Shah set two glasses before me, one salty and the other sweet, asking me to choose them.

'Salty first,' I think I remarked, 'and sweet later.' He burst out laughing. 'I'm glad that you are amused,' I said, 'but what's so funny?'

'You,' he replied.

'Well, if I'm such a figure of fun,' I answered, 'at least one's doing something useful with one's life. I mean, what's your function?' I burst out indignantly. 'You say you're a Sufi Master but you haven't yet made me laugh.'

'I'll tell you a Nazrudin story,' he responded. Nazrudin is, of course, the Robin Hood of the Middle East. 'Once upon a time, Nazrurdin was on hard times, down on his luck and living in straitened circumstances with his wife. A rich relative came to visit and he brought Nazrudin and his wife a freshly-slaughtered duck and suggested that it be cooked for their dinner. Very good it was, too! The rich relative departed on the following day; and two days later, there was a knock upon the door. "Hallo, Nazrudin, I am a friend of the relative who brought you the duck." "Come in!" Nazrudin the Mullah exclaimed warmly, "dinner is served!" Two days later, there was another knock upon the door. "Hallo, Nazrudin, I am a friend of the friend of the relative that brought you the duck." "Come in," said Mullah Nazrudin; "dinner is served." Two days later there was yet another knock upon the door. "Hallo, Nazrudin, I am the friend of the friend of the friend of the relative that brought you the duck." By this time, the host's wife was berating him for his feckless hospitality. "Come in," sighed Hodja Nazrudin; "dinner is served. Here is the soup of the soup of the soup of the duck that my relative brought me." '

I couldn't resist a chuckle at that one and, in order to encourage my host further in his purveying of anecdotes, I offered him a brandy 'or anything else you might like'; and he told me calmly that a glass of neat Scotch whisky would suit him best. This sounded like a jolly good idea so I decided to join him.

'Seen your Yogi friend?' I enquired.

'No,' Amin Shah replied. 'He's been delayed and won't be here for a couple of weeks or so: but I assure you, he is worth meeting. Another man you must meet is Sir Richard Bellingham.'

'Thank you.' It was hard to maintain a straight face. 'But I've known him for years.'

'I know.'

'Then why did you ask me to meet him?'

'Simply to observe your reaction to the suggestion.'

'You are a very curious creature,' I replied.

'Yes,' he said simply. 'And I hope you don't make the mistake of the vast majority of creatures, which is continually to confuse something with what it isn't. For instance, there was once a bear who was told by his father: "For hibernation, son, never forget to take plenty of *berries* or else you'll starve to death." This bear was later found in a cave by the bunnies, starved and frozen to death. Upon his head, paws and feet, he had *berets*. Most people are just like that.'

'Yes, I've had similar sufferings on account of misunderstanding,' I replied. 'I'm slightly short-sighted, and a few years ago, I was on a railway journey, sitting in the buffet car and hoping to order a spot of lunch. Unfortunately, I'd forgotten my glasses and my monocle and so I couldn't read the menu properly. I asked a pleasant-faced woman, seated opposite, to assist me in telling me what the bloody hell was on the thing. She told me and I ordered – probably just a cheese and tomato sandwich. Then she said: "You mustn't be embarrassed, you know.

There's nothing of which to be ashamed." "Not ashamed at all of anything," I retorted indignantly. "Six weeks is all it would take," she responded, "and please listen, for a new world of truth and beauty would open up before your eyes." "You sound like some sort of crusader," I remarked. "Yes!" she cried; "for I teach the noble arts of reading and writing. Come to my Adult Illiteracy Classes!" ' Shah chuckled.

'Communication, so-called, is so frequently so conditioned by preconceptions so as to be socially dysfunctional,' the Sufi remarked. 'Have you ever heard of the fabled American Western gunfighter, Wild Bill Hickock?'

'Of course.'

'It happened during the Civil War of the American States, so we're told,' said Amin Shah, 'in wide-open North Platte, Nebraska. Bill Hickock, Union scout, Indian fighter and dead shot with a lightning quick draw, hitched his horse, Black Nell, to a post and entered a saloon for supper. A waitress approached him nervously and whispered that she had *heard two men plotting to kill him*. One was going to come in the front door and the other the rear, guns blazing before Mr Hickock could whip out his Colt Dragoon .44's.

'Hickock, this gentleman pistoleer,' Amin Shah continued, 'swept a lock of golden-brown tresses off his shoulder and chucked the trembling bearer of Death's tidings under her chin. "Little girl," he said, "you get to one side. You might get hurt in the overflow." The waitress fled to the kitchen. The resulting carnage has been described by a biographer, Mr O.W. Coursey, though I quote from memory: "Wild Bill, facing the desperate character who entered the front door, had shot him with a revolver in his left hand, while with the right hand he had thrown the other gun over his left shoulder and shot the man coming in from the rear. History does not record a more daredevil act, a more astute piece of gun work".'

'Marvellous!' I exclaimed. 'What's wrong with that?'

'As a story, nothing,' said the Sufi. 'The episode fits nicely with our picture of Wild Bill Hickock as the fearless square-shootin' hero who triumphs over the damnedest odds. "*Marvellous!*" indeed, as you say, sir. The only trouble with it is that there isn't a shred of evidence that it ever happened.'

CHAPTER TWENTY-FOUR

The finest whore for the best fuck that I met in Madras was Janine, who was half English, a quarter French and a quarter Indian.

'My dear Horby,' she murmured as she licked my stiff prick, 'I am glad that you are drinking brandy.' She wriggled her soft and rounded bottom delectably as her long, dark, glossy hair cascaded over my belly. 'Gin is too depressing for men and takes all the starch out of their pricks. You know the saying: "Whisky makes the love hot but brandy makes it long." For my part,' she continued after a long, deep suck on my cock, 'give me a man who can keep his place well and go on with his fucking, getting stiffer and bigger inside my cunt, until he stirs my blood, raises all my passions to such a pitch, that when at length both come together, it is really the melting of two souls into one and leaves you to fall into that blissful ecstasy afterwards which,' she sighed languidly, 'only true and experienced fuckers really understand. Fancy a bottle of fizz?'

'Yes, fetch the fizz,' I replied, 'my impudent cheeky beauty. I hope to give you a new sensation for, despite the impending chill of the champagne, you look warm enough for anything.'

'Thank you for the compliment. I own I'm not a lump of ice but I'll be quick as I'm curious to experience your style.' She vanished briefly to reappear with a bottle of Veuve Cliquot, which she opened expertly, rather as though she were bringing a penis to orgasm. She thence pledged me 'a long life and plenty of fucking.' Slipping off her dressing gown, which at once revealed that she had only her corset, chemise and drawers to hide her person, set off to best advantage by pink silk stockings, pretty gold-buckled blue garters and elegant high-heeled French slippers, she lay over the end of the sofa and bared her exquisite backside. 'As hard as you like, darling, but make it long and slow before the finish.'

'I'll be all there when my pounding makes you spend, Janine,' I answered as my prick penetrated her delicate labia and I commenced my thrusting. 'And afterwards I wouldn't mind sucking up every drop.' My belly slammed against her truly magnificent olive rump and her vaginal squeezing of my stiff cock possessed all the stock-in-trade of as handsome and pretty a young whore as any man could wish to experience. 'And I'll begin as I mean to go on.'

My deep penetration, with the tip of my penis touching the outer lips of her womb, made her writhe with exceptional joys of sensation. Her face flushed as the blood tingled in her veins. She shivered with emotion and voluptuous desire.

After about five minutes of fucking in depth, slowly and rhythmically, Janine gave most evident signs of the impending crisis. She closed her eyes and hung her head over the end of the sofa, her bottom and thighs fairly quivering with the excess of her emotions; and I rushed upon my victim with all the energy of a lustful satyr, thence turning the girl over on her back and burying my face between her thighs to lick and suck up every drop of spendings from her quivering quim. I kissed her sweetly-scented cunt and said: 'I must fuck you again.'

She fell upon her knees and seized my cock between her lips, engulfed it within her mouth and sucked it with raging delirium.

'Oh!' she gasped. 'I just can't resist that beautiful, rubicund head!' Turning over and lying upon a Persian rug, she exposed her irresistible buttocks. In a twinkling, I had penetrated her rosebud of an anus, filling it up with my instrument which on this night appeared to know no rest. Ah! How she helped me by opening and shutting the cheeks of her backside, by writhing, twisting and swooning with joy.

I roared like a lion when I came. We lay closely together for a while and then I ordered more champagne, more brandy, lobster and prawns, requesting that she dress for a little supper. Janine responded by donning a black gown of shining silk with a wide belt of gleaming black leather and a silver buckle. Her thrusting breasts threatened to split the fabric at the front and her small, tight bottom looked fit imminently to burst out of the erotic fabric in which it was so tightly wrapped, making it quite visually devastating. Her white petticoats of satin rustled each time she moved her slim legs. After our meal, I could not bear it any longer.

I crushed out my cigar in the ash-tray and rose from my chair. Janine sucked in her breath, her dark eyes widening supremely, and in mock horror, tried to fling herself backward at my approach. I put my hands out to those splendid naked globes of her bosom and lovingly squeezed and stroked them, feeling her nipples stiffen and tingle as my palms lingeringly grazed those crinkly tit-bits. Then I lowered my hands under her skirt and suddenly yanked it up.

'Oh, sir!' she shrieked. 'Don't do that! Why, and I

thought that you were such a gentleman!' In moves of intoxicating tantalization, she lunged this way and that, whilst her beautiful breasts jiggled and danced in a most delicious choreography.

Her skirt, although it squeezed her hips, was exceptionally full around her peeping ankles and there was also the matter of her petticoats. When I had grasped all this fabric in my left hand and lifted it up to her waist, I found to my rising excitement that she had surreptitiously sheathed the vulnerable targets of her loins and bottom in dainty, lace-trimmed pink silk drawers, whose legs reached nearly to mid-thigh and whose snugness defined the shape of the plump prominence of her mound of Venus. Through the transparency of the thin material, I could see the thick bush of black silky curls which crowned her luscious cunt.

'Madam,' I said, 'kindly lie down upon the couch like a goddess who disposes herself to receive adoration from her followers. You have a lovely warm cunt so tender it to my warm, sweet mouth. And thus we will give one another the true kiss of peace!' Blushingly, she took her position and I slipped my hands beneath her bottom and put my mouth to the raven thicket of her mound of Venus, applying a long, sweet, sucking kiss.

'Oooh! Ohh, Horby, what're you doing?' she squealed. When I perceived that Janine's hips and loins had begun once more to wriggle and lunge and when I heard her inarticulate sighs and groans and knew her to be further along the pathway to paradise, I seized her by the waist and pressing her down upon her back, inserted my near-bursting cock into her moist slit and with a single mighty lunge, thrust myself home to the hilt.

Janine uttered a strident cry, flung her arms round my shoulders and, nimbly wrapping her legs over my sinewy and jerking behind, arched up to meet me in the frenetic gymnastics by which we both attained our climax. Happily, considering that I had poured forth such a deluge of essence into Janine's cunt, I discovered that my cock retained its rigidity even after it had spurted forth to acclaim the heated reception this lady's quaking love-canal had bestowed upon it.

I was resting after our embrace and watching with rapt fascination as Janine moaned feverishly, one slim hand now slyly frigging herself as she posed with heels planted upon the couch, knees up and yawningly straddled, her skirt and petticoats all in disarray. I chided her teasingly:

'I will give that little hand something better to play with. Reach out and I'll be there!'

'Ohh, *yes*, Horby dearest,' she sighed, opening her moist eyes and uttering a joyous gasp. 'Oh! that'll be ever so much better!' Janine grasped my ramrod and guided it into her twitching, damp, pink crevice. And once again, with a single, mighty lunge, I impaled her to my very balls and then commenced to fuck her with long, hard digs, as she was clutching me with her arms and stockinged legs, moaning and kissing me feverishly until she poured down her furious tribute.

Gallantly, I then retired, for I had left double the money which she had expected and I feel that delightful ladies of the night are entitled to a period of rest. I shall always recall her fondly as a damn fine fuck, with grace to match it, and I fully intended to visit her again but my plans were to be changed without my knowledge prior to the event upon this very night.

The mysterious Sufi, Amin Shah, had invited me to take some refreshment with him at midnight at a house he was renting in the centre of Madras so as to meet his friend the Yogi who had finally arrived. A huge Sikh proceeded to usher me into a bare room consisting solely of a large round table and ten straight-backed chairs of teak where Amin Shah was drinking fine old malt whisky with Aleister Crowley. We greeted one another warmly and Shah's malt whisky was of surpassing excellence.

'This is a very pleasant surprise,' I said, 'but where is your friend, Amin, the Adept of Yoga?'

'Here,' said Shah, indicating Crowley. 'I have been waiting for him.' I looked more closely and discerned that Crowley was positively glowing with good health and high spirits.

'Got there in the end, Horby,' he told me, 'thanks to the teaching of Allan Bennett. After I saw you in that brothel bar, I went back to Allan and positively raced for results. Twenty hours a day,' he said calmly and with sincere conviction. 'Eventually I achieved the exalted trance of *Dhyana*.'

'Sorry . . .?' I enquired.

'Contemplation,' he replied. 'In analysing the nature of this work of controlling the mind, two things are involved: the person seeing and the thing seen; and the person knowing and the thing known; and one normally regards this as the necessary condition of all consciousness. But what happened to me is that this consciousness of the Ego and the non-Ego, the seer and the thing seen, the knower and the thing known, was blotted out. There was an intense light, an intense sound and a feeling of such overwhelming bliss that the resources of language have been exhausted again and again in the attempt to describe it. *It is an absolute knock-out blow to the mind*. By its light, all other events of life are as darkness.'

'Quite agree,' Amin Shah responded. 'And thank heavens, Mr Crowley, that you are a strong and genuine poet whose use of language may eventually give your readers some intimations of this experience. I don't think that you'll be one of those semi-educated stutterers wallowing in oceans of gush.'

'Too kind, sir.' Crowley smiled. 'And incidentally, Horby, it might greatly interest you to know that the practice of Yoga has greatly improved my sexual performance. These days I can go four hours of rod-ramming without coming. Take up Yoga for that reason, Horby, if for nothing else.'

'So what are your future plans?' I asked.

'Tonight I'm going to have a good dinner and a good fuck,' Crowley responded. 'Then I'm going to escort my dear guru Allan Bennett through the swamps and jungles to Burma, where he wishes to take the Yellow Robe as a Buddhist monk. That is his vocation in life and I respect it immensely but it is not mine. I'll be off after that for some big-game hunting in the jungles with a good chap called Edward Thornton. Now I *would* go tiger-hunting with him.'

'And then?' I queried.

'You sound just like my father,' he answered with a smile. 'Various Rajahs and Maharajahs have kindly invited me to their palaces. I also have appointments with a variety of holy men such as the estimable Mr Shah here.'

'I'm not "holy",' Shah demurred, 'whatever that word may mean. 'I simply endeavour to apply my intelligence.'

'I hope the other ones do, too,' Crowley retorted. 'Then it'll be time to link up again with my dear friend Oskar Eckenstein and climb K2, the second highest mountain in the world.'

'Good luck,' I said.

'You may need it,' Shah added. 'And what of your studies?'

'I shall pursue my studies in Cerebral Neurology;

Psychology, both Western and Eastern; and Philosophical Metaphysics, hoping by reason to persuade men of Science to investigate extra-ordinary states of consciousness as being the next step in human evolution.'

'Good luck,' said Shah, 'for you will need it. And if you come up with a genuine discovery, you will be lucky to escape the prison bars and financial ruin. I predict, though, that at some point in your life, within the next five years, you will encounter an Intelligence way beyond your own which will make of you a true Prophet yet ruin your reputation, which will survive for some generations solely as a classic of infamy. Such is the lot of those who seek too openly to improve the condition of this planet.'

'It may be so, sir,' Crowley answered, 'but I'm always on for a good adventure.' He rose and shook hands warmly. 'Excuse me, gentlemen, but I'm just dying for a fuck. Look after yourself, Horby,' were his last words to me, 'and don't do anything that I wouldn't do. If you can't be good, be careful.'

Today (1925), contemplating my *Memorandum 1023*, I recall the prophetic words of Mr Amin Shah. Allan Bennett did indeed take the Yellow Robe as a Buddhist monk and thence brought Theravada/Hinayana Buddhism to Great Britain. Crowley did indeed win a formidable reputation as a hunter of big game, stalking and shooting the tiger, the leopard, the crocodile and that most dangerous of all creatures, the water buffalo. The Eckenstein-Crowley expedition to K2 smashed more world records and even though they did not succeed in reaching the summit, no one else has either; and the height reached at 22,000 feet has only recently been surpassed. 'An Intelligence way beyond your ken?' Well, Crowley claimed to have encountered this in Cairo in 1904, where it dictated to him an intensely beautiful prose poem called *The Book of the Law*. As a result of endeavouring to preach its doctrines and put them into practice, I gather that Mussolini has expelled Crowley from his 'Abbey of Thelema' in Cefalu, Sicily and he is regularly excoriated in the gutter press. Personally, I cannot believe that he is any worse than I am and for all I know, he may well be a damn' sight better. Certainly I don't believe the salacious tales about him manufactured by 'journalists' unfit to be the smegma in his foreskin. Peace be with thee, friend, where e'er thou be.

Now, I was about to take my leave of Amin Shah when his Sikh butler and bodyguard ushered a familiar figure into the room. Shah greeted him with a few ceremonial formalities.

'Douglas, you old bugger!' I exclaimed. 'It's always a pleasure to see you but what the fuck are you doing here? I thought that after our charming Nile cruise, you had to attend to your business and political interests.'

'I have,' he replied. 'And I am a Master of the art of delegation. First-rate people hire first-rate people. Second-rate people hire third-rate people.'

'You sound just like an adviser to our present Prime Minister,' I replied, 'whose advice has been ignored.'

'Quite right, Horby,' he responded smartly, 'my political and economic advice on Tariff Reform and Imperial Preference *has* been ignored and the Cabinet is merely a menagerie of mediocrities. I have handled my financial interests accordingly. They can all get on as best they like without me for the time being. Anyway,' he took a crystal glass of malt whisky from Amin Shah, 'you chaps simply must come with me on a sea voyage. It's aboard one of my ships going back to England.'

And that was how I came on board the S.S. *Albion* with Douglas and Amin to see an astonishing sight in the bar.

My dear Rosemary was there and so was my darling Claire! And Bellingham and Davina were quaffing champers too! It was a joy to see Emily Ward-Bishop again. The willowy Lady Alison Utterley and the voluptuous Lady Jane Fortescue were there too as well as the strange Mr Ram Singh and the ship's Captain, good old Jack Rivers. The finest of French vintage champagne was flowing freely.

'Welcome to Albion,' said Douglas.

'Rule Britannia!' Emily exclaimed.

'Britannia rules the waves!' sang Davina.

'Britons never, never, never shall be slaves!' bellowed Bellingham.

'Aboard the Good Ship Venus, perhaps . . .?' Ram Singh murmured.

'Or possibly the Ship of Fools?' Amin Shah suggested.

'Land of Hope and Glory!' Captain Jack Rivers roared.

'Mother of the free . . .' sang Rosemary at strong alto.

'How shall we extol thee?' Claire sang in exquisite soprano. We all paused to recharge our glasses.

'Wider still and wider!' sand Lady Jane.

'Shall thy bounds be set,' Lady Alison chimed in delicately.

'God who made thee mighty,' I sang.

'MAKE THEE MIGHTIER YET!' they all responded; and then we all joined in the rousing chorus of:

God, who made thee mighty,
Make thee mightier yet.

'Speech! Speech!' Sir Richard Bellingham shouted.

'Ladies and gentlemen,' said Douglas. 'It is my pleasure and privilege to welcome you on board. By staying on board, you will enable me to realize a dream which I have for long cherished. I don't know just how many of you have read that wondrous and miraculous book, *Gargantua and Pantagruel* by Rabelais.'

'Who the fuck has, Douglas?' Sir Richard cried out. 'Just tell us your point, old chap, and please, no sermonizing.'

'I was expecting you to say something along those lines, Sir Richard,' Douglas retorted coolly. 'My point is simply that in this book, there is an Abbey of Thelema, the Ancient Greek word for Will, in which the only commandment is: "Do what thou wilt." That is the rule on this voyage from Madras to the Port of London. I trust that you will all find your cabins to be comfortable. There is a double four-poster bed in each one of them. For those of you who might be in the mood for calmer pleasures, there is a good library. Others of you may prefer billiards, cards or quoits and, naturally, there is provision for all of these activities. Deep-sea swimming in the Indian Ocean is a delightful activity; though when we come into colder waters, there is a heated pool in which we can swim or paddle. I trust, furthermore, that my chefs, Abdul of Turkey, Marcel of France and Chang Ku-Wei of China will be able to delight your palates in addition to improving the condition of your stomachs. Then there's Mario, our Italian barman, who will give you any drink you want in whatever quantities you order; and Dr Aziz, the ship's medical officer, who will treat your ailments and also give you as much opium and hashish as anyone could conceivably desire. Absolutely everything upon this ship is voluntary, although one hopes that you might choose to be sociable. If, however, you prefer to stare at life on the ocean wave, read pornography and frig yourself, that is your right too. Any questions?'

'Yes,' said Davina Bellingham. 'Why are you doing this?'

'Oh, I've done so much harm to some people in my life,' Douglas responded, 'that I felt it was about time that I did something good. Horby, will you be joining us for the journey?'

'Yes,' I said. 'Yes.'

CHAPTER TWENTY-FIVE

The arrangements on the S.S. *Albion* proved to be admirable in every respect. One could hardly call my luxurious suite 'a cabin': I delighted in the sight of a huge four-poster bed and noted that there was a crystal chandelier firmly affixed to the ceiling should the rocking and rolling of the ship inspire me to essay experimental sexual positioning. I had thought that my desire to join the boat might be impeded by delays occasioned by the difficulties in transporting my possessions but the Ship's Purser, a Mr Clarke, dealt with my query in a trice, proved to be a model of efficiency and organized the matter immaculately.

Clearly, he was doing the same thing for Bellingham for I saw a steward carrying baskets of birches and canes to his cabin, which adjoined that of Davina.

'Got to have all supplies on board, y'know, Horby,' he chortled, having padded up silently behind me, a brandy in his hand and a cigar in his mouth. 'It'll be a long voyage and so the wife and I may be wanting a good bit of flagellation to pass the time. Anyway, they grow good bamboo out in these parts. After all, we don't want our voyage to be all rhubarb and custody.'

'Ah, Horby!' Douglas exclaimed, joining our company with a glass of champagne in his right hand and a black Russian cigarette tipped with gold reposing within a cigarette holder of ebony he was cradling in his left. 'Everything going all right? We're weighing anchor and casting off at dawn – and let it be a golden dawn – but there'll be scrambled eggs on toast with champers and brandy at the Captain's table for anyone who wants the stuff at 4:00 a.m.'

In fact, all the passengers joined the Captain's table at that hour for refreshment that was absolutely delicious. There I gathered the information regarding the various adventures that had brought us all together, here and now, at this moment. Ram Singh and Claire had travelled together at the former's instigation from Rajasthan to Madras upon the Indian railway built by the British after word had been received from Douglas, who had encountered Claire earlier. Douglas himself had travelled with Emily, Jane and Alison, linking up with Mr and Mrs Bellingham in Bombay and then proceeding by rail to Madras in order to meet Rosemary, who had come by sea from North America.

I felt in the mood for a fuck but I wanted to make sure who was going for whom. Rosemary clearly wanted Douglas and he clearly wanted her. Claire and Emily both competed for my attention. I had wondered whether Claire might be engaged to Ram Singh but he did not seem to be at all put out by her flirtatious behaviour towards me and instead flirted with the blonde and buxom Lady Jane. Amin Shah appeared to have taken quite a shine to Lady Alison. Sir Richard Bellingham appeared to be enjoying his honeymoon with Davina so much that suddenly they slipped beneath the table and commenced a noisy fuck. Nobody batted an eyelid.

'Have you gone below decks and looked out of the portholes?' the willowy Lady Alison asked in her, high, clear, slightly lisping, lilting voice. 'They're absolutely *wonderful!* You can see all these brilliant tropical fish swimming around, eating one another and having what passes for sex.'

'What *passes* for sex?' Douglas queried, as Bellingham humped Davina amidst grunts and groans beneath the round table. 'I think that human beings enjoy it more than fish. But do they? Rosemary, my dear, you've just joined us from the Yukon so perhaps you can tell us all about it?'

'Certainly,' said Rosemary. 'And I might add that I am rather pleased to be heard'. She drank some champagne. 'My sea journey from Anchorage, Alaska to Madras, India was a long and arduous one, as the actress said to the bishop.' She laughed merrily. 'Douglas, you're such an enigma, a dark horse, yet I would not exactly classify you as being a skeleton in the cupboard; even though,' she smiled at us, 'he is still to me a man of mystery.' Douglas remained impassive.

'What can I say about my journey?' Rosemary continued. 'I saw some Pacific grey whales. They are such beautiful creatures. Do you not remember that line from Shakespeare's *Hamlet*: "Very like a whale"; an assent to an absurd statement. At this time I can only reminisce in a retrospection, a rather self-indulgent survey of the recent past, of the Arctic Circle, where the weather is always so bitterly cold. Semi-nomadic peoples do actually live in igloos, relying upon the trapping and trading that will provide them with essentials such as guns, provisions . . . sustenance; the general contents of the larder.

'Sometimes I gazed at the ocean and reflected upon my time in the Yukon. I recall coming across a strange saloon: *Diamond Tooth Gertie's Gambling Hall*, with can-can dancers, beautiful women moving with the tinkling of the piano player's ivories: high kicks with a display of long legs, exposing frilly petticoats. One of the dancers came over and introduced herself, sitting beside me.

' "Hi! My name is Bessie. If you are looking for Wyatt Earp," – which I was, and how did she know? – "he has come and gone." I felt rather disappointed. I did so much want to meet that infamous gunman, the most feared lawman in the West! "But you may never know when he might show up," Bessie told me, adding: "His brother Virgil is sometimes an effective double."

' "What do you mean by that?" I queried.

' "He walks in his brother's boots."

' "How well do you know Wyatt Earp?" I asked.

' "For a while I was employed in his gambling parlour." I could understand why. She had such fine chiseled cheekbones, deep, dark, brown eyes and hair as jet-black as a tar-barrel. "Would you like a drink on the house?" she offered; and I accepted. "I must treat you to the speciality of the house: a Sourtoe Cocktail!"

' "I have never heard of a Sourtoe Cocktail."

' "Not many people have," she responded, "but let me tell you how this drink came into existence. Our winters are extremely cold and you can often suffer from severe frostbite. During an exceptionally cold winter, a miner had his big toe frozen off and so he pickled it in a jar of rum. After the drink is consumed, the toe is returned."

' "I think a glass of rum straight without the big toe will satisfy me," I said.

' "You British are all alike!" she laughed. "You know, at one time I was courted by an Englishman, a poet, the Bard of the Yukon?"

' "Robert Service?" I asked.

' "One of the best – yet I had many other lovers. Shookum Jim, Tagish Charlie and George Washington Carmack."

' "These were the founding fathers of the gold rush,

weren't they? Were they all, in your opinion, rather lusty men?"

' "Yes."

'Darlings,' said Rosemary to us, 'I loved her joviality so much and the way in which she conducted herself with such dignity, elegance and grace without any sign of vulgarity. Unexpectedly, she kissed me upon the lips and I was sensitive to the fact that my cheeks were blushing. "You suffer from *mauvaise honte*," she declared in Quebec French. "Why is it that you British always pretend to be so modest, elusive and oblique?" 'She pronounced it '*oh* blique.'

' "*U*blique," I replied.

' "Like a herring?" she pressed.

' "The *herring* is a way of ascending a slope with one's skis pointed outward."

' "Yes," she replied. "However, the descent is easier than the ascent and I would love to reach your muff."

' "I am not wearing a muff," I responded, even though everyone else in the bar was wearing this fur to keep their hands warm.

' "It is the *other* muff that I want to reach," Bessie retorted, "the soft, fine hair that enhances and adorns the bedizenment of my desires." Escorting me to her apartment, she then gradually and slowly unloosened the stays of my basque, so painfully stiffened by whalebone. Kissing me gently upon the breasts, she gently caressed my papilla to arousal: and how my nipples did stand up! She took each one in turn between lips so soft; and she playfully nibbled upon each, dallying with temptation, incitement and an attraction which plucked upon my very heartstrings. Bait to entrance? I was overwhelmed by her presence, an omnipresence, diffusion with a desire to permeate, pervade, saturate and, in her way, penetrate into my body.

'How she did activate and stimulate my yoni! Ladies, do you not know that exquisite feeling? As her finger entered my vagina, I could feel an uncontrollable tremor between my thighs, a pulsation throbbing to build up a climax to the ultimate orgasm.

' "Let me lick your cunny," she requested softly.

' "On one condition," I replied, "that I can do justice to yours." My tongue slowly penetrated her labia, the colour of incarnadine, brilliant crimson. While I nibbled, she stroked me so gently upon my head, fondling my hair. Suddenly, she took my hands in hers, grasping each in a moment of frenzy.

'I drank her orgasmic fluid with such voracity, possessed by an insatiable, inordinate desire, a thirst that may never be quenched. We then kissed each other upon the lips, savouring the flavour of our exchanged juices and relishing its swallowing with great gusto. Before we fell asleep, I gave her a butterfly kiss upon the cheek.

'She wanted to appear so tough; yet I could discern the tenderness within her heart. In the morning I had to leave and she prepared me coffee in a tin-can kettle. However, I saw a sadness within her eyes.

' "I will miss you," she said. "I have slept with several hundred men, including the most notorious and infamous outlaws; yet I would love to come and visit you in London to attend one of your tea parties."

'I would be pleased to invite her,' said Rosemary, 'but, as I had to inform her, I will not be in London for quite a while. So much for my sojourn within the Arctic Circle: now I wonder how unending another sea journey can be. I am so grateful that I do not suffer from sea-sickness! Anyway, isn't my tale enough for today?'

We all agreed that Rosemary had told us an excellent tale but now there was the question of bed. Despite all the enticing advances of Emily, I could not resist the temptations of Claire. I must confess to a twitching of my private parts, a trustworthy and never-failing indication that she had already begun to arouse the basest carnal desires of which my bachelor nature was capable.

Her body, five feet nine inches in height roughly, was magnificently proportioned for that stature. Her hair was worn then in a popular style of that time: a delicious little fringe of affectatious curls all along the top of her high, arching forehead and a prim, huge oval-shaped bun at the back of her head, which suggested somewhat the semblance of a crown. Perhaps it was symbolic, for surely she would be my Queen of Lust for these hours until we cast off. I vowed to myself that I would have her hair unbound and falling in a glossy sheath against her naked skin before she would be allowed to dress and return to her own cabin.

I noticed that her nose was a trifle snub, which gave her an aspect of disdain, quite in keeping with what I already knew about her. Her nostrils were widely flaring, quite sensuous, as was her mouth, somewhat small with a pronouncedly ripe upper lip that completed the delineation of insolence. Her eyes were a dark, imperious blue, very widely set apart from the bridge of her exquisite nose and surmounted by exaggeratedly thin-plucked eyebrows and extremely short but thick lashes.

During this period, to be sure, it may fairly be said that women wore far too many clothes for the immediate savouring pleasure of one of today's rakes. Myself, I cannot concur. I must admit that it was always delightful to prolong the moment of my conquest by having to remove the many garments turn by turn. This paradox heightened my pleasure a good deal as there was always the element of suspense in wondering just what treasures I should at last espy naked when all the outer conventional costume should be removed and the bare flesh come into ardent view. And from the lady's viewpoint, it was far more thrilling, as her suspense was being constantly augmented until the supreme moment of finding herself Eve-naked in my presence whilst I remained fully clothed.

Seeing Claire dressed at the height of fashion gave extra impulse to my own lust as I recalled her physical charms and delightful curves. I fondly remembered that she had had a somewhat slender waist from which – if her bustle's contours could be faithfully believed – there flared impudently rounded, full and ample hips. Perhaps she did not have so curvaceous a form as Emily Ward-Bishop but she nonetheless gave in every way the prospect of being an absolutely breathtaking morsel of pulchritude when she should finally be stripped down to the indisputable state of helpless nakedness that I meant to exact from her.

'I'm going to be cruel to you,' I told her.

'Oh, simply *soopah!*' she responded. '*When*?'

We excused ourselves from the Captain's table. Jack Rivers beamed benevolently, for he had been casting his eager eyes upon Emily for the past two hours. Sir Richard and Davina continued to hump away beneath the table, blithely oblivious to everything other than the act of fucking. The moment we entered our venue, which was my cabin, I flung Claire down upon the bed and stripped her naked. I unbuttoned my fly to release my stiff cock and simply pranged it into her.

'Oh, Horby . . .' she sighed as we both came together,

'sometimes you can be so crude . . . but it's been such a long time, hasn't it?' She touched my balls and kissed me on the lips. '*Bon voyage*,' she said.

The ship's siren sounded and our boat weighed anchor in the golden dawn as we enjoyed our orgasms.

CHAPTER TWENTY-SIX

'Jolly good show, the British Army!' Sir Richard Bellingham declared. He relaxed in his chair and regarded the glass of fine old Burgundy he was cradling in his hand. We were all now cruising pleasantly in the Indian Ocean and had enjoyed an excellent Lebanese *meze*, a selection of all sorts of tasty dishes prepared well by Abdul. 'And I'm all for the *British* traditions,' Bellingham continued. 'Oh, yes, the public school is a damn fine thing. Those people who didn't go there strike me as being a pretty grisly set of oicks. No manners and what-not.' He dug his fork into a dish of thinly sliced raw beef and crammed it into his mouth, biting on it so hard and with such satisfaction that blood flowed down his chin and had to be wiped away by Davina.

'I gather that your English public schools are very strict,' Amin Shah commented mildly, helping himself to more bread and *tahini*, a delicious dish made out of sesame seeds.

'Oh, yes, Amin, and quite right too,' Bellingham retorted. 'Lots of beating. Why, when I was at school, we used to get six of the best every day. Made me what I am.'

'And what *are* you?' Rosemary enquired.

'Oh, just a bloody fool, Madam, same as all the other men here.' Bellingham seized a plate of prawns and devoured five of them in one mouthful. 'The nature of Man is to penetrate and the nature of Woman is to enclose. This is why we men, although we sometimes make the odd discovery that advances human evolution, usually just carry on making ruddy pricks of ourselves. Let's face it, men are stupid sods and women are silly bitches and if we only were to realize that basic truth, we'd all get along a jolly sight better.'

'Slightly pessimistic, perhaps . . .?' lisped Alison.

'Not at all, my dear.' Bellingham seized a spoon and dug greedily into a bowl of *hummus* – mashed chick peas with yoghurt and spices – and then popped three *falafels* – compressed and fried chick-peas – into his mouth.

'There's only one way to stop Bellingham declaring his opinions,' Douglas observed drily as Bellingham chewed. 'Keep feeding the bloody man!' He helped himself to one of the delicate little pastries which enclouded spiced minced meat with onion. 'But continue with your military theme. One hopes that it might lead to something profitable.'

'Yes,' Ram Singh muttered, 'sales of armaments to under-developed countries.'

'All right,' said Bellingham, 'here's a joke. The Commanding Officer calls in the Regimental Sergeant-Major as the men are on parade. "It's bad news for Private Smith," says the C.O. "His father's just died. Break the news to him, Sergeant Major". So the Sergeant Major goes out onto the Parade Ground and bellows: "Private Smiff!" "Sah!" "Your faver's just died!" Private Smith keels over, has a breakdown and time in hospital but after three months he's back on parade again. The C.O. calls in the Sergeant Major and says: "More bad news for Private Smith, I'm afraid. His mother's just died. Break the news to him, Sergeant Major." So the Sergeant Major goes out onto the Parade Ground and roars: "Private Smiff!" "Sah!" "Yer muvver's just died!" Private Smith keels over, has another breakdown and it's time in hospital for him again. After six months he's finally back on parade. The C.O. calls in the Sergeant Major and says: "Poor old Private Smith doesn't seem to be having too much luck lately. His wife has just died. Break the news to him, Sergeant Major . . . oh, and Sergeant Major . . . *Sergeant Major* . . . I understand there's been a spot of upset in the past. Now, gently does it, Sergeant Major, gently does it. Tact and diplomacy, that's what's required heah." So the Sergeant Major goes out onto the Parade Ground and yells: "All those wiv a wife take one pace for-ward . . . *Smiff*! you 'orrible bleeder, where you fink you're going?'

The women hooted with laughter as the men looked slightly unhappy.

'What is the point of this story?' Ram Singh enquired.

'It's a cruel, hard world,' said Bellingham.

'And you approve of the British Army?' Ram Singh pressed the matter. Bellingham took more Burgundy.

'As the Iron Duke of Wellington said,' he answered, ' "I don't know what they'll do to the enemy but, by God, they frighten me." As he also said "The battle of Waterloo was won on the playing fields of Eton".'

'I see. Officers and men,' Ram Singh responded. 'Somewhat class-ridden, wouldn't you say, Sir Richard?'

'Not at all!' Bellingham snorted dismissively. 'As Wellington said when some upstart tried to embarrass him at a ball with "Good evening, sir. Mr Smith, I believe", he replied: "If you believe that, you will believe anything." '

'Thank you, Sir Richard,' Ram Singh replied. 'You have just shown me precisely why the British Empire has won and now covers one-fifth of the entire globe's land surface.' Bellingham quaffed his wine and nodded approvingly. 'You have also shown me,' Ram Singh continued, 'precisely why it will in due course be lost: in the end, the whole remaining territories will not amount to a greater size than one of your smallest English counties.'

'Oh?' Bellingham raised a quizzical eyebrow. 'And why's that?'

'I think it would be unkind to tell you,' Ram Singh retorted.

'Well, it's no disgrace to be honestly mistaken,' Bellingham replied. 'And you are.'

'Quite right, Sir Richard,' Ram Singh responded with a gentle grin. 'Only time will tell.'

'I suppose that fighting and fucking are the activities in which two people come closest,' Rosemary observed. 'And fighting is all very well, though I find it to be a game for boys. Enough of fighting, Sir Richard! Tell us about some fucking.'

'Gladly, my dear lady,' Bellingham replied. 'Oh, how I lust after a grand fuck!' I noticed that his wife Davina was gazing at him approvingly. 'There can be no male who cannot find the opposite sex fascinating and provocative, who cannot tremble with hardly suppressed excitement at the anticipation of fulfilling all his most lustful whims. I dare say that in each of us, an incipient sadism lingers, product of earlier, less gentle ages when women were slaves and men their lawful masters. Who, for heaven's sake, has not chafed under the scorn of some haughty girl, baffled and raging at the knowledge that no retaliatory move is possible under the code of society that treats the female as being an helpless, weak creature that must be shielded at all costs from villainy and violence? Therefore, I unashamedly admit before you tonight, that in the days before my marriage to my darling lady wife here,' Davina smiled at him, 'a bitch made a fool out of me and I resolved upon revenge.'

'I adore revenge,' Jane murmured dreamily, 'for cruelty is rarely dull.'

'It can be,' said Alison, 'if it is executed without appropriate imagination.'

'I am merely erotically excited,' Emily declared, 'by tales of dominance and submission.' She was sitting at the right hand of Captain Jack Rivers, who looked at her with appreciation and approval.

'The facts are,' said Sir Richard, 'that at one point in my earlier days, I was engaged to the beautiful and charming . . . let's call her Lady Arabella. I had a jolly good chum called . . . well, Lord Horace Somebody, and he was engaged to . . . shall we say Lady Henrietta? Now, a woman I shall call Patricia was a close friend of both of these ladies and Horace and I found her to be exceedingly attractive. Patricia proceeded to seduce me away from my lady love, an heiress, charmed me and after our fuck, swore undying love to me; though I must confess that I wasn't on particularly good sexual form that night. However, I departed feeling utterly infatuated.

'Horace,' Bellingham continued, 'had always sworn to me that he would never make a pass at any woman with whom I was involved. He congratulated me on my success: yet the next thing I knew, and at least he told me to my face, was that *he'd* deserted his affianced for her alleged best friend, Patricia, who had declared her undying love for *him*, and had departed utterly infatuated. I was really rather offended. It all rather spoiled the relationship between Horace and myself; but there was worse to come.

'Patricia, who was called with some truth "the best lay in London" at the time, now endeavoured to blackmail Horace and myself with the indiscreet letters of infatuation we had foolishly written to her. Well, I emulated the

Duke of Wellington in saying: "Publish and be damned." So did Lord Horace; but the consequences were unfortunate. Patricia exacted her vengeance by sending copies of our letters, which revealed sexual acts which our respective affiances would not countenance, to Arabella and Henrietta. I think that probably the most embarrassing moment of my life was when Horace and I were confronted by our intended partners in holy matrimony – heiresses both, I might add – waving these bits of paper in our faces and spitting self-righteous scorn all over our heads. Patricia had furthermore told everyone in London that Horace and I were utterly useless in bed. She nicked-named me "Woody Woodpecker" and she called him "Droopy".' And we had enjoyed a reputation as rake-hells! She had just spun us around her little finger and made of us a pair of clots.

' "I can forgive you for an affair," each lady said to us separately, "but I cannot forgive you for making such an idiot of yourself in public." And so ended two intended marriages which could have been most fortunate.'

'Good,' said Davina Bellingham. 'It would never have worked anyway.'

'Glad that's your attitude, my dear,' Sir Richard responded, 'but I was determined to exact my revenge for this appalling humiliation. I invited Patricia to one of my houses, swearing my own undying love for her, no matter what she had done. It was an invitation to afternoon tea, as I recall, and I had it set before her, all the while behaving with the utmost deference and gentlemanly courtesy. For if you have never had in your home an arrogant and cruel young woman who has treated you as if you were beneath her notice whilst at the same time you are conjuring up visions of her rosy lips deferentially fixed about your manhood, then you cannot begin to understand the riotous images that filled my imagination and the shuddering impulsions which titillated all my nerves and sinews.

'After having poured tea and added cream and demerara sugar to my preference, I seated myself opposite her and fixed upon her the most intent and gracious look it was in my power to muster. An uneasy silence fell over us and then, after a ladylike switching and swishing of her skirt and petticoats, she fixed her dark eyes upon me and declared:

' "What chiefly brought me to agreeing to visit you, Richard, is the inexplicable part of your note to me. I cannot for the life of me understand how you could possess any kind of information about my future happiness, as you termed it, that would be of the least concern to me. Will you please explain your meaning?"

' "Certainly and gladly," I replied, as I put down my tea-cup with a *chink*. "Since we last met, I have developed psychic powers. You're interested in marrying a rich and powerful man, aren't you? Well, if you just close your eyes for a moment and hold out your hands, thinking of the spirit world all the while, I can forecast your future." She smiled slyly and, as if to humour me, closed her eyes and held out her hands. That was all I need to snap on the steel handcuffs; and my butler Robert quietly inserted a large lump of cotton wool within a mouth gaping with astonishment and gagged her with a pair of women's drawers. Her feet kicked out furiously but the two of us soon secured them with black leather thongs. She struggled and twitched to no avail as we carried her downstairs to the chamber I had prepared for the purpose of punishment.

'This chamber consisted of a bare room with an altar upon which reposed a marble statue of Priapus with red-tipped, erect phallus, with a tall white and a tall black candle on either side. Within the centre, there was a flogging-block, purchased from the firm which supplies these to Eton. As you probably know, it's a piece of stout furniture arranged like a low platform with a central "step". Patricia had to kneel on one end, bend across the step and have her hand-cuffs fastened at the other end so that her luscious bottom was elevated to precisely the correct angle. The attached restraining straps of brown leather secured her ankles. I then pulled away her skirt, threw up her petticoats and tore down her silken drawers to expose her pearly white, neat and naughty buttocks, twitching in furious affront and indignity. I removed her gag and she began to shriek and yell and howl.

' "I'll have the Law on you!" she screamed. "I'll ruin you!"

' "Oh, do be quiet; you've already tried to ruin me," I sighed wearily. "Your shouting does no good, Patricia." Now, the hobby of my butler Robert, whose forebears have been with the family for many a generation, happens to be photography. I'd hired a whore called Olivia that night, a pleasant black girl from Jamaica, and she inserted her fingers into Patricia's cunt and shoved her arse against Patricia's face as Robert took photographs.

' "You fucking bastard!" Patricia hissed. Robert and Olivia left the room silently.

' "Shut up, you silly bitch!" I snarled back. "You have endeavoured to blackmail me and now I'm going to do exactly the same thing to you. If there's the slightest sign of misbehaviour from you in the future, copies of the photographs just taken will be circulated among members of Society as proof of your decadent enjoyment of Satanism, black magic and perversion in some low-down Paddington brothel, leading to the ruination of all your marital prospects. And if you manage to find some wealthy pervert of a husband who is actually attracted to you on account of the fact, then they will be circulated as cheap and filthy post-cards for the sniggers of street-urchins."

' "I hate you!" She spat the words.

' "Good!" I exclaimed. "At last we've got something in common! Anyway, my advice to you is simply to submit to your chastisement for all the wrongs that you have done; and if you squawk too loudly, I'll simply double the number of strokes. Now be a good girl and raise your bottom obediently to suffer my just and punitive measures." She continued to writhe in a frenzy and fury and I must say that this made of her pearly white, curvaceous bottom a most appealing sight.

'Now, I decided to use a variety of instruments and there was indeed a method in my madness. As my friends know, I take a great deal of interest in these matters of flagellation. The reason for this lies in the essential natures of the three classes of punitive instrument: smack, cut and lash. To give but one example, a properly administered caning will leave prominent red and blue weals across the lady's stern. These marks last for days and are a necessary part of the terror of the cane but there is, in my view, no point in overdoing it. The answer is, surely, to inflict the second chastisement with another class of weapon, whose effects can safely and usefully be added to those already *in situ* because although it punishes the same target, it does so in a different way and with different emphasis. A bottom lacerated from a recent caning can therefore still be punished if necessary, provided that the second correction is inflicted with a birch, a tawse, a tapette or the palm of one's hand.

'Taking the same line of reasoning a little further, it is

therefore obviously possible to achieve still more variety and choice of disciplinary method when it is realized that two or more different instruments may be used, in succession, during a single chastisement. Instead of ten cane-strokes, do what I did to Patricia, which was to give her a sound spanking followed by three hard swishes of the cane. Let's face it, a bottom well reddened beforehand by a lusty encounter with a strong hand will be in even more sensitive condition to receive a few whippy strokes from a good, flexible cane.

'As it was, I could see that my loud and heavy spanking, each slap of which echoed throughout the chamber, ensured that her bottom was well-reddened and twitching, wearing thin my delinquent's reserves of energy and endurance and causing her to sob her apologies. As a result, the number of concluding stripes could be confined to a minimum for the sake of remembrance. I am not a cruel man; but I do enjoy attention to detail and an appreciation of nuance.

'When it comes to caning, I'm a great believer in "three-inch grooving". By that, I mean that the stripes should be confined to the three-inch zone at the centre of a woman's bottom, with one strip at each inch. Patricia howled and squealed as I lashed her twitching red bum at each one of them: ho! ho! Again she sobbed out her apologies for her shabby behaviour and promised that she would never conduct herself in such a shameful manner ever again. For my own part, I stepped back to enjoy the sight of her scarlet bottom, formerly so snow-white, trembling and wriggling and writhing on account of its weals and stripes whilst strapped helplessly to the flogging block. Oh, yes! There's a real pleasure in watching a flogged girl's bottom change its colours – better than watching a sunset.

'It's very erotic, so I took out my stiff prick and shoved it up a helpless cunt that had become wonderfully moist in the course of her chastisement. I took only a few thrusts and then I came quite gloriously. Yet when I stepped back and saw her glowing bottom changing colour, well, I just had the hots for her again. This time I shoved it right up her burning arse, I can tell you, and I groaned in the sheer ecstasy of my come as she squealed. Afterwards, I had my servants untie her, give her a bubble bath and send her on her way.'

'What happened to her?' I asked.

'Oh, she'd learned her lesson,' Sir Richard retorted. 'And she's since proceeded to marry a very rich, boring old fart.'

'Oh, Richard!' His wife Davina burst out laughing. 'Sometimes I just don't know whether you're a complete fool or the Devil himself!'

'If you're going to be a fool,' said Bellingham, 'make sure you spell it with a capital "F" and be a Great Fool.'

CHAPTER TWENTY-SEVEN

'You're obviously fond of games, Sir Richard,' Ram Singh said as the port came round. The ladies had withdrawn for coffee and liqueurs and probably also to get away from the men.

'Very much so,' Bellingham replied. 'And my favourite game is called "Jenkins." Every player gets a bottle of Scotch and has to drink it standing up in one go. The last one left standing up is Jenkins.'

'And what is the point of that?' Amin Shah enquired.

'What's the point of anything, my dear fellow?' Sir Richard retorted. 'I mean, what do you chaps do to enjoy yourselves?'

'I once gave quite an interesting dinner-party,' said Douglas. 'Electricity was wired to every seat of the eight snobs I had invited. Every time that any snob committed the slightest breach of dinner-party etiquette, he or she received an unpleasant and jolting electrical shock.'

'And how did your guests take it?' Ram Singh asked.

'They were all very shocked,' said Douglas.

'Serve them right,' Ram Singh as he seized the decanter of excellent vintage port, poured it out expertly with his right hand and passed it along to me. It was a perfect accompaniment to matured Stilton cheese with thin Captain's Biscuits, although, as Jerome K. Jerome has said, 'I mean the biscuits were thin, not the Captain.'

'Too many of the English people who come out to India are bloody fools,' said Captain Jack Rivers. 'I mean in the old days, it was actually the youngest sons of the gentry and the aristocracy trying to make their fortunes through trade. They had respect for the culture of India, which was a civilized society when us lot . . . hell's bells, we were just running around with blue woad on our faces yelling: "Wogga! Wogga! Wogga!" But the sons of our upper class understood that, which is why they often intermarried with the Indian upper class and came home sailing as enriched *nabobs* or *nobs*.' Ram Singh and Amin Shah nodded approvingly. 'The problem arose, in my opinion, with those bloody middle-class public schools and their bloody missionary Christianity.'

'Quite right, Captain,' Ram Singh responded. 'They had no respect at all for our culture, when they came out here. The missionaries tried to convert us to their wretched religion of sin and guilt. The only ones who went along with them were the Untouchables, the filth, slime and scum.'

'No one is an Untouchable in my religion,' Amin Shah declared, 'but there is no notion of sin or guilt in Islam. You bear your Fate with manly fortitude. We call it *kismet*. And,' he glanced approvingly at Ram Singh, 'the Hindus call it *karma*. It is essentially the same thing regarded from two different angles. Which apex of a triangle is the "correct" one? And who would choose to exchange this sense for Christian missionary nonsense?'

'No one,' Ram Singh answered, 'except a slave. Another mistake that's been made by the British Empire has been to send out their middle-class women. For a start, they cannot stand the climate. Nor can their husbands, who become impotent. The English women, meanwhile, who itch for sex, eventually allow themselves to be seduced by Bengali servants. In consequence, the entire mystique of the Great White Sahib vanishes altogether. The Bengali servant boasts of his conquests and the white man and woman become, not subjects of veneration, but objects of ridicule. Then the missionaries come and inform us that we should convert to their primitive, tribal beliefs. Frankly, Sir Richard, Lord Horby, Mr Douglas and Captain Jack Rivers, the average inhabitant of the Indian sub-continent much prefers your swaggering swashbuckling swankiness, which will leave him alone, to the mealy-mouthed moralizing of the mentally retarded missionary.'

We white men all raised our glasses to toast that.

'Please understand,' said Ram Singh, 'how you chaps came to conquer India: it *suited* us. India absorbs all its conquerors. You ruled a country of many millions with just your proverbial "thin red line". Many of us wanted that for we thought that we could learn certain things from you. And we did: your technology, for example. Your rule gave us efficient railways and civic transportation. You made the waters clean, cured disease and, insofar as you could, you made sure that the hungry might be fed. Your system of Justice could not be bribed, an unusual phenomenon for us, and although, of course, your courts always found in favour of an Englishman, which we expected, you nevertheless were utterly fair and impartial between our various castes in Hinduism, between Muslim and Sikh, between Parsee and Jain. This is why, when the British Raj ends, we will still like you and want to make friends.'

'Oh, steady on a minute,' Bellingham protested. 'I think you're quite wrong there, Ram. You're talking about the British Empire upon which the sun never sets, y'know.'

'It *will* set, sir,' Ram Singh answered, 'within roughly fifty years.'

'Bah! Humbug!' Bellingham snorted and tossed back his glass of port. 'Shall we join the ladies?' He followed that statement with a colossal sneeze into his scarlet silken handkerchief.

We all gave him a good 'Bless you!' and I must admit that at the time, I thought that Ram Singh, good chap though he was, was talking absolute bloody nonsense. Today, however, (1925), looking at the situation in India and reading about those curious fellows, Gandhi and Jinnah, and learning of all the agitation for independence, I have to admit that he may well have foreseen something which may be coming.

'Let us eat, drink, and be serious; hardly a recipe for a good time, is it?' I murmured as we joined the ladies – only to take a pace backwards in shocked surprise. Our eyes were greeted by a scene of sheer debauchery. Lady Alison had her head very much inside the voluminous skirts of Lady Jane, whose head lolled backwards with her pale cheeks flushing as she moaned softly in her rapture, twirling her high heel of her shining leather boot upon the back of Alison's white, satin blouse. They occupied a sofa. Rosemary and Claire had declined to take a love-seat and were sitting back-to-back. This looked perfectly proper until one realised that the left hand of each one was buried deeply within the other one's skirts and that they weren't sighing and groaning and panting on account of the beauties of the view. Emily had had her corset unlaced by Davina, who had released her full breasts and was licking and sucking at her nipples.

'Men sorting out the world can be such a bore . . .' Rosemary sighed as she came to orgasm.

'That's a statement that's all very well,' Douglas

responded coolly. 'Gentlemen, I have the feeling, somehow, that the ladies always find us a bore unless we have stiff pricks. And don't we find it a bore when we haven't?'

'Oh, well, I've got one,' Bellingham declared. 'Davina, d'you want to fuck with me or with some prick-less bitch?'

'Both . . .' Davina sighed dreamily, then melted into a warm and loving embrace in Emily's arms as her caresses brought off the latter.

'It seems to me,' Amin Shah remarked, 'that for these particular ladies, only the best will do.'

'YEAH!!!' they all screamed out with a ferocity some might have found to be positively frightening: but by this time I was used to the many moods and modes of Woman; and the sight before my eyes granted me much delight. I was about to approach Claire when the boat rocked and rolled so alarmingly that the ladies were all deposited sprawling upon the floor.

'Oh, hell,' said the Captain. 'I can sense a typhoon coming. If we're going to get through this one, I'll have to be at the helm. Kindly excuse me.'

The ship shuddered again and the women ceased their lascivious activities and looked alarmed. There was a howl of wind so loud that we were all aware of it within our chamber of pleasure and especially since a wave made all our bottles and glasses roll over and crash on the floor. I seized Claire in my arms, Bellingham grabbed Davina, Ram Singh and Amin Shah separated Jane and Alison; and Emily announced that she would be going to the assistance of the Captain.

'Oh, damnit!' Rosemary shouted as another big wave caused her glass to crash over and she fell into the arms of Douglas. 'We haven't got anything to drink!'

'No problem!' Bellingham cried out. 'I'll just get a

bottle from good old Mario in the bar!' Unfortunately, the next wave was so heavy that as Bellingham tried to walk, he missed his step and was flung across the room. 'Take more than that to knock me out,' he muttered through gritted teeth as he hauled himself to his feet and staggered forward on unsteady pins. 'Brandy!' he exclaimed defiantly, 'that's the way to get through a typhoon!'

The ship lurched as much as Bellingham as the man made his exit. I looked out of the window and saw a raging sea whose huge waves were washing up on deck and which were threatening to engulf and swallow our tiny ship.

'If the typhoon and the ocean are going to drown us all,' Jane declared in her plummy voice, 'why can't it be done now rather than keeping us all in suspense? Anyway, I'm going to go down fucking. You up to it, Ram Singh? Or is *Ram* a misnomer?'

'Not at all, my dear lady,' he answered. 'Let us fuck and die together.' Thereupon they fell down upon the floor, utterly oblivious to the stormy weather. Jane shrieked out her joy as he tore up her silken skirts with one hand, unbuttoned his fly with the other and then pronged her with his great big fucking whanger of a rod.

The boat tilted so sharply that I lost my balance and fell flat on my face. I was up in a trice, only for a heave of the mighty sea to send me flying into the arms of Claire. As I lay upon her breast, I saw Amin Shah sitting calmly in a chair with Alison on her knees before him sucking his stiff cock.

'Hmmm, rather like a lollipop, isn't it?' she mused in between sucks and licks. 'Oh, well, if I'm going to die at sea, I might as well die well.' Thence she returned eagerly to renewed cocksucking, her mouth and thin lips clinging on so hard to his prick that she was still hanging on for dear life when the next wave and the roll of the boat threw him out of his chair.

'Either we die or we don't,' Douglas was saying to Rosemary. He had pulled up her skirt and petticoats and pulled down her drawers; they were now fucking. 'Let's just move as the ocean takes us. If we die, it will be the *mors justi* – the death of the righteous in our noble act of fucking.'

'And if we don't die,' Rosemary returned as the boat rocked quite hideously, 'it will be the life of the righteous in the noble act of fucking.'

'Where *is* that bloody man of mine?!' Davina shrieked as the next wave made her chair tumble over, leaving her sprawling on the floor. At that moment, a member of the crew staggered into the room looking like a drowned rat.

'No one on deck!' shouted Able Seaman Higgins. 'Captain's orders!'

'D'you think we're all fools, same as you?' I asked.

'Oh, frigging in the rigging . . .' Davina sighed as she masturbated openly upon the floor as the ship swayed perilously. 'There's fuck all else to do.'

'Quite right, Madam,' I said; then knowing it could be the last fuck in my life, I hurled Claire down upon the floor, ripped down her drawers, buried my head inside her skirts and kissed, licked and sucked at her gorgeous, pouting cunny lips, with my tongue coming to tickle her clitoris. Thinking that if I were to suffer the dismal fate of being drowned at sea, I might as well go out with a bang, I prodded my rod into the gorgeous vagina of this girl, swiving her back and forth until death seemed really rather irrelevant. She gasped and sighed as I pounded her pudenda. I whirled my prick all the way around her cunt as the ship swayed, at one moment so violently that we were hurled against the room's wall. The winds screeched and the waves tossed us forth as we came together in sensational ecstasy.

A period of calm followed as we held one another close and tight. Was it the eye of the typhoon, in which case more would be coming that might be worse; or had we just sailed into one of its circles? None of us knew the upshot of the issue. We hoped to high heaven that nobody had been washed overboard as Able Seaman Higgins led us up to the forecastle. There we discovered Emily Ward-Bishop fiercely gripping the wheel as Captain Jack Rivers was giving it to her up the arse. None of us criticized him for his effective method of steering us through a storm: but where was Sir Richard Bellingham?

We all searched high and low, praying that the high seas hadn't taken him in a fit of absence of mind: and we eventually found him way below decks in a cabin that must once have been used to amuse the children of passengers. He had his dick in his hand and was singing softly to himself as he held a bottle of brandy in his other hand and swayed gently back and forth upon a rocking-horse.

CHAPTER TWENTY-EIGHT

It soon became evident that we had weathered the storm, owing to the Captain's unorthodox but excellent manner of steering the ship. Yet our perils were not yet over. On the following morning as we were all playing quoits on deck, suddenly a pirate ship appeared on the horizon.

'Piracy on the high seas?' I queried. 'In this day and age?'

'Oh, yes,' Captain Jack Rivers replied jovially, having just won money from Douglas at quoits. 'The South China Seas are still infested with pirate ships. It's less common in the Indian Ocean, but it happens. They see a passenger ship such as this one and they espy easy pickings.'

'And what do they do?' Alison enquired nervously.

'They ram the ship,' said Rivers, 'or else they board it via long-boats. Then they kill all the men and rape all the women, after which they throw 'em overboard down to Davey Jones's locker. If the ship's better than theirs, they take it over.' There was a pause while this information sank in. Everyone was trying very hard to keep calm.

'Could we simply out-speed them?' Rosemary enquired.

'Not as far as I can see,' the Captain replied. 'Here,' he held up a spy-glass. 'Take a look for yourself. It's hardly the colourful pantomime Jolly Roger.'

'How exciting!' Emily exclaimed. 'I do hope they'll be a good fuck.'

'Stop being such an idiot, Madam!' Captain Jack Rivers roared at her. 'Don't you realize that once they've fucked you they'll simply slit your throat? Meanwhile us men will have our balls cut off and stuffed in our mouths before they drown us.'

I took a look through the spy-glass and my blood ran cold. I don't think I have ever seen a more evil band of ill-intentioned cut-throats. I resolved to sell my life dearly.

'Any weapons aboard, Captain?' I asked.

'Pistols and cutlasses, that's what we need!' Bellingham declared. 'And we'll cane these savages yet!' The captain responded by having Able Seaman Higgins distribute precisely these weapons to all of us as the pirate ship drew nearer. I braced myself for the forthcoming conflict, resolved either to do or die.

'I admire your calm,' I said to the Captain. The women were visibly nervous. They knew that their men were no cowards and were resolved to fight until the last breath: but would we survive against a pack of professional pirates who vastly outnumbered us?

'You'll soon see why, Lord Horby,' Jack Rivers replied. At that moment, Able Seaman Higgins wheeled a cannon onto the deck and positioned it, peering through a gap. 'You see, I wouldn't sail these seas without one of these.' Actually it wasn't a cannon in the Nelson style: it was more the sort of field gun used in the Great War to come. The pirate ship fired a few shots which landed in loud splashes a few hundred yards away from us. Emily squealed, realizing that it wasn't a game any more. 'Bloody fools,' Jack Rivers muttered. 'They're way wide of the mark.' He lit his curved briar pipe. 'No idea of range at all.' He slightly adjusted the barrel of the gun. I stared at the steam-ship heading toward us. 'They still can't hit us,' he murmured, 'but now's the time to hit *them*'. He fired the gun. The shell smacked straight into the engine room of the enemy and their ship blew up in a whirl of smoke and flame.

I don't know how many died at that moment or after, when the ship was sinking slowly, but the pirates were resourceful. Now it was their turn to do or die and they swiftly abandoned ship and piled into long-boats, brandishing pistols and cutlasses, rowing in a zig-zag pattern that made of their vessels an elusive set of targets. The Captain fired three times and missed, swearing heavy oaths and uttering imprecations. The women gripped their swords and pistols fiercely but grew more visibly nervous.

'No problem at all,' Douglas said coolly from behind us. We turned to see him carrying one of those (then) new-fangled machine guns. 'As the poet has it:

Whatever happens, we have got
The Gatling Gun, and they have not.'

Captain Jack Rivers helped him to set it up on the ship's rail. I watched with fascination as Douglas smoked a cigar and waited for the pirates' long boats to come closer, yawning like a lazy cat as their pistol shots failed to find us and plonked in the water, at least a hundred yards short of the distance. At a nod from Douglas, the Captain proceeded to turn the handle of this ingenious machine and the former pressed the trigger. A volley of bullets drilled holes in the pirate boats and killed a few more blood-bespattered victims.

'But now, and as I like to say, Ladies First!' Douglas declared and we could all see that the pirate boats were slowly sinking. One by one, Rosemary, Claire, Jane,

Alison, Davina and Emily stepped up to the Gatling and pressed the trigger as the Captain cranked the handle. It was really rather like going on a pheasant shoot. Anyway, the women bagged the whole bloody lot of them and afterwards hooted with delight. By the end, there was a ship slowly sinking and two long boats already sunk, with all men dead and spreading skeins of blood in the water.

'Splendid shooting, ladies!' Bellingham bellowed. 'As I've always maintained, *English* women are absolutely top-hole!'

It was a dark and stormy night indeed as we all sat down to dinner but a gale was considered a mere flurry following from the typhoon and the endeavours of the pirates who had been literally blown out of the water by superior Western technology, if that's the right term. I keep hearing it used more and more these days (1925). Marcel was on duty as chef and he gave us the delights of fish in the Indian Ocean as a *bouillabaisse*, a fish stew that was absolutely fabulous. We greedily chewed, licked and sucked meaty morsels of crab, lobster, crayfish, prawns and hefty slabs of sea-bass after which we slurped the soup.

The next course was *steak tartare*, raw minced fillet of beef with spices and capers and crowned with a raw egg, served with a multifarious variety of breads: dry toast, rye, granary, white, black, brown and so on. All of us relished the matter of feasting after a good kill. We then ate lambs' tongues and lambs' kidneys in an exquisitely delicious sauce of cream and brandy and herbs. The cheese board was tremendous: *always* have the cheese board, I say, *provided* that the chef is French. This was followed by a delicate apple tart with cream, which proved to be delicious.

We were all as happy over coffee and brandy as people

who have just fought off a pirate ship can be. Naturally, the matter had affected us: I saw that Ram Singh was going after the willowy, lisping Alison whereas Amin Shah now wanted the plummy-voiced, buxom Jane. Claire seemed to be besotted by the bravery of Captain Jack Rivers, who had steered us through two crises, and Emily was sucking up to me, so much so that she had unbuttoned my fly and was indeed sucking my stiff cock beneath the table. This was hardly bad etiquette at the Captain's table since Douglas had plunged his head beneath the skirts of Rosemary, who was sighing with pleasure as he licked her cunt and sucked her clit. Sir Richard and Lady Bellingham promptly fell down beneath the table yet again and commenced fucking like a pair of pigs. I therefore put Emily upon my lap, whipped up her skirt and petticoats to discover an ingenious slit within her silken knee-length knickers, and prodded my rod into her. As I came, the world seemed to explode before me; and as I came *to*, I noticed that Jack Rivers was exploding within the loins of Claire, whose own loins were astride him.

'I don't think we're doing too badly.' A sweaty Bellingham arose from beneath the table and helped himself to copious quantities of biscuits, butter, Stilton and port. Davina arose and brushed down her skirts demurely. 'Fighting and fucking! That's when two people come closest!' he declared. 'Mind you, I'd rather fight *with* a good man on the same side rather than *against* him: but when it comes to a good woman, I just want to fuck her!' Davina burst out laughing. 'D'you hear her?' he demanded. 'I do. And I tell you, if a man doesn't listen to his wife, he's just a bloody fool. If his reason for not doing so is that he claims that she's thick, why then, he's a *double* bloody fool for having married her in the first place.'

'Quite agree,' said Douglas. 'And that's why I think it's pointless to have separation of the male and the female at this table tonight. Let's all compose ourselves with all due decorum. We've heard stories told by Rosemary here and by Sir Richard; but Emily, my dear, surely it is your turn. How is the Society for the Promulgation of Petticoat Government?'

'It is *thriving*,' Emily replied. 'Why, just before I left England to enjoy this intriguing journey, I enjoyed the occasion of accompanying Mrs Joan Smythe on a visit to the marital home of two of her former pupils: Lady Charlotte and young Jeremy, her husband.'

'We were there!' Lady Jane chortled as Lady Alison smirked.

'Oh, indeed,' replied the Hon Emily Ward-Bishop, 'and your presence added greatly to my own joy. Well!' she continued animatedly, 'Jeremy and Charlotte have a stately home in Sussex. And that's just where we went. Jeremy's ancestral hall has become a shrine to Petticoat Rule. The four of us women were greeted by a maid and ushered into a drawing-room where Charlotte was seated. Behind her stood her husband Jeremy, looking *so* sweet in his skirt and *so* charming as he executed a perfect curtsey to us. We sat down to sip rare *fino* sherry and delighted in the sight of this formerly arrogant youth now reduced to petticoated servitude.

' "Jeremy has been a very naughty boy today," said Charlotte. "I was awaiting your arrival so as to punish him publicly. I really cannot *bear* his impertinence and insolence. Jeremy, you will bend over that chair, lift up your skirt and petticoats, lower your drawers and bare your bottom!" His bottom! I have long ago come to the conclusion that the cruellest part of the punishment of a man by a woman is that she invariably whips the bottom and delights in it. It is so shameful for him, so ignominious, so utterly degrading, so *absolutely humiliating*. In that, too, we ladies delight and glory. There are very few women who do *not* delight in the idea of whipping; the sense of complete power and the joy of acutely punishing the animal nature of the male has to us an irresistible attraction.' She laughed throatily. 'There are none who have once wielded a birch against a man's arse who do not consider it the most exquisite pleasure they can have, one which they ever after perpetually love to enjoy. It is a pleasure I regard as being essentially feminine.

' "Kneel down, Jeremy," Charlotte commanded, "Kiss the birch that I have had pickled in my urine especially for my attention to your bottom – isn't it neat and soft and sweet, ladies? – and now kiss my hand." He had been schooled into obedience and so this slim and delicate young man trembled, obeyed and began to sob. "Now say: 'Madam Charlotte, my darling lady wife, will you favour me by birching my bare bottom for being naughty? Please give me six of the best for that; and another six for the audacity of having been under your petticoat." ' He sobbed out the humiliating words as we girls just giggled.

' "What is the particular piece of insolence on account of which you are punishing him?" I enquired.

' "He had the sheer impertinence," Charlotte replied indignantly "to express the wish that he might some day be 'emancipated' and *freed from the petticoat!*'

' "Shocking!" we all declared in chorus.

' "Precisely," said Charlotte. "His wickedness all arises from his masculine garments. In consequence, I have deprived him of them. My husband has to wear a skirt before me. He is also subject to the regime of the corset and the stay-lace." How we all tittered and how flushed our faces became! Peradventure we might desire males that we could put into petticoats.

' "Speaking of petticoats," Charlotte continued as her husband's small, tight bottom trembled at the thought of her impending wrath, "can anyone here lend me one?"

' "Oh, you darling girl!" Mrs Joan Smythe exclaimed. "I think you're probably my prize student. Oh yes, I can certainly spare one. I put on two this morning as it was so cold but they can be too much and I shall be glad to sacrifice one to productive usage."

'As it happened, Jane, Alison and I had also put on two petticoats that morning and now were only too pleased to take off and offer one to Charlotte. I'd forgotten to put on any knickers that day and so mine was soaked in my erotic juices and I strongly suspect that the same was the case for the other ladies present. Charlotte smiled graciously on receiving our four moistened petticoats, reeking with femininity, then slipped off one of her own. Mine was soft, white and silken; Joan's was of red flannel, trimmed with white lace; Alison's was of yellow satin; Jane's was of royal blue; and Charlotte's was of a stiffly starched white linen that crackled.

'Charlotte proceeded to make a bag out of them, warm and redolent with the juices of our femininity. She then slipped them over the head and face of Jeremy. There he knelt, this formerly arrogant and insolent young prick, his drawers around his ankles, his skirt and petticoat that he had to wear before his wife tucked up above his trembling bottom, cruelly exposed for the amusement and delectation of the ladies.

'Charlotte tapped his slender, firm bottom with her birch, commanding him to raise it higher. She proceeded to lash it in a way that made it smart and burn for our amusement. This wealthy, young and handsome young man twisted, writhed and howled before us with the petticoats, multi-coloured, of five women smothering his head, face and shoulders.

'This chastisement had the advantage of permitting me to observe closely the lovely forms of the fair disciplinarians and Charlotte's graceful movements as her birch rose and descended. I'm sure that the pain was very hard for Jeremy to bear and the worse it was, the more we tormentors smiled and enjoyed it. I held my breath. *Swish!* And the blow descended. The first few strokes were given with great precision and very scientifically from both sides, well over the whole of his bottom, which I'm sure was so thoroughly warmed that it felt on fire. Charlotte then asked Joan Smythe to pass her a fresh birch, which Joan smilingly supplied.'

'The sight of the weals rendered me quite furious with lust,' Lady Jane confessed as her ample bosom heaved.

'Oh,' said Lady Alison, 'I just kept frigging myself because I *so* like to see a man's pink bottom twitching beneath a lady's birch. The petticoats were then removed.'

'The succeeding strokes,' Emily went on excitedly, 'were divided into a particular punishing of each buttock; and the birch was very elastic – it had been well soaked and each one of the strokes made Jeremy's bottom jump. He sobbed out his apologies as his lady wife gave him permission to stand up and curtsey to the ladies. I noticed that his prick was upstanding, as if, despite the punishment, it still wanted to tear through the feminine frills which enshrouded it. The French maid, Hortense, looking rather dishy in her silken black dress with a white frilly apron, entered to present Jeremy's fishing rods to Charlotte.

' "A petticoated male," Charlotte snapped, "has no use for such things." She broke the beautiful, delicate rods across her knee and, striking her husband's cheeks with the fragments, ordered them to be used for firewood. "I have packed and sold your guns to a secondhand dealer," she declared sniffily. "In future, you will sit and sew and you will embroider my name, CHARLOTTE, the name of your wife, upon the petticoats that you will forever wear." '

'Oh, it was *such* a pretty piece of petticoating,' Alison sighed.

'And more, as you may well remember,' Emily said. 'Then Joan Smythe gave Jeremy a special present, with his wife's permission. Long, very tight suede gloves, twelve buttons each, were put by her upon her former pupil's hands and arms. A thread was wound around the buttons and sealed with a little gold seal, pinned to the wrist and bearing the coat of arms of her family.'

'And more than that!' Jane looked as though she were about to enjoy an orgasm. 'His corset and stay laces were secured by a small padlock, so that they could never be removed without his wife's explicit permission; and she wore the key on her pearl necklace, dangling just within the groove of her cleavage.'

'Lord Jeremy then had to go and stand in the corner,' Alison reminisced; 'face to the wall, knickers around his ankles, his gloved hands holding up his skirt and petticoats to reveal his scarlet glowing bottom, well whaled and wealed. We ladies took tea and admired the sight of this strong young male's firm buttocks changing colour. We gossiped and chatted and then agreed with his wife Charlotte that he should be given permission to pull up his drawers and lower his petticoats and skirt, provided that he crossed his hands behind his back and that our own petticoats were once more placed over his face as a token of female supremacy. Gosh! aren't we such bitches when we have a male cornered?!'

'Absolutely,' Jane declared firmly and approvingly. 'And as I recall it, Charlotte said: "Men are such pompous, vain creatures. But consider the shame of a man having the most animal part of him flogged by a girl!" '

'What degradation!' Emily laughed. 'But I think a husband should be perfectly helpless before his wife, turned up like a baby and spanked as she might choose in her good pleasure. It takes the conceit and nonsense out of a man. The worst part for a man of being whipped by a woman is clearly not the suffering; it is the power she thence derives over him by means of the exposure and by the experience of the pain she can inflict and the intimate relationship into which this places her, as she looks disdainfully at his abject condition. Why, she can never regard him as any sort of lord and master when she has made him twist and turn under the anguish of her lashes and when he knows that over his bottom, she can always brandish the rod.'

'What man,' Jane demanded, 'could hold his own with the woman who at any moment might say publicly: "Just wait until we get home and then I shall birch your bottom!" '

'The holy sceptre of the birch cannot be defied,' said Alison. 'And I recall Charlotte's words about her husband, young Lord Jeremy: "Sometimes, if it is my whim, he has to kiss my quim. For quite two hours I insist upon being pleased and amused thus. This is my construction of conjugal rights and the bondage is the most severe imaginable; there is no escape." Quite right, too!'

'Then,' Emily took up the thread of her tale, 'Jeremy was released from his corner. He had to curtsey to the ladies again and he did so with a huge, pulsating erection protesting as well as projecting through his skirt. Oooh!

what a sight! His face was as crimson as his bottom! then he was sent upstairs to dress for a vote at the House of Lords. Charlotte's maid attended to his *toilette*. He is always compelled to wear, underneath his male clothes, Charlotte's lingerie: long stockings and a tight corset; also a penis cage which permits erection and urination but which can only be unlocked for sexual purposes by his wife. This attire has a most subjugating effect upon him but it has made of him a complete dandy. We ladies love to flirt with a petticoated male and he is the envy of many men whose wives are always twitting them over being outshone by Jeremy.'

'The division-lists in the papers must be a perpetual nuisance to him,' Jane said maliciously. 'Charlotte always knows how he votes and he has to vote as Her Ladyship pleases. I was there on one occasion when he didn't. "You disobeyed!" Charlotte exclaimed, looking most uncommonly beautiful. "You disobeyed *me*! I don't care for Government whips or for any other whips except my own. Bend over *at once*! And Jane, kindly be my witness to this punishment." '

'Well, I've always been a good one for great games!' Bellingham exclaimed. 'And if the result is that my old chum, Lord Jeremy, consistently votes for more enlightened and libertarian measures, as he does, then so much the better for petticoat rule. Anyway, what's wrong with a good spot of fladge, eh? Let's all have some more brandy.'

Our revels were rudely interrupted by the abrupt intrusion of a stranger who was literally armed to the teeth, for he carried a dagger in his mouth, a pistol in one hand and a sword in the other. Clearly he was a pirate who had survived the battle.

'Good evening,' said Douglas. 'Why don't you just throw down your weapons and join us at our table for something good to eat and drink?'

This idiot responded by firing his pistol at Douglas but it misfired and went *phut*! Debate still rages among us as to who drew first and shot most accurately but no one denies that amidst this devil's Dozen, we all drew our guns, cocked their hammers and squeezed the triggers; and that there were twelve bullets in the body thrown unceremoniously overboard.

'The clitoris and the penis,' I observed as the ladies and gentlemen placed their smoking guns upon the dinner-table. 'Now: are we going to shoot each other or fuck instead?'

CHAPTER TWENTY-NINE

I have noticed that women love to swish their skirts and push out their bottoms after a particularly bloodthirsty triumph and this night was no exception. Some men tell me that they are frightened by both the manner and the matter: but to me it is simply an erotic sight that is worth seeing; and even worth going to see.

'Has anyone read the tales of Dauntless Dick?' Captain Jack Rivers demanded; and a number of us nodded for we had occasionally read of his exploits on purchasing the London *Evening News*. 'In one episode, Dauntless Dick is captured by the evil villain and hung by heels upside-down over a vat of sulphuric acid. His limbs are secured by chains as he hangs from a rope with a gas-jet flame burning through it. "Ha! ha!" the villain laughs. "Farewell, Dauntless Dick!" and the episode ends with the villain leaving the room and Dauntless Dick hanging by a thread over a vat of acid; and this thread is about to be burned through. Can anybody guess how the author solved the problem of getting Dauntless Dick out of this one?' We all shook our heads and waited for a relation of a masterpiece of writer's ingenuity. 'The next episode in the ensuing edition began,' said Jack Rivers; "With one mighty bound, Dauntless Dick was free!" Anyway, I've had enough of all this petticoat government!' And with one mighty bound, the Captain had seized Emily, thrown up her skirts and petticoats, pulled down her drawers and was noisily fucking her under the table.

'Ram Singh,' Douglas addressed him coolly, 'you're usually so silent; but do you have an erotic experience in your past with which you would like to regale us?'

'There was a most interesting one, Douglas,' Ram Singh replied as Jack humped Emily and she cried out her joys, 'On my last visit to London I entered a Circle Line carriage of the Metropolitan, District and Circle Line at Victoria Underground Railway Station, my destination being High Street Kensington. Unfortunately, the carriage was exceedingly crowded, and there were many women who could not find a seat. I found myself standing behind a most attractive and enticing Englishwoman. She was tall with a slender waist but a full figure, clad in a most delectable walking costume of black satin and wearing a black hat with a lace veil. Her gorgeous bottom threatened to split the skirt of her suit and her head was adorned by glossy blonde hair. The very sight of her gave me, I must confess, an instant erection.

'Now,' Ram Singh continued, 'normally I would never molest a woman, and I would certainly not make sexual advances to one I had never met before and who was simply standing in front of me in a crowded carriage on the Underground Railway. However, the train suddenly lurched, I was thrown back against the strut to which I was clinging and she lost her balance and it was she who fell back against me, her bottom inadvertently pressing itself upon my rampaging erection. I had expected her to jump away quickly but instead, she screwed the cleavage of her buttocks onto my erection with a slight wiggle. The wool of my trousers and the satin of her skirt were preventing full, fleshly contact, of course, yet she showed temporarily no desire to move. She moved away only when the train reached Sloane Square, but she did not leave the carriage.

'I stood up and, as the train moved on, the carriage being still as crowded as before, took the risk of allowing my stiff penis to brush against that gorgeous bottom, swathed so tightly in her smooth and shining satin skirt. She responded by pressing her arse against my rod all the way to South Kensington. On the journey to Gloucester Road, she softly rubbed her bottom against my prick. None of the other passengers had the slightest idea as to what was transpiring; and my impression of her face, which she kept turned away from me, was confined to its reflection in the glass windows of the carriage.

'The feeling of her gorgeous bottom rubbing against my trousered prick was quite exquisite and I came, endeavouring to disguise the matter with all due decorum; though I did emit a sigh. Seconds later, I distinctly heard *her* sigh and I felt her bottom, thighs and legs tremble. We left the carriage together at High Street Kensington, mounted the steps, handed in our tickets as though nothing untoward had transpired, and as we reached the street, she suddenly turned to face me. What a beautiful and voluptuous face she had! And she proceeded to astonish me by saying: "You're Ram Singh, aren't you, that chap whose come over here to lecture on Yoga? What a delightful man you are! You simply must come to tea." '

'Absolutely!' Lady Jane Fortescue hooted with laughter. 'That's just how we met! And I don't mind admitting that on the Underground Railway, the prick of Ram Singh was so bloody stiff that my cunt soaked my knickers all the way down to my knees. It was a delight to meet you, Ram, since I was *so* tired of my husband at the time. Husbands!' she snorted indignantly. 'They're never there when you need them and they're always there when you *don't* want them.'

'Jane, I had no idea that you were married,' I remarked.

'*Was* married, Horby,' she replied plummily, 'just the same as Alison heah. Oh, and we were Spanking Wives, weren't we, darling?'

'Certainly,' lisped Lady Alison Utterley. 'The only way to keep a husband in order is to make sure that his bottom is well-reddened before his daily kissing of one's arse.'

'And where are your husbands now?' asked Amin Shah.

'Oh, pushing up the daisies,' Douglas informed us casually. 'One went from malaria in the jungles of Bengal and the other one died on an expedition to the Arctic: frostbite, I think. Needless to say, they were encouraged to undertake these adventures of heat and cold by their wives. Quite right too: they were rich but quite ineffably boring. I call these ladies the Black Widow Spiders.' Jane and Alison did not exactly look displeased.

'It sounds as though the pair of you had American marriages,' Davina commented. When Jane and Alison looked puzzled, she proceeded to explain. 'It was either the wife of Morgan or Vanderbilt – or it could have been Rockefeller – who held a curious party in New York City about a year ago. Fifty couples were invited. There were two doors to the reception and one of them was headed: BOSS. Forty-nine married women walked through that door with their husbands walking through the other one. The fiftieth man swaggered boldly through the door headed BOSS with his wife walking humbly behind him. "How did you manage that?" the hostess enquired. He replied: "Wife's orders." '

'There doesn't seem to be much talk about love here,' Amin Shah observed with wry amusement.

'And what exactly *is* "Love"?' Jane demanded.

'You remind me, Madam,' Amin Shah returned, 'of the Cambridge professor who was lecturing his students and who said: "We all know what Electricity *does*. But can anyone tell me what Electricity *is*?" "Sir! Professor!" shouted some bright spark who'd jumped up at the back, "*I* know." "Then speak up, young man,' said the Professor. The student faltered and stuttered. At last he said: "Sorry, Professor, I *thought* I knew but I have forgotten." "Just my luck!" the Professor exclaimed; "There was only one man on this planet who could tell me what Electricity *is* – and he has forgotten." '

'Love?' A flushed Captain Jack Rivers arose from beneath the table and zipped up his trousers as Emily arranged her skirt and endeavoured to compose herself with all due decorum. 'Well, a man goes into a London pub, orders three triple whiskies, drinks them fast and bursts into tears. "Now, now," says the barman, "what's *your* trouble?" "I have spent a year of my life writing this beautiful love song," the man replies, "and I am a musician and poet of absolute integrity. *Not one word or note can be changed*. Unfortunately, whenever I have offered it in London, and I've been trying for another year now, if I'm not turned down flat, I have demands for changes. Being a man of total artistic integrity, I cannot agree. And so no one wants my beautiful and truthful song of Love." Whereupon he orders another triple whisky and bursts into tears again.

'Well,' Rivers continued in between gulps of cognac, 'the barman says: "There's a piano over there. Why don't you play us your love song and I'll give you my opinion?" So the man sits down and starts playing his love song; and, very slowly, people start listening. It's so haunting and beautiful that conversation dies in the saloon bar and the entire public bar comes over to hear it. People walking down the street are attracted by these haunting strains and the bar is packed out well over the limit. As the man reaches the climax of his love song, the hardest women are crying their eyes out and strong men are weeping unashamedly. As he finishes, there is a moment of reverent silence. Then they all burst into a frenzied bout of enthusiastic applause. "In my opinion," the barman declares, "that was absolutely fantastic. I just can't understand why anyone would turn it down or try to alter these marvellous lyrics or anything else. By the way, what did you say the title was?" The man replies: "*I love you so much, I could shit.*" '

'Ho! ho! ho!' Bellingham bellowed. 'Well,' he grinned broadly at Davina, 'that's not exactly the way in which I feel about you, my dear. Who cares what is love and whether or not I love you: here, now and at this moment, I *lust* you. In fact, I just can't wait to pull down your drawers, whip up your skirt and petticoats and plunge my tongue into your absolutely luscious cunt.'

'Oh, Richard . . .' Davina giggled, 'you do rather have your own way of putting it.'

'Always do what the Captain says,' Sir Richard responded, with a quick look at Rivers, accompanied by a wicked smile. With that, he seized his laughing wife and they both tumbled to the deep-piled carpet. Bellingham was as good as his word and lost no time in tearing down Davina's drawers, ripping their white silk in his urgency, and as she shrieked out in mock indignation and then billed and cooed with delight, he licked his lips greedily at the prospect and plunged his face eagerly into Davina's writhing vulva.

Captain Jack Rivers promptly seized Emily once again and they dropped beneath the dinner table to recommence their vigorous fucking, accompanied by loud yells and gasps. I looked up to see that Jane had stood up and that Ram Singh, who had previously been surreptitiously ogling her ostentatiously low bosom cleavage, had now embraced her from behind, taking her copious breasts within his palms, and pressing his rod against the writhing, generous bottom of Jane.

As Ram and Jane essayed their *frottage*, I noticed that Amin Shah had lain down upon the carpet with the back of his head resting comfortably upon the cushion of the sofa. Earlier I had seen him whisper into Alison's ear and her pale and haughty face had briefly flushed with pleasure.

'This is the best way to talk to you,' he said calmly, 'and anyway, you have a gorgeous and slender, twitchy bottom.' Alison preened herself, fluttered her fan, threw it down, swished her way over to Amin Shah, whipped up her skirt and petticoats to show that she wasn't wearing any knickers and, with a demure flutter of her blue-shadowed eyelids and a spiteful smirk, placed her bottom upon Amin Shah's face.

He groaned in an admixture of agony and ecstasy and Alison's bitchy face shone with sadistic pleasure. Her white teeth gleamed in a grin of glee. By and by, her expression changed, though, as her blue eyes became increasingly dreamy. She began to sigh and shiver and quiver, squealing as she squirmed out of control.

'How about a straight and very crude one?' Douglas said to Rosemary.

'I was thinking that you'd never ask me,' Rosemary responded; then arose to bend over a chair, throw down her fan and thrust out her derrière, beckoning Douglas to do the honours of unveiling her bottom, which quivered with anticipation. Douglas unbuttoned his fly to produce a stiff, thick member and without further ado, he rammed it right up inside Rosemary's arse. He roared like a lion as he did that and she shrieked out with the sheer unexpected ecstasy of it. He stuffed it in, back and forth, as she writhed and squealed.

Claire and I took one look at one another and at the scene around us and, with gasps of delighted astonishment, fell into one another's arms and tumbled down onto the carpet. She hitched up her skirt and petticoats to indicate that her white satin knickers had been deliberately sewn open so as to give her a slit of access. It was a joy to plunge my rampant rod right through this satin slit and on through another slit, the interior of which was silken. My palms grasped and caressed her beautiful bottom and my forefinger lovingly stroked and prodded the rosebud of her anus.

The boat rocked and rolled on the waves as we came together gently, having some improved idea of what love is.

CHAPTER THIRTY

Happy is he who rejoices over calm waters was a proverb with which both Amin Shah and Ram Singh concurred; and so did I when at length I saw this sight. The ocean seems to stretch for all eternity and yet one feels a unique calm of mind and a love coming back. I was very happy with Claire; indeed, everyone appeared happy with our pairing, however temporary. I seized the opportunity to take lessons in Yoga from Ram Singh and lessons in Sufism from Amin Shah; as well as lessons in shark-and swordfish-angling from Jack Rivers, finance from Douglas and boozing from Bellingham. After all, there's not much point in a long sea-voyage unless you learn things that you will never forget.

The lessons of Ram Singh were certainly physically productive. He proceeded, at my request, to teach me *Hatha* Yoga, which consists of mastering posture and breath control. *Ha-tha* refers to a union between the Sun and Moon, the male and the female in Nature, brought about in this system by use of the body. The theory holds that providing the posture is right – the first and most difficult step – the Sun and Moon can be mated within the human body via the action of breathing. It is held that breath through the right nostril – *Pingala* – affects a certain part of the central nervous system: and the same is allegedly true for the left nostril – *Ida*: as it is also for breath between both nostrils – *Sushumma* – which affects the central spinal column, or so it is stated by the masters of Yoga.

Well, I don't know really, about the theory. The facts are that by practising Ram Singh's postures and breathing exercises, I became quite murderously randy and a much better performer in bed.

Claire was certainly pleased with the results and I was pleased too when it was her turn at the dinner table to tell an erotic tale a few days later. She began:

'Back in 1899, I recall a time in Oxford, sitting in front of the fireplace with a mug of tea, to which I had added a dash of spirits, and wondering where all the good men were as I stared into the flames of the hypnotic light burning and blazing within the inglenook; but matters would soon improve.

'Samuel Pepys said of Oxford in 1668, "a mighty fine place." I cannot disagree. I met such an interesting man there, William Richard Morris.'

'Ah, yes,' said Bellingham, 'he's done splendid work for arts and crafts, particularly in printing and book design: the Kelmscott Chaucer, for example. I quite like his poetry and his novel, *News from Nowhere* isn't bad at all. Mind you, and to be quite frank, although he's a charming chap in person, he does shout rather a lot and I simply can't stand his impassioned advocacy of his bloody Christian Socialism.'

'No, Sir Richard,' Claire retorted, 'I am not speaking of him. This is a *different* William Morris, one who attended a Church school in Cowley, leaving at the age of fourteen to repair bicycles, then gradually set up his own business and became the local cycling champion. When I met him, his exploits and his ingenious machines were becoming increasingly well known and he had just opened a shop in

Oxford's High Street. Oh! we had such a silly day together!

' "Let me take you to the River Isis," he urged. "It is the most beautiful river bank that I can envisage." Whenever I think of Isis, I am reminded of the Egyptian Goddess, the wife of Osiris and the mother or Horus in yet another story of the creation of the World. Isis? Is she not the Goddess of love, fertility, intuition, inspiration and secrets? She begins as a maiden, a virgin, finally coming to reach fulfilment of her sexuality in a growing and maturing love.

'This young man worked so hard to impress me. He lent me a bicycle to ride and to intrigue, absorb and claim my attention. He himself rode upon a Penny Farthing. I felt so intoxicated by the fresh air. The front of his bicycle supported a basket containing a hamper, including sandwiches, a variety of pastries, fresh fruit and cheeses and a bottle of mead that his mother had so kindly concocted. Home-made mead can be so intoxicating! and, given its honey base, also aphrodisiacal.

'It did not take us too long to arrive at our destination: and he had chosen a beautiful site by the riverbank. Cows mooed contentedly in the background while, upon the waterway, ducks swam, occasionally plunging their heads beneath the surface in the hope of finding fish. We spread out the picnic blanket and proceeded to feast upon the delicacies that had earlier been prepared. However, the mead was much more potent, intoxicating, temilent, than I had originally anticipated. Yet how we did guzzle this mead, fermented honey, the nectar of flowers and the sweetness of life! Gradually, William began to lose all his inhibitions, the restraints and discipline that too often can control and shackle a good man.

'When I kissed him upon the cheek, he reddened with

modesty, rather as though he were making a misguided attempt to maintain his fecundity through chastity.

' "Would you like to ride upon my Penny Farthing?" he asked me.

' "I would delight in this pleasure," I replied in a gracious and courteous manner. He assisted me in placing my bottom upon the saddle. What a hardened seat it was to my delicate posterior! And I found it virtually impossible to control this particular two-wheeled conveyance. Unexpectedly, the hem of my skirt was caught within the spokes and the machine began to wobble and I could no longer keep my balance; then I felt myself falling and hit my head upon a stone and then the world fell silent.

'I do not know how long I was in a state of unconsciousness, so defenceless and vulnerable. Slowly I climbed back into awareness to find that I was lying naked upon a picnic blanket with William Morris nibbling upon my breasts.

' "My darling," he said, "you looked so beautiful just then that I simply could not contain myself any more. My intrinsic and essential desires were so aroused that I found it so necessary to . . . to . . ."

' "To do what?" I enquired.

' "You appeared even more lovely and fair than The Sleeping Beauty," he answered. "My member began to pulsate and throb so hard!"

' "And what did you do then?"

' "I asked graciously for your permission to penetrate: unfortunately, you were not quite in a fit state to answer my question."

' "Would you like now to perform that action?" I asked.

' "Mademoiselle – or should I call you Milady, a much more appropriate term – I do not want to appear too vulgar yet I must confess and acknowledge that your cunt is absolutely beautiful, being sure that many a lover has compared it to a lotus flower. In my opinion, yours is more like that of a honeysuckle, often with a humming-bird hovering overhead, rapidly vibrating its eager wings."

' "They all want to reach the honey and acquire the nectar in the end," I replied. "Did you?"

' "I plunged my stiff rod into your beautiful cunny," he responded. "I had hoped that I could arouse you. Please do not feel too offended by my actions."

' "Not at all . . ." At that moment, I was still feeling a bit dazed. "Did you reach a climax?"

' "Why, yes, I did," he answered with great rapture. "My organ pulsated and throbbed within your most gorgeous quim and I felt like a fountain, a veritable geyser spouting out grand jets of spunk!"

' "Now that I am conscious again," I told him, "one finds it essential to repeat the process."

' "Milady, I am so willing."

' "Then let us do so." There is nothing more sensual in life than spontaneous orgasms. Our love-making on the river bank was better on the second time; and as for the third, I felt like Alice coming out of Wonderland!'

(Note, 1925: William Morris became one of Great Britain's leading industrialists and manufacturers of motor-cars: my chauffeur insists that a Morris Cowley is the most convenient for driving in London on informal occasions and I cannot disagree: The Author.) (Note: 1993: The Morris Minor and the Morris Mini-Minor have achieved legendary status as classic cars, with the latter being especially suitable for town driving: The Editor).

'Did anything else happen?' Douglas enquired.

'Oh, yes!' Claire exclaimed, her face flushing ever so gently. 'You see, when he had done, I could not help laughing. He asked me the cause of my merriment. "Nothing," I answered, "it just reminded me of something." Not wishing at any risk to cause him the least shade of vexation, I insisted that he lie by me and told him how I was led on to procure sweet pleasures for myself.'

' "Ah, darling!" he exclaimed. "What would I not have given to see you frig your delicious little cunt?" He asked me many more questions about my solitary habits and I went so far as to tell him that on the evening prior to his invitation, I was so full of thought of him that I had done it there and then.

' "By Jove!" he answered, "this is truly curious. Confidence in return for confidence, dear angel, to know that the same night and probably at the same hour, we were exchanging our souls in mutual spending! Once I had seen you, I went home madly in love with you. I could not believe that I should be happy enough to possess you but all my efforts tended towards that desired end. I went to bed and thought only of you. I was in a fearful state . . . you can guess how! I put out my light and conjuring up your image, covered your face with imaginary kisses. Then I did what you were doing and the pleasure was so great that I am sure we emitted at one and the same time . . ."

' "What!?" I exclaimed in mock horror and astonishment. "*Can* men frig themselves, as we do?"

' "Certainly. Why should this natural means of relief be denied to them? Your pretty hand and my ugly paw both perform for the purposes of solitary gratification."

' "But there should be *mutual* gratification," I whispered into his ear.

' "Oh, I pray you! Grant me this pleasure!" I responded by disclosing his instrument, which was sufficiently excited by our conversation to have shot up once more in its most splendid condition. I took his hand and placed it upon his throbbing member.

' "No, really . . ." he protested, "this is rank folly!"

' "No, sir!"

' "But I would sooner have *your* fingers or *your* beautiful bubbies, if you will only but lend them to me."

' "But me no buts!" I cried out. "I *command* you to make haste and do it to the very end, or I will no longer love you." My dear lover could refuse me nothing. He began, and leaning over him, I followed his convulsive shaking with a singular feeling of pleasurable curiosity. I soon took pity on him, however, and kneeling down on the river bank before him, made him finish between my breasts. Yet shortly after this caprice of mine, he began to caress and suck my nipples once more.

' "Now show me your little cunt," he sighed, "and frig yourself with your left hand." I obeyed his instructions, all the while wondering what was to come. I now wanted to spend again fearlessly. My lascivious instincts began to blaze yet again. The operation that I had begun jokingly to perform, on account of a bicycle accident and only to please him, had become serious in the extreme. There was William Morris, with his trousers down, insinuating his organ, rampant in a state of nature, under my right arm. The originality of this fantastical idea inflamed my imagination more than ever. I bent my head and avidly contemplated the beautiful tool, the tip of which appeared and disappeared at each stroke of my dear lover, who kept his own eyes fixed on my left hand, which was frigging away for dear life. Soon we mingled our rites, we warned each other that the end was nigh and our double discharge took place simultaneously.

'My next position was to place my body atop his face, my bottom reclining upon it and my legs stretched asunder as he began his adorable, lecherous licking. My eyes were closed and I was wrapped up in my enjoyment, tasting every one of the thousand delicious sensations that his tongue conjured up, when suddenly he drew away and motioned me to do the same. Instantly I saw why; for there was a boat coming along the river and both of us knew some of the passengers. And I was just about to spend in his mouth! Quick as lightning, we were on our feet at once, our dress arranged, and then seated at a proper distance. We waved casually to our acquaintances as they sailed by. I felt terribly giddy but nevertheless managed to collect my scattered senses.

'It was an interesting encounter,' Claire concluded her tale, 'but I then had to go upon my travels to sample many more.'

As soon as I decently could, I escorted Claire to my suite, leaving the others to smoke and drink and fuck, and tumbled her down upon the bed.

'Oh! You adorable girl . . .' I sighed. She clasped me in her arms and, as I slipped my hands beneath the silken skin of her gorgeous, rounded bottom, she took hold of my member and frigged it bountifully for some exquisite time and, when it was in a most glorious state of erection, she slid it into her slit.

I rammed my rod into her with a joyous abandon, pounding her pudenda, all the while regaled by her cries of lascivious delight. I roared like a lion as I came: and it was immediately afterwards, with my prick in her cunt, that I asked her to marry me and she accepted with a squeeze of her vagina that left the issue of her acceptance in no doubt.

CHAPTER THIRTY-ONE

It might well take another volume to describe our sea voyage back to England on the S.S. *Albion*, and our adventures at our various ports of call. The facts remain that the company was delighted with the news of my engagement to Claire and a good time was had by all during our return to dear old Blighty, which occurred in late December 1901.

Those of us who had been involved with the Hermetic Order of the Golden Dawn returned to find a scandal that was all uniquely frightful – and all over the headlines of the popular press. There I found allegations of the Satanism for which I had searched in vain in Paris. The Golden Dawn, of which Bellingham and I were still passive members, was receiving a great deal of unwelcome publicity on account of the trial for rape of one Theo Horos. His wife, Madame Horos, was charged with aiding and abetting the matter.

I took a great interest in this case, since the couple in the dock appeared to be blaspheming things which I had discovered to be holy. Mr and Mrs Horos were an unlikely looking couple: she was remarkably fat and he was remarkably thin. It came out in court that, in 1888, she had served six months' imprisonment for swindling a Mr Luther Marsh out of his Madison Avenue house and, a year later, she had served two years for larceny in the

State of Illinois. Her husband, whose real name was Frank Jackson, had been Treasurer of a 'spiritual' movement his wife had founded, 'The Koreshan Unity', but had had to resign from this position after meeting with some difficulties in attempting to balance his books.

(Editor's Note: 'Horby's' account is consistent with the evidence produced at the trial, save that he does not mention *The Flaming Star*: 'Official Organ of the Koreshan Unity movement': it is worth observing that the recent mass cult suicide and shoot-out with the FBI occurred in Waco, Texas; and that the cult leader was a David *Koresh*. Connections with the movement founded by Mrs Horos have yet to be thoroughly investigated).

According to the testimony given at the trial, Madame Horos said that she and her husband Theo had been appointed to do God's work, for Theo was a new incarnation of Jesus Christ while she, the Swami, was none other than the Mother of God, bent upon establishing the theology of 'a Theocratic Unity.' In late 1899, they had travelled to Paris to meet Mathers, Head of the Golden Dawn. Madame Horos, described by one witness as 'the slickest and most accomplished crook-swindler ever known,' nevertheless managed to convince Mathers that she was the real Anna Sprengel of Germany by repeating to him details of a private conversation he had enjoyed with Madame Blavatsky many years before. It was fortunately not long before Mathers realised the nature of the fraud and denounced it: but not before Madame Horos had stolen some of his property, thence decamping to London where she had carried out some peculiarly nasty pseudo-occult sexual rites in Gower Street in the name of the Golden Dawn.

Mr and Mrs Horos wanted to attract as many people into their orbit as possible, put these people through fake

Golden Dawn initiations based on the documents they had stolen from Mathers and obtain every penny and atom of sexual satisfaction they could from the idiots who believed them. Now, at that time, it was often difficult for men and women of the lower-middle classes, desirous of matrimony, to meet one another socially, and so advertisements were a common feature in the popular press. One Evaline Mary Maud Croysdale, commonly known as Vera, was lured to the Horos couple from her home in Hull. Theo Horos pretended that his wife was his mother and married her in a 'pagan' ceremony, climaxed by going to bed with her in order to confirm its consummation. Apparently Vera had her doubts as they essayed sexual intercourse but these were soon resolved by the presence in bed of Theo's saintly mother, the soul-reading Swami, who knew and approved of this action and sighed as they fucked. Vera was thence persuaded to 'lend' Theo some diamond ear rings, a diamond pendant and a golden brooch, all of which she never saw again.

It was not, however, for obtaining Vera's trinkets by means of a fraudulent promise of marriage that Theo was sentenced to fifteen years of penal servitude and his wife to a similar sentence of seven years: it was for the rape of a sixteen-year-old girl named Daisy Pollex Adams.

Daisy, later described in court as a 'pretty little thing' and who came from Birkenhead, had been invited to London with her fourteen-year-old brother 'in order to complete their education;' and their parents, a Master Mariner and a Police Court missionary, had met the Horos couple and given their consent. Daisy would be taught shorthand, typing, music, drawing and painting; while the boy would be taught singing at St Paul's Cathedral. This proposition turned out to be not as attractive as it initially appeared.

My heart sinks even today as I ponder her testimony; for I do not feel that she was lying. Theo told the naive Daisy that she had to spend the night in his bed. This was essential, he said, for him to expound privately certain secret teachings of the Golden Dawn to her. In due course they retired for the night where, after being informed by Theo that the Spirit of Christ was in him and that she was to be his 'little wife', Daisy was initiated into the practice of mutual masturbation. A few days later, full sexual intercourse took place with the consent of Daisy, who told the court that she thought that Theo was the Son of God and therefore could do no wrong.

Unfortunately, on August 27th, 1901, Daisy was 'initiated' into the bogus 'Golden Dawn', using Mathers's original rituals and thereby blaspheming their nature. The Horos couple continued to preach the virtues of vegetarianism to Daisy whilst themselves indulging in both beef and beer. Having fallen into arrears with their rent, they moved to Gloucester Crescent; and it is here that Daisy began to doubt the divinity of Theo and resisted his advances: so he raped her.

A newcomer to this unlikely menage, one Laura Falkner, brought in by a matrimonial advertisement published in *The People*, stated in court that she had been instructed to bring Daisy to the 'Swami's' bedroom; this she did, and subsequently heard the girl crying out: Oh! Theo, don't.' Later she saw Daisy leave the bedroom, her eyes swollen and red with weeping and said that, within the hour, Daisy had told her that she had been raped, saying: 'You don't know the treatment I received this morning. The Swami held me by the head.'

Despite this, Daisy was stupid enough to write a letter to Theo stating that she was very sorry that she had wronged him and 'would vow on her knees before God to remain true to him . . . even if . . . tortured to death.' The Horos couple were finally arrested as guests at the home of Daisy's mother, who had managed to cling to the purity of their ideals, surely a considerable tribute to the persuasive powers of Mr & Mrs Horos.

On 20th December 1902, Mr Justice Bigham was confronted with the statement of Mrs Horos that her husband was incapable of sexual intercourse. 'Bloody rubbish, Horby!' Aleister Crowley exclaimed to me in later years. 'I stayed with that pair of confidence tricksters once for a long weekend and he was always boring me by walking around naked with a rampaging erection.' Fortunately, Mr Justice Bigham was of the same opinion and after rightly stating that it was difficult to conceive of more revolting or abominable crimes, passed a stiff prison sentence on these two rather seedy sexual perverts and confidence tricksters. Myself, I applaud his action; but it was hardly good news for the Golden Dawn, whose Neophyte ritual had been (incorrectly) described by the Solicitor-General as being 'most blasphemous'. Even to this day, some who followed the case associate the Golden Dawn with the Horos perversions. Others view the members, not as the Great Adepts they considered themselves to be, but as a set of amiable lunatics. Bellingham and I saw no alternative other than to resign, as did so many other members of repute.

Since that time, one gathers that the Golden Dawn continues in its way despite schisms and much undignified squabbling. There are various groupings which purport to be *the* original Golden Dawn. Who knows? Who cares? I am inclined to agree with Amin Shah that if you faithfully follow the Golden Dawn theory and practice of the 1890s, it will make you an excellent individual of the 1890s: but that is of no use to me in 1925.

To my knowledge, Mathers carried on with his sincere beliefs until, after a severe quarrel with Crowley, he died in the Spanish Influenza epidemic of 1917-19. Crowley, of course, is still going, though who knows where *that* will lead. Yeats is in line for that thing they call the Nobel Prize; or possibly he's already won it. Myself, I feel that the Golden Dawn did much more good than harm.

As for Satanism, I had to tell British government agents that it doesn't exist, save among tiny and utterly insignificant groups of perverts. I'd rather like it if there were an international gang of Satanists bent upon wrecking civilization and seizing power, among all their other alleged perversions, since it would be such tremendously good fun to crusade against it. Alas! there is no such beastie.

I certainly needed a breath of fresh air after the court case and that is why I joined Claire to play tennis on the hard court that Douglas had recently established at a home he owned in Roehampton.

'I know it's supposed to be called *lawn* tennis,' he jested, 'but why can't we play it under other circumstances too?' Winter tennis in the open weather certainly gets the old muscles moving, and the blood, brain and sinews. Servants put out copious quantities of mulled wine, steaming softly as we played our games. The idea was that we all divided into teams for a tournament of Doubles, with penalties for the losers and rewards for the winners. Douglas and Rosemary appointed themselves to be impartial umpires, taking high chairs at each side of the net. Douglas wore a blue blazer and baggy white flannel trousers; Rosemary wore a white, tight, silken dress, and as she settled into her seat, her white-gloved hands opened up a white parasol.

The sun shone out of the arse of the Universe on this

cold, crisp, clear day as we drank our hot mulled wine, seized our tennis racquets and gathered before Douglas to hear the luck of the draw, gathered from slips of paper we had earlier tossed into his top hat held for him by Rosemary. He announced that the first match would be between Amin Shah and Jane Fortescue against Ram Singh and Alison Utterley, the reward being a thousand guineas each for the winners; and a public spanking followed by standing in the corner for the losers, the match to be best out of three sets. All concerned consented to the match.

Amin Shah wore very short shorts and a white shirt. Claire commented approvingly on his slender, wiry arms and strong, slim thighs. Jane wore a frilly but loose-fitting blouse with a long, white pleated skirt. As she grasped her racquet fiercely with her right hand, her left delicately whisked her voluminous skirt. Ram Singh wore a Cambridge pullover and immaculately creased white flannel trousers. Alison wore a frivolously frilly but loose dress of shocking pink.

The play in the first set was fiercely competitive. I soon enough had a rampaging erection on account of seeing beautiful female bottoms bent over to receive a service; and I suspect that Claire and Davina got similar joy from watching the men. Jane's service was so absolutely smashing that she won some of her games to love. By contrast, Amin Shah served a ball so slow that, on its bounce, it looked like a sitting duck. Alison missed its spin entirely the first time and the bold swipe of Ram Singh sailed way out of court. Ram Singh's own serve went straight like a bullet and almost as fast: its return was a set-up for his smash. Alison's serve came in a curve, spinning in a way to set up a defensive return.

Both men started to play on the ladies' lack of mobility

in their skirts, perceiving that when both women were positioned for the ball, they struck home and hard. The forehand of Jane was a devastating stroke; yet the spinning backhand of Alison more often than not resulted in a futile swipe of the ball into the net. Shah and Singh were all strength and scintillating agility, conducting brilliant volleys at the net. At 4-4 in the first set, I overheard Singh say 'Play on her backhand' to Alison; and Shah saying: 'Play on her forehand,' to Jane. However, as luck would have it, it was Shah's service to Alison, which played upon the weakness in defence, of her forehand drive to make it 5-4: then Alison's serve to Jane's backhand spun back as a lob in the air, Singh lobbed it back and Shah smashed it. This pattern of play took the game and the set 6-4.

Shah and Jane established a dominant pattern of play during the second set. Jane took the base-line, banging in solid shots of tremendous power and Amin was neat and nifty at the net. Ram Singh and Alison, trying to outplay them at mid-court, had no answer to these tactics and lost the second set 6-2. It was time for the punishment and leather stools had been thoughtfully provided. The losers of this particular game bent over them obediently.

Amin flicked up the skirt of Alison, pulled down her white drawers and commenced spanking her pale, slim bottom with his tennis racquet. Simultaneously, Jane bared the bottom of Ram Singh, attending with her racquet to the condition of his athletic buttocks with enormous enthusiasm. Six strokes each sang out as if the racquets were striking tennis balls: and two bottoms writhed, twitched and reddened. Once the punishment was over, Ram Singh and Alison Utterley, as agreed by forfeit, had to stand in diagonally opposite corners of the tennis court, hands behind backs and upon glowing bottoms, faces to the wire, thus unable to see the next match.

This was Bellingham and Davina against Claire and myself. Bellingham was wearing a white cricket shirt and long, baggy shorts. I wore a plain white shirt and old white flannels. Claire now astounded one and all by peeling away her long fox-fur coat to reveal a white, short-sleeved singlet with a knee-length, white pleated skirt that jiggered every time she twitched her bottom. By contrast, Davina was wearing a costume quite impossible for the playing of tennis. All that could be said in its favour is that it was white. The excruciatingly tight dress of shimmering satin rendered it impossible for her to take more than a six-inch step at a time; and, judging by the way in which her breasts jutted, her corset was so tight that any fast step taken would cause her to fall out of breath.

'I'm just hopeless at these things,' said Davina as Claire popped over an easy serve. It bounced before her, she essayed a faint stroke and she missed. Claire's second serve to Richard was much harder and faster. He swung mightily and missed. For all their many virtues and saving graces, Sir Richard and Lady Bellingham were not terribly good at tennis. Whenever she served, the ball was lobbed feebly into the net. Whenever he served, he hit the ball so hard that it was way out of court. Whenever Claire or I served, either she hit the ball into the net or he hit it out of court. This match went by very quickly, with Claire and I winning a point-less win of six-love, six-love; and Douglas and Rosemary both declaring it to be the worst game of tennis which they had ever seen. Now there was punishment to follow; and Douglas and Rosemary added to it by ordering Richard and Davina to drink a paper cup of orange squash each and to eat a dry and boring biscuit.

'Oh, do spank me,' Davina entreated me sweetly as she bent over.

'I can hardly wait,' Bellingham murmured as he bent

over. With one accord, Claire and I moved into action. She stripped Bellingham of his shorts and underpantaloons. I took my time in unfastening the garments of Davina but took delight in exposing her rounded bottom to the afternoon air. Soon the tennis racquets of Claire and I were whanging down on two red, writhing bottoms, the pale skin of which looked like neat lattice work. It was the corner for both of them as the final commenced.

We lost the first set 6-1, since we were completely outplayed. Whenever the ball was placed for Jane's forehand, it proved to be virtually unreturnable. Amin was putting so much spin on his balls that any return rendered one liable to a smash.

It was then that I saw something. Claire and I had been playing with her volleying at the net and I was driving the strokes in from the base-line. What would happen if we emulated Amin and Jane and proceeded to play it their way, only taking it further? And I recall Claire whispering to me: 'Just defend.'

This strategy confused our opponents, for they certainly were not expecting Claire's top-spin back-hand, fired from the base-line. As for the net play, I took my partner's advice and instead of trying to slam through the skilled defences of Amin Shah, I encouraged him in endeavours to slam through mine and concentrating upon returning every ball as if I were a rubber ball. We won the next set 6-2.

In the third and final set, Claire, in her short and fluttering skirt, took advantage of Jane's lack of mobility within her heavy pleats, and scored repeatedly with neatly placed shots. It was an erotic sight indeed to see Claire time that drop-shot perfectly, causing Jane to run in a flurry of skirt, just too late to reach the ball, yet forced to bend over and shove her bottom upwards as she reached.

I returned the most athletic of Ram Singh's skilful endeavours to take the deciding set six-love.

'Punishment now!' Douglas grinned wickedly and rubbed his hands with joy. Rosemary had dismounted from her umpire's chair and was walking towards us with an arrogant swish of her skirts and petticoats, as four penitents paid their forfeits by standing obediently in the corners of this wired cage.

'A good spanking, is it, Horby?'

'That depends,' I replied, 'upon what my partner, co-victor and affianced declares. After all, ladies first!'

'The penalty,' said Claire, 'is that Amin Shah will *not* bend over and expose his bottom to me, much as he may be dying to do so, for all I know.' Rosemary smiled broadly at her star girl pupil. 'No, no, I want him to bend over *backwards* for me!' She wriggled her young, athletic bottom within her short tennis skirt and the pleats appeared to flutter gleefully. 'Mr Shah, in payment of your agreed forfeit, I request kindly that you lay your back upon this leather clad stool here and expose your rampant rod for my delectation.'

'Your wish is my command, Madam,' Amin Shah responded graciously, rather as if he were a genie in some tales of *The Arabian Nights*. Obediently, he stretched back upon the stool, unbuttoned his shorts and produced a long, thick, stiff ramrod of a penis.

'Splendid!' Claire shouted with joy. She whipped off her drawers and in an impudent piece of cheek, she threw them at Douglas, who merely smiled. 'I'm going to ride you, Amin, as I would a stallion!' So staying, she plucked up her tennis skirt and with a hop, step and a jump, landed directly upon his stiff rod and sighed with the pleasure of the sensation. In no time at all, she was rocking back and forth and shrieking out her delight in it as the man beneath her whirling loins heaved his hips and sighed with pleasure.

I had my own penalty in mind for Lady Jane Fortescue. Although I rather liked her, she had always struck me as being quite unnecessarily haughty; as the lower classes say, she was 'a right bossy boots'. It was a pleasure, therefore, to have this typical Girls' Head Prefect at my mercy. I commanded her to bend over the leather stool and with her own hands to expose the gorgeous golden apples swathed by her skirts. It was such a pleasure to see her rounded bottom bared in the afternoon sunlight upon the tennis court and an even greater pleasure to thwack my tennis racquet upon the quivering flesh with a sound *ping!*

Her bottom jumped up and down in sportive fashion as I gave her a strong, overarm first service; a spinning second service that made her gasp as her rear twitched to the right; a sizzling forehand shot that made her jump; a slicing backhand which made her squeal; and a final, overhand spanking good smash which made her beautifully reddened behind shudder and quiver. As she surrendered utterly, I rammed my rod within her soaking quim, whipping it through her so swiftly that she screamed out and came at the instant that I did.

A gong sounded and the game was ended. Claire, who had just come all over the shaft of Shah, dismounted and smoothed down her skirt. Jane rearranged her dress as I endeavoured to observe all due propriety. Rosemary blew a whistle and, with all forfeits paid, Richard and Davina and Ram and Alison joined us joyfully for a glass of mulled wine.

We all enjoyed a very good dinner that night but I shall never forget Claire's words as we composed ourselves within a true four-poster bed around midnight:

'I feel so content now,' she sighed, 'knowing that I have experienced life to the fullest . . . my travels were most enjoyable. I would not say that I have been terribly promiscuous, no, never indiscriminate in my manner, though there is still a *wanderlust* within my soul.

'Life,' she said, 'is a pilgrimage, an exploration. One can gallivant around the World for so long before it becomes rather tedious. At the present time, it is so important that I can be here in England as I have been invited to a wedding and it is so essential that I should attend.

'I know the groom so well,' she murmured dreamily. 'What a handsome, intelligent man; with such charm and attraction and such powers of seduction! As for the bride, I know it will be the happiest day of her life – that slow walk down the aisle to the altar, accompanied by her father, she herself sequestered and camouflaged by a veil . . . to finally reveal herself before her husband!'

'Let's fuck,' I said.

CHAPTER THIRTY-TWO

I married the woman referred to in these Memoirs as the Hon Claire Woodrough shortly afterwards. (Editor's Note: Horby deliberately does not give the precise date; research is still being undertaken into the various couples who wed in December 1901 or January 1902). On account of our social position, we had to get married C. of E. style – at least the service is short – and then host a whole load of society bores.

The true wedding came a day after and was held at my country house. Claire and I just wanted a few special friends to be present. A long-forgotten ancestor of mine had constructed a network of caves beneath the property, although as Claire mentioned to me: 'I feel there an eeriness, spookiness, a frightening sensation, rather macabre and eldritch.' Well: this particular ancestor had been an associate of Sir Francis Dashwood, he of so-called Hell-Fire Club infamy. Much planning and consultation was devoted to the course of the ceremony. Eventually, we were all agreed.

When the moment came, I donned a black silk robe and gladly accepted a brandy in my study from Sir Richard Bellingham, a cigarette packed with hashish from Amin Shah, an opium pipe from Ram Singh, a Cuban cigar from Douglas and a tankard of mead from Captain Jack Rivers, all of whom congratulated me warmly on making a wise choice of wife. No doubt Claire was receiving similar encouragements from her lady friends.

'Since we're coming along during the Season of Yule,' said Bellingham, 'I shall tell a joke: did you know how the Fairy came atop the Christmas Tree?' None of us did. 'Well,' he explained, 'one Christmas Eve, Santa comes home rubbing his hands together and going: "Ho! ho! ho!" But Mrs Claus is sitting there with her arms folded and looking rather fed up. "I don't see what's quite so funny, Santa," she informs him. "I've hardly seen you over the past three months and whenever you do bother to come home, I find you to be quite scandalously drunk. Santa, I simply can't take it any more and I am leaving you," and she goes. So poor old Santa's wife leaves him on Christmas Eve and he has to cook all the Christmas dinners for the poor people himself. Well, he's not terribly good at cooking and he proceeds to cut himself and he burns himself a few times but finally he shoves all the dinners in the ovens.

'Then off he goes to the factory to make sure that the presents have all been wrapped. But the elves and dwarves and gnomes and goblins and imps and pixies are all sitting there with *their* arms folded and looking, quite frankly, rather pissed orf. No presents have been wrapped. Santa says: "Come on, what is this? It's Christmas Eve and we must surely wrap the presents." They reply: "Sorry, Santa, we want a wage increase." Santa says: "Look, I haven't got it. Business is bad and the Christmas spirit isn't what it used to be. Come along, chaps, have a heart and wrap the presents." They retort: "Sorry, Santa, it's a wage increase or nothing," and when he shakes his head, they go: "Right, lads! Everybody out!" So Santa has to wrap all the presents himself.

'Then Santa has to carry all the presents out to his sleigh

and load it up. Unfortunately, he's just finished doing that when a runner comes away. So Santa has to take all the presents off again, fetch his tool box and repair the sleigh – and he goes and smashes his thumb with a hammer. Finally he gets the job done, loads all the presents onto the sleigh again and thinks: "Better go and check the reindeer, I suppose." Well, Donner's suffering from rheumatism, Blitzen has a bad case of arthritis and Rudolph has a cold and so his nose isn't glowing. All in all, they're a very sorry crew.

'Santa goes back to his house. Now I did mention that he wasn't exactly terribly good when it came to cooking. The Christmas dinners are all burnt into a black, charred mess. Santa is just contemplating this string of disasters when there's a ring upon the doorbell. Santa opens the front door: and there is this exceptionally beautiful fairy smiling happily and saying: "Hallo, Santa! Merry Christmas! And I've brought you your Christmas Tree. What would you like me to do with it?"

'Well, what do *you* think Santa said?' Bellingham concluded. 'And that's how the Fairy got on top of the Christmas tree.'

Joviality reigned as the men escorted me underground and into the tunnels that led to the caves, eventually to reach an artificial river called the Styx, the channel of the dead. I paid Bellingham a golden guinea, since he was playing the part of Charon the Ferryman, and he punted us across.

Fires flared and candelabra flickered throughout the various chambers, causing a melting of the stalagmites and a dripping of the stalactites. Finally, there was the major chamber. I entered to see Claire lying naked upon a four-poster bed that had been transformed into an altar. Upon its wooden base was the sign of the Eye in the

Pyramid. Behind it, there was a quartet of statues: at the head, the androgynous goat-god, Baphomet; at one side Priapus with a red-tipped phallus; on the other side, Venus was caressing her cunt; and, nearest to the bed, Bacchus and Venus were entwined within a loving and lustful embrace.

Douglas as the High Priest and Rosemary as the High Priestess solemnly conducted me to the bed and altar as Claire twitched her thighs and moaned. Behind us was the Priest, Ram Singh, and the new Priestess, Emily Ward-Bishop.

Organ music resounded throughout this Temple as Douglas and Rosemary intoned solemnly:

Thou who art I, beyond all I am,
Who hast no nature, and no name,
Who art, when all but thou are gone,
Thou, centre and secret of the Sun,
Thou, hidden spring of all things known
And unknown, Thou aloof, alone,
Thou, the true fire within the reed
Brooding and breeding, source and seed,
Of life, love, liberty and light,
Thou beyond speech and beyond sight,
Kindling as my intents aspire.
Thee I invoke, abiding one,
Thee, centre and secret of the Sun,
And that most holy mystery
Of which the vehicle am I.
Appear, most awful and most mild,
As is lawful in thy child!

At that instant, I rammed my rampant rod right into Claire's gorgeous cunny and inhaled the sweet perfume of sandalwood as she squealed and squirmed in ecstasy. At that instant, they all started singing:

For of the Father and the Son
The Holy Spirit is the norm;
Male-female, quintessential, one,
Man-being veiled in woman-form.
Glory and worship in the highest,
Thou Dove, mankind that deifiest,
Being that race most royally run,
To spring sunshine through winter storm.
Glory and worship be to thee,
Sap of the world-ash, wonder-tree!

Thus inspired, I slammed into Claire, laughing happily as I caused her belly to writhe and squirm with pleasure.

'Glory to Thee from Gilded Tomb!' roared the men.

'Glory to thee from Waiting Womb . . .' the woman sang. Then, as we fucked joyously, they all joined in a chorus:

Glory to Thee from earth unploughed!
Glory to thee from virgin vowed!
Glory to Thee, true Unity
Of the Eternal Trinity!
Glory to thee, thou sire and dam
And Self of I am that I am!
Glory to thee, beyond all term
Thy spring of sperm, thy seed and germ!
Glory to thee, eternal Sun,
Thou One in Three, Thou Three in One!
Glory and worship be to Thee,
Sap of the world-ash, wonder tree!

A gong was struck and I came at that instant, fiercely and

firmly pumping all my juices into the luscious cunt of Claire, who was awash in her own floodings of lust and who came with me.

As we rested upon the bed that was our altar, the Priestess collected our mingled love-juices from the chalice that was my wife's vagina and, with a long silver spoon, placed them within a diamond-encrusted chalice of platinum. The contents were then mixed with mead, and offered to me. I indicated that Milady should drink of it first and she responded by graciously insisting that this chalice should first pass my lips. Having supped of this delicious delectation, I presented it to her and she relished her full swallow. The congregation then drank of it and subsequently smacked their lips with satisfaction.

Was there indeed a secret magical ingredient within this Love Potion? Certainly I felt myself spinning into a state of consciousness which was unlike any I had experienced before, entwined delightfully as I was within her writhing white limbs. It seemed somewhat to have dispelled the initial solemnity of the congregation.

'Yo! ho! ho! and a bottle of rum!' Sir Richard Bellingham was bellowing as he ripped her thin silk dress from Davina and proceeded to fuck his wife upon the floor.

I suddenly noticed that at the end of this chamber, there was a stake to which was attached an iron chain with hand-cuffs. Captain Jack Rivers must have noticed it too, for he had snapped the cuffs upon Emily, ignoring her status as a Priestess, pulled up her silken black robe and was now giving it to her up the arse with shouts of joy. Emily was shrieking with delight too.

Douglas and Rosemary had slid to the floor very softly and slowly but they were now fucking swiftly and slickly.

Jane was bent over the lap of Amin Shah, gasping out her pleasure as her rounded white bottom glowed and started to writhe on account of his solemnly administered spanking.

Alison was furiously riding the stiff prick of Ram Singh, who lay upon his back and gasped with satisfaction. So did this randy bitch soon enough.

I had been unable to resist inviting Mrs Joan Smythe, for she was now married to that awful poet, Wilfred Sedgewick: some member of his family had left him a fortune, allowing him to leave the Colonial Service for service of a somewhat different nature. Joan lay back in her chair, arrogantly tossed her long black satin skirt and petticoats over the head of her kneeling servant and sighed with deep satisfaction as, no doubt, his tongue licked her cunt. Personally, I think it was giving rather more pleasure doing that than spouting terrible poetry.

My penis was stiff. Claire's vagina was wet with the juices of her desire. I prodded my rod into her for an ecstatic union. At the instant of our orgasms, we saw the infinitely great in this vast and starry Universe and the infinitely small in the grain of life-giving pulsation within the atom: and from this conjunction between the infinitely great and the infinitely small come all things in an ecstasy of Creation. In an agonising shudder which shivered my timbers – yes! thus and not otherwise did I come to the Temple of the Holy Grail, to pour within it the very last drop of my life's blood.

'The male and the female,' Claire said. 'Energy! Energy!! Energy!!! THAT'S IT!'

We shall draw a veil over our honeymoon, for as I said to my wife, the rest is silence.